Book Reviews

"Deck can write. In the *Land of The Story Tellers* he writes up a storm… and war, and festa, and… He writes with a seemingly infinite range of styles from sparse Hemingway to rococo—Faulkner and beyond. Amazingly, at least to me, he's mastered them all. From this exceptional observation of details comes vivid and luminous images, and from the juxtaposition of these images he builds his stories."

—JOHN M. DEL VECCHIO
*The 13th Valley, For The Sake of All Living Things,
Carry Me Home, The Bremer Detail, Demise: A Novel of Race,
Culture Wars, and Falling Darkness*

"*Dolly Dagger* is a story in *Land of The Story Tellers*. This is a tale of accuracy and truth. We endured the threat of injury and death every day. To survive and come home to a largely hostile population bred among us anger and a sense of revenge. The climate today is a 100% reversal of goodwill for veterans and support long overdue."

—CPL. ALDO MARTINELLI
United States Marine Corps, Tour of Vietnam 1967-1968

Note: *Aldo was shot through the chest by an NVA sniper on April 19th of 1968, far north in Quang Tri Province. He survived from the love of his fellow Marines, the doctors and nurses at Chelsea Naval Hospital, and now lives in Florida with his wife Shelia and daughter Julie.*

Dear Stephen,

"Thank you for your copy of the short story, *The Mexicans*, kindly inscribed. You know how I love to read! And thanks too for the engaging photo. President Bush joins me in sending our best wishes."

—LAURA BUSH
Note: *The Mexicans is a story in Land of The Story Tellers.*

"The choice of words in *Land of The Story Tellers* are like brush strokes of an artist…they capture and engulf the reader into the expressions of great storytelling.

The author's abilities to capture the essence of the environment and conduct the readership through the windows of time, sparks the imagination.

The story of *May Rain* in penned through a true event, the author fishing on Ashfield Lake. The tale ends— "Sometimes in fishing, the lessons go beyond deep waters and the catching of fish." This story allowed me to reflect on many of my life lessons learned while fishing along my grandfather and memories made. Some books find us at just the right time."

—DONALD WILDA, WILDLIFE ARTIST

"Simply stated, Stephen Deck is a natural born storyteller who is able to tell his stories (and his poems) on paper with the same eloquence and spelling binding as if he were sitting across the room and regaling the reader in person. *Land of the Story Tellers: 24 Stories and 7 Poems* is a compendium of short stories whose deftly crafted prose raises them to an impressive level of literary eloquence.

The signature of his storytelling is breathing characterization with unusual subject matter, and protagonists who bear very deep scars, both seen and unseen from the whipping posts of life.

—MIDWEST BOOK REVIEW

"Stephen Deck's *Land of the Story Tellers: 24 Stories and 7 Poems* is a diverse and captivating anthology that pulls the reader through various experiences, periods, and emotions. The book's long journey to publication feels like the culmination of an author's dedication to observing life and carefully crafting what matters most in storytelling. The anthology is a rich tapestry of variety in subject matter and tone. These stories excel in exploring the rawness of human emotions and relationships.

The variety of stories and the calming layout piqued my interest, and I knew this was a book I had to read. I wasn't disappointed. In *Texas Hardpan* told in Hillcrest Cemetery, Deck seamlessly moves between thematic introspection and the supernatural, offering compelling and thought-provoking stories. *Practicing Law* ventures across the Atlantic to Ireland, combining history, tragedy, and political tension, while *Dolly Dagger* is a poignant Vietnam War tale. Deck's portrayal of a wounded veteran grappling with physical and emotional scars is authentic and honors those who served. Deck's ability to create engaging settings and solid, well-fleshed characters makes this a thought-provoking read that will appeal to readers of all ages and genres. The poems are as good as the stories. My favorite is *Schools Out* because it's so nostalgic, and *Swamp Serenade* is a close second with its portrayal of Poe's *The Lake*. *Land of the Story Tellers* is an unforgettable anthology that sticks with you for its diverse storytelling and the masterful way it's written."

—REVIEWED BY CAROL THOMPSON
FOR READERS' FAVORITE

"Stephen King once revealed along the lines that a writer must be willing to roll in the words. Read all the classics of literature—for here is buried the magic key that can move mountains in storytelling. I have fond memories of curling up at my dad's feet on a Saturday night when the family gathered by the fireside for a night of storytelling. Dad had a great voice for telling stories and a great number of books full of stories. Stephen Deck's *Land of the Story Tellers* reminds me of those cherished childhood moments. His collection of short stories and poems reflects the profound and sometimes very simple nature of life. *The Old Lady* is a story about volunteers who devote their lives to caring for others while Pencil Box is a tale from the heart of Central Park in New York, where an iconic green park bench is inscribed with the words: *For All the Dreamers.*

Stephen Deck's book, *Land of the Story Tellers: 24 Stories and 7 Poems*, is an anthology of words of wisdom and reflections on life. The author/poet's ability to control the power of the English language to tell a simple, yet compelling story, time and again, is paramount in this collection. He is well-read in the classics as he writes in a wide range of styles, a master of the artistic ability to spin a great tale. He writes about real-life events, as well as fictional themes that reflect life. This is a fascinating collection of stories and poems to be savored and enjoyed each day, one entry at a time. Profoundly artistic, thrilling, adventurous and captivating."

—REVIEWED BY EMILY-JANE HILLS ORFORD,
FOR READERS' FAVORITE

"*Land of the Story Tellers: 24 Stories and 7 Poems* by Stephen Deck is an anthology of American fiction, featuring a collection of stories and poems that span 25 years. The tales range from war veterans in *The Old Lady* to familial love in *May Rain*, from sanctifying grace in *Texas Hardpan* to the scars of war in *Dolly Dagger*. Each story delves into the human experience, exploring themes of love, loss, redemption, and resilience, with vivid characters facing life's challenges in raw and moving ways. This is a brilliant collection of classic American tales that showcase a variety of attitudes and ideals across the diverse landscape of recent American history. There's both a disparate and unifying feel to the work, with dialogue and descriptions that bring American politics, humor, satire, and deep personal drama to life, but also subvert stereotypes for surprises and realism in each plot.

Stephen Deck's keen observation of people and conversations infuses the stories with authenticity, making each character and setting feel remarkably real as the dynamic and often very witty dialogue leaps from the pages to make you chuckle or gasp out loud. His versatility as a storyteller lets readers experience different emotional landscapes as well as physical ones, taking them in one moment through the horrendous pangs of loss and grieving, and in the next, the giddy highs of love, nostalgia, and hope. His ability to explore deep scars of memory and experience through his protagonists adds vulnerability and truth to every tale to make the characters feel all the more real. The anthology truly captures the age-old humanism of storytelling and the culture of stories themselves. Overall, *Land of the Story Tellers* is a poignant, thought-provoking, and memorable read that fans of accomplished short-form fiction everywhere are sure to adore."

—REVIEWED BY K.C. FINN, FOR READERS' FAVORITE

"*Land of the Story Tellers* by Stephen Deck is a collection of original short stories and poetry, each one reading independently. They all range in length, tone, and tenor with most leaning into themes of conflict and consequence. *The Long Wait* follows Nick, a devoted deer hunter who remains in his tree stand, waiting for the mystical buck to appear, with a twist ending. *Watering Cans* describes the experiences of an American stationed in Cessole, Italy during WWII, who engages in vineyard work and witnesses the local impact of Benito Mussolini's downfall in the broader wartime context. *The Jackass in the Road* tells of a paralyzed jackass during the devastation of war, shifting to a vengeful Russian assault on Germans driven by a history of suffering, and a death march to Siberia.

Stephen Deck's *Land of the Story Tellers: 24 Stories and 7 Poems* demonstrates Deck's command of storytelling, showing us his keen eye for detail and a unique understanding of human profiles. I found the writing to be authentic, and the author captures the essence of his characters with striking clarity, whether depicting personal loss, historical events, or true-to-life relationships. I loved the incorporation of poetry and, my very favorite aspect, the inclusion of pop culture pieces with a special shout-out to Led Zeppelin. While all of these might seem like a mixed bag, the amalgamation absolutely works on account of Deck's skilled handling. Overall, this collection stands out as a singular anthology in its exploration of universal themes through engrossing and persuasive storytelling."

—REVIEWED BY ASHER SYED,
FOR READERS' FAVORITE

"*Land of the Story Tellers* is a collection of 24 short stories and 7 poems by Stephen Deck. *The Old Lady* follows a woman who, after spending over three decades volunteering at a soldiers' home, is plagued by pangs of loneliness in her elder years. Two men with checkered pasts try to make amends for their former misdeeds on Easter Eve in *The Mexicans*. *Land of the Story Tellers* follows the adventures of a Croatian fan in an Irish pub on the matchday of the 2018 World Cup Final. In *Field of Dreams*, a man stops by a farm road to pick some berries and develops a deeper appreciation for the amiable farmers on a hot summer's day. A young boy helps a batch of baby turtles experience water for the first time in *First Steps*.

Land of the Story Tellers is an enthralling anthology that will delight short story lovers and poetry readers alike. Stephen Deck's tales explore many different facets of the human experience, narrated through the POV of protagonists who face their own unique challenges and situations in life. These stories feature some vividly drawn and grounded characters, who come from diverse backgrounds and are at different stages of their lives. Each tale has its own set of surprises in store for the reader, adding rich and distinct flavors of life to the narrative. The book also contains seven captivating poems that are bound to bring joy to any poetry enthusiast. Overall, I thoroughly enjoyed this anthology. If you're looking for a quiet evening read and love short stories, this is the perfect book for you."

—REVIEWED BY PIKASHO DEKA,
FOR READERS' FAVORITE

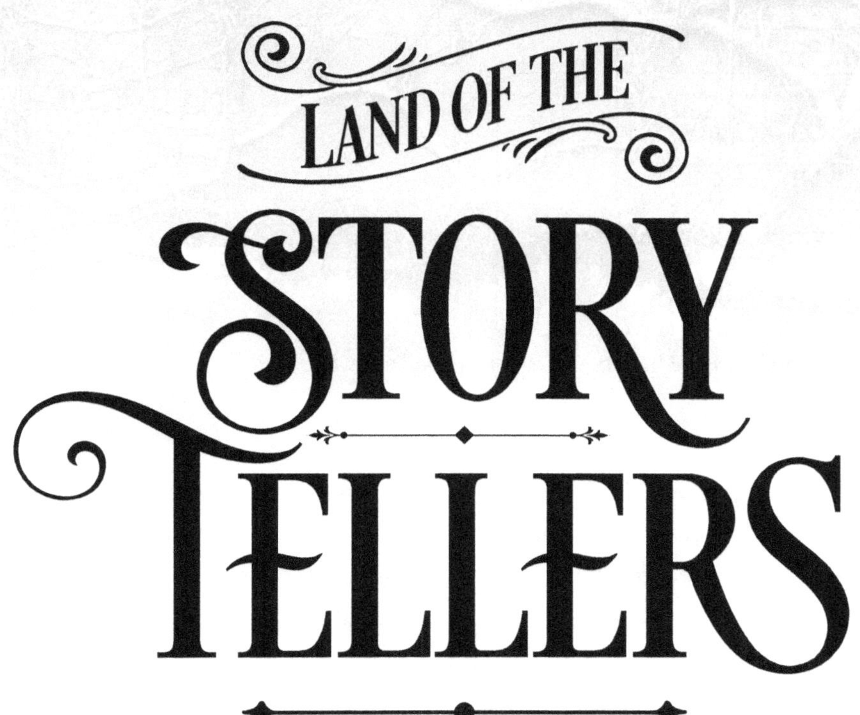

24 Stories and 7 Poems

Stephen Deck

Contents

7 POEMS FOR MY READERS

Artwork by Stephen Deck

Preface

The first story of this book was written long ago. It's one of my first short stories. Some of the earliest stories are *Field of Dreams*, *A Long Wait* and *May Rain*. The last short story in this collection under *Direct Object Formula*, was written during the past Christmas season. The tales in this book span twenty-five years of telling stories.

You will find many stories in this book. There is a story here for just about everybody. All readers that believe in God and mystery of the Holy Ghost — will love all of them. *First Steps* was designed to read a very simple story; something grade school children could grasp. Reading from the other hand, the story *When the Subject Matter Caught Up with Everything* was inspired from *Banal Story* by Ernest Hemingway. It's one of those choppy-whoppy stories you see around on rare occasions, with the company of several plots twisting and weaving around, a facet of many diamond faces twirling in your mind. I've got no favorites in this collection. All of them have brushed me against the superclusters of adventure; many strange things were revealed in dream-like worlds.

These stories were written in many places. I've converted my hotel room at the Mountainside Inn at Telluride, into a combination bachelor pad and boutique writer's station, and wrote stories necked up to the boxed canyons. Some were written on the second floor of the Stowe Inn, and down below they had a free breakfast nook and a long wooden bar for night drinking where I could slug down a few red wines. During those very casting of words, was when I inched behind a real man with a nasty scar running his cheek ordering a maple frosted doughnut — and that's where *Dolly Dagger* formed in my brain. I've written in a sagging-floor old white cottage of The Maples, dead summer months of Grand Isle, and sat on a stiff stool in stifling heat waves, beads of sweat pouring off the brows, wafts of cow manure drifting through the screens and electric fans beating the dead air. But it was here a precious vein of gold was stricken — *Land of The Story Tellers* was born inside that Vermont cottage. Always addicted to the pens, I once wrote for a solid week on a city park bench over inside Dearborn Park of Northbridge, California. But most of this writing over all these years, was penned here at home, down in the cozy silence of my cabin-like station.

Stephen King once revealed along the lines, that a writer must be willing to roll in the words. Read all the classics of literature — for here is buried the magic key that can move mountains in storytelling. This is all true: without the inspiration from Edgar Allan Poe, the novel of *Salem's Lot* would have never been fabricated under those dark curtains of horror. Edgar taught Stephen some fancy moves behind the scenes.

It seems looking back, that I've read a million books. Worn jackets right off books. I've read *After the Storm* no less than fifty times. There's a gripping meter and pace to that sea tale, that I wanted for my toolbox. Ernest gave it with open arms to Stephen.

It's hard to pick a winner. There have been so many wonderful books and stories. My bookcase is full of them. But the most beautiful story I've ever read, was *The Story of Pandora* by Emilie Kip Baker.

In the first opening of the ornate chest, served with a soft-feeling cord of gold strands in a curious knot — which was delivered to Pandora by an old man who was none other than Mercury the messenger is disguise — a host of tiny creatures like brown-wing moths poured from the chest. The malicious little sprites were so numerous, they clouded Pandora and bit and stung the curious woman, and they hovered about her husband Epimetheus with the same nasty medicine. It was not, however, until later they realized the extent of Pandora's folly, for the little brown-winged creatures were all the spirts of evil that had never entered the earth. Some of their names were Pain and Sorrow; Pride and Jealousy; and Poverty and Hunger.

But in the second fondling of the ornate chest with carved figures that had faces which changed at each glance ... she heard a wee soft whisper in the chest, and it said, "Open, Pandora, please, please open and let me out." In spite of her blunder of turning free the host of evil beings, Pandora was curious to see what was begging so plaintively for freedom. So, with the consent of Epimetheus, she lifted the lid once more, and out fluttered a tiny little creature with beautiful gauzy wings. She flew straight to Pandora, then to Epimetheus, and upon her touch all their hurts were healed, and all their pain forgotten. The name of the gentle messenger was Hope. She had hidden in the chest, after hearing that Jupiter was sending so many ills to fret mankind. Hope knew that once the evil beings were set free, could never again be shut up in their narrow prison of the chest; but wherever these evil spirits flew — even to the remotest corners of earth — Hope followed them and brought healing with her wings.

And that's why *The Story of Pandora* is the most beautiful story to me, because the world has the wings of Hope in the salient clouds, and even in the days when man neglects the altar of God, the virtue of Hope will still be remembered in the votive offering from the beds of suffering, and remedy against the bites and stings of the brown-wing sprites.

These are the necessary things learned from reading. They form the cartridge belts of silver bullets for the writer. In all these books and stories, these are the writers who had meaningful lessons and formed the author of this book:

Junior writing instructors, set premise between the margins. Maynard Hershorn out of *Winning* magazine, was one of the best short-story men in the business. He gave me tight sentence blocks, which are very useful in a street fight, when you want to pepper a reader with combinations. Willian Nack was a sportswriter out of *Sports Illustrated*, and he taught me about the proper formation of paragraph blocks. Mike Barnicle once covered Metro Regions in the *Boston Globe*, and what he revealed was the best stories are often told by beating the pavement of foot, and reporting from the ghetto blocks of Beantown. A ballpoint pen writing the journalism alive and breathing along the curb belts.

But the only newspaper man I ever loved, a frictionless kind of mellow guy born with midwestern charm out of Chamberlin, Illinois — was the best sportswriter who ever lived. His name was Bill Lyon, and he was the sensitive interloper who covered all the big cheese stuff out of the *The Philadelphia Inquirer*. Bill Lyon had his way with words; and they rubbed off on you. Some of them still live inside of me. There's not much room in the newspaper column, and he came at you right away with such a beautiful flourish of words. Take for instance the beginning of "Successful Seniors":

We begin with the basic premise of golf, the very bedrock upon which the sport is founded, and that is: This stupid game is impossible to play.

You got it, partner, agreed Lee Trevino, cheerful as usual. Once you understand that, it'll keep you from cutting your wrists.

Take for instance the opening bell of "Is Ryan Mellowing?"

In windbreaker, green shorts and white sneakers, Buddy Ryan showed up for his first official post-mortem of 1989 looking down-right natty and nautical, almost as though he had just come in from a morning of sailing. He was ruddy and relaxed. But then the view from the bridge of his ship is all seashells and balloons and red sails in the sunset. For the moment, at least.

It crushes my heart that Bill Lyon is not around, so he could have read my collection of stories, let alone sign the book's jacket. I've got a good feeling about everything, one of those premonitions where you hear cannon fire in the cloud banks and see a flash of pink in the Tabernacle of words, that he would have been pleased.

Some of my Senior writing instructors were novelists. Take for instance when Vardis Fisher saddled up rugged Samson John Minard, and brushed me across the virtues of courage, fortitude, and mercy for the weak and defenseless in *Mountain Man*. Take the time Russell Annabel penned two sourdoughs on an Alaskan shale buttress, with buckhorn sights on the ribs of a mountain goat, loafing in the immaculate sunbath of white snow fields. Take the efforts from the sweltering jungles of Vietnam, when John DelVecchio wrote *The 13th Valley*. A writer with very little experience, who persevered to write the blockbuster where conflict is steeped in meticulous realism and seeping with philosophic musings. This effort was monumental, and the two sentences that always stayed with me were: *We think ourselves into war. The antecedents are in our minds.*

Cormack McCarthy was never my writing instructor. Done plumb missed the lessons. Watched the movie. My favorite movie. Them damn Cohen brothers. So damn good. But I've read the sheriff's prologue in *No Country for Old Men* maybe three or four times. Four times. Wasn't it somethin' though when McCarthy necked up those two nasty nouns of gas and chamber in the first sentence? Jesus Christ Almighty Man. They jacked you in place didn't they though. You could already feel the doom-soaked prose rising from the Texas southwest plains, long before Llewellyn Moss tries to dump a pronghorn squinting down through a Unerlt telescopic sight, let alone when you stumbled on the drug deal gone bad with all the dead bodies, large dog gutshot and dead, the desert floor riddled with brass shell casings and coagulated blood everyplace; the tin sides of the desert rigs walked with the linear tracing of automatic weapons, all the tires shot flat; and over there in the golden sands a shotgun with a pistol grip and twenty-round drum magazine. Jesus Christ Almighty. .00 Buck is one thing. But no kinds of fancy moves will save your hide when sprayed with that kind of firepower. There's no rolls on the dice for that medicine.

Those are the kinds of things I learned in Senior Writing III. There were other voices on the podium, but through much time and suffering, many of their names escape. But thinking back now I recall the rhyme and meter sewn under my rough and tumble hide, from William Carlos Williams, Archibald MacLeish, and Walt Whitman.

Things got real pinched on the top floor of Master Writing Instruction. Three figures which had risen to the symbolic creams of perfection. The best short story men who ever lived.

You should have seen and heard what Edgar Allan Poe told me up inside the chamber, behind the black velvet curtains, and thus gloomy hall, shut out from the morning moon and sun and tabernacle of blue sky; and it was here with gangs of flambeau burning with the ghastly lights falling across Poe's face, where I needed to pull back because the wild colors of stained-glass windows had painted such a multitude of colors extreme on his countenance. But what he told me was priceless.

Nope. Sorry. Can't leak or won't be telling. Poe made me swear on a stack. Must have been six or seven bibles. Seven bibles. And if you saw the glints in his eye in the reveal, the candlelight falling on his black eyes ... you wouldn't talk either.

Stephen Crane taught me to paint with strokes of colours, and write pointed sentences with vivid and explosive prose, where the reader is witness to symbolic grids and jabbed with specks and flashes of tumultuous forces.

It must be said, nevertheless, that Stephen Crane's thought process in the sentence blocks is singular in his masterful construction, and students could stand on their heads for years with copy-cat pens, but never find that shifting meter where the reader feels a constant patter as if stricken by hail.

Ernest Hemingway had the most influence on this writer. He revealed all the things you must know about in telling stories. Write in short declarative sentences. Use riffs of one-syllable words. Listen very close to what you heard in the café, but only write what was really important. The things that grabbed you. Don't tell the reader everything, only what they need to know. The dialogue moving as sunken logs through the subject matter, is very powerful in story telling too.

The Lord was my salvation. He provided the writer's gifts.

But it was the writing instructors stricken above, who sailed sparks from their die grinders and cut open my gut chamber, fussed around and hard wired the planetary drive gears, then stitched me back up for combat with husky rivets swedged with blows of ball peen hammers. And let me be perfectly clear, that without their pivotal groom and calibration jobs, I would never have been able to pen the collection of stories here to follow.

The best way to read these stories, is one by one. The way they have fallen on the pages. Treat them as a box of chocolates. There is no room here for jumpy fellows, nervous types, or speed readers. Read slowly; feel the words. Let the syntax and pictorial language complete its work. Goals here are to rise emotions.

It's time to snuggle up in an easy chair, under the yellow glow of arc lights. Lace up your well-oiled boots, slip on a honed Buck belt knife with a razor edge, and above all pack a liquid-filled Silva compass.

We are embarking on far places in *Land of The Story Tellers*. These are stories with hands-on approach to subject matter and spun in the timeless themes of courage in the face of defeat and personal triumph. I dare exclaim in these stores here stricken, if I'm not greatly mistaken, the assembly of readers will be more well-rounded and with a good deal of their souls nudged back straight into position.

Stephen Deck
2021

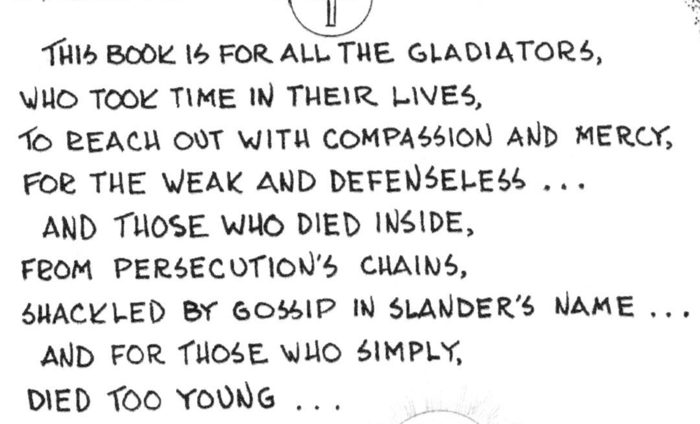

THIS BOOK IS FOR ALL THE GLADIATORS,
WHO TOOK TIME IN THEIR LIVES,
TO REACH OUT WITH COMPASSION AND MERCY,
FOR THE WEAK AND DEFENSELESS . . .
AND THOSE WHO DIED INSIDE,
FROM PERSECUTION'S CHAINS,
SHACKLED BY GOSSIP IN SLANDER'S NAME . . .
AND FOR THOSE WHO SIMPLY,
DIED TOO YOUNG . . .

Ｙᴇ ᴡʜᴏ read are still among the living; but I who write shall have long since gone my way into the region of shadows. For indeed strange things shall happen, and secret things be known, and many centuries shall pass away, ere these memorials be seen of men. And, when seen, there will be some to disbelieve, and some to doubt, and yet a few who will find much to ponder upon in the characters here graven with a stylus of iron.

The year had been a year of terror, and of feelings more intense than terror for which there is no name upon the earth. For many prodigies and signs had taken place, and far and wide, over sea and land, the black wings of the Pestilence were spread abroad. To those, nevertheless, cunning in the stars, it was not unknown that the heavens wore an aspect of ill; and to me, the Greek Oinos, among others, it was evident that now had arrived the alternation of that seven hundred and ninety-fourth year when, at the entrance of Aries, the planet Jupiter is conjoined with the red ring of the terrible Saturnus. The peculiar spirit of the skies, if I mistake not greatly, made itself manifest, not only in the physical orb of the earth, but in the souls, imaginations, and meditations of mankind.

SHADOW – A PARABLE
~By Edgar Allan Poe

The Old Lady

The old lady in her black coat, curious grey plastic bonnet tied under her chin, came along the trampled edge of the parking lot on a winter morning, and the weak sun peeked on a horizon where gliding pale streams of basest clouds mingled; the rags of time hung on the old lady.

The old lady was still good size. She was still over six feet tall, ninety-six years, and still driving. Her dark blue Rambler was necked in a stall which provided the shortest distance and the flattest ground for her black boxy shoes, and the faded blue skin of the automobile was dented here and there, and both fenders had been in brushes. Twinkling in the faint rays of sun, were the white beads of a rosary chaplet that hung from the rear view mirror; its silver cross dangled and twirled when the Rambler chugged down the road.

Confrontation assembled — a flight of eight stairs challenged the old lady's access into the Soldiers' Home. She'd been that route countless times, the steep river of concrete steps. This figure in the habiliment of black, was on no account a strange face on the premise. She'd been a volunteer who tended on soldiers for 37 years now, an ordeal which began out of loneliness after her husband died of a massive heart attack in night sleep.

A warning chante was rising under her breath, which was the sign of those who live alone behind four walls. "Down with the good…up with the bad. Down with the good…up with the bad." Her meter of words was parrot-like, a lexicon of internal monologue she had recited many times.

The furrows of her finger bones were deep hollows of fields that had seen many of harvest, felt the soft touch of love, and as she tugged herself up the black handrails of cold steel, a spray of blue veins ran hither and tither across her backhand. "Down with the good, up with the bad." The old lady put her good leg down — steady, oh how very steady! — and then dragged the bad knee and worn joints up and over the cornice. This practice had considerable worn the shoe leather. The top grain cowhide of her black shoes, was now battle worn on the toe boxes. She was too old for polishing shoes, and her vanity had been enveloped with dignity and sagacious conduct in part of frail bones. She once quizzed the chaplain inside the Soldiers' Home on these things.

"Why did I live so long?"

"To set examples," said the chaplain. His face did not change in the reveal. He'd pressed her shoulder down with a firm assurance. A spark had been seen across her grey eyes.

The old lady crested the eighth stair. She entered through the double glass door trailing her bad leg and wood cane, and into the tempest of figures and voices. It had been a full week since she heard conversation. Voice carried well in her home, but they were the company of television and radio stations. She checked herself against the spilling of mumbled words and waded into the stream of figures.

The old lady tried desperately to break into conversation. Frequently she seemed about to address people, her mouth on the edge of words.

She spun like a bear reared under the golden nectar of a honey tree, wheeling in her black coat, arms with fur cuffs sweeping the crowd, wide-eyed trying to manufacture a smile that would draw somebody in close enough so they could be cornered for exchange.

But the floor was in gear, there was a bustle in the crowd, and many in foot traffic knew her reputation as a talker. These people were on pinched time and were holding back emotions for their loved old soldiers on higher floors. Three nurses were spilling their weekend into the crowd, speaking loud enough across the lobby so nobody missed any of the fine details, walking brisk toward their duty stations in white pump shoes and sky-blue scrubs. Even the hunched men in wheelchairs rolled past, cupping the big wheels with fast jabs of their ancient hands, gliding swiftly over the tiles and past the woman.

At last, however, the old lady spotted two suitable victims for conversation. The pair of lovely young women were at the sign-in book. All volunteers needed to sign the book, and at that point attached their name badge for proper address from the old soldiers. They were well-dressed on this Sunday morning, and one of them was an over-strawberry blonde who was wearing a stunning peach blouse with a pleated chest and long puffy sleeves that were well-ironed into fashion of a full-rigged schooner with sails set. They seemed to have plenty of time, and with timid smiles and all giggles, were carrying on exceedingly polite conversation across the counter with a telephone operator.

The old lady nestled in close and looked over their shoulder. Her height was advantageous in this observation, and the girls had not detected her presence. The old lady listened to them for quite some time. Their zest brought an impulse out from the old lady, and she suddenly exclaimed off her lips,

"Excuse me… but do you know anybody who travels over the mountain? I'm getting too old for driving myself."

The two girls spun and looked up at those large eyes turned down on them.

"I'm willing to pitch in a few dollars for gasoline."

In that instant the two girls had braced their hands on the sign-in book and stared at the figure that loomed them. The old lady had arrested their attention. For the two girls saw in her wisdom and thick skins of resilience of those who have lived through war.

They seemed about to exchange a smile with the stranger, but suddenly checked against it and froze up. The lonesome countenance of the old lady had zapped their halo of babyhood. The girls could see the miles on her face, the wrinkles on her baby-soft cheeks patted down with rouge powder, and the varnish of fire-engine red lipstick across her wide lips. The red really popped her face in the bath of window light.

"I'm sorry," said the young lady in the pleated peach blouse.

"I'm so sorry… but I'm driving my father's car. We are not allowed over the mountain."

"Coming over the mountain can be dangerous business. The guardrails are a menace, and there's no telling what could happen on ice. Your father has done well in his guidance."

The ages tried desperately to claw at the edge of a congenial offering. It crossed the mind of the closest girl to grab her wrist with mercy, but when she saw the sad eyes and blue veins with a shrunken wrist, she imagined how cold the old lady's blood must run, and that the sensation of casket people might be running under her skin. So she patted the fur cuff. The other girl in the window light, gave a symbolic peace sign. Both girls finally gave a smile, but they were sensitive smiles, on the edge of personal sorrow.

"I'd be willing to walk to the school bus stop," pressed the old lady. "They have a wonderful green bench under cover, and I could wait for my ride."

"I don't know anybody," said the strawberry blonde with a rueful face.

Silence engulfed the atmosphere. The telephone operator was measuring all their faces. Although yellow sun streamed through the window glass, a dark shadow of disappointment fell across the old lady's face. It was almost like another year suddenly slipped away from her.

"Don't you?" mustered the old lady. Her voice had risen into a state of despair.

"Well, no, ma'am," softy replied one girl's tender heart, "I don't know a soul who crosses the mountain."

The girls finished signing in the large book on the blue lines and fastened their name tags. They were white name tags with Roman letters. Their names were Giselle and Valentina. No personal information had been divulged between the baptism of conversation. The old lady's eyes were poor for reading under scrutiny; she averted the name plates and pinched back on her wanton imagination for any reveal.

Then the girl sheepishly continued as those precariously walking the cornice of a ledge — "But if you give me your number and address, I may find someone in my travels, and if so, I will certainly let you know of it."

The girl produced a stock of card and with a blue inked pen, and wrote down what came out of the old lady's mouth.

"My, you have fine penmanship." The old lady had taken miniature bear steps toward the girls and snuggled up tight. The girls could see a new light around the old lady, and her jowls were casting a baby smile.

"Thank you so much!" She gave the girls a thumbs up, but the grip of arthritis had arrested her thumb in the anti-aircraft position; nevertheless, the message sailed clean.

The old lady opened her coin purse. The girls pulled back slightly from a tip. She procured three hard candy. They were holiday candy with red and white marble. She plopped one each with the girls, then expertly unwrapped the plastic jacket with her long bookkeeper fingers, and pushed the candy past her lips of fire engine red.

Then the old lady wheeled and disappeared into the crowd. Sunday Mass in the chapel had just broke, and a vast sea of men in wheelchairs and holding themselves with canes, visitors and loved ones alike, formed tight waves of figures as they moved with haste toward the free coffee and doughnuts up in the canteen.

Having flung her black coat with a soldier-like move across the sofa, she could be seen through the gauze of people, loading the old soldiers in wheelchairs on the elevator. At her size of over six feet, she was marked well in the tide, and with her good leg and bad leg she sailed the men inside with vast spurts of energy.

The next week the old lady waited across the mountain, down in the pinched valley inside her small brick house. She waited all through the day in the silence for the telephone to ring, and with the spark of hope of those living on the edge, waited for the mail. But there had been no takers, and nobody offered.

The telephone remained dead — Oh! So dead that she checked for dial tones several times in the clock's circuit — and there had been no mail from good Samaritans who would cross the mountain, even though she had offered the bonus of gasoline money.

This had been no big surprise to the old lady, for the calendar on the wall in the kitchen revealed the whole story — episodes of check marks in the day boxes had made runs on 157 days straight, where nobody had checked on her. It was hard to kid yourself with that kind of evidence.

Time had hardened the old lady, as she'd kept herself in the bounds of her singular reality inside the small brick house. Loneliness in many ways, had become her Red Badge of Courage.

On the grey and silent afternoon of Friday, a huge storm engulfed the mountain. They closed the mountain pass. A gang of yellow sawhorses sealed the road, and two smoke pots sent a pother of raven smoke into the sea of white flakes.

That night in the kitchen, the old lady was into a Boston cream doughnut, its crown laced with chocolate frosting. It was six days old. She'd warmed it inside her toaster oven. She ate very slowly, and opened her mouth wide, and some of the frosting was on her lips. Under the yellow glow of her table lamp, she sipped on black tea and licked back in the sweet chocolate.

It was a Soldiers' Home doughnut. The head cook had given her a dozen. The donations from the bakeries across the village had been generous, and after everyone filled their belly, a surplus with hundreds of doughnuts remained.

The head cook knew well of the old lady's sweet tooth. He'd seen her around for many years now, the old lady who volunteered in the blue battered Rambler, who never missed and was reliable as time. So free doughnuts were really nothing.

The old lady pushed in the last of the doughnut and slugged down the last of her second cup of tea. She took the last look out the window. It was very dark, the snow twirling down through the rock maples, and a clutch of sparrows was huddled on the porch's cove against the ominous whispers of the storm. Then she retreated to bed.

On the wall of her bedroom in close quarters to the bed post, was a favorite poem of the old lady. It had been there a long time. The poem had been a favorite of her husband too. A warm glow from the electric flambeau cast a yellow ray across the plaque; but on this evening the old lady did not pass an eye over the poem. She was more anxious of an ancient calling, to snuggle under the home-spun love of the colorful quilt, and brace herself against the storm.

Just before she killed the switch, the voice of the Medieval Morning Poem seemed to call across the chamber; there was a desperation in the response of frequency:

> *Jesu Lord, blyssed thou be,*
> *For all this nyght thou hast me kepe,*
> *From the fend and his poste,*
> *Whether I wake or that I slepe.*

The old lady wiggled her toes. She was on her back with ankles crossed, and had retired with a silk evening gown. It was shell pink in colour, and ran the length of her calves. The satisfaction of eating chocolate doughnuts was still with her, an inner peace in the storm, and the old lady fell sound to sleep.

That evening the telephone rang. The ringing came long and sharp across the kitchen.

There was urgency in the night call, and the tintinnabulations of peal carried into the parlor. Then a sudden hush fell over the chamber, and the clock's perforce of ticking carried into the night, and the refrigerator's motor hummed in the silence.

Well into morning, the telephone rang again. The storm had stopped in the late night, and sun was streaming through the eastern window of the bedroom. The phone rang a long cry. What seemed only minutes past, the crying of rings resumed, and made challenge to the prior sequence of dings.

But there was no answer, and a sea of silence returned in the chambers. The old lady had died in the night. She was still on her back, with both hands crossed over her chest. Outside a million diamonds of fresh powder sparkled in the sun, and below the blue sky in the looming rock maples, a pair of cardinals sat angel-like on the limbs. They perched in silence over the glitter of immaculate whiteness, and basked in the field of yellow sun bath.

On mountain's crest, they'd pulled the sawhorses of construction yellow, and snuffed the smoke pots. The snow plow operators had shoved back the banks. Sanding operations were completed, and the roadbed had been captured. Automobiles streamed over the summit. A vendor was selling coffee from a road stand on the shoulder, and was doing quite well in attendance.

Way across the mountain, down in the hamlets, a figure had just finished shoveling of walks and stairs. They'd rested the red shovel against the clapboards, stomped their snow boots on the threshold, and entered the home where a fireplace was banked with cherry coals.

But there was still a conscience that hung above the figure. It had hovered about through the storm. They picked up the receiver, and dialed that same number on the white card stock fixed to the cork board with a blue-head thumb tack. The phone on the other end was ringing loud and clear. Valentina and Giselle had carried through with the word.

May Rain

Travis killed the truck's motor. The black wipers came to a sudden halt. They never made it all the way and the black rubber hung at a cocked angle across the windshield's view. The drops of rain quickly took over all the wiper's work. The capture only took a few seconds. The spring rains streamed down the glass, and past the drops Travis could see the budding maples across the lake. They showed in light green flecks and blotches.

Travis opened the door. He stepped out on the gravel lot. All the heat trapped inside the cab by the truck's defroster, now went with Travis. Soon the glass was enveloped in fog vapor, and the vinyl seat had started its contraction.

Travis moved off the bluff and down the steep slope. His fish pole was still in the cab. It was broken down in two sections and cinched with red bands of rubber. The heavy rains had made the chopped-out trail very slippery and Travis went down descending the embankment with hands out and palms down, weaving down the path with his boots skidding on mud, moving around and over the bare tree roots that had gone black in the May rain. He could see the lake and the raindrops were peppered all over its surface. The falling rain had made quick work of soaking Travis's shoulders, as his grey sweatshirt lacked value for fighting bad weather.

On the shore was a grove of trees. They were hemlocks. They still had not taken on new growth, and their coats of needles were casts of forest green. Out in the center of the lake, a thin veil of fog was moving in trailing wisps across the waters.

The largest hemlock of the stand leaned at sheer angles over the waters. It survived its whole life clinging to an undercut banking, with its roots sipping from the lake. But its limbs were slight, and no kid ever thought of putting a Tarzan swing on its frame. They swam on a gravel sandbar across the way all summer, but it was too cold for that thinking now — the swim raft was still beached where it was pulled up on the sandbar last fall. Some of the steel float drums showed rusting, but the planking was still a coat of gloss enamel.

Under the groves of green buds were three silhouettes of bright colour. They were fishing. Two figures of construction yellow and the last of baby blue. Their raincoats glistened in the flat light of dawn.

Travis cupped his hands and shouted down the slope. The grove of hemlock seemed to swallow his voice. "Hi guys! …any luck?"

"Naw, nothing yet." answered one of the yellow men.

Travis moved down closer over a bed of moss. The man who had answered met Travis under the forest and said, "The spring runoffs have the Deerfield River in high banks, and we moved into these calm waters an hour back."

The other two stayed fishing. They had hushed dialogue. Travis watched the rain come off the man's ears. It was almost a steady flow of drops running from his lobes, but the man still smiled wide and swept hands in his conversation and his white teeth and weathered wind-burned flesh stood out well inside his yellow hood.

This is a funny thing, pondered Travis. If the boss at the factory asked us to work sweeping in the rain, we would put on sour faces and complain all day for our pay. But out here in the countryside away from pay stubs, we could take nasty weather all day long and go home happy as larks.

The three fishermen had come into the Berkshire hills from the sand swept dunes of Cape Cod. They'd all been born on the arm of seashore. This trip for them was about adventure, and it felt good to breathe the mountain air, said the spokesman still all smiles in the rain. It was also for them, an escape before the tourists came in caravans of cars that clogged up roadbeds. Then travel would be a thing of the clock, fighting out a break in the colorful stream of automobiles and working the side streets, so they could end the day taking cold pulls on a bottle of brown beer, and glance across the blue chop where white sails were framed in a setting ball of orange.

Travis threw another funny thing around. It was about people in general. A person could live at the base of Mount Washington and take all its splendor for granted. Live in Alaska and dream of white sands in Hawaii. They could live in Florida and say it's way too hot and the Maine folks would swear winter was finally getting to their bones, and then the whole clan of them could meet in Arizona while on winter's vacation. And then they would complain and in the same breath brag about their home state. These were good signs, concluded Travis. People need change.

The other two had turned around. They were not all men as Travis had first thought. It was a father and daughter team. The man was working spin baits and had cast his daughter's pole far out from shore. She was fishing with worms and the father had set it up with a red and white bobber. It stuck out boldly on the gloom waters. The girl in the baby blue slicker watched the bobber. Her father had propped the pole in a crotch of a sapling he cut from the sucker brush. It looked like a slingshot shoved into the gravel shoreline. His Queen Stag jackknife had peeled off the bark, just to let the daughter know she was special.

The blonde shocks of her blunted cut were at angles outside the blue hood, the rain seeping into her highlights. The cuffs on her slicker were turned over at least twice over her wrists, and the bottom hem was near her Maine hunting boots. It happened to be her grandmother's old rain slicker.

The father and Travis traded fishing stories. Then the secret fishing spots leaked out. Travis gave out a few and zeroed the trio onto a sweet pond inside Boone and Crockett Reservation, a place with easy casting from the woods and lurking with lunker browns. That put some spark in all their eyes. Then the father gave back some beach heads and tides that worked swell while live lining mackerel on the bottom. Now both men felt good. They had taken the first step into friendship. It was too bad, they would never see each other again.

They shook each other's hand. Everybody said goodbye. Travis went back up the slope. He fired the truck's motor, flicked the wipers back into flight, and motored along the bumpy road to the sandbar on the other side. The boat was upside down in the truck's bed, and the bow lurched in all the heaves. Travis pulled into the gap between the guard rails and parked in a small lot. He looked out his side window that was cranked all the way down. He sat there for a while and watched the rain die off. Fine mist from the grey clouds sifted across his knuckles. Then a small chop took over some parts of the lake. But the cove way up the north side, was still as glass. Monstrous chain pickerel lived in that cove, and all minnows stayed clear of those slaughter beds, unless they wanted to spend the night inside the pickerel's stomach.

There would only be two more hours of daylight and Travis was now contemplating if he should break the boat free. Even in his soaking sweatshirt that put chills up his back, he already knew this would be his winnow of straws.

This is a short life, Travis reasoned. No sense hoping for perfection. He changed into a dry pullover shirt and then slipped on his red checked Mackinaw. Now it was a different world. The wool soon made warmth against his body, and Travis knew he could take whatever blew down the lake.

He lashed off the rope and pulled the boat's bow down onto the sandbar. Then the tugging started. It was not a long distance to the water, but far enough the labors would drain out three rest stops. The aluminum hull made a scuffing sound on the wet beachhead. From where Travis pulled walking backwards, he could see how the keel in his backtrail had knifed into the sandbar. When the boat's belly was in the water, Travis went back for his fish gear and electric motor. He walked the keel's trail in the wet sands back to the boat. Then he shoved off and was out into the freedom.

His rubber boots made fidget scuffs on the boat's hull as Travis fussed over hooking up the motor leads — the sounding of his feet went through the aluminum and into the water and came back to Travis's ears like the sounds movie makers made for those sounding submarines in the old-time movies. This was the first time since fall lockup that Travis had wet any lines, and it felt really good inside to be at the whole thing again.

At first, he wet no fly. He just cruised the craft along the stone face of the dam in deep waters and enjoyed the evening. The boat's bow lifted with no other riders, and Travis could flair the turns on a dime. He listened to the whine of the prop far below, and watched the three raincoats of color on the other bank.

When Travis rounded the dam and was into straight waters for a spell, he let out the first level of line off the stern. On the very end of the leader, a Royal Coachman trailed behind.

The fly was just under the surface and made no wake. Its white high-back wings flexed back when Travis pumped the pole. Its red body looked very real to trout in these actions, and it did not take long to raise some. Several hundred yards after passing and giving a wave to the trio, Travis was on to his first fish.

The fish took him by surprise. His reflexes were not tuned, and he was not expecting action so soon. He turned around in astonishment and watched his pole tip bending toward action. Then the fight was on. He was a good fighter, this rainbow was, and a smart one too. Near the boat the rainbow sensed the danger and veered and dove and then darted away from Travis's net. The trout made another short run out from under the boat, and Travis turned him with high tip angle and went to scoop the fighting fish into the net's webbing. That's when the fat rainbow spit out the fly.

Travis could hardly believe his eyes. He leaned out over an oar lock and watched the trout for just a few blinks of time. The lake was still clear from all the snow melts and Travis could see him clear as day. The trout was finning in fixed position. His eyes blinked a couple of times, then the trout opened and closed his mouth very slow. Then it was gone with the flick of its tail, and all Travis caught was the silver sides flashing off as the rainbow dove into the deep dark depths.

No great loss, reasoned Travis. Good for him. A good rise was working the surface. Trout were feeding. He slid his hand across the stern thwart and into the lake. The trout's world felt warm against the May snap. Travis keeled his fingers in the wake, and lessons his father once taught him mysteriously surfaced through the lake. This revelation prevailed after death.

Travis scudded toward the cove where monster chain pickerel lived. He used the breasthook of the risen bow as a gun sight. The summer lily pads had not surfaced in the cold waters. In August the weeds and green pads had the cove choked in tight, and the only residents that seemed to love the weed beds were the bullfrogs. They were quite fond of loafing the day away on the green pads and croaked deep into the night. But now it was clear sailing and Travis cut a wide arc around the cove's mouth, then sighted back towards the spillway.

Some showers still fell from the sky. But for the most part it was just drizzle, a fine mist that drew the skin taught on Travis's face. Some fish had started to rise, and things were looking up. Travis trolled along the cove at slow speed. Then poor timing advanced under the glass waters — he hooked up with a lunker rainbow right in front of the father and daughter fish team. He had swung hard way beyond her red and white bobber, and that's when the fish sucked in the fly.

But Travis knew this was a keeper and fought him for all he had. The leaping rainbow put on quite a show for the man's daughter. It came out jumping and fighting, then would dive along the bottom at new angles. It would be over in a few minutes. This time Travis won. The bright bands of color on the fish's side, seemed to vanish in the creature's death. His yellow Queen Trapper jackknife went to work. Travis slipped the opened fish into the wicker creel. He had placed fresh ferns there, so any prizes would stay clean and in neat order.

The other man in yellow was all worked up after seeing Travis land the fish. He ran along the banking in huge bounds, then leaped across a deep slash in the slope. Then he walked out to the tip of this point and started casting a great distance. Excitement now ran the man. He was one of perpetual motion, cranking the handle with vast speed, lobbing the golden spoon into new water in hopes of a nice rainbow. He had pulled the yellow hood from his head, but a smile was still on him.

The father hauled in the bobber to check the worm. He worked his hands around the hook, then casted it back out. The red and white float sent rings of tiny wake, and the daughter watched the scene while seated on a boulder.

"Nice fish!" he shouted back to Travis. "How big?"

"About two pounds… a real fat one!"

Travis held up the fish so they could both see it well. Then he put it back in the creel and closed the woven lid.

"What did you get him on?" The father's voice came back very clear across the lake. That's how calm the May evening had become.

"Royal Coachman," answered Travis.

The sounds were so clear on the waters, that Travis could hear the daughter ask the next question. "What's a Royal Coachman?"

"It's a wet fly you troll under the water and the trout get fooled into thinking it's the real thing."

"Oh… do you think we could try that back home on Muller's Pond sometime Dad?"

"Why sure we can, Sweetheart," said the father as he leaned down and pulled her far shoulder in for a hug.

Travis trolled along the broken stone face of the dam. The wake of his electric motor made tiny laps on the stones. The raging brook had done more than its share to fill the lake. The spillway spit a sheet of white veil over the flash boards. Travis could see how the rips grew ominous near the gate valve and turned quickly away from where trouble may lurk.

Dusk had fallen on the lake. A pair of Canada Geese flew over the scudding boat, and they honked a ritual on their flight path up to the north cove. They had a ground nest there, a slight depression that was lined with dry grasses and goose down.

Travis turned to make another run. May rain had brought ruddy colors to his cheeks, and the veins on his back of hands had turned blue. He glanced to see if the trio were having any luck. But in the short span of time it had taken for turning the boat, the three had already packed and were walking up the steep slope. The man in yellow rain suit, was cutting across the high slope in a grove of husky beech trees. Their stout trunks dwarfed the man. The father and daughter went up and over the crest. A small patch of brightness glowed in the western sky. It was as if the father and daughter could feel Travis watching down the lake. They both turned and the father gave a wave. Travis could see his hand well in the skyline. Travis gave them back a round-house wave. But neither man said nothing.

It was as though deep inside their hearts, both men knew and understood this had been a very special evening on the lake in May rain. The short conversations between the father and daughter had cut for the better both ways:

The daughter was glad her dad cared enough and happy just knowing there would be another day on the waters with him; the father had known for some time in his heart, that these days with Veronica would soon be over with high school days coming soon, and he felt proud inside the daughter still asked to come along.

Sometimes in fishing, the lessons go beyond deep waters and the catching of fish.

— A short story for all those who made the times.

The Mexicans

The green parrot was perched in the ponderosa pine. This tree grew on a crested bluff in a tight grove of other pines high in the Chiricahua Mountains. The bird could look a long way off into the distance and across the Mexican border. His green feathers with wings capped in scarlet, were now absent from sight. It was dark and black. The parrot was a silhouette in the night. He had perched high in the canopy on a stout limb, when he knew the snows were coming. It had snowed heavy that night of deep powder across the mountain caps. The bird sat still in the blackness and sang softly into the night when the storm was waning to thistle down flurries. He sang to his other three companions roosted in the sister pines. There had been five parrots. They had flocked through the winter's migration when they banded that spring before the summer. But now there were only four parrots.

Just that morning before the snows came, a red-tailed hawk had dive bombed from the blue zenith into the green pine boughs and pummeled the placid bird. The morning air erupted in a powder puff of green feathers. The claws of the hawk pinned the green parrot, and the predator's hooked beak crushed its skull. Clutching its prey, the red-tailed hawk glided silent to the forest floor. He tore away the parrot's breast and commenced to drink its blood. The hawk feasted on the flesh and picked everything clean. Then he beat his wings over the pine needle floor and soared down the valley air currents and landed in a Joshua tree.

Down in the desert town of Bisbee, a man was rubbing his forehead. His name was Father O'Shannon, the pastor of Saint Patrick's Church. He was dressed in a black shirt and sat in the rectory cloaked of white stucco walls and was talking to himself. He had been listening to the tube radio and could hardly believe the reports of heavy snows in the mountains. Who would ever dream deep snows would fall the evening before Easter Sunday. Father O'Shannon whispered out loud and thanked the Lord for keeping the snows out of the valley. It would have been a tragic experience and would have ruined everything for those involved in the Holy Day celebration. He could not picture little girls walking in deep snows with spit-shined shoes and those colorful dresses. The priest was still talking to the high dome stucco ceiling, when he realized shafts of morning sun were falling through the pane glass and falling at his feet.

Father O'Shannon had gone to great lengths for Easter. On the morning of Good Friday, he had sent two Mexican gringos up into the desert hills above the town valley. The both of them were retinue around the church, offering their free time for tasks without the payments of money. The two of them had been dire whore masters driven by outbreaks of straight whiskey, and the short one with the scar on his cheek who went by the name of PaJoe, had been under the sickness spell of money poker in smoke-draped saloons, long before most people could remember. And that was really saying something, because PaJoe played poker-faced on both sides of the border for years. So then, the two of them had offered their labors to the Lord for forgiveness of their sins, hoping to clean out some of the stains on their souls.

Now the two Mexican gringos were shuffling and stumbling across the high desert plateau. Their footprints in the sand beds weaved through the stands of cactus. The winter winds had ebbed the sand dunes and swirled out fantastic patterns around the plants of thorn. PaJoe recognized this beauty and did his best to skirt around and not trodden the designs with his boots. But Father O'Shannon had sent them there to collect spring flowers from the cactus. So, it was impossible for PaJoe not to trample some art works by Mother Nature. The most beautiful and deep colors always bloomed in spring. It seemed to be a signal for all life to begin. Father O'Shannon had provided the two Mexicans with plastic tubs. The bottom of the tubs had been fitted with beds of sponge that had been sopped up with tap waters. The two Mexicans wielded Green River knives. They had carried the knives for a long time, for both of them had worked the date groves down in Yuma County, and knew about what bud scars to prune for production. Hence, it was second nature for them to sever the cactus flowers with the sharp blades. They shoved the stems into the sponge folds, which extended the blossoms life expectancy. Some of the flower brackets were bigger than cantaloupes, and of all the colors found in the flower world. The tubs filled very quickly. The Mexicans took a double smoke break before coming down off the ridge; they lit the second smoke from their clips. A soft cool breeze was raking the plateau, and their exhalations were scattered down the bluff lands. They knew well these kinds of days were precious in the desert lands, because soon the summer suns would bake the desert sands, and they remembered very clear two seasons back when the heat wave made a run at coming on strong for three weeks consecutive.

The plastic tubs filled with flowers, were light as feathers. They carried like air. PaJoe opened the rear door of Saint Patrick's Church with his shoulder blades, and both men delivered the grey tubs to the pastor. Father O'Shannon sorted and spread the flower heads on a white oak table in the vestibule. Milk glass panes of the side window that was sashed out in the past century by craftsman's hands that were now long dead, illuminated the beds of flowers. You could even see the hushed tones of the stamens. Father O'Shannon now had the ornamentation he had pictured. The three men used the first tub for accents spattered across the altar. The white cloths spread over the altar, made sharp contrast for the colored flowers. Several of the cactus blooms were tucked around the candle box, where match heads could be struck for those souls loved. The dancing of candle flames flickered on the church wall, and shadow boxed the beautiful flowers. The last two cactus flowers, pure red twins, were cupped around the holy water vessel just inside the front entrance. Those who dipped two fingers for anointments of the blessings, would be under the token gesture of the desert's beauty through the brace of red flowers. With the field of Easter lilies across the altar's stair, flecked now with cactus blooms, the church looked spectacular. Pungent wild scents drifted and hugged the pew rows. Father O'Shannon was now ready for the telling of preacher's lessons and honor the Resurrection Mass of Easter Sunday.

High in the ponderosa pine, the green parrot had begun to shake out the sleep. He hopped along the stout limb towards the new day. Soft morning light spilled across the desert floor, and the green bird husked out seeds from a pine cone.

It was Easter morning in the Chiricahua Mountains. Through his big set of eyes, the green parrot could see very clear. He saw the blanket of fresh snow across the desert morning, and how the platoons of green cactus stood out against the white carpet. He looked across the grandeur landscape and down into the drought basin where the snow had melted on the hot beds of yellow-orange sands, and the blue stream that wove through the arid gulch, where the cobblestones along the banks were baked white from the sun, and off in the distance the groves of Engelmann spruce hugged the ridge, where a French blue was hung over the Arizona landscape.

The night's storm had not been driven by backing winds. The grove of ponderosa pines had held its defense against the deep snows. A few inches had sifted past the stout boughs. The parrot pecked its breast. It looked down through the ring of limbs to the forest floor. He could see the death bed of his fallen comrade. Some of the feathers were masked by the storm. Both scarlet-capped wings stuck through the snow, and flecks of green plume peeked out past the snowflakes. A berth of crimson had seeped into the storm. The bird blinked its eyes, and recorded the sacrifices paid below. But in the large theme of all things, the green parrot standing rigid on the limb had no reasons for worry. Even though the green bird had no soul, the Lord always showed mercy for the weak and defenseless. The green parrot would find its maker in the end.

But down in Saint Patrick's Church on this Easter morning, the consequences were being played out for higher stakes. The two Mexicans seated two rows back from the altar under the effects of amber electric lights, sheepishly bowed their heads and clutched fast to strings of rosary beads.

The Mexicans made small peeps with their lips, moving their fingers up and down the black beads and kept the penance of the prayers inside and to themselves, because they had both lived fast lives inside strange bedrooms and much time on stools that spun in barrooms, and they wanted to make certain from the heart with all their convictions.

Three mission nuns were seated five rows back, and they followed suit to the Mexicans. The wafer-thin sister with full lips, seemed to be measuring the scar across PaJoe's face.

Father O'Shannon braced himself in the pulpit and took a long hard look across the sea of faces and bright colors of those in attendance, hoping they would get the drift of things and remember a man had taken steel spikes through both hands for their sins, so they could get a free ride out like the birds perched in the forest of pines.

Showering of the Sparks

Mister, you never saw odds like that. The Parque de Vida in Cortez was jammed. It was the 4th of July. Counting the five police officers on the corner of Mildred Road and Montezuma Avenue, myself a drifter from out of town, and maybe ten other stragglers in the crowd, there were perhaps fifteen white people. Maybe twenty. That's it. The rest of them were Navajo Indians. There must have been a good four thousand of them.

Well…not all of them were Navajo. A big bronze faced Navajo with an Angels ball cap, told me there was Utes mixed in the crowd. A white fireworks watcher like me, only saw Indians who were very polite and orderly. But that Navajo guy, Chester Nez as he introduced himself, could tell the difference alright. Chester said by Jesus, the Navajos were blood brothers of the Apache nation, and they could spot a Ute a mile away.

It was sure a swell event. You never saw such green grass on the high desert. For a heat spell, the sport's field was greener than a sheep meadow in Northern Belfast of Ireland. Huge puffy white clouds filled the sky. There was not a stitch of wind, and across the field a few silhouettes of men in cowboy hats, were setting up what looked like a row of rain barrels. But Mister, they were no rain barrels, but a series of charged high-showering fireworks. They were wired to ignite by electric hand plungers. I could see a rancher with a white hat moving hither and thither in the detonation zone; and just then he opened more crates of fireworks. Two other guys were running wire, and the biggest of them was shouting orders, while the skinny guy payed out the spool.

Many of the Navajo tribe who'd driven from the reservation, were early birds. Their iron armada that had proceeded from the south-west through the high plains desert on the black ribbon of roadbed, began spewing in on the green clipped fields in the crux of morning tides. The grey slate hue of dawn was sliding its last trace into the zenith. The sun was climbing. Many of the big white clouds had not formed by then. Pale orange and carmine streaks were on the hori-zon. The Indians had marked these colors exceedingly well. For them it was second nature. Later that morning the dew had burned off and a vibrant green spilled across the playing fields, and under the sky of cerulean blue the sunlight flamed on the tips of mountains.

The Indians streamed in all through the sun-kissed after-noon. The thing that had struck the red man's notice, was that in the higher elevation of Cortez's high plains desert, the needles of the sun took less out of the tribe — there was a cool breeze going down your throat. Indians holding back grins with open win-dows in automobiles wearing the veils of tawny dust of the high plains, necked tight in a stream of colored tin up Montezuma Avenue. A patch-work of Indian blankets covered the green grass, and many bronzed figures were seated in folding chairs.

Those Indians sure had good gear. Sound equipment from the chain stores. Their sun tents and roped cinched awnings, had no rips and were not faded by the sun. The Indians knew how to set up tents too. All the ropes were taut as guitar strings, and the stakes were well driven. Looking across the Parque de Vida was a sea of colored sunshades, the white ropes anchored into the green turf. The Indians were all over the angles of the sun. They were always one move ahead of the sun. When the yellow sun was rising from say Durango, they shifted their sun flaps in accordance.

The Indians made a day of it. Independence Day was a big thing. They left nobody home on the reservation. All family members had taken the ride. There was a mother in a calico dress that brushed her ankles, breast feeding a baby with jet black hair. A grandfather was drinking orange soda through a straw while seated in a blue lawn chair; I never saw the guy at first, but he was making so much noise slurping the orange beverage between his teeth, he caught my attention and there he was in the next tent. All dimensions were present. In my rounds around the grounds, I saw two Indians on battery-powered oxygen machines.

Because of the shade pockets across Mildred Road in Centennial Park, none of the Indians over there needed to pitch shade tents. Elm groves with mushroomed crowns and massive silver limbs, set back in the tree belt, casted a cool veil of shade over the park dwellers. A blue-collar paradise had been assembled. The Indians had circled the furrowed trunks with their blankets and ice chests. Further back in perspective, dappled shade fell from the canopy of a cottonwood stand. Many voices of children were rising from the playground. A gang of kids were spinning in wild orbits on a giant metal dish known as the tilt-a-whirl; their tiny hands held on in defiance of their speed. It sure was a swell park. There was a duck pond. There was a genuine water bubbler that was adorned in green enamel, and with all kinds of water pressure. I saw some kids testing the spigot, to see how high they could shoot water.

It was too bad though, about that odd duck in the pond. The other ducks did not like him. He had shabby white feathers, and motley pin feathers with very poor plume. That duck was a mess, and his face was dirty.

Brother, those black ducks with those flashing orange beaks, really put the screws to that odd duck. They chased him from the pond, up the trampled foot path, and got him in some kind of headlock with their beaks.

They had his neck pinned to the ground and were really giving it to him. He looked like a dead duck. But after a while, the gang of black ducks let go of the pasted underdog and swam away quacking. The dusty oddball duck shook his feathers, and watched the other ducks circle the pond. After a while he took the hint. He puffed himself in the bath of sun and loaded away in the field of rays. A Navajo girl with twin black braids, witnessed the whole ordeal from the water bubbler.

I'd been under Chester Nez's tent for some time. It was very satisfactory to be out of the afternoon sun, and the pupils of the Indian's brown eyes had grown large in the shade. Chester was a good storyteller. His daughter Violet had just graduated from high school in Albuquerque, and she could not tell you any authentic stories about the reservation — she only knew about traditions and Indian lore handed down to her. Chester had all the memories though, and both his parents were buried into the desert sands of the Navajo Nation.

Violet was sitting on a beach chair. I was standing. The shade tent offered all kinds of head room. Her legs were kicked out in buckskin Navajo boots; silver conchos glittered in the flat light.

"Can you see that mountain far off in the distance?" said Violet with a blank face. She was pointing to a singular mountain with her trigger finger, and all her fingernails were painted blue.

"Where?" I asked bending at the knees. The clouds were flying low, and way off in the far horizon, the cut shades of mountains were painted in graduations of Air Force blue.

"There," she pointed. Violet grabbed my shoulder and said "Look — use the peak of that silver metal roof as a gun sight."

The tin roof heliographed in the sun. I sighted up on the hip roof — and there in the distance a flyspeck was on the frontier.

"That lone mountain that looks like an Egyptian pyramid?"

"That's it," said Violet. "It's called Lone Cone Mountain. We are going fishing in that high country over the weekend. It's a good place to escape the heat. We'll work the rivers below the steep pitches in the valley, then hike up into Trout Lake."

"Catch many fish?"

"Dad's a professional. I'm still learning. The fresh air in the mountains is my calling card. It's another world up there. The wildflowers are exploding in the high meadows, and the colors should be spectacular."

Violet found it very satisfactory to camp in the high mountains of summer. She liked it best when the temperature dived in the blackness, and Chester banked the campfire with dead pine snags. She marveled at the plumes of sparks climbing in the smoke pearls, red-orange embers that died in the forest's black veil under the galaxy of twinkling stars. There was something about wearing a long-sleeve flannel shirt against the chill, that brought Violet security. The pungent bite of fire smoke in the evergreen cathedral, stayed close to Violet's heart a long time. It was one of those potions that got her through winter, when the windstorms peppered her panes with golden grains of sand.

Five hours would advance the clock, before fireworks would be exploding in the black curtain of night. Thousands of Indians were seated in orderly fashion looking out over the athletic field. Just then, the irrigation heads popped, and watering of the athletic fields commenced. I guess the way the orders were spilled, was that the head honcho of the fireworks wanted the ball fields sprinkled, to arrest any chance of grass fires from the shower of sparks. The giant industrial heads, fanned vase shapes of water across the playfields.

The Navajo boys caught on quick. They'd been pushing a soccer ball down the chalk line. The skinniest kid with fancy footwork, was showing his ribcage sheened in sweat. His black belt was cinched on the last hole; a good ten inches of cowhide was flapping on his blue jeans.

But when the boys saw the heads of water, the white ball died. They raced across the turf with a new zeal. The afternoon sun was steeping the boys in yellow rays, and we could hear their echos sounding across the field, the pointed yelling and screaming with a boy's excitement. Pure innocence filled the scene.

The boys ran through the water zones. See the boys run. The skinniest boy ran the fastest. The others charged ahead, zigzag through the maze of heads. They flailed their arms wildly, always running. It was a great deal across. The water zones covered two football fields; the Indian boys were screaming in happiness. All of their chests glistened in the sun, and a raven sheen was painted in their black locks.

The skinny boy broke free from the pack. He carved a wide turn on the turf, his high-top sneakers cutting into the green blades. The day had grown brighter, the sun banking his full radiance upon the bronzed boy, and in these rays of light, a vision enveloped my mind: signature brush strokes from an Andrew Wyeth egg tempera painting, formed suddenly around the Indian boy. The tones of earth colours were very convincing. The image was hit aslant with realism. The boy running at cocked angles down the farm field in his black winter suit, the painting on gesso board which had been given the title of *Winter*, had enveloped a symbolic linear passage to the Indian boy. Even the pictorial language in their faces had taken on this resemblance, and in the mind of this drifter I could picture him inside the picture frame. It was a very convincing hallucination. It's been recited many times that the power of art can provide symbolic significance as a linear thread into the living. Watching from the distance from under the brim of my cowboy hat, the Indian boy was coming to life in the palate of sun rays.

Three of the five police officers on the corner of Mildred Road, were leaning on a white sawhorse drinking from cans of soda. The two others were directing motor traffic, and the fattest of the two was rubbing his belly. And that was really saying something, because the cop next to him was pushing over two hundred and fifty pounds on the short side. All the cops were getting hungry. A great deal of Indians were hungry too, and the sweet smell of frybread was making my mouth water.

A white baker's tent was pitched in Centennial Park behind the navy-blue uniforms of the police. The tent was reminiscent of the canvas proportions used to feeding army men of battalion strength. The Indians had hooked up gas bottles to a large iron grill set on blocks of cinder, and under the coppice of high limbs a huge pit of glowing coals was searing red meat. Puffs of confederate grey smoke waxed and waned in the dead stillness, a gauzed lamp of mellow sun sleeping in the forest, and here and there through the trees, flashes of orange and blue could be seen from the fires.

The Navajos were selling food. Under the white tent, the Indian women were taking orders. It was a blueprint of simple math. All the orders were printed in blue ink on scrap paper, fixed with your first name. The orders were clipped with a wood clothes pin on a tag wire that ran above the cash register.

Most of the native plates were on the black board. The staple of the Navajo nation, corn and mutton soup with two slices of blue bread, was a big seller. Many of the Indians had come back for seconds. They were not bashful about putting real butter on their bread.

There was rabbit stew. It simmered in a big aluminum pot. A Navajo woman with a wide headband in the bold shade of satin magenta, long double braids of raven locks flowing across her shoulders, was stirring the stew pot with a big wooden spoon. When she spooned it out into bowls, you could see it was the real thing. It teemed with hominy and thick brown gravy. Some big Navajo — he must have been seven feet tall and built like Thor — was cooking over wood coals. His job was grilling up dogs and burgers. He looked like he could put away burgers like Wimpy.

But the biggest seller was frybread. Those fried discs of dough were bringing in a lot of bread. The money was coming in hand over fist, and the two Indian girls raking in the dough, had to keep pressing down on all those green bills into the metal cash tin. The tin was adorned in the hues of juniper boughs. The Indians had used this box for a long time. The enamels were worn from the corners of the lid and revealed silver tin. The old box was showing its age. It came to a point where no more money could fit, and the Indian cook in a black cowboy hat took away the money. He put the sheaf of green bills in a steel chest and locked it down with a padlock.

That frybread was a hot item and sailed out the white tent. It was golden brown and big as dinner plates. The customers were backed in line under the dappled shade, and the blades of grass were showing poor colors from the scuffing of boots. After your order was taken on scrap paper, you were asked to stand under the grove of trees and make room for the other people standing on edge for food. They called everybody by first name. I was inside the circle of people waiting to hear their name.

A guy in the circle near me was white too. He was wearing a straw rancher's hat, and a NFR black T-shirt embossed with white threads: National Bull Riders Final. His oval belt buckle was very large and looked very old. A bull was bucking on the silver. His Justin cowboy boots were scuffed and banged, and when I looked close on the shaft, there was a gash which looked like a bull had tried to get him.

When I turned back to look at him again, I saw that he had a silver front tooth and a scar running up his cupid's bow. The bull must have been mad.

We were the only two white guys around. All the rest were Indians. The smell of smoke was winding through the trees, and all of us were getting hungry.

"Felicia!" called the order number lady. "Seven fry breads and two corn stews."

Felecia came from the shade pockets and under the tarpaulin awning. She was a big lady with a round face, and her Navajo complexion was golden and still like a kid. It glowed so radiant in the cool shade of the summer elms.

A lot of customers were like Felicia. They bought full plates of food. It was all going to a noble cause. None of the Navajos working the food concession stand would be getting a penny. All the money was going to be given away.

A plywood sign was screwed to the trailer. It was a homemade sign, white house paint with black letters. It read: All profits of food sales donated for the funeral costs of Rajani Tahoma.

What an awful thing. It was tragic. Half of the Navajo people, men who had held back the tears, found themselves feeling bad for weeks later. The whole Navajo nation had been in mourning. There had been no warning. Absolutely none.

Rajami was a grandmother. She had been holding the hand of her granddaughter Fulki Shooting Star and making certain she got safely on the yellow school bus. From holding hands, part of the old lady was feeling young again, and Shooting Star was standing very firm on the sidewalk and was confident now about many things. Ominous dark clouds choked the sky, as the little girl skipped onto the bus. She blew a kiss through the bus glass at her grandmother.

The bus pulled out, and got smaller, and then smaller down the lane. Rajami was holding tight on the metal post of the red stop sign, when everything went black for her. She had felt very little. There had been a thunderclap. A silver-blue bolt had shot from the charcoal sky. It had been a direct hit. Rajami crashed over dead on the sidewalk. She had felt only a quick jab of electricity. Then she was dead.

The lightning bolt had done considerable damage. She never had a chance. The metal sign conducted electricity well. The storm's charge ran the metal post, and in a blinding blue flash, had burned hair away. The right side of her head above the ear, was singed to the scalp.

She had no arrangements. Discussion had never been made inside a funeral home. McCutcheon Funeral Home performed the embalming out of their pocket. It was a pinched casket. The cheapest wood coffin. It was an open viewing. A Navajo scarf of beautiful tapestry had been fitted around her skull. No trace of the horrible incident was visible. The undertakers had used a blend of secret serums, known only inside their circles, to fill in the seared groove across her cheekbone from the lightning bolt. But Billy McCutcheon was a businessman. It was a simple process. He needed to get paid. Billy gave the Indians a one-year note. No interest was tacked on. But it was expected they come around square.

So, you could see why the Indians were so free with their money, and a lot of kids shelled out most of their allowance.

But a lot of their hearts were still heavy. They still held Rajami's tragedy deep inside. It was a distant kind of grief, although most of them had stopped crying for more than six months.

You had only heard the statement of her loss. You had no idea if her arms flailed wild as she went down. You could only picture those things in your imagination. You knew the grandmother died on the corner of Tumbleweed Drive and Zuni Avenue from new reports. You pictured she had fallen very suddenly and must have laid dead on the sidewalk motionless as a burlap sack of spuds. You might have heard the lone siren of the sheriff's patrol car from a thousand miles with sharp perception, and here and there, saw blue flashes between the row of houses behind your doll eyes. But it was a distant death. You did not see her die.

Those were personal grounds. Afterwards some of the tribe picked up more details from the ambulance crew who was attended by their own people on the reservation. They had been painted in with realistic details; and a lot of them were sorry they asked. This information circulated all around the Navajo nation, and the gravest details stayed with the tribe behind sealed lips.

But, in spite of these things, it was a marvelous revel, and there was a rising and falling of all kinds of laughter from inside the white tent.

It was my turn. That lady with a nice round face and skin like copper looked around the corner of the white tent and shouted right at me. "Roger — orders up!"

I moved real fast. I was sick of watching other people eat. My mouth was watering bad. Say, it sure was something though when that lady called a drifter like me by my first name. I'd almost forgot my first name. Nobody had called me by my name Roger in over two years. I'd been living out of a glorified hobo sack, riding trains and drifting around, and nobody had known my name. But now the Indians knew my name on account of my food order, and I was never so happy to hear my name again. Those Indians sure had a keeper friend in me now.

I'd been watching the local customs real close. A drifter like me knew nothing much about Indian customs. Gee, those Indians sure had a sweet tooth. They covered the frybread with confectioner's sugar. They became so generous with the sprinklings, the picnic table looked like dusted snow. I'd even seen a few kids sprinkle their palms, then lick the white dust. When in Rome, act like the Indians. I sifted on some nice dust, grabbed my cup of lemonade with ice cubes, and headed over to the duck pond. It was a very satisfactory place for eating. Most of the Indians were holding down blankets. There were four vacant tables. The pond was dead. No ducks around and no quacking. I proceeded to eat my frybread, and sip lemonade. It was good to have lemonade to swig down the white dust. The water on the pond was dead flat, and in the reeds a bullfrog was singing. He carried nice notes.

Just then a visitor arrived. It was the white duck with the dirty face. I'd not seen him. He must have been hiding in the cattails. But he was coming alright, his orange webs waddling towards me, and he was quacking.

"Quack! Quack!" said the duck.

Wow — you never saw a duck like this. He was a real mess. His face was so dirty, and he even had sleep in the corner of his eyes. He looked really bad.

This duck looked up at me with his black eyes, as if to pour out love on me. The white duck quacked again. He pecked my boot with his orange bill, then laid down and tried to snuggle on me. I think this duck thought I was his mother. Was I ever feeling bad for him.

He was a pleasant fellow. The duck not only allowed me to pet his head, but you could hear a soft purr in his throat; he seemed exceedingly happy to be wanted for a change.

I told the duck to stay still. He listened. This was very strange in itself. You would expect a dog or cat to listen, but not a duck. But he listened alright and sat on his haunches right away. Then I walked to the water bubbler of green enamel and wet my napkin.

It was too much on me to see a duck with a dirty face. You should have seen how happy that duck was when I wiped his countenance. He started marching around in a tight circle and said, "Quack! Quack!"

I turned away from Mister Quack-Quack and started eating my frybread. What a nice treat. It was going down fast, and the pink lemonade really hit the spot. Tranquility filled the scene.

But then that duck started piping up again. He was really giving me the business. Quack! Quack! Quack! He would not be quiet. The duck was trying to push a hint on me, that he was hungry too.

I ripped my frybread in two. You saw what the black ducks did to him. He'd been through enough of hell already. I wanted really bad to give my new friend some food now, because he'd been treated so badly all because he was an odd duck with a dirty face.

The duck dove in. Both of us ate in silence. The duck was a very fast eater, and his bill moved a million miles an hour. In the prominence of these effects was the bullfrog croaking in the reeds.

Dusk had descended. Electric light bulbs could be seen burning in the homes past the Parqe de Vida. Many residents had taken to their roofs. The homeowners with flat roofs, had piled coolers and lawn chairs up there too. Chester Nez was looking at them through his binoculars from under his tent.

I needed to make tracks. It was time to find a good spot for watching fireworks. I rummaged through my sack; drifters like me always tried carrying three-day old baked goods, which we could buy many times under the dollar. An old and hard oatmeal cookie was dug out. I gave the cookie to the duck. He clutched the cookie in his bill, waddled down the bank, and I saw him dart into the cattails where he must have had a sound nest.

Mother Nature was calling. I needed to make tinkle. There was no way of making it through the fireworks. I needed to go bad. Those two cups of lemonade were going through me.

Lined out down the shoulder of a white pea stone parking lot, was a row of green fiberglass Porta Potties. There were eight of them, with a vast crowd out front waiting to use them.

I got in line. All the figures in line were Navajos. We shuffled over the bed of pea stone. Many people were looking for relief, and it was a long line.

A Navajo mother with her four children, were directly to my front. Her little boy, maybe nine years old, was pinching himself. He was holding tight on his trousers' zipper. He needed to go bad and was prancing in place with tension on his brow.

Just then, an old Irish guy with his wife that had silvered hair, cut across the white pea stones. They pressed towards me. The Navajo mother and her children had worked to the very front. They were next in line. Watching the Irishman close his gap, his face had been caught in the flat lights which cast from the falling sun. You never saw such white skin as on this guy. A spray of blue spider veins ran across his temple, just under the baker white skin. His complexion clashed against the sea of red men.

The Irish guy bade me with a desperate plea — "Sir, could I have cuts in line? My kidneys are shot. It's tough getting old."

"Sure Mister," I told him. You never felt sorry for anyone like him. The poor guy. I put my hands on his shoulder blades for assurance. The Irishman held his head in bashfulness, and both eyes were seeping crust.

The Navajo mother surprised me. "Come," she told him. She gave the old guy free cuts. Her children parted to make room. The old Irishman shuffled in with his white loafers. His arthritic knuckles palmed the cane. He was shaking bad. The boy was still pinching the crotch of his blue jeans. His red sneakers were prancing and rising dust. The candor of needing relief was all over the boy.

A green stall had become vacant. The old man broke for his chance. He closed the green door and fumbled with his zipper. The silver haired wife braced herself against the door. She smiled back at the Indians.

A silent courtship was conducted over the heads of the throng about the beds of pea stones. Independence Day loomed across Cortez. Foreshadow of sensitive revelation assembled. Numbers and dates were stricken on the dusk sky. History came to a screeching halt: The documents had been signed with a crow quill laced with black ink on July 4th of 1776. John Hancock and fifty-five others had thrown down their signatures, which permanently freed American colonies from British rule. That we were united, free, and independent figures. In no shape or form on the documents, were the American Indians included. Roger could feel this in the air.

Then things turned a sharper side of ugly. Time had wheeled exactly one hundred years on the button. The murders had taken place on the 25th of July of 1876. It happened on a tranquil summer day, birds chirping and Indian kids swimming in the Little Big Horn. The thumping of horse hoofs rose notes on the prairie floor, and slashing sabers glistened in the sun rays. General George Custer had shackled orders on the 7th Calvary to slaughter the tipi village in cold blood. Everybody dead. And even though the brave Indians pulled a power flank and gave Custer his last stand, what really happened on the blood-stained golden sands was the doom was sealed for all Indians to be locked inside places called reservations. Exactly one hundred years after we got the idea of exploding fireworks was a grand celebration, just like Roger revealed in his story line.

I kept my mouth shut and lips tight though. The crowd was sailing in high spirits, and I didn't want to bring about sour matters. Saying the wrong thing might start trouble.

"Lovely night."

"Sure is," said the Indian next to me in line for the potty.

"What a lovely crowd."

"What a nice showing."

"Looking forward to the fireworks."

"Our people come off the reservation every year to see the fireworks."

"God bless you," I told her with a dead serious face.

The old man finished shaking himself. Three drops of yellow piddle sailed through the air. He appeared in the green door opening. The old Irish couple beamed towards the Indians. Very few people alive, even the deepest thinkers around Cortez, would ever know the generous consequences of his cuts in line.

The last threads of darkness were sewing on the horizon. Cortez was stitched in raven colors. Things were getting close. Looking far across the Parque de Vida, three flashlights of the fireworks men were plain as day, and the yellow beams were darting hither and tither over the charges and spaghetti wire. It was a wide-open view. All the Indians had taken down their tents. The Indians had taken care to fold their tents with love and affection. They were not like some white men you see around, who make a mess of folding tents and cram everything into the trunk and call it close enough.

I came across Mildred Road with a sea of Indians. There was much excitement in our cadence. We could see the din of explosions were right around the corner, and my eyes were growing wide with wonder in the effects of night vision.

The fattest of the two cops was pounding down a second can of soda. Next to him near the sawhorse on Mildred Road, were two used paper plates; and one of them was all splattered with brown gravy. He must have ordered a couple of helpings from Rajani Tahoma's benefit, and when you saw the size of his belly, all second thoughts went away.

Indian kids were skipping in the theater of night with glow sticks. The effects of the soft colors were very satisfactory, and two girls skipped past me with pink and lime green sticks. The glowing colors washed on their faces, and above them, there was a twinkling of star beds in the sky.

I moved through the Indians. There was over four thousand Indians, and I was the only white guy around. Most of the Indians were in lawn chairs, and the rest were on blankets. Every bench in Parque de Vida was full, and in some cases, you saw five people crammed into a green bench with children on their laps. Even in the curtains of night, you could see against the skyline that a great deal of Indian braves were sporting cowboy hats. No matter how many angles you looked at an Indian in a cowboy hat, they looked exactly like an Indian wearing a cowboy hat. But by the same token, when you saw a wrangler wearing a Navajo bandanna around their forehead, both wrists ladened with turquoise stones set in silver bracelets, they looked like imposters. Many black and white cowboy hats were cut out against the sky, and the profile of their nose and high cheekbones pointed them out as Navajos.

Here and there in the forest of Indians, were jar candles burning. The yellow flames licked the night, and I moved out through the flicker of candlelight. This dancing of fire brought a magnificent effect to the atmosphere — it touched on a super-natural world.

The first barrage of fireworks caught everybody by surprise — Whooooosh… Kaboom! Then again as cannon fire — Kaboom! The crowd tightened and gasped. " Oh my God," exclaimed an old Indian grandmother near me. She was braced against the night holding a carved wooden cane, and the wash of fireworks had brought a sudden color to her face.

A speeding rocket suddenly exploded into the black night, and the orange sparks falling into the night casted a glow of pumpkin orange across her grey hair.

The gleam from the explosions had set a spark in her brown eyes, and I could see she was missing two teeth. These kinds of things had no bearing on the old lady's thrills during the explosion of fireworks.

A war-like veil of smoke was drifting in the night, and when the men in the detonation zone got a sniff of cordite, they moved with a quicken pace and appeared to riding the waves of adrenaline. Soon after they went wild on the plungers. The sky was pumped with mad minutes. Rockets with blue slip streams raced into the night tides. Plaboom! Plaboom! A mushroom of tangerine sparks pursed a Hail

Mary halo under the watch of sympathetic heavens. High shooters exploded with needle rays of red, white, and blue. The hunched figures of cannon cockers fired Roman Candles of giant proportions in rapid fire — Phyffit! Phyffit! Phyffit! Gold and silver stars split from the candle's heads. The fireworks men broke the fused bombs from crates with claw hammers and sent them on split shifts of self-destruction. When those kinds of guys see the aftermath of their fingers stabbing the detonation buttons, they become riddled with child-like passion for lighting more fuses. Caught in the hot flashes of euphoria, they delivered a boom-boom show — sudden thunderclaps made people jump. Blaboom! Boom! Blam! Blaboom! The voice of the fireworks could be heard clear into Crow Canyon.

Caught there in the concussion, the fat cop had a flashback of his Grandpa Charlie, who once told him the story of what it was really like when the Marines had stormed Red Beach on Iwo Jima. Grandpa Charlie never revealed and pointed details of blood spilled across the beachhead. But the fat cop always remembered what really stuck inside him from the subject matter — "If it were not for the six Navajo Code Talkers assigned to our task force, the Marines would have never taken Iwo Jima. They had worked around the clock for two days with no sleep and had sent over 800 coded messages without a single mistake."

A sudden revelation came over the fat cop, for he was enveloped by over four thousand Indians while standing on the roadbed in the black of night. Under the umbrella of silvered sparks and colored plumes, he saw these Indians with their high cheekbones with silhouettes against the bright explosions, in a new light. He saw them as heroes who had helped win a terrible war for the native land.

The fireworks had brought about a wretched chill across his round countenance. The finer points of combat were well concerned.

He saw Grandpa Charlie's face in the stentorian speeches of gun powder exploding with pink flashes.

This poor fellow with tight buttons across his uniform, had reeled back in the raven shadows of park elms, and broke out a Milky Way to curb his distress. No ordinary experience could have excited such sensation. In truth the intoxication license of death was a rare visitor. It would have been folly to pretend and keep in pace with the external world. Charlie's face was the avatar, and there was no wiggle room around.

The police officer had eaten his candy bar in two bites. Food had always been his secondary reaction to the tight quarters of bad emotions. The weight he carried was in direct proportion to emotion. They say fat people are jolly. This individual fit the mold. The size of the man carried into his disposition, and he was revered as the most cheerful police officer on the second beat of Cortez Police Department. The guys were all over him, because he could blunt the crux of their bad days.

The sky suddenly took on tangible forms of colors. Multitude of explosions occurred — the grand finale had arrived. The fireworks men had detonated platoons and squadrons of rockets, which in face had so many novel effects, volley of indefinite decorum seldom seen, the crowd gasped in astonishment. Plumes of palette and luminous fancy thronged the night ink, and a barbaric luster fell over the mountains.

The glittering trails of orange sparks, casted wine-tints across the duck pond. The white duck had awakened in the raucous, and he was seeing all kinds of stars about him in the sky. Gleams of silver and gold, here and there in the curved sky, fell upon the Indians.

In the prominence of these effects was the old Irishman. His white skin showed as snow. His neck was craned to the fireworks.

The mouth box was pulled back, and he was squinting.

The malady had stricken the old man. Its progress was rapid. Macular degeneration had creeped into his eyeballs. Central vision was shot for the old timer. Neovascularization had made a mess behind his retinas, and blood was sloshing around from blood vessel failure.

High above the crowd, under the star beds, glancing rays changed people's faces to pink hues and silvered the windshields of automobiles. The old man cocked his head sideways and looked through the cup of his singular eye. He smiled wide and with passive love on the show. Flowers of colored explosions were swimming in his cut-rate vision and climbing above the Indians grey smoke was curling and seated into clouds from the burned powder.

"Roger," said Chester Nez leaning forward from the black curtain while grabbing my shoulder, "that old timer must have feebleness of the eyes."

"It sure looks that way."

The old Irishman was leaning on his white cane with an elk antler handle, and as he watched the shower of sparks falling with eyes seeping a crusted film like an old Plott hound. The Irishman was sure glad those Indians gave him cuts in line, because the last thing he wanted in that sea of celebration was bright yellow stains on his white boxer shorts.

A man would have to comb through tablets a long way back, to find a more poignant act of Divine Mercy appointed to the Irishman, given with compassion from a mother whose son was pinching off his zipper, because it was the white man who sentenced her people to the reservation.

They were sure a generous nation. How many people with red blood could have made her decision?

That night we lay on the floor in the room and I listened to the silk-worms eating. The silk-worms fed in the racks of the mulberry leaves and all night you could hear them eating and a dropping sound in the leaves. I myself did not want to sleep because I had been living for a long time with the knowledge that if I ever shut my eyes in the dark and let myself go, my soul would go out of my body. I had been that way for a long time, ever since I had been blown up at night and felt it go out of me and go off and then come back. I tried to never to think about it, but it had started to go since, in the nights, just at the moment of going off to sleep, and I could only stop it by a very great effort. So while now I am fairly sure that it would not really have gone out, yet then, that summer, I was unwilling to make the experiment.

— Now I Lay Me by Ernest Hemingway

Texas Hardpan

It was very hot. All the soil was cracked from the sun. The Texas sun, and it had not rained for a very long time.

The cemetery was in the Texas Hill Country, and the soil between the name plaques was cracked this way and that way, and a great crowd had gathered.

The little girl had never deserved to die. She was only ten years old. She had never expected to die that day, when the shooter walked into her classroom with an automatic weapon. But she died alright. Nineteen kids died that day, and both of their teachers.

It's not very pleasant to talk about. The first teacher and the shooter had met face to face. They had looked each other in the eye, standing there in the doorway. Then the shooter backed her into the classroom, and still looking her in the eye, shot her in the head. She never knew what hit her.

Then he shot the other teacher. She took the lead, and managed to live for quite a few minutes. She had managed to pull her cellular telephone and talk with her husband. They had last words. To this day the conservation was never revealed, and held tight to the chest as a private matter between the family.

The others died in the same manner, in cold blood. It was a good thing God had Sanctifying Grace in place. As all the kids were ten years old or thus younger, they all got instantaneous Sanctifying Grace. All of them went to heaven, just about the time they hit the floor inside the classroom.

But nobody talked about this at the time. Some never would. I'm glad I reminded them.

A great crowd had gathered for the burial of Nevaeh Bravo. Just about everybody was sweating, and the soil was cracked, and the first cousins of Nevaeh Bravo were crying hard. Their mother did not try to stop them from crying. She knew it would be good for them to cry, and get everything out of them. It was hard to watch the young girls cry. They were crying very hard for Nevaeh. They were part of the immediate family, and they were standing under the tent procured by the funeral director.

The rest of us were in the baking sun. The soil was deeply cracked, and we were scuffing the ground with our shoes and boots. About the only nice thing about the funeral of Nevaeh Bravo, was that they were giving out free water. The plastic bottles of water were in a galvanized cattle trough. It must have been a Texas thing. There were hundreds of bottles of free water; and I grabbed one for myself and slugged it down. There must have been ice in the beginning, but now it was all melted away in the Texas heat, but there was still moisture on the plastic bottles of water, and several people were slugging them down.

The first cousins had never stopped crying. They were sobbing away very loud, and the mother was patting them on the back for assurance.

Reverend Eduardo Morales of Sacred Heart Church, was doing

his best to keep things under control. His voice boomed loud across the cemetery. There was a Latino ring in his voice. Just about everybody around the open grave was a Latino, and they were all over what he was saying. All of them knew the priest first hand, and many of them called him Father Eddy.

Reverend Eduardo Morales spoke some of the words in Spanish, and some of them in English. He mixed things up in the dialogue, and was dressed in priest vestments of cream colored silks that hung to his black shoes, and the silk was swaying over the cracked soil of the burial grounds, when Reverend Eduardo Morales had swung his arm across the Texas sky. I saw his lips move, but could not put together the words.

White boys like me might have missed some of the message, but not too much you know. It was general knowledge for the dead. The priest read from the Bible. I could not speak any Spanish, but when Father Eddy switched to the native tongue I learned many things from what was on his face. And the rest I picked up from the crowd. I'd been a high plains drifter for a long time, and knew how to read things from the street.

Reverend Eduardo Morales had flipped the page of his Bible, and back over to English. All of us believed every word. It was very easy for us to believe, because the name of Nevaeh, is actually heaven spelled backwards. All of us could see everything very clear now. The priest had an easy sell on us. The complete crowd was convinced the little girl was in heaven.

A guy next to me who was on the free water and pouring sweat, blessed his forehead out of the blue from under the filtered shade of a nut tree. The Texas sun was wringing it out of us now. All of us believed every word, and following suit, I blessed my forehead with a giant cross of saliva under the yellow sun.

The two first cousins had stopped crying. It was strange to have silence now in the cemetery. They had been crying for a long time now, and the crowd had become accustom to their weeping. The mother kept on anyhow, patting their shoulders and rubbing their hair.

Two of the funeral men, on cue from reverend Eduardo Morales, had inserted hand cranks and lowered Nevaeh Bravo's casket into the graveyard. They were very proficient at this task, and their hands worked the cranks at a good speed.

Her casket disappeared into the ground. The priest was sprinkling holy water across the grave. Under the white tent for the family members, many of the faces had began to cry. The first two rows were sittings very close to each other on wooden chairs, and many of them had joined hands across their laps in sorrow. The first two cousins had opened up again, their brown faces averted to the cracked soil, and they were crying loud as ever with big tears running down their cheeks. The priest did not falter, and kept on praying. He'd moved closer to the family on the edge of the tent. Father Eddy as he was know under the white tent, closed the Bible, and now was saying things off his head that had worked out very well at previous grave funerals.

It took a great deal of time for the cemetery to clear out. Hundreds of people waited to say something to the family. It was a very long line. Reverend Eduardo Morales had intervened the line. He was telling people under the tent may things that would help them out later on. His voice had a resonating quality under the white canvas, and the big crowd under the cemetery trees could hear him well.

The priest reminded them do not let death take you into darkness. Hold the keepsake of their faces, and remember the departed through love, just as Jesus continues to be in our soul. Try to keep your heads clear of too much sorrow, realizing through faith you will see your loved ones again in the Promised Land.

I could have sworn I'd heard Reverend Eduardo Morales say that prior in the week. I'd been to ten funerals and calling hours that week. All of them had been inside the school classroom. The shooter had killed all of them. But though much suffering through the funeral parlors, and the Funeral Masses that afforded no vacant seats, I could not remember the church service or how many times, and only that Reverend Eduardo Morales had told us inside the church at some time.

The line was still very long. It moved slow in the Texas heat. Hundreds of people wanted to say something to the family. The mourners knew that this would be perhaps the best time to say something, while the family was seated and trying to deal with personal sorrow, and when there was so much hugging and cheek kissing going on under the tent. A few close relatives tried to put on a smile and tell a quick story of back in the old days, but they were pinched smiles on the edge of deep sorrow, and their story telling backfired and only brought on more tears. The line wound around in the dappled shade under the sparse cemetery trees, and many people were still taking the free water from the cattle trough. I took a second bottle, and when nobody was looking, I spit behind me on the cracked soil. It was sure some kind of hot. My black funeral shirt with silver pinstripes was soaked across my back, and I chugged half of the second bottle in a slug.

I stayed a long time after the lines departed. The funeral director had walked the family and Reverend Eduardo Morales back to the black limousines. There had been a massive funeral procession parked up on North Lovers Lane. They were double-parked and bumper to bumper, and the lines of cars had taken a long time to reach the highway. Police had been in strategic positions during the funeral. They had been tucked back in their cruisers at all the crossroads. The police were the last to leave the cemetery, and converge into the cortege. They did not hit their blue lights, and the funeral procession motored towards the city limits.

I was sure glad to attend. It was a moving experience. I had not fallen in love with Nevaeh Bravo at the time. That would happen later. It's a very strange phenomenon, indeed, when you start loving the dead. Having conversations with a person that never crossed you path. We were complete strangers. But, nevertheless, that's the way it happened under the Texas heat, and I think, perhaps, that the little girl must have entered my soul from the graveyard. I'd been measuring the crowd and standing very close to the free water trough, but I never felt a thing. Nobody saw anything, but it happened alright. She must have come through thin air. Many of the other victims would follow her path. That part of everything was a true story.

After the procession departed, it became very still in the cemetery. Nobody was around. My white Comet was the only car parked on North Lovers Lane. I walked the cemetery. Everywhere you looked, the soil was cracked. Hot Texas sun. You could see a long way in the cemetery, because there were no headstones. It was all flat burial with ground plaques. The graves were adorned with flowers in brass vessels. It was a very colorful experience looking across the sea of flowers.

There was fresh soil in a pile. Grave diggings. Eliahana Cruz Torres was right there. They buried her maybe fifty yards from Nevaeh Bravo. The sexton had dug the graves straight down. They were razor sharp on the faces. The Texas soil was good for digging graves. The diggers never hit a stone, and they went straight down with the shovels.

The grave of Eliahana Cruz Torres was still open. It was a long way down. I'd creeped near the edge and took a good look, and the grave diggers had already placed the lid over the burial vault. Her name was on the concrete cover in blue letters, and many flowers lined her grave.

Those flowers were arranged on giant wood easels, like you see around in art school. The easels were just about six feet tall, and the flowers were very spectacular and beautiful. They must have cost a fortune. I sniffed the flowers. They sure smelled good. It hit me just like French perfume. Nobody was around, and nobody saw me. The scent of the flowers sure had a punch, and they were very much alive. Some of them were big as teacup saucers, and had yellow stamens.

Things sure went full circle in the cemetery. I'd attended the funeral services of Eliahana Cruz Torres that morning. It was a singing chapel service over at Rushing Estes Knowles, and the praying and gospel singing commenced at eleven bells sharp.

But because the female soloists belted out quite a few songs from their hearts, and the funeral preacher rendered a plainspoken praying with universal love to the Lord, the services lasted a good two hours. I was in the funeral procession to the cemetery, and when I checked my watch, there was less than an hour before the funeral Nevaeh Bravo. Time was too tight. So I pulled out of line and took a quick shower back at the hotel.

The calling hours and funerals were sure stacked high in sorrow. This day before the sun went down, I'd pay respect to Jacklyn Cazares, hug the casket of Miranda Mathis, and pray that evening over the caskets of Jayce Carmelo Luevanos and Julia Silguero, which was a double calling hours on account they were cousins. I was sure a busy guy. Praying for the dead had me running.

But now in the dead stillness with the Texas heat cloaking over the burial grounds, I could say my last words to Eliahana Cruz Torres. I said something. I'd gotten too close to her grave, and a spray of baby pebbles plinked off her casket.

It was getting late in the day. The grave diggers had already punched the clock. It was clear now, the girls would sleep the night away under the open beds of twinkling stars. The next morning the grave diggers would shovel the soil over their graves. But for this night and this night only, Nevaeh and Eliahana would have a crystal clear view in the blackness of night across the sparkle of stars.

I pulled back and sat on a bench. It was a green bench with curved slats for your back, and it was good to take a breather. I could see the two graves of the girls wide and clear. They were right in front of me, caught in the field of perspective, and my white Comet was there in the blazing Texas heat.

The funeral men had not pulled the tent over by Nevaeh Bravo's grave. I could see all the rows of empty chairs. They were very old folding chairs, and the varnish had turned them dark brown over time. The galvanized cattle trough was still there too, and there was still plenty of free water bottles. I thought about walking over and cracking another bottle, but looking around the cemetery and seeing all the fresh graves with tine marks from the rakes and the kids' dolls around the graves, I stayed in place on the bench. There were still a lot of funerals in the next few weeks, for it takes time to prepare those kind of victims riddled by automatic gunfire. They would be needing the water bottles for the next funerals. I was certain the funeral men in both parlors in town, were not only one step ahead of death with plenty of ice bags on hand, but would be dumping the ice cubes into the cattle troughs very soon. They were professionals, and knew how to figure all the angles around the pangs of melancholy. With the way the Texas heat was coming on, and so many funerals in the habiliments of sorrow, they would be needing those bottles of water down the line.

A heavy blanket of heat enveloped the Texas High Country. There was a curtain of orange sun below the cobalt blue sky, and threads of purple were showing on the horizon. I walked back to North Lovers Lane. The dry soil made easy work for powdering your shoes. I'd stomped both shoes on the road, and fired the white Comet. Now on the horizon the sky had turned into a darker ribbon of purple, and a huge flock of doves were in formation towards the grain field. There appeared to be hundreds of grey doves, and the birds of peace were caught in the orange rays of sun.

That night there was a crescent moon rising. A galaxy of silver stars twinkled over the cemetery. Faint yellow needles of the crescent moon, had painted a soft halo over the grain fields. Both girls were on their backs in the open charnels. Constellations from other worlds gleamed in the black velvet night, and millions of sister stars winked across the bed of graves. Deep into the night, a pair of shooting stars streamed valiantly across the shimmering Texas night.

The city had become very dark. It seemed even darker over on Old Carrizo Road. The pecan trees in full leaf, loomed over the houses and casted a darkness of black ink.

Inside the bungalow house on Old Carrizo Road, the two first cousins were in their pajamas, and just had commenced their night praying. All their prayers were for Nevaeh. They offered no prayers for anybody else, or did any other faces come to them. They only thought about their cousin Nevaeh, and whispered to her through all the praying.

The mother had been watching her daughters pray. She'd been standing over them in the bedroom next to their bed.

The girls rose. Their cheeks were adorned in tears. They had been crying again. Their mother wiped away their tears with a Mexican handkerchief which was embroidered with colorful themes, then tucked them in bed. She kissed them several times on the cheeks, and then hit the lights. The bedroom became very dark, and the mother closed the door with a tender touch.

The mother listened a long time in the dead silence. She listened from her bedroom on the edge of her bed, and had cupped her ear to the wall. There had been a short spell of pouting in the girl's room. Then the silence returned.

It had been a very long day for everybody involved. The girls had closed their eyes in the night, and all of a sudden they felt everything go out of them, and they drifted into sound sleep. The two girls rested in far away worlds of new and old dreams, and stayed huddled very close in their pajamas all through the night.

It was sure good the mother had known enough to let the girls get it out of them. They had sure been on a crying jag at the cemetery. That night and many nights to follow, the family would get more out of them. That was part of the healing.

But over time they got a grip on themselves, and began to dwell on certain things that Reverend Eduardo Morales had told them under the blazing curtain of heat in the cemetery. They began retreating from their veil darkness, knowing now and believing through faith their dead walks with Jesus. Zeal returned to their souls, because they believed in Sanctifying Grace, and were very confident they would embrace their angels once again in the Promised Land.

<u>CAST</u>

<u>Main Characters:</u>

Nevaeh Bravo
Reverend Eduardo Morales

<u>Primary Plot Characters:</u>

Two first cousins
Mother of the two children

<u>Lead Support Character:</u>

Eliahna Torres

<u>Support Characters:</u>

Jacklyn Cazares
Maranda Mathis
Jayce Carmelo Luevanos
Jaliah Nicole Silguero

<u>Cast</u>

First teacher — Irma Garcia
Second teacher — Eva Mireles
Funeral directors — Hillcrest Funeral Home
Police
Female soloists
The shooter
Author as the high plains drifter
Jesus

Settings

Robb Elementary School
Hillcrest Cemetery
Sacred Heart Catholic Church
Rushing Estes Knowles
North Lovers Lane
Old Carrizo Road
Bungalow house of two cousins and mom

Texas Hardpan was completed on the morning of July 4th, 2022. Independence Day. The author spent a week in Uvalde, paying respects to the victims of the Robb Elementary shooting. He attended many of the wakes and funerals, and buried Nevaeh Bravo up in Hillcrest Cemetery.

Texas Hardpan is a story told on true events, laced here and there with fiction. Only the residents of Uvalde, Texas will know for certain, where the barbwire fence line of storytelling begins and ends. This story is dedicated to the memory of Nevaeh Bravo.

A Requiem for Fredes Mendez

Fredes Salvador Mendez was on his last legs. He was on his deathbed, on the second floor in the old section of the Hospital Santo Tomas, over on Balboa Avenue. The doctors had inserted plastic tubes in both lungs, and there was a gurgling coming up from his chest cavity. It must be remembered, these were the days before a true immunization had been invented against pneumonia, and any kind of vaccine in the choked Isthmus of Panama against the green ocean with the breaking white caps, was a rare and cherished item.

So they had Fredes Salvador Mendez on sulfapyridine shots, but detection had not been caught until the last stages, which foretold most of his chances were tinged with calamity, and he was a dead man still holding on stretched flat on his back, with beads of sweat pouring from his forehead.

The Santo Tomas was called by some as the white elephant, a low squatted hospital of white masonry, with big stout pillars out front. From Fredes Salvador Mendez's room, you could look out the front window on the singular giant palm tree that grew on the front lawn; and in the heat wave of Panama City, the fronds were all flagged down and not looking so good; and inside the hospital bed laid out on his back, Fredes was not looking so good himself. He still had a full head of silver-grey hair combed back, but his cheeks were sunken, and the nurses had pulled his upper partial. On a wooden shelf above his bed, was a saucer plate holding his false teeth, and a statue of the Hail Mary painted in semi-realistic colors, was looking down over the dying man.

When they first began the squirts of morphine under his tongue, Fredes had seen a supernatural vision of guardian angels circulating in the hospital room over his situation. Under the effect of the narcotics, he witnessed the soft white feathers on their backs, and the rosy cheeks of the cherubs. He had begun to believe in some kind of recovery, from the pensive doom over his presence. But now Fredes Mendez had forgotten about the Virgin Mary, the first and last name of his deceased wife, and could not tell you the month or day.

It was a tragic thing, to see him in this condition. When the nurses put two and two together on his name, they'd begun crying in the shifts, sobbing at his very sight. Fredes Salvador Mendez had once been the national pride of Panama. He would live on in the highest memories of the homeland and many around the world.

Fredes Salvador Mendez had been the reigning Featherweight Champion of the World. He'd held both NBA and IBU featherweight title belts, for seven years consecutive. In his third professional fight in the Club Tropical, he fought in his signature style with pouring on the gas with a cloud of speed, and dropped Kid Fortune deep into the fifteenth round, winning the Panamanian Isthmus flyweight title. The crowd had almost gone berserk. Half the population of Colon was there or glued to their tube radios, and inside the smoke filled arena there was screaming, yelling that rose veins on their throats, and more screaming louder and then louder; and when Kid Fortune's head bounced once on the white canvas with his eyes closed, the crowd's voice began to become hoarse from all the yelling, and the hangers-on at ringside, who'd been cheering for Mendez, threw their arms into invisible fight gods in the veil of gray smoke.

But now Fredes Salvador Mendez was out of commission, down for the count of death inside Hospital Santo Tomas. The hospital room offered a street view, and when the window was cracked, Fredes could hear the humming of automobile tires passing below. His son, Jose Pedro Mendez, was holding his father's hand through the bed rail. He'd been there administering comforts for over three days now, and his shifts of devotion went nearly around the clock.

Jose was having a great deal of pain, in facing his father's death. Fredes had told the head nurse three days prior, he wished to live no more. The feebleness in his chest had become extreme, and because he had no faith in the sulfapyridine injections, he'd lost all his zest for living. Tapioca pudding made with coconut milk, was the only thing he'd eaten in days. His weight had plummeted, and now the fearless Champion of the World, had gone under one hundred pounds.

Jose had to fight back tears. When things got too bad for watching, for instance when the nurse squirted climbing doses of morphine under his tongue, Jose would cross the hall into the vacant room where two people had recently died. The clothes of the dead were still on the hanger, as if living patients still resided in the room; but what threw everything off was the drawn curtains around the beds, cinched back up after the funeral director and his helper had removed the corpses. He could look out the window on the back of Hospital Santo Tomas, and there was a long tile roof running above the first floor, below two more floors of the white elephant, and for the entire week three DeSoto automobiles were in the stalls.

Jose Pedro Mendez had picked up the jitters. He was very nervous and questioned some of his moves. For instance, he was constantly shifting the position of an electric fan, trying to gauge the proper amount of air blowing across his father's face. He tried many positions and angles. Sometimes he moved a miniature nightstand with the fan. Sometimes the electric cord was too short. One time, he'd placed the spinning blades so close, his father's hair began dancing in the wind. He moved the fan several times a day. Jose had been a bundle of nerves. He was constantly thinking his father might be starving for air; and later he was scared the air bursts of the fan would give his father the deep chills and advance the march of pneumonia.

Finally, the shift nurse set him straight. She informed him his father had been jacked with 5 liters of oxygen. After Jose got a grip on things, he'd set the rheostat dial on low, and supplied his dying father with only a caressing stream of soft air — something like you might feel along the seacoast just inside the Golfo de San Miguel, while sitting on a beach blanket in the afternoon sun, watching the smacks work a chum line out across the blue chop.

Jose had procured a tube radio from home and had been playing music for his dying father. It brought a great deal of comfort to the hospital room, because a lot of the notes and tunes were the same stuff they'd listened to in the good old days.

Back in those days, one of the hottest radio channels in the whole isthmus, was WXBY Panama out of Curio, and that's where Jose had his dial set. They played a wide taste of Latin American music, mostly Panamanian, from modern back into songs of the past century.

It seemed the disc jockeys played music in shifts and set moods for the day. It was custom of the station, to play almost solid Cumbia throughout the forenoon, then follow up in the night hours with local hits.

It was very satisfactory for Fredes to listen in on the music, and just the raw sound of the beats always moved him, so you can just imagine what kind of sensation he must have felt when on morphine. The belt of the music carried well in the Santo Tomas, moving with great ease up the tile floor in the fort-like masonry; and one afternoon two visiting relatives of separate patients down the hall, requested to increase the volume a few levels, because their loved ones in dire straits also dwelled on the music.

With Cumbia, the accompanying sounds of the caña de millo, accordions, and mejoranera were always present. And because this kind of music sensation can be romantic, sometimes Fredes Salvador Mendez thought of all the women he'd bedded in his life-time, withering away in the hospital. When a man is Featherweight Champion of the World for such a run, they are enshrined with a movie star status, and the most beautiful women in the world come with the ground. Fredes had a black book filled with names and numbers.

But the tragedy of his love phantasms, like his very own wife, Fredes could not remember any of their names. For all those women, except Margharita Carmona-Medina, he could not even put faces on them. The best he could do was remember some of the scents from perfume while making love and feeling the lips passionately kissing his neck and the lobes of his ears.

In the late afternoon, WXBY Panama stood things on end.

They knew the day shifts were ready to punch out, and the jockeys started spinning perhaps a steady hour of nothing but Tamborito. A great deal of historical evidence could prove that Tamborito was introduced into Panama by the African slaves, going back into the 16th Century.

Because slave boats worked the seaport of Colon, many of the raven skinned blacks had sailed with their conga drums and began playing their native land's percussion in their free time. The vivacious potion of drumheads filled the hospital room, and over the speaker Fredes could feel the long slender fingers of the negroes tapping the taut rawhide skins with all kinds of zeal, the rhythm sinking deep into his spirit. In Tamborito there are three separate small drums, one for high tones, another for low tones and caja, and the third putting out a symbolic conga beat of jungle cadence — more than once Jose had seen his father's fingers tapping with meter, and although his complexion had turned clammy and looked ghostly pale, Fredes had worn a wide happy smile from a man who had sunken cheeks and devoid of his upper set of false teeth.

In the background of this traditional Tamborito, coming from inside the plastic Nile green radio housing, was a field of women's voices. The lead singer brought across a flowing melody into the Hospital Santo Tomas, her cantante voice raising goose bumps on Fredes' arms, while the rest repeated a chorus line with chants and clapping. The effects created a musical song of question and answer, and for Fredes Salvador Mendez and many others in the hospital ward, reminded them of the singing from tropical birds rising from the sweltering jungles of Panama.

Young bucks were glad he retired forty years back, because they could only sometimes do what he did in the ring, and very few could make a speed bag sing like Fredes. He was the sharpest featherweight to ever come out of Panama's bloodlines, and even ten years into his professional career, nobody still could touch him. He was like a blur in the ring, a phantom ghost stalking and often peppered his opponents with such a flurry, they felt caught in some kind of squirrel cage version of a torture chamber, driven by a donkey engine. Like all of them who come along from neighborhoods where food itself is a pinched item, climbing on dreams from poverty to clutch championship belts, Fredes Salvador Mendez had an unmistakable cruel streak, fighting as if he'd caught them trying to steal his wife.

When Fredes was right, he could tell you the names and personal traits of every prize fighter he ever faced and go round by round and get everything straight to a T and remember the judge's score cards at many increments through the fight.

Fredes Salvador Mendez faced many men inside the ring. All of them were wildcats once they stepped inside the ropes; many of them put on game faces at the shaking of gloves, very certain their willpower could clutch victory. But all of them were proven wrong, and the bravest who'd worn the sternest game faces, seemed to be those who left their blood stains on the white canvas.

Take Ernesto Foramenti, who'd been a lot of mouth around the sport's writers of the Corriere della Sera newspaper, predicting he would emerge the chosen son of champions. But when things got heated up in the Palazzo Dello Sport, in the third round to be exact, Fredes Mendez stunned him with a barrage of fancy combinations, then finished him off with a tomahawk right hand to the frontal skull plate, that dropped Foramenti like he was pasted with a 12ga. shotgun.

Take Albert "Baby Face'" Aruzemendi, who was a physical specimen like seldom seen, a gym rat who had a 38 BPM resting pulse at daybreak. Aruzemendi came out for the first six rounds like a man possessed, working Mendez with a machine gun shellacking of body shots, hunting for the liver and kidney box, organ shots that could weaken Mendez.

Many spectators in the Queensboro Stadium of Long Island, watching Fredes Mendez's coach yell strategy into his ear, were gasping in astonishment, feeling their bets slide toward the bookie. Even the hot dog man selling the skins had pulled up in row twenty-seven of B Section, all eyes on the ring. Wearing a red and white vertically striped hat like seen on a Navy ship, the frankfurter man was eating his own profits on a chunk of dog with yellow mustard; he was talking to a potential customer in a derby hat, talking and chewing, asking and telling in the same breath this thing might go to the underdog.

But in the tenth round Mendez opened his bag of tricks, as well as a two-inch gash over Aruzemendi's right eyebrow. It was the kind of nasty wound that even had the cut man's hand tied, the red crimson seeping past the orange salve as Aruzemendi rose from the corner stool. Then when Fredes smelled blood, he painted Baby Face into a neutral corner, came home with a textbook uppercut, and followed with a crushing right hand. Slumped on the ropes, Baby Face was seeing a galaxy of stars behind his eye sockets, and the referee almost jumped from his trousers exclaiming a TKO. The ring announcer was from Brooklyn, and his deep borough's accent came over the microphone which had been lowered from a rope-pulley into the ring and announced Fredes Salvador Mendez the winner. Another big-buckled champion belt had been defended. Fredes danced around the white canvas one revolution on his toes, then blew a kiss toward Jesus in the heavens.

There was a lot of Jersey talk going on in the departing

crowd, bumping and shoulder rubbing coming out of the stands.

A tall thin detective who worked undercover homicide out of Jersey City, who'd been off duty and taking in the battle, said to his partner, "Brother, that Mendez moves like the wind, and hits like a freight train."

"All those guys south of the border from the jungles, are tough cookies," said his partner puffing on a butt. "Let's hope we can move fast out of this joint," blowing a stream of gray smoke into the night. "With this kind of crowd, we'll be lucky to get across the bridge into Jersey City before the cow jumps over the moon."

Walking point down the stadium stairs, the tall, thin detective reached under his vest while caressing the hammer of his snub-nose .38 cal. revolver, making sure the holster was in place. Descending the wide stairs, both detectives studied the back of the crowd's heads out of second nature and pressed toward the distant lots where yellow arc lights shone over the thronged row of automobiles.

But of all the gladiators Fredes Mendez ever faced in the boxing ring, spanning the globe into the European theater, there was only one fighter who ever won a portion of mankind's love from Mendez's heart.

The fighter's name was Nelson "Nella" Tarkington, who fought out of Blackpool, England. In the month before the fight, scheduled for fifteen pounds inside Kings Hall of Manchester, Fredes and his coach, Rafael "Zoro" Cabrera, had poured over Tarkington's boxing history. They turned his fight game on edge, looking for a vulnerable angle. Fredes Mendez did not have to read far, because on the first page of Nella Tarkington's medical chart, was evidence that froze Mendez in his tracks: at the tender age of two years old, Nelson Tarkington had begun living life on a single lung.

Mendez was speechless. The fight at that altitude would provide no problems for Fredes Mendez. He'd been skipping rope for months, was toned and lean, and was in condition to pour on the gas for all fifteen rounds. But face a man with one lung?

"Are you kidding me, Zoro?" as Fredes often called his coach, "a professional fighter with one lung?" You could tell Mendez was deeply moved, and Zoro needed to stay on him during the training with sparring partners. His coach was gravely worried that Mendez was not taking the fight seriously and would let the virtues of mercy for the weak and defenseless become a factor.

The night of the big fight had come. Everybody knew Tarkington never had a punch. He was a technical fighter and won on points. Rafael Zoro Cabrera was tugging on a white terry towel around Fredes's neck, giving his fighter the last lines of a pep talk.

"Don't slack off… this guy's a pure points man," said Zoro looking mad. "This guy holds two Lonsdale Belts. Take him seriously before he works the score cards for a win."

For the first six rounds, Mendez was all over him. It was easy picking. Fredes felt certain he could drop him at will. But he wanted to see how much guts the Englishman with one breathing chamber had inside.

In the next six rounds, Tarkington showed his stuff. First, he was here, then there. A phantom man gliding the ropes, cutting the ring with his pretzel thin body. A wide band of astonishment filled the baker-white faces of all the Englishmen in the grandstands. Nella Tarkington was certain the Queen was watching on television, which was true; and the fighter dug in his calf muscles around the duck canvas, pouring out some nice cut and weave moves for the Union Jack.

He peppered Mendez with feather-like combinations, none of them with enough power to inflict pain. But the blows were making contact, scoring the points, and at the end of the 13th round things were too close to call. The judge's cards actually had Tarkington ahead by the frailest margin.

Just after the bell made its commencement for the 13th round, Panamanian pity was traced all around the eyes of Mendez, knowing well it was not inside him to finish off a man with one lung. Fredes got close enough to give him a bear hug and said, "For Christ's sake, Nella, let's throw the fight. I could have knocked you cuckoo in the third round."

"Sounds good," said Tarkington, who threw back a wink from between his brown gloves. "My breath is taxed from putting on a show for the home blood — but make it look good."

"Break!" the referee was shouting, "Break!"

"Let me run this circus act for the next two rounds, "Fredes told him, seeing the sweat pouring off of Tarkington's face. "After you catch your breath, finish off the 15th with fancy stuff. "

For the next few rounds, both fighters threw wild shots, Mendez in pursuit. Loud snorts were coming from the fighter's nostrils, and Mendez kept tapping his forehead with the brown gloves, as if trying to catch a rhythm for a knockout. Fredes Mendez then threw a roundhouse right, telegraphed across the ring, and missed by a mile. Tarkington was not putting on the dog with his shallow panting, but continued the light pattering of shots.

After the 15th round, for what seemed like eternity, the judges had tallied their cards. It was proclaimed a dead draw. Both men would take part of the fight home. But it was more than a split decision, because a lifetime of friendship had been born.

There was never anything like it when Fredes saw the postal stamps from Blackpool, England in his mailbox. The two friends had become pen pals, across the blue seas. Fredes always ran the scissors around the foreign stamps who'd been branded by postal seals. He saved them in a candy tin for little Jose's stamp collection. Every Christmas season Fredes went on a certain corner where a pay telephone was available and shoved large amounts of coins for a few light minutes of conservation with Nella. Fredes still had a photograph of Nella's first-born daughter, yellowed now, tucked in his bedroom mirror.

This business of throwing the fight, was never revealed beyond family. It was seldom spoken. This knowledge had never even reached the ears of Rafael Zoro Cabrera, who had departed to the grave for several years now.

But his son Jose knew the story well, and still had the tin of his stamp collection. Looking down on his father breathing hard in the hospital bed, hearing the gurgling of the air apparatus, brought back the old story of the soft spot in Fredes Mendez's heart, and choked up his son.

With the river of swollen tears coming down his cheek, Jose Mendez left the room and crossed into the vacant room. He was sobbing out of control. Jose reached between the buttons of his short-sleeved dress shirt, and grabbing the crucifix began praying for the reinforcements of fortitude. Below in the parking lot, a custodian who owned one of the DeSotos, had pulled out of the stalls. Ricardo's Place had the best rice and beans, and the hospital worker could no longer hold off his appetite.

But in his state of sorrow, still in the crying jag, Jose had failed to notice him driving away. He'd been watching high above through the windowpanes, still crying, where specks of seagulls were circling Santo Tomas in the air currents.

"Is everything all right?" asked the shift nurse. She'd come into the vacant room very silent on her white nursing shoes and handed Jose a moist face cloth. He pressed the cool towel against his eye sockets.

"Oh... everything is alright," Jose told her. But in the back of his mind still remembered Nella Tarkington with his singular lung, and how his father had shown him the gift of mercy.

Jose Mendez walked back into Room 204. He adjusted the radio a bit higher, so he was certain the chords and singing were reaching his father's ears. Fredes Salvador Mendez had lasted longer than expected. Most men would have been dead. A priest with a starched white collar under a sable twill shirt, had given the last rites to Fredes two days past, and had sifted holy smoke over his body laid under the bed covers. His excellent condition from youth was giving him an edge, but in a lot of ways he'd been reduced to the breathing capacities of Nella Tarkington and was no less a goner.

Jose had noticed the stubble of his father's beard, two days back. It had been on his mind. The grey stubbles had grown and begun to fill in a beard, and the whiskers around his cheekbone were growing in the sunken hollow. Jose reminded himself to procure some kind of shaving implement and shave his father's beard before he passed. Fredes had rubbed his chin one afternoon, and said to his son, "I could use a shave."

"For certain, Papa," said Jose. "I'll tend to it very soon."

But because of all his emotional suffering, the agony of staring death in the face, planning the funeral, writing his father's obituary late into the night by desktop, his father's last wish had slipped his mind.

Back in those days, less was known about pneumonia. Blood had been seen in the orange phlegm, the day he was admitted. The head surgeon was thinking about sawing open his breastbone and looking around inside. Sometimes the infection could be scraped away by the ribcage. The surgeon knew from experience, there was no question the alveoli in the lung lobes was seeped with fluids tinged in death, and white blood cells were racing to the scene, trying to fight infection.

But because the head surgeon had lost the last seven patients on this procedure, he found himself with cold feet. He'd chosen to insert a plastic tube thrust deep inside Fredes's cavity, under the effects of laughing gas.

Before going off to never-never land, Fredes Mendez had come clean with the surgeon. Fredes had told him the happiness in life was much more innocent, before he turned professional. "There was not the weight of the world on me then," confessed Fredes.

"I understand, my friend," "said the surgeon, as he rubbed some assurance into Fredes's shin bone.

Before Fredes got the quick blast of sleeping gas, he held himself tight in the fetal position and kept asking the surgeon if he would leak information under the influence.

The surgeon did not reply. They cranked open the valve on the green bottle, and Fredes breathed in through the wide mask.

A few minutes later Fredes came out of everything, and said, "Did I reveal any secrets? What did I say?" He hoped nothing was slipped about Nella.

"You only said something about wanting a big plate of black licorice."

"I can recall it in my after-dreams from the laughing gas," said Fredes, rubbing his eyes. "All the licorice was stacked in rows, like straws when laid out in order."

"Me encanta el regaliz negro," said the surgeon. It's one of my favorites."

"Yo tambien," added the nurse.

So that was it for the day. All involved in the infirmary bay had come clean and made confessions. Everybody seemed to like black licorice.

Crowned with Featherweight Champion of the World, much fame and fortune had come to Fredes Salvador Mendez. Photographers were always hunting him. Ring Magazine had featured his photograph twenty-seven times over the years, glossy and bold on the front cover. Everybody knew him, and that was the part that bothered him the most, that he could not dodge the public eye. He'd tried everything, dark cheap sunglasses, with hats pulled down low. But somebody always seemed to put a make on him, and his personal space in the world had become obliterated.

Up in Room 204, Fredes was really sailing now. The narcotics had really kicked in, and he was on cloud nine. When a man is on his deathbed, and time itself is a pinched item, a man's memory only seems to focus on the most significant data. This was the way everything was being played out for Mendez, and he went a long way back in time, when a halo of innocence was over him as a boy, in his childhood inside the town of Chepo.

Fredes could see very clearly. His imagination had been sharpened by death's urgency. He could see the tiny schoolhouse. The school was run by Iglesia Catolica Parroquia San Cristobal. Many of the teachers were nuns. Fredes who was running a slight fever, could see all his classmates. All of them were just about ten years of age. They were seated in rows of wooden desks, with hinged tops that could hold many books, and the desks were grooved for pencils and drilled for ink bottles.

A thin nun in black and white habiliments was teaching Geography. Knowledge had been disclosed, their country of

Panama was hemmed in on two sides by sea water — the Pacific Ocean and Caribbean Sea.

Up to that time, many students in the classroom, had been completely unaware of oceans in their proximity. They'd been too busy working hard weeding and hoeing crops, and the strongest of boys had been allowed to single-plow furrows behind a mule.

All this new information, fascinated Fredes Mendez with marvel. That summer vacation, Fredes Mendez hit the stacks inside the town library. He memorized all the countries in South America. He'd been aware of Colombia. But he was exceedingly proud of himself he discovered Paraguay and El Salvador. The next summer, he went overland to the Pacific Ocean, hanging on to the back of his Uncle Pedro's gasoline scooter. He was awestricken with the ocean's power, the crashing of foam-lipped breakers, combing the rocks with surf. Years later, when he was fighting professional out of Curio, his bare feet would run on the wet sands of the Caribbean Sea, staying limber before lacing up.

Fredes's nurse had been constantly checking the bottoms of his feet. There had been the telltale signs of creeping death, a rush of red blood gathering under the skin. But a short time later, the deep crimson welts would be vanquished; and then an hour in advance, show themselves near the ankles. Fredes's blood had begun to settle.

Part of Fredes had already gone to the backside of the mirror. He'd felt his soul going out of him, and through a great effort pushed it back inside. He was having too good a time, in his reverie of the boyhood days in Chepo. He was hoping to put everything off for a few more days, before he needed to venture off and see the Lord.

In a lot of ways, the San Cristobal Church was a lot like Hospital

Santo Tomas, in that both were constructed of heavy masonry, spackled in white stucco, and with plenty of brawn to take any hurricane blow that came screaming across the seas.

Back in those days, you could look out the massive doors of the church and see the town square through the lattice of tropical plants. In the prominence of the well-groomed common, which sported a hand-pump water fountain for drinking, was the Arcada de Campones. This is where Fredes Mendez learned to fight as an amateur, and where his fondest memories of life were seated.

The Arcada de Campones was nothing more than the town bandstand in the park, converted on Friday nights for boxing matches. This is where Fredes Mendez was sharpened in the fight game, a place inside his element where he could seek out his calling. There were always Christmas lights burning year-round on some rooflines of the vendor's shacks, and with the swelling of crowds, and the colored strings of light bulbs in the black night, painted a festive scene on the arcade.

There were many other descriptions of colors saturated around the Arcada de Campones. From his position of failing health, Fredes could recall many other versions of tincture, the sweat wicking into the bed garments around his spine.

Colors bristled. Behind his eye sockets were colorful people. These visions were not contrived by fantasy. In his youth Fredes had seen San Bias Indians emerge from the jungle, who stood in the back rows during the Friday night fights. The Indians brought their women; the women wore huge nose rings, metal discs in their ears, necklaces of trade coins; they painted long black lines on their nose bridge, looking for the illusion to present themselves with longer noses. Colorful dark-skinned natives from the jungle.

Colors. The morphine was doing a lot of painting for Fredes

Mendez. The skin of his forehead was very taut from losing so much weight, the globe of his skull was exposed, and the shift nurse was looking over the blue tints around his sockets. Below the covers his big toe was meager violets. His arms were all pricked up with raspberry welts from the needle jabbers. Fredes's face was very calm, and he was drifting in a colored pencil world.

It was not a far stretch. These kinds of sightings were very common. They occurred mostly in the hottest months, in the highest humidity. Spoilage was quicker then. Loaves of bread, although never wasted and eaten three days stale, needed to be thrown out when the green mold appeared. Kernels of yellow corn had also been known to turn bad in the humid cloaks of weather, when moisture seeped inside the storage barrels. The stale breads, buckets of discolored yellow corn, were sprinkled around the town arcade for the birds.

In the high bell tower of Iglesia Catolica Parroruia San Cristobal, and in the musty steeples on other jacked roofs around Chepo, lived the wild parakeets and parrots. Like the Indians, they too had ventured from the jungle for easy pickings, and the sound nesting quarters of the bell tower.

The children of Chepo were caught in the hot flashes of fondness for the colorful birds. The old people had completely lost their stomach for pigeons, after having parakeets eat from their hands. Fredes had tried many times to catch a parrot, using a homemade trap fashioned from a wooden crate, pulled by a heavy waxed line. But Fredes's father had caught him employing the box trap in the park, hunkered down behind the trunk of a bitter orange tree with wild eyes, and sternly warned him to capture no pets — they belonged free in the wilds, high in the jungle's lattice of fronds with the monkeys.

Colors. Fantastic colors were coming to Fredes Mendez, in his journey to six feet under from Room 204 in Santo Tomas, in the comfort of his son and the three DeSoto automobiles in the back lot. Flocks of colorful birds were soaring in his mind. Green parrots with yellow heads, were perched in the thickets of smilax, and perhaps a thousand parakeets were squadroned on the red roof of Arcada de Campones. Fredes saw an old man from his deep valley of death, heaving a pail of yellow cracked corn across the cracked soil. An explosion of colored wings erupted, the kaleidoscope of colors swirled the sky, and descended in a mad feeding frenzy.

Tamborito music filled the room. He'd revealed nothing of his dream escapades, through facial expressions. They had stopped the sulfapyridine shots for a good five days.

The conditioning of a prize fighter can make him hard for dying. There were tough times coming up for Fredes Mendez; make no mistake about anything. Fredes and almost every amateur fighter trained on horse meat. It was the most affordable staple, very lean and good for building muscle, and these the young men fought very well on horse meat.

All the release forms to enter the ring, were signed by crow quill pens by their parents, or in some cases for those who did not have any, or lived in an orphanage house, where the waivers were signed by the boxing coach, or the assistant coach whose main position was manning the water bucket in the corner, or the reluctant hands of a nun in the orphanage.

Perhaps the biggest hardship for those who fought in the Arcada de Campones was the invention of the ice machine had not been introduced, so when the fighter got banged up in the ring, there was no option for icing down. The fighters took their lumps standing up. The best which could be accomplished, was a wooden staved pail filled with cool water from the hand-pumped well in the town arcade and immerse their throbbing head into the pail for relief.

For broken noses, however, there was little remedy. The busted noses needed to be set in the home, and the nostrils packed with cotton. With no ice machines, the swelling lasted for weeks, with puffiness migrating to the cheeks, the white cotton turning scarlet from the seepage of blood.

Fredes had only gotten clocked on a lone occasion — an over-zealous sparring partner two weight divisions above Mendez, pasted him in the kisser with a straight right. Fredes had heard the bone crack, only crack, and got away with a greenstick frac-ture. Removed from the fight game for two weeks by his coach, Fredes hit to the streets and jacked up his miles. The white cotton congealed of carmine colors, brought a red badge of courage to the young fighter. Gliding on his featherweight frame, Fredes ran laps around Chepo, throwing his bare-skinned chest to the admiration teeming from the sea of wayfarers, a thread of dried blood running down his cupid's bow.

So then, it's very easy to understand, why Fredes Salvador Mendez would never trade off any of his precious childhood memo-ries of Chepo, quite understandable. But then in the next breath, after letting everything sink in that just rolled off his tongue, tell everybody he'd never give up his champion belt for anything. That's the way it always seems for those who rise the hard way, from the meager side of town.

Jose was watching his father's face. A graduation of silver-gray hair was filling in on Fredes's expression. The faint yellow sun coming through the window, illuminating Fredes' face, and made him look very old. The whiskers on the flank of his wind-pipe were growing in whirls and painted him a disheveled victim on his deathbed. Jose could see the stubble was too long for the straight razor. Listening to the music on the green radio, Jose Mendez tapped his shoe to a player jingling zills on a tambourine, and thought everything through in giving his father a clean shave.

Fredes died the very next morning at sunrise. The ball of orange sun was coming off the sea, and in the falling tide on the beach flats, the seagulls were feasting on things squirming on the slickened sands. Word spread exceedingly fast. The attention cast on Mendez's death, was near that of a national holiday, or more pointedly, a hero nativo, which of course he was. The obituary for Fredes Salvador Mendez was stricken by the iron stylus worldwide. It had been translated into many languages. Colored supplements were in all the newspapers.

The day of Mendez's funeral, the streets were lined twenty deep in mourning. Over half of the crowd was crying.

Some men saluted the casket in the open hearse, lined with colorful flowers for the native son. It was one of those caskets, where length of iron pipe as seen in plumbing, was fastened to the sides in mind of the pallbearers. Even the fishermen in their skiffs and smacks, had pulled anchor for attendance. They understood there would be plenty of days left to drift lines for mackerel and red snapper, and all kinds of time for men to hold their breaths and dive for pearl oysters, but only one chance to acknowledge the man they had loved in and out of the boxing ring.

At 9:00 a.m., which was one hour before the procession through town, the pier was lashed with all the skiffs and smacks; up in the scale house, the fishermen were scrubbing down to remove the fish slime, and then combing their hair for a proper farewell. Down back along the water, a powder blue smack bobbed placidly on the sea. She was lashed by her beam to the pier head. Hand painted on her sternpost in canary yellow, was the name Jonquil. The boat belonged to the oyster divers. It had been a remarkable morning. In the cracking of oyster shells, they'd found two good market-sized pearls. In their reverence for Fredes Mendez, rushing and very nervous, they'd left a double-lensed diving goggle on the bow's seat. The lenses were quite large for good peripheral vision and connected by a red rubber strap across the nose bridge. A sandpiper had landed on the seat and was studying the goggles. The bird saw reflections of quick flashes with other birds like him in the glass lens. But he was the only figure to touch down anywhere near the pearl diver's goggles, because stealing around the wharf from other fishermen was dealt with in the most severe keys, where the practitioners of lifting items could be severely punished on the docks — getting your fingers smashed with a gaff handle, was in the cards.

They buried Fredes Salvador Mendez on the hill, next to the tomb of Jimenez. The scores of mourners ringed the cemetery, and several people were still hiking up the hill on the narrow winding road, when the priest had already begun the graveside service. The pallbearers had already lugged the casket by the iron pipes, and they laid out Fredes over the open grave on wooden cribs.

Many of Panama's top fighters were present. Some of them were very old now and could never beat Fredes in his prime; and in the champion's death they blessed their foreheads in the public eye and buried all their shortcomings of past jealously along with Fredes.

Some of the new blood who fought below in the Arcada de Campeones attended the service. Like all young men full of sincere idealism, they'd fashioned black arm bands, in respect to the featherweight champion. Just knowing the actual soles of Mendez's boxing shoes, authentically danced by sticking and moving on the same canvas floor, and that Fredes had parted the very heavy ropes, was enough to keep the new bloods hunting in the ring with plenty of pep.

Inside the dressing room, Fredes Mendez's old locker room had been turned into a shrine, his name still on the sheet metal door, locked tight against the progression of time.

Long before his death, Fredes had made arrangements. He'd met in private inside the rectory of San Cristobal Church, and paid Father Zabula in cash money. It was only thirty balboas for perpetual. The priest assured him with the utmost confidence, that for that kind of money and being who he was during his life as Fredes Mendez, that Father Zabula would make certain the grave keepers would sickle the weeds around his tomb, at least once a year.

Francisco Jimenez had a big brown tombstone, with boxing gloves hand carved into the face. Below his chiseled name and the dates of his birth and the day he died, was an italicized passage:

"No peleo tanto por ganar, sino por ver quien tiene mas agallias. Francisco Jimenez — Panamanian Junior Welterweight Champion of the World. 1941-1942-1946"

But Fredes Salvador Mendez had chosen the most spartan means for burial. His request was that of a common wooden cross, painted in the simplicity of immaculate whiteness. At the cross's foot, Mendez's wish was for a small tablet, inscribed with the significant information about the late departed. The priest, Father Zubala, knew he could go many years perpetual, for what Mendez paid. The sexton was always encouraged to manufacture all wooden crosses, with a long foot section that was buried below grade. Even in the tropics, a cross could last a good eight years before decay set into the shank. With the reserve of wood built into the lower cross, why, the sexton could re-point the cross, and bury it home for another eight years. Father Zubala liked this kind of thinking, because it only cost a few centésimos to paint over a cross, instead of making a whole new run with expensive lumber.

After the last of the funeral procession departed the tombs, the mourning of Fredes Salvador Mendez carried well into the night. But the revere had turned more to cheerfulness, knowing Fredes would have wanted it that way. This kind of cheery conduct, always part of the healing process, played out in all towns of Panama. Men lined the barrooms and recalled the old stories with warm hearts about the national pride in Fredes Mendez. The television showed a special on the boxing career of Mendez, but the reviews were very poor, because the reporter never knew Fredes Mendez on a personal level, and there was a lack of authority in the story line. The best stories were being told on the night of his funeral, on the bar stools of the Vasco Nunez Club, by the men who'd seen sweat pour from Mendez.

And on a more intimate level, one of the hottest stories of gossip was swirling around town, about a heavy-set lady in a silken tangerine dress, white buckle shoes, and pearl necklace, who'd been seen crying on a hill during the priest's sermon. Nobody could put a name on her, and her eyes were shielded by a gauzy funeral veil, but the tears had been streaming down her cheeks alright. Between her sobbing episodes, the last and only thing the stranger ever said, was in the pinched cry, "I love you, Fredes." Her emotional voice had seemed to slip out beyond all control, and she cupped her mouth against the crowd. The groups of women around the open-air tables of the street cafe were really digging into the gossip story, and many of them on the second glass of red wine, had filled in many parts about the incident, which had only taken place in their imagination.

Even the children of Chepo, where all the grade schools in Panama had been closed in respect to Fredes Mendez, were still on the multitude of swings in the courtyard of Arcada de Champions, pumping their legs high in the blue sky.

Two boys who had sneaked inside the Vasco Nunez Club, hiding under the big round mahogany table and eavesdropping on the stories from older men, were now outside near the seesaws and telling the girls what they'd heard under the table about Fredes Mendez.

So whatever you heard around the streets, it was a million times better than what the news anchors were reporting.

The death of Mendez really stirred up a lot of people's coals, and there was no shortage of authentic stories on the Isthmus of Panama. Inside the rectory of San Cristobal Church, seated behind his desk with checkered sunbeams pouring past the window screen, Father Zabula had already opened thirty-two envelopes, each holding four balboas, which was the standard fee in those days for a memorial mass. Fredes Salvador Mendez's name was the benefactor on every card. The fighter had not only sold out around the world in his reign as champion, but now had booked the Iglesia Catolica Parroquia San Cristobal on memorial masses, breaking all kinds of records that even caught Father Zubala off guard.

It was really something though, the way the fisherman paid in the nets, and hand-bailed their lines back on spools, for reporting to Fredes Mendez's funeral procession. The world had stopped dead in its tracks, in honor of Fredes. The most reverent of the followers, the most devoted friends and hangers-on of his corner, including the cut man and two of his loyal sparring partners, carried on with the mourning long into Sunday afternoon, which was a good three days after the sexton shoveled dirt over Fredes Mendez's grave. People really poured out their hearts and gave Mendez a universe of condolence.

Even the birds seemed to play a part in Fredes's farewell. Seven brown pelicans were perched along the bow rail of a pale-yellow smack. The cream-colored heads and necks of the pelicans, the commanding battle gray plumes of the wing plates, struck a supernatural pose against the yellow boat. With their long beaks, the pelicans groomed themselves, working the shimmering feathers with passing of bills. The birds were in no shape or form, pressed for any time. The skipper and two deck hands of the yellow smack, were still up in the Vasco Nunez Club taking long pulls on hard liquor cut with Indian quinine water, still caught up in the memorialization of Mendez.

But the most classic act of reverence, took place up in Room 204, in the very minutes before Fredes Salvador Mendez died. His son Jose, treading water in the last striking of the clock, sat on a chair turned backwards, his hands on the spindle back, looking at his father.

The son's face was full of child-like esteem. He'd returned to carry out his father's last wish.

"It won't be long now," said the shift nurse. Three days of morphine dripped under his tongue had arrested his shallow breathing to a tortoise pace.

The nurse looked under the covers. The marbling of blood returned to the soft flesh of Fredes's ankles. "He's going to be going soon," said the nurse. She brushed Fredes's silver-grey hair with her hand, rubbing her fingers three consecutive passes along the side of his head. Then the nurse, with the case-hardened move of a professional hospice nurse, reached over and pulled the air line from Fredes's nostrils.

"He won't be needing this anymore," said the nurse. She never looked Jose dead in the eye. "Sometimes we need to do things that make it easier on us too." Then the nurse coiled the air line and left the room. A guy down the hall had been pushing the electric buzzer-bell many times over, and the nurse went down to check on him.

Between Jose's legs on the chair, was a handsome set of Pippa electric shears. They were fitted with pearl grips, and they were a smaller scaled-down model of the big brother shear.

Actually, the Pippas were livestock shears. They were very, very sharp cutters, and the Mendezes had used them for years to accentuate the mane on their pet donkey, Wilbur, and trim the face hairs on the jackass's long snout. Wilbur had become accustomed to his clip jobs, and stood mannequin still and never shuffled around, under the electric humming of shears.

Jose Mendez would never chance giving his father the last shave, with a straight razor and hot foam. Shaving a man on death's bed with surgical steel, could be a tragic mistake. Fredes had a lot of extra skin below his chin from losing so much weight and running a stropped blade in that kind of countenance, would be very dangerous.

Jose prepared for his task. The green radio had been turned off the day before, when it was realized Fredes would be singing no more songs in this lifetime.

Jose uncoiled the Pippa's power cord and pushed the brass stakes into the wall receptacle. The electric cord, served with a black and white textile material, paid out with plenty of slack to his father.

Jose was very pleased with the provisions he'd made in advance. The night before, he'd meticulously groomed the Pippa with an old toothbrush, and rubbed down the cutter blades with a white crew sock, doused with a solution of ammonia and water. His son wanted to make sure, there were no bugs hanging around or clipped donkey's hairs, which would encounter with his father's face. His son was doing the best possible under the circumstances — it would be a few more years down the line, when men's electric razors reached these remote third world regions.

Clutching the livestock shears, Jose realized this would be his last father and son reunion.

Drawn over the hospital bed, Jose tenderly cupped his father's chin, and with the other arm began shaving the beard. His son was very experienced from giving Wilbur haircuts, and he glided over his father's face with the greatest of skill. A sea of grey whiskers immediately fluttered down on the pillowcase. Jose had come in on the cupid's bow and worked clipping hairs of Fredes's stubble to the ear lobes. He even ran the electric shears into the father's ears, cutting free all those long hairs.

Then Jose saw the rising and falling of his father's chest arrest, and there were no signs of breathing. Then his father kicked back on and breathed a few more times. A gasp followed. Then there was nothing. His father's heart rhythm slipped in his hand, and Jose could feel the life slip out of him. Then Fredes Salvador Mendez was dead. Jose pulled back in the shock of despair. He blinked his eyes, fighting back tears. Jose had not finished the task — only half of his father's beard had been passed over by the Pippa. The other side of his face was still a meadow of silver whiskers.

The nurse, who'd been beholding from the background, grabbed Jose's arm and said, "He's not with us anymore." Then she went in for a closer look and flipped his eyelids for verification. "He was a good man," said the nurse in a sorrowful cry. She did not cry. "The world will miss him."

Jose explained his dilemma. The nurse obliged him. She clutched Fredes's head with both hands, holding him tilted and rock steady. Jose brought the Pippa to life and moved forward with his task. He would never have a clear mind, if the job was never completed. Jose leveled the shears, and the last gray whiskers began to fall.

Very soon, Fredes was a new man. The pillowcase on both sides of his father's head, was sprinkled with gray whiskers. Jose moved in close and intimate with his father. He filled his lungs and huffed and puffed the gray stubble into space. His fingers quickly whisked away the few lagging hairs from the pillow.

The nurse pulled back and made two beautiful hospital corners. She folded the sheets military-crisp at the footboard. The blanket was straightened over Fredes Mendez's corpse, tugged into a presentable fashion. Then she completed the vision with nurse tidiness, folding a neat hem back over the man with the brown blanket, riding over his chest bones.

Strange but wonderful subject matter would fill the land after Fredes Mendez's death. You saw the lady in the silken tangerine dress, white buckle shoes, conduct a crying jag behind a face veil in the cemetery. The fishermen pulled anchors and rode their boats in on a chop for Mendez's procession. The blue skiff of the pearl divers, bobbed in the wharf's slip, the big-lensed diver's goggles on the stern seat. Brown pelicans with cream-colored heads and silver-gray plumes revealed themselves standing at perch on the pale-yellow smack. Father Zabula counted the stack of balboas, and filled in thirty-two mass dates with a crow quill pen inside the black jacketed book. The manager of the Vasco Nunez Club, a short fat guy by the name of Renya Gonzalez, who had enough on the ball not to run out of Indian quinine water, three days into the stiff for Fredes Mendez. There was all kinds of marvel coming around the town of Chepo. But at that time, in the minutes after Fredes died, only the prophets could look that far into the future. Jose was still in the dark, on just the kind of subject matter which would cast its color around town.

Jose Mendez wrapped the Pippa's extension cord around the shears and shoved them in his back pocket. He leaned over and said something very soft to his dead father. Then his son licked his fingertip with his own saliva, and pressed down very firmly on his father's forehead, making the sign of a cross. Then he whispered something else. The spittle of holy markings was glistening on Fredes's forehead. Jose stood up rail straight, and pulling back his shoulders, felt quite good about everything. He'd found some kind of blessing inside Room 204, where he got peace of mind after carrying out a least a very crucial number of the Ten Commandments—honor thy mother and father.

Jose grabbed the green radio to bring back home. He was feeling much better. Mysteriously, the tears had suddenly arrested their shedding. Jose caught a second wind of fortitude, not only because he'd filled all expectations of the family tree for the champion prodigy, but also because it's always a good idea to grant the dying under the Sacraments of Last Rites, exactly what they implored as the last wish.

Land of the Story Tellers

I'd heard it many times before. That a great deal of the staff at the Rirá, put on fake accents. They weren't even Irish. An English teacher told me.

That phony accent thing got me in hot water one morning coming down the Vermont highway. The world was very green in the flush of summer. A herd of black and white cows were grazing near Shadow Cross Farm. My green Land Rover putted along the countryside. I'd called the RiRá from my cellular telephone, requesting which exit to embark, for reaching their fine establishment on the pinched street. Croatia and France were playing for the World Cup championship in a few hours. Time was pressing. I was real hot for soccer.

It was Sunday morning. The phone rang a few times. A man picked up, and said in an accent thicker than Irish butter, "RiRá."

"Listen man," I told him, "I'm coming down to watch the soccer match — what's the best exit?" I could hear many voices in the background. The place sounded packed.

"Fine chap! Please do come. We're just about to bring on a fine breakfast."

"Let me find the place first," I told him pulled over on the shoulder. "What exit?"

"Oh… let me check on that." I could hear an Irish woman's voice filling him in on the other end. He spoke again and said, "Exit ——." He'd put on such a phony accent, it sounded like Martian talk. I could barely hear a word he said.

"Man, you're breaking up. What exit?"

Again, the Irishman muffled out directions, "Exit ——."

"Did you say Exit fourteen," I begged. This guy's put-on voice was thicker than pea soup.

"Oh no, it's Exit ——," said the Irishman. "One…Three. That's Exit ——."

"I'll see you soon. Save me a chair."

"Butter hurry," he told me. "This place is fillin' up mighteeee fast!"

Why that son of a gun. He gave me the wrong exit. I should have gotten off on Exit 14 West. The way he had me get off, for heaven's sake, I came sailing off the exit ramp, and plowed into heavy construction. They had Proctor Avenue shut down for road work. The traffic was backed up three blocks. Just about then, I could have killed that Irishman with the phony brogue. The line of cars never moved in ten minutes, and a guy two rigs up in a Chevy pickup, was on the horn.

It would be hard to make up this part of the story. I was sitting in traffic, steaming mad with the heat rolling off the pavement, side window down, when a guy who looked like he just skipped a boat direct from Belfast, sauntered up the sidewalk.

"Hey Mack," I yelled. "what's gives ahead?"

"There's been a hell of a pile up," he informed me clutching the newspaper. "Take a peek for yourself."

We were already mired down and dead. A few guys had already

peeled out for a quick smoke. I jumped out for a quick look, and sure enough, there was a pile up alright. A tri-axle had pulled out of Flynn Avenue, a big beautiful blue beast of a Western Star with chrome stacks; the truck driver was trying to slip across and wiggle up Proctor Avenue with his load of crushed stone. But a lady in an avocado green Fiat, tried to play push and shove with big iron, and lost big time. She got herself so clobbered pushing the envelope, her driver's front fender was demolished, and the front axle was shoved back under the motor. Her fancy driving moves, just gave her spanking new Fiat a ride to the car crusher.

The lady was incredulous. Steaming mad. She looked like she might have a blown head gasket and was stomping her feet in front of the driver on the pavement. The lady was trying to push the blame over on the trucker. In the distance, the far whine of a police cruiser was racing toward the scene. The lady was pointing her finger in the guy's face and scolding him like nobody's business.

But there were plenty of witnesses, that she'd tried to play chicken with a dump truck. In the pandemonium, the owner-operator of the Western Star, had made a stab for the air horn; but bouncing around in surprise, his fingers brushed the knob for the air lock tailgate — a good portion of crushed stone spilled out. The concussion of the accident had given the lady's car a shot across and blocked the other lane. Things were tied up tight.

The guy with the newspaper, was still next to my passenger fender and looking upon the scene. I extended my hand across the engine's bonnet, and said, "My name is Nick — I'm up visiting from Chattanooga, Tennessee. Pleased to meet you."

"Hello son," said the Irish looking guy. "My name is Bill Murray." He put the newspaper under his armpit and spoke again, "I live right on the corner place." He pointed in the direction of the crash.

"I'm really pressed for time," I told Bill. "I'm heading up to a local pub on Church Street, to watch my team Croatia in the World Cup."

"Where abouts?" asked Bill.

"The RiRá," I told him.

"I know it like my own church," said Bill with a glint in his eye. "I've been up there for holy water many an evenin'," said Bill with big eyes. "A few jiggers never hurt anybody, and they got a hell of a selection on tap."

Just then, Bill anxiously tapped the newspaper across his palm, and exclaimed pointing up towards the crash site, "Listen Nick, bang a left right here on Furguson Avenue, and at the first main way, take a right. That will take you right up through town, and land you within walking distance."

"Thanks man." I slipped out of traffic, and gunned the old Land Rover around the corner, and headed up Furguson Avenue. Bill gave me good directions. On the crest of the hill near Burlington Town Hall, I hooked around towards Lake Champlain, and parked on the side street near the Unitarian Church. There was already a tide of wayfarers on the walks, and a few bicycle riders sped by on rentals.

I headed up Church Street at a good clip. I could not wait to put a face on that phony accent man inside the RiRá. Church Street is a walking area only, where motor traffic is prohibitive. Right there in the middle of the street, in front of the Crow Bookshop, a yoga class was in full swing. The instructor with salt and pepper locks and dark circles under her eyes, looked like she was only a few years away of stepping into the casket. A guy in the back row over an orange yoga mat, was dragging his beer belly on the brick roadbed. A skinny guy up front with his girlfriend, had so much wither traced on his face, he would remind many people of a captive in a Chinese torture chamber. He was grunting and making enough noise too, to cover everybody in the class, and below the cheek pockets on the brick pavement, was a spattering of sweat beads.

I pressed down Church Street with long strides. A wash of summer sun was spilling across the walkway. Weather forecasters had predicted a heat wave. I was real hot about seeing soccer. It was do or die for my Croatia team.

I went through the threshold of the RiRá, cool long shadows inside, and ran face to face into a redhead Irishman. Well, he looked Irish. He spoke like one. He had the kindhearted mannerisms of the old Green Isle; kindred to the regard for duty carried by World War II veterans, when men were still real men. Five other staff were sailing around like bumblebees. It would be almost impossible to find out who the dummy was that gave me those awful directions. Besides, with the place packing by the minute, the last thing I had time for was doing any Dick Tracy work off the clock.

I pressed into the crowd. My Guardian Angel must have been flying with me. A single wooden chair, was void of any figure. All the other seats, luncheon booths, and every stool on the bar was taken.

"Anybody sitting here?"

"No sir," said a young fellow with a crew cut. He had a spray of freckles across his nose bridge, and the front of his hair was plastered straight up with Crew Stick. His girlfriend was rubbing his forearm.

I pulled up a seat. It was the best seat in the house — I could see the gigantic television screen wide and clear, and the bar was just to my right. On everybody's table, was a small white paper that read:

GAME TIME BREAKFAST MENU	
Rasher, Eggs, and Cheese	$6
Banger, Egg, and Cheese	$6
Breakfast Poutine	$8
Gaelic Hash	$8
American Breakfast	$8
Irish Breakfast	$13

The dropping of the soccer ball on Russian turf, was still over an hour away. I ordered the rasher, eggs and cheese, with a coffee. The last thing I needed at this time of day, was to start getting hammered. But all the young bucks swarmed around the bar, were really putting them down; you better believe it too. Four guys on my right flank, standing and loud, were ordering double drafts with every round. They sure were sucking suds. They'd work down a glass, gripping the other draft, put the dead soldier on the bar, and instantly press their lips on the second round. I could see a lot of people were going to be in rare territory.

A good twenty minutes had passed. No breakfast sandwich or coffee had arrived. I told the guys with the freckles to hold my seat, and worked my way across the sea of party people,

angling toward the kitchen doors. The doors had been swinging to and fro, and the plates of breakfast meals sailed by in the waitress's arms.

I pressed my nose into the port-hole glass of the kitchen doors and took a look inside. Three cooks in white T-shirts were moving double time. There must have been a million crushed eggshells heaping from the trash can, and on the big iron skillet, rows of eggs were frying. A guy was slabbing off ham with a butcher knife. Placed very carefully on the warming rack near the range, were hundreds of beautifully baked buns. Their domes were a perfection of golden brown, and I was getting really hungry just looking through the glass.

Memorabilia filled the Irish pub's walls. Many photographs of dead Irishmen drinking in far off establishments, decorated the walls. On the far side of the room — for there were many rooms and nooks in the pub — was a map of Ireland. The map was framed in an old wooden frame, its wood marked with patina of time; the rendering itself was drawn back in the days, when the hands of men drafted in India sepia ink.

Running the ceiling, were platoons of crystal chandeliers. The ornate lights were glowing over pockets of long shadows, and a wash of coziness filled the pub. Many people had passed by under the embellished lighting, and caught in the game's prelude of excitement, moved wiredrawn in the back nooks in search of vacant seats.

I sat back down. The television set on the side wall was big. It looked almost eight feet across.

"What a big television set," I said to the freckle man.

"It's not real," he told me.

"What?"

"It's a projector — look on the ceiling."

Just above our heads on the stamped tin ceiling, was a black projector box. All the glitter of the chandeliers had drawn attention away from the magic box that threw pictures. On the big screen, the players were walking single file from the locker room.

I was still twisting and turning, looking for that phony accent man. Many possible suspects floated past. But the RiRá was really beginning to rake in the dough, and the guys I wanted to run through a shakedown were too busy chasing the buck.

A waitress with a Cleopatra face brought my egg sandwich and coffee. Her face looked just like stone. I looked very close into her eyes, and she blinked and gave in with a smile. I fanned her a twenty spot, and she disappeared for my change.

Those golden-brown buns sure were soft. Your teeth sunk right in. The Canadian bacon hit the spot. I hate to admit it, but it was worth the wait. I put down the sandwich like nothing. Second thoughts crossed my mind, about ordering two more.

It was a long time, before I'd seen coffee like that. It tasted like ordinary coffee. The coffee went down against the sandwich just fine. But near the bottom of the cup, swirling things around, I spotted a silt field of coffee grounds. In disbelief, I used my fork to spin around the coffee, then took a sip. The bottom of the cup was full of grounds alright. I downed the cup. Drinking grounds was part of the adventure, like in deer camp when you did those kinds of things.

I was just wiping some egg off my face with the back of my hand, when a wave of fans drifted past. Two of the ladies were talking exceedingly loud and one of them said into the crowd, "What an accident down on Proctor Avenue." The blonde scanned the crowd's faces to see what kind of attention she had risen. "I heard a dump truck turned over on its side, and the road is covered with stone," she informed.

"When did you hear that?" I butted in.

"I just heard it down on Bank Street."

"Who told you?"

"A guy selling red candy apples from a cart," she said as a matter of fact.

"That's not true," I told her. "You must have run into a real storyteller."

"How do you know that?"

"Because I was on the scene," I told her while trying to get another drop out of my coffee mug. "The truck never went over. The truck driver was just trying to make a weekend delivery to keep the job rolling. But a dizzy dame in a green Fiat, cut him off. There's stone in the road alright, but it's from his air lock on the tailgate bumping open."

"I see," said the blonde. She immediately changed the subject and was filling her friend's ear about how thirsty she was.

Many sights and visions were now taking place in the establishment:

A huge mob had formed going down the left wall. Many of the swarm had spilled on the intimate dance floor and had rummaged wooden chairs. A large number of their jubilant faces appeared to be in France's corner. The chair sitters were a good ten deep, their wooden seats necked tight, and packed in like sardines. In the prominence of these figures, was a man who struck the crowd with a slight resemblance to Ernest Hemingway. The older man had the grey beard, the same kind of face, and was sporting reading glasses thicker than soda bottles. From my table, I could look through the old man's glasses; all the background on the television screen was blurred and fuzzy.

Standing behind this floor section of fidelity for France's victory, were three college boys who appeared, at first glance, to be wearing Superman capes. But, under closer scrutiny across the sea of faces, what they had draped over themselves, fastened around their neck with twine as seen around butcher shops, was the French flag. All three of them seemed to lack confidence in their public display of colors, and were huddling tight against the luncheon booth, where their girlfriends were peeking out over their heads into the crowd.

A guy with his ballcap on backwards had wedged himself between patron's stools behind the bar, shaking his money at the barkeeper and trying to order. He turned back to me and said over his ruddy complexion, "Give me that draft beer on the table. I can't start this game without beer." Still in the seated position, I passed the glass up through the crowd; the guy's fingers stuck out between the people and pulled in the golden draft.

On the television screen, both teams walked double-file into Luzhniki Stadium in Russia. Escorts of children were at their sides. A ceremony man was standing on the green turf off to the side, standing next to a bombshell in a golden dress. The ceremony man placed the golden World Cup trophy on a pedestal. It seemed like a million in the crowd followed in applause.

The guy with his bill pointed backwards, had scored bigtime. He got two more drafts of Guinness, filled to the brim. He put the warm beer in his hand bottom-up to the ceiling and slid it down his throat.

The French national anthem had begun playing over the stadium's speaker system. The patriotic notes drove the French fans inside the RiRá into a state of delirium. They leaped around as those jabbed with electric prods.

That France fan who looked like Papa with the grey beard, sprung from his chair and began singing La Marseillaise. He stood rigid and proud, the blue light of the television spilling over his red flushed cheeks, and the fellow really belched out the tune. He really knew all the words too, and there was no lip-synching about him. His voice carried into the chatting crowd, and many of the ladies around him in chairs had begun chanting, with their voices very melodious as a backdrop.

Standing behind the seated choir across the dance floor, were those three figures draped in the flags. They were singing too. They were drinking, but the booze had not got to them at this point, and they were still on the timid side.

The tallest and the skinniest, was so thin draped in the flag, almost no parts of his body protruded against the colors. Half-hidden behind his two friends, the rail thin guy sang La Marseillaise down the back of his friend. It looked like he was trying to sing tunes past the starched collar, down into the spine of his friend. They were extremely cautious about spilling beer on the colors and held their beer glasses at a great distance.

Just then, a guy walked by with a plate of Breakfast Poutine, and a mug of black tea on a tray. I remembered him right away — he was the guy sitting in a chair next to the grey bearded soloist. I made a double-check, and sure enough his chair was empty.

You could not miss a guy like that. His hair was dyed the most unrealistic black you ever saw, and he had miniature veins of spider webbing across both cheeks. But his green eyes had the whitest whites, and when he looked your way, Brother you knew it.

So to say something, I said, "Wow — that guy from France really belted out the tunes."

"Him?" said the guy holding the tray. "Impossible!"

"Why's that?" I wanted to know.

"Because I know him well," said the over-black man stooping lower. "His name is Marcel Lapierre, and we both come from Ville Marie up in Quebec."

"I'm surprised he could remember all the words and sing so well," I offered.

"You're not the only one. It's been the biggest surprise to many of us here this morning."

"Why's that?"

"Because I'm married to his sister. She's told me many things about him in private."

"Can you tell me anything?"

"Not really," he said looking around. "But let's put it this way — he's not the brightest bulb that ever came out of Ville Marie."

I took him serious, but after the guy went away, I laughed, and the guy with the freckles was laughing too.

Over in the sea of chairs, his brother-in-law with the Hemingway beard, was sitting down. La Marseillaise was over. The guy sat down in the chair throwing all his weight around, like a man trying to push air out of himself. He patted down his brow with a red bandana. Many of the women in his assembly, were rubbing him with love and patting him with affection.

The soccer field was a whirling of colors. Men darted at all angles. The game for all the marbles had begun.

Hunting in the middle triangle, Luca Modric, Ivan Ratitic, and Marcelo Brozouic, stormed around with all the gusto men could muster. The war had done this to them. You could see it in their faces, feel it across the stadium. They moved with a great deal of honor; they realized that victory could take some of the people's pain away, from a long time back when the bombardments came.

At just over twenty-seven minutes into the game, the first of the bad omens for Croatia, drifted as a prelude across the green grass, for things to come between the white lines.

Croatia was deep inside enemy territory. They were pulling the stops on all the defenses. Something was in Modric's eyes. If you'd been watching from the very beginning, when all the countrymen were singing Lijepa Nasa Domovino for Croatia's patriotism, Luca's eyes were in the heavens someplace. He could have been talking to all the dead of his people inside. But now his eyes were on the field behind a game face, and it was very clear he was trying to check the French machine, with calculated moves close to the book, or just as well, behind the referee's back.

Marcelo Brozovic, had picked up with a lot of this kind of thinking. But he got pinched with a foul for pushing the envelope in front of the referee's face.

And that referee put the screws to him right away: Christmas came early for France with a free kick. As if insult came to injury across the field, the free kick bounced off Mario Mandzukic's head, with Croatia scoring for France in enemy grounds. Turning in the state of shock, Mandzukic's eyes revealed his pain, and walked with the aspects of those experiencing bad luck around the goal posts.

Far away in the television set, the crowd in Russia went into a crazy yelling. Soccer fans from around the world were screaming inside Luzhniki Stadium. But even inside the RiRá many voices went crazy alright, and those three French flag men had shifted into second gear. They were on the beer now, and the effects of false courage were falling into place. The skinniest of the flag boys, had forgotten altogether about singing into dress shirts. Now in the command of some new voice, he took one timid step into the crowd, and without even making eye contact with anybody, he began chanting.

"Allez Les Bleus! Allez Les Bleus! Allez Les Bleus!"

His other two friends were saying the same thing. The chair sitters followed suit. Behind in the luncheon booth, the three girl-friends were sitting still, placid with extreme calm demeanors, and one of them was dipping a straw in and out, and back into her fancy strawberry glass of alcoholic beverages.

Soon, our side would have reason for celebration. Croatia found a weak spot out front, and Ivan Perisic drilled a left-foot screamer into the net. A huge uplifting of voices, rose inside the RiRá to the tin ceiling. Still wearing my bucket hat with the brim turned up above the eyes, the draw chords dangling down my back, I catapulted myself off the chair's seat, and went into a flurry of hands like you see around the gymnasium when boxers work the speed bag. An esprit de corps was riding high in the Croatia fans, and all of us were on our feet. A wake of fans had risen in the far platform of seating, and a man was blowing a party horn. In the front of this electrified crowd, was a stout lady with a buzz cut in a white T-shirt. In bold black letters across the chest, Genuine Croatian had been printed. Below the letters was a red heart. The lady was waving frantically my way, caught in the hysteria of merriment; and she was giving me both thumbs up, jabbing them high into the space above. I gave her thumbs back. She was on her toes now, skipping around in circles. Many of the France fans were looking at us with shifty angles and mouths open, almost shocked we had not given blind allegiance to them. But we were the underdog people, and we loved fighters. None of us would have sold out Croatia, for any kinds of paraphernalia or money.

The sea of voices boomed. There were perhaps a hundred people talking at once. All kinds of voices mingled. It was a miracle, but I thought I heard something... the faint jingling of bells. My perception had not been mistaken.

Twisting in the chair, I observed a figure in a white shirt and black tie, speaking into the telephone at the greeting station. He appeared to be putting on the dog, trying to fill in as the maître d'hotel. I knew this was the case, because prior to making a lavatory visit for washing my hands, I'd spoken at length with the real maître d'hotel. He was an older gentleman, polished in manners, sincere, a well trusted figure of the RiRá, and without any question was of full Irish descent.

I said to the freckles guy, "Hold my seat." For insurance, I'd put my half-glass of Manager's Irish Cider on the table, put my bucket hat down, and went for investigation.

I caught him red handed. He was blabbing away over the black telephone. It was the phony Irish man alright. He was giving a lot of free advice, and I was right behind him.

"There's nooo seating available in the en-tire premise," he was saying. "This place is bloody full to the gieels my friend." There was nothing real about his phony brogue, and up close and listening, I could see he was not more than an imposter.

"The score?" said the phony Irishman throwing out his chest. "It's One taaa One."

Why that son of a gun. It was him alright, the same smart cookie that gave me that Exit One-Three stuff and got me tangled in the Proctor Avenue crackup.

Just knowing was enough. I said nothing. There was no sense starting trouble with an imposter of brogue. When the telephone man hung up, he said to his waiter friend, "Some kind of hot around heeear," in a Vermonter twang. He no more came from Ireland, than the Man in the Moon. I went back to the table and pulled back on my bucket hat and took a heavy swig of that Magners Irish Cider. Brother, it hit the spot. The cider had a tangy apple taste, and I could feel the glow. The effects were causing my memory to fade about that phony Irish rascal.

The rest of the forenoon's medicine was a hard pill to swallow. France seemed to have gained an edge of sheer motion. The calls were going their way too. A hand-ball foul against Croatia — some called controversy — spelled trouble. France scored again from a Croatia blunder. Then farther down the clipped green blades, France scored again.

You could feel it across the room, the sensation of a balloon being popped along the parade route, and the kid's grasp of excitement now slipping away into the enameled blue sky, caught holding the slack string in his empty hand.

All kinds of singing came out of the woodwork. The France fans in the RiRá, had gone into a salvo of mania. Some fans even invented songs. After that third goal of France, the fans pulled all stops. The heavy drinking had made them that way.

The three drunk boys draped in the French flag, were singing loud into the rafters. The veins on that skinny guys' neck, were really sticking out. His face was flushed red. There was a glassy look in his eyes, like sailing in the clouds. The three of them were at the top of their lungs, belting out, "La la la la Pailade! La la la la Pailade!" The three girlfriends in the luncheon booth, had jacked themselves on their knees in the seating arrangement, and were looking over their boyfriends who had taken on rare form.

That grey beard guy from Ville Marie, was back on his feet. He was half-popped and needed to hold himself up on the chair arms. Throwing his fist across the crowd, he put everything into his barrel chest and sang, "Les gens veulent savoir, Qui nous sommes ! Et nous le leur isons, Qui nous sommes !"

A fan in front of me, showing her heart for Croatia, was telling them with hand signs to buzz off — the game was far from over. The lady with the "Genuine Croatian" T-shirt, was also giving them the business.

Just then, the grey beard guy who struck a slight resemblance to Hemingway, changed tunes. He began singing over an over with all kinds of energy, "He' Montpellier! He' Montpellier — la la la la!" With that recital, he completely blew his cover about having papers into France. He was singing the fan song of Montpellier Herault Sport Club.

His brother-in-law was motioning to me from his chair. Under the thin thread of light from the chandelier, I could see his jet-black hair and green eyes very clear. He was turning his eyes up at the tin ceilings, and circling his finger around his ear lobe, suggesting his brother-in-law might have popped a few screws loose.

This went over very big around my table. Many of us in our sea of faces, found this pantomime quite hysterical, and were laughing out loud. The grey bearded soloist was now making the circuit of a clock around his fan base, pointing his hands and singing, "He' Montpellier! La la la la!" Caught in the hot flashes of this revel, the flock of France fans around him had chimed in too, some of them experiencing head rushes from too many highballs.

The script of this soccer game had been seen many times in the world of sports. The last few chapters for Croatia, were of men wanting victory so bad, they abandoned all the game plans and textbook drills, and seemed driven against the nets of desperation. They had lost the fluid spontaneity of moving the white skin up the green field toward victory, and instead of the practitioners of deadly set-up men, they were pushing things and taking hero shots.

Nobody would ever know everything for certain — upon both teams had a lot of games in their legs — upon who was masking injuries — upon how long the Croatian men could run on second wind?

Watching the field clock's face gobble up precious time, boxed them to embrace the forlorn hopes of blind destiny. They shot at things that were not open and sailed wide open ringers into space.

Nevertheless, France knew quite well their opponents were

fierce warriors of a war-torn nation, and that the Croatians were extremely dangerous around the box. The French players already holding the psychological edge, brought the moves of impenetrable defense around the hot zone, and stifled their chances for clean shots. This kind of game plan ran Croatia out of gas; the savage bursts of running had sapped Croatia's legs.

France won 4-2.

The RiRá was clearing out. This took a great deal of time, and the French fans had plenty of time to mingle, pushing laughter around between themselves. I cut through the crowd, passing the kitchen doors, and descended into the basement restroom. It was better to be away for now, far from the crescendo of France's fans. The sight of yellow cards being flashed over the green field, were still very clear. The loss was hard to take, especially with the embarking crowd yelling and screaming, with booze all over their breath.

Coming up the long flight of stairs, I spotted the three French flag boys. They were getting ready to split. Two of the three girl-friends, tilted back their heads, making sure they killed the last of their strawberry drinks. Digging around the edges, I'd purposely gave one of them a shoulder nudging, and said, "You guys going back to Montreal now?"

Stumped, the guy told me as a matter of fact, "All of us were born right here in Burlington. We're college students."

"Oh," I said. "Somebody told me that tall skinny guy with the French flag, was a national of France." Nobody had actually said that, but I made it up to spur him on.

"Hey," said the guy in defense, "that guy's great grandmother on his second cousin's side, was born in France."

"No kidding?" I said with a straight face. I just about laughed in his face, and he knew it too.

I shoved my way back through with my blue bucket hat. I'd had enough of that French stuff for the day. Buying time for clear sailing out of the RiRá, I pulled up a bar stool and let the crowd disperse.

Twirling around on my bar stool, studying the menu, I spotted those two in-laws from Ville Marie wading through the crowd. Man, I knew that grey bearded guy who liked singing was short, but now in the tide of faces, I could see just how short he was. You could see the shape of his skull, the grey beard down to the mutton chops, and flashes of those rosy cheeks bouncing in the crowd; but it was him alright. The brother-in-law gave me the high sign above the shuffling crowd, and shouted, "Ce fut un plaisir de vous rencontrer, Monsieur!"

"Same to you," I offered with a sincere smile. I had no idea what he just said, but I wanted to send him back to Ville Marie in good spirits.

I was sure hungry. All that yelling and screaming, the feinting of hands through the air for the hope of victory, had made me good and hungry. Looking over the bold print of the menu, I told the bartender, "Give me a Cottage Pie."

"You made a fine choice," said the bartender. He was an older gentleman in a black vest and carried a lot of extra weight. "It's sooo good," said the Irish chap wiping down the copper-cladded bar.

"Anything to wet your whistle?" he asked, suddenly arresting the circular motions of his bar towel.

"Absolutely — give me another glass of that Magners Irish Cider." High above the bar was a slate blackboard with a list of all drinks on tap. They were scribed in white chalk. Next to the selections, was the alcoholic content of that drink. My hard cider was running at 4%. You wanted to be careful, because even on hard Irish cider you might catch a nice buzz.

Just then, that lady with the Genuine Croatian T-shirt was heading in my direction with big smiles. She had the sleeves of her white T-shirt rolled up tuffy style. Her complexion was golden brown, and when she got close to me, she bristled the buzzy sides of her auburn hair. Short hairs above her ears, fanned out like a porcupine. Choppy rock-star bangs fell across her eyes.

She had pretty big guns for a woman. Across the biceps of her right arm, was the tattoo of a burly ship's anchor in raven black ink. It was the work of an artist, with fine detail. Above in the arching font of stylized Roman letters, was inscribed, "Sailors Give the Best Screw"

"Man, tough loss," I told her.

"Sure man," she said.

"Hate to say it… but France played a good game. They played smart."

"That they did," she said in begrudging tones. The woman sat up on a bar stool and spun around to face the bottles of booze. As she was perched to my left, her elbows riding on the copper bar skin, I could see her tattoo very close and intimate. It fit her to a T.

Her emotions filled the pub. She was at the time buried in profound dejection and stone indifference, for the spell, when the bravest and most enduring champions fail, and the ship goes down. Our team had, willy nilly, been out gunned on the green blades. This made us sad.

Looking over at her golden tan, soccer T-shirt, I took a wild guess and said, "Are your people from the coastline of Croatia on the Adriatic Sea?"

"Croatia?" she asked in wonder. "I'm not Croatian. I don't even know where it is on the map." I could see she was dead serious.

"I'm Clementine," she offered. "I was born and raised in the sticks of Powder Springs, Georgia. Still live there too."

I extended my hand over the copper bar, and said, "My name is Nick." We shook off real hard. Clementine really grabbed your hand with a lot of give back.

"I'll be honest," confessed Clementine, "the only reason I rooted for Croatia, is because I'm in love with Luca Modric."

I shelled out a fin, and said to the bartender, "Give the lady a drink."

"Give me a Guinness Blonde," said Clementine without hesitation. In her Georgia drawl, she came right back to the subject matter:

"Let me tell you Nick — that Luca Modric is my kind of man. I like my men light and frisky. And that rock-star hair just about puts me over the top."

In the wan lights, her complexion was copper and chestnut casts were across her bangs. Her eyes glinted in strange ways, as if Clementine was casting her imagination about for Luca. To change the subject matter, I'd asked what airline she'd flown into Vermont from Atlanta.

"Not us," said Clementine. "Me and my Aunt Cadie don't have any notions to become birds. We rode the train up to Essex Junction." She pulled a train ticket stub from her buckskin pouch and showed it to me.

"Aunt Cadie is over next to City Hall in the park reading a book. She likes reading books in the park while we're here in town." From where Cadie was reading, there was a spattering of shade from the park trees, and from the green benches you could look a long way off to the distant mountains. On the hot summer day, the mountains showed in graduations of grey-blue on the horizon.

"May I offer a selection?"

"Sure, why not?" said Clementine.

"Try the Cottage Pie."

"Sounds terrific," beamed Clementine. She ordered up with the bartender.

I rubbed my forehead. It sure had been a hell of a thing alright. I'd started off the day with a dial-up to the RiRá, and that phony Irish accent guy gave me a bum steer off Exit 13, right into a crackup on Proctor Avenue in the construction zone. Good thing that Irishman Bill Murray came along and gave me insiders dope to cut up Furgeson Avenue, and swing around the traffic jam.

I ran into that short grey bearded guy from Ville Marie, who painted a notion inside the RiRá that he was from France, when his brother-in-law revealed he scored bad on report cards at Ville Marie High School.

Then there was the vendor with the wooden cart on Bank Street, selling red candy apples into the tourists, and telling tall stories how a tri-axle down on Payson Avenue rolled on its side, spilling an avalanche of crushed stone across the roadbed.

I saw three human flag men out of Burlington, who gained a lot of liquid courage from draft beer, then made a huge stretch into French bloodlines from a distant aunt on the second cousin's side.

Out of the blue, I had a Clementine come clean with her Genuine Croatian T-shirt, and report she was born in a satellite hospital in Powder Springs, Georgia.

All along, and through these escapades, there were numerous American flags flying over the cobbles on Church Street.

That sweet Clementine grabbed a fork, and we began digging into the Cottage Pies. Steam was lifting past our forks. It sure was good pie. It was the best we'd ever had. Sitting there in silence of long gone faces, the combustible crowd of fans now extinguished, now wandering someplace in the thongs of village people... it was good knowing those French fans could never be a part of our humble experience.

Looking over at the Georgia peach, I said, "Sure is some pie."

Clementine's hand went up behind my shoulder blades, and patting me a few times, said in her southern drawl, "Isn't it though?"

Out on the cobbles, yellow beams of sun were shining across the wayfarers. A procession of rays streamed past the RiRá's windows. Many visitors of colors and spectacles flashed past the panes.

In the light of the world, I didn't have the heart to tell sweet Clementine her chances of sinking claws into Luca under the satin sheets were just about zero, and those round-trip tickets she had riding in that fringed pouch of buckskin, would never get her anyplace close to the Adriatic Sea, so she could hunt down her lover boy Luca.

Sometimes in the telling of stories, it's best to let some ride for the dreamers.

The Long Wait

Nick sat still. He had been that way in the dark, long before dawn, crouched up there on the hillside in the oaks. First light had come in dead stillness. Then he picked his spot.

His back was to a blowdown, and above his stand a jagged ledge grew from the slope. Nick's view to the front and flanks was clear. He sat on an old wool blanket folded into a small square. The warmth of the seat felt good seeping into his Johnson pants, past the long johns and into Nick's flesh. He cradled a Winchester Model 70 in his arms, both set of knuckles against the green wool.

Nick scanned below. Down there on the basin floor, two deer trails crossed in the beeches. The milky greyness of first light had now faded. The view across the valley was crisp and clear. A chipmunk scampered up and down a stump, husking out acorns on the flat end grain. The brush down there grew tight and thick, but under the cover of darkness, Nick had sneaked down to trim side suckers with his Queen's Trapper jackknife. Now there was an oval gap where a bullet could crash through, without being deflected. This was the third day of deer season. So far only a press of does had sauntered through the forest, the trio in single file, each set of eyes taking turns scanning for the herd's survival. A decent fork-horn had passed opening morning, keeping inside the brush line like smart bucks do, moving quickly with its head down, the rack floating right above the forest floor.

But Nick was only after the king of bucks — Mister Majestic. It would be him or nothing. That rule was made long before season.

Nick was stiff. He had been that way since rising. He tried stretching his legs in troughs that had been scuffed free of those leaves cloaked in hoarfrost. That way a man could move free,

not worrying about giving away his position, sending noise to where cupped ears may be listening.

It was the third day in a row of all day hunting, and today had been a tough one to spring from bed. The flannel sheets were snug. Majorie was under them. She was a good wife, he thought in the dark. Nick had leaned over in bed and planted a kiss on her lips. He looked over her forehead out the pane window — bright stars twinkled out there in the blackness.

Majorie had never moved. She was still asleep on her back. Her lips were dry from deep sleep, nothing like when she had just stepped from the shower. Nick gave her another wet kiss on the cheek, then got dressed. Leaving through the door with gear in hand, Nick never glanced back to where Majorie still slept sound.

Nick thought often of the giant buck. It became his passion, something he could not clear in his mind, a dream that circled in his thoughts. He watched the big buck feed on blades of green summer pasture, while the sun fell west for nightfall. Made mental notes of its rounds and pattern. Knew all the deer trails and runs. Scouted the woodlots flushed in green lattice of summer's browse.

But so far, Mister Majestic had not shown. Only grey squirrels were in sight, digging beech nuts in the grove below. Although Nick could not see small movement that far away, a handsome box turtle had crossed the deer trail not long ago, its bright yellow marking very beautiful in the wash of soft sunlight.

It's always like that, Nick thought. You can pattern a trophy buck in the off season like clockwork, but once the pressure is on things change, right along with your theory. It's amazing how fast the human mind can work — in a blink of time Nick's mind had raced over every woodlot, all clear cuts and open pasture, and stream bottoms within his walking radius. Doubts descended in the forest. Nick questioned his deer stand up there on the oak bluff.

Then he peered down there into the basin where the deer run crossed. Truth was scribed in the forest. Many saplings and a stout baby beech the thickness of a Louisville Slugger, were torn and shredded to smithereens. A wide rack of horns had raked in deep scars. Nick could see the rubs, tucked into his ground blind up in the forest.

Then he looked again. There was a big primary scrape down there. A place where hoofs of bucks had scraped a circle the size of a car's hood. They had cut in down deep, not a single leaf left inside their calling card, raked into the forest floor. Every doe in the woods knew exactly what its meaning was. Time to make love.

Nick's mind revolved again. Yes, he confirmed, this was the spot. Stick to your guns, Nick. No sense moving now. We have almost three days into this stand, all the signs are here. There are plenty of heavy tracks cut into the frozen blanket of leaves. The big boys are just running nocturnal, that's all. Sooner or later, he's going to show. The buck he had dubbed Mister Majestic had to be somewhere.

It was. It was dead. On the second day of the season, three ridges and a wide field over, the deer had been shot. Errol Runshaw had been the lucky hunter. But Errol wasn't hunting, only tending his penned chickens, when he spotted the big buck. Errol had been stooped over, casting handfuls of feed past the diamonds of chicken wire. He found it amusing to watch the birds race for the cracked corn. Raising up straight to move with a galvanized grain pail in hand, his eyes caught movement. They had locked on the huge rack bobbing above the brush, its ivory tips in sharp contrast with background of sassafras shoots.

Mister Majestic had every muscle fiber trained on a large doe who was in heat. She would feed on lush clover, take a few steps, then lower her head again. He would follow. The buck's guard was completely down, with only one thing on his mind. That would cost him his life.

Errol had plenty of time to grab the loaded rifle leaning inside the stud bays of his chicken house, steady the semi-buckhorn sights of the Winchester 25-35 on the buck's ribcage, and squeeze off a shot.

Blam! The huge buck faltered, lunged and sprung forward a few bounds, then crashed in a lifeless hump. It would not move again.

Errol Runshaw was a peculiar man. Something like a hermit who lived alone in a rundown place. Some folks thought him to be a total recluse, but he did talk to certain people on certain visits to town.

Hunting season meant nothing to him. He shot deer year-round. You could see it in him, when he reached the buck. It was in broad daylight of legal deer week, but Errol's reflexes were drawn tight as piano wire. His neck jerked around nervously, scanning the field's perimeter. He hunkered low, grabbing the antler beams and pulling in spurts of tugs toward the barn. The role of outlaw was all over Errol. It was part of his nature.

The measure of that trophy or tally of those wide horns meant nothing to Errol. His only measure was in the meat, how much he could knife off the bones. The huge buck was dragged off just short of the brambles, where grass blades grew tall. A small jack knife that was always with the man, slit the animal's belly; and after slashing the diaphragm from both ribs, the gut pile rolled out into a soft depression.

By the next afternoon, Errol had most of the deer's tougher pieces sliced thin and jerked out on wooden racks. The two chunks of hindquarters were stacked on the homemade ice blocks inside the ice chest. And Errol Runshaw was back outside doing what he did a fair part of each day — tending chicken and chewing snuff.

Nick pulled his collar up. It had reached mid-morning and nothing so far. The excitement of the day was now with Nick. The air smelled good. Something pure. Made a man feel alive. The sting of dawn's watch had finally left his toes. The frozen soles of his packs had regained some warmth. That gift was the pinnacle of living.

A lone blue jay scout had just passed, gliding from tree to tree. Nick did not move. The sun beamed its rays right past Nick's eyebrows; but still, he did not blink. He knew the blue bird would sound alarm at any intruder. The blue jay is not one to sit still, and soon was gone. It never saw Nick.

Funny how the hours passed in the woods, and what a man thought about in that time. Nick had been thinking of Majorie. It was noon, and he figured her to be long up and about. He could picture her down there at the kitchen table, sipping coffee while reading over the kid's school papers. That thought made him proud.

He thought back to the days when love first swept them both away. Their first date, when after walking Majorie to the front porch, how he very gently had lifted her hand and planted a kiss on the inside of her wrist. He remembered the wedding. How the special gift of the children had come.

Then he thought of Danny. He was their middle child. Danny was not with them anymore. He had died two summers ago, a day before the 4th of July.

Nick had been driving the tractor, bailing dry cuts of hay. The sun baked the field. Danny ran behind the tractor. Footfalls of his tiny red sneakers floated across the meadow, threads of cut-off jeans fell across his knees, and golden locks bounced in the afternoon sun. He seemed happy to be with Pop.

The bailing machine was almost new, and it should have never happened, but it did anyway. The right-hand gear box off the PTO exploded during a power surge, and a flying fragment of cast steel caught Danny in the skull. He died three nights later, with a priest and Majorie and Nick at his side. He was only ten.

Nick reached for the Thermos. It held hot coffee with heavy cream. He poured some, then thought some more. He took a few bites from a liverwurst sandwich, but discovered he was not hungry.

About two hours before dark, a spike buck had passed. Nick stayed locked on its movement, as the animal fed uphill. He noted all the pockets vulnerable to rifle fire. There were not many. He marked them well.

Dark grey cloud cover had taken over the sun. It smelled of snow. Soon the flakes started falling, tiny crystals that sifted down. They made a slight sound when landing on the frozen oak leaves.

This looks good, thought Nick. Small deer ... big deer. Perhaps the snow will get the deer moving. A favorite bedding ground of Mister Majestic was those raised moss beds of Belvidere Swamp. That tangled expanse was just over the ridgeline to Nick's back.

Nick slowly opened the bolt action. The big brass shell was still there. It shone bright in the flat light. He closed it back inside the chamber, very softly. He brought up the gun and trained its scope on the pocket in the brush. The sight picture looked perfect. It would be an easy shot. Nick buttoned the top of his red-checked Mackinaw coat, and settled in. It would be a long wait.

—A short story for Ernest Hemingway,
who knew how to tell those things better than most.

Direct Object Formula

Things has been festive. Colored strings of lights had been burning. Fairy threads of sun were breaking in the fog bank. The vapors hovered above the deep snows that cloaked the land. It was early morning, the colored lights were out, and it was four days before Christmas.

There was a line for coffee. I was in the line, and it was moving very slow down a shoveled path. Figures in the back of line were enveloped by the grey plumes, and wafts of pipe smoke lingered through the customers. I shelled out three greenbacks from my wool trousers. Hot coffee would be very satisfactory at this hour. I was coming off a bender of night drinking over at the Sons of Poland, a wonderful club that offered pickled pigs-feet for $2 each with crackers, and wanted coffee to bring my head around. My boots trudged up the line in the snow. It was a powder storm, and the brown fur of my arctics were snow dusted. I held very fast to the green bills.

An orange bulb of an arc light burned above the coffee stand. The attendant had a blue cut-stone on her forehead, and the orange beams angled across her dark skin, and presented a glow of copper about her complexion.

The attendant's name was Pretty. Her father and mother gave her the name back in Pakistan. The city of Jacobabad had given her the copper skin. Weather forecasters liked to coin that city, the hottest place on earth. Numerals stricken on record heat waves on weather charts, could back up their thoughts. The story had been told many times over, that little boys looking for mischief on the streets of Jacobabad, had been successful at frying quail eggs on hot cobble stones.

"Medium coffee, one shot of cream," I told Pretty.

"Two dollar and one dime," said Pretty in heavy accents.

I slid the green money across the plank counter. Pretty grabbed the bills. She liked holding money. Back in the old country of Pakistan, her family had little. But in America, especially selling coffee at this prolific and very profitable coffee shop, Pretty could run her hands over all kinds of money. She smiled wide and had big lips with big spaces between her teeth and was in the communion of copper provisions from the sun.

She glided my coffee across the green counter planks and placed 90¢ in my hand. Her hand was warm against mine. She was heavy on the change. Many of them were copper coins.

I clutched the coffee and took a slug. It went down nice against winter. Then I plomped 50¢ in her tin jug. On the tin in black marker, it said Tips. The two quarters clinked inside the metallic jug.

"Thank you very much," Pretty told me. Her black eyes twinkled, and the manager of the coffee shop was looking over her shoulder and eavesdropping.

"At least you will not be working on Christmas Day," I told her with a big heart.

But everything went over her head. She missed the message. "Oh no … I work everee days. No days off." She had become stone cold serious, her lips had pursed, and she had locked-up ramrod straight like a soldier.

So, I pointed my thumb to the sign. Somebody had stuck a wood sign on a picket into the snowbank. It read: CLOSED ON CHRISTMAS DAY.

Pretty had shoved her head out past the counter, blinked a few times, and said, "No work on number 25 days."

So that was it. She had caught on. Part of Pretty was still arrested though, and she wore a foreign look of those believing they may have cheated between the lines.

Pretty was still learning customs and spoke with heavy constant phonemes. When she got in trouble with the language barrier, she fell back on the phonetic frequency of Pakistani.

Many times, in street conversations out of her native tongue, she switched around conventional syntax, with sentences that began with a verb before the subject, then snuck in the direct object formula.

But she was coming along exceedingly well and worked very hard. Pretty picked up elementary English back in Jacobabad, from old grammar books with hide glue binders. She practiced writing alphabet letters on slate blackboards; and there were no fans in the scorching heat waves with sweat bands over the black brows, as she sharpened her skills under white chalk.

Pretty did some things backwards. She'd bought an old car in perfect shape from an old lady who lost her license from lost vision. It was a faded blue Pinto wagon, and it had perfect seats, but both bumpers had dents from the old lady. Pretty bought the car with coffee money. She only paid $300, because the lady liked her.

But there was a problem — Pretty had no driver's license. She was not comfortable with the road laws in the United States. The signs and painted lines were not part of her pictorial language. She was enrolled in driving school. Pretty practiced driving her car in the driveway, with the motor killed. She sat on the seat with a pillow, for she was on the short side, and held the big steering wheel with both hands, while gazing with child-like enthusiasm out through the windshield.

The father of Pretty, had been thinking about it for a long time. He wanted the best for his daughter. He'd been thinking about America and was trying to the find courage.

All across the lands of Pakistan, there was little opportunity for making good money. Trust was a hard thing to find, because of rampant corruption. A great deal of people on the top were skimming. You could never escape the sweltering heat, and because of poverty in many sectors, there were a lot of bugs crawling near the baseboards. So, all of these things were eating at him, but the last straw was when Fagil Sajid Bhutto got assassinated.

It happened just past dead noon, up in the Blue Pearl Hotel over on Tower Road. It was a horrible and brazen murder. Fajil Sajid Bhutto was on the throne of a white porcelain toilet, his trousers and boxer shorts down by his dress shoes, when it happened. He'd been reading the paper, and the assassin must have taken him by surprise, because there was a point-blank hole from a .38 Special in the center of his forehead. No shell casings were recovered. The assassin must have been packing a revolver.

When Fajil crashed over dead, his shoulder had jammed against the flush lever, and water was rushing into the toilet bowl. The slug had torn out the back of his skull, and huge amounts of blood was spattered across the salmon tiles.

It was only Fajil's first month on the seat of the 4th Union Council, a fixed job he got from the mayor, who was his brother-in-law. The assassin had jumped out the window into the alley. The police detectives could see where his boots had made scuff marks in the cinders. He'd jumped two floors, and then must have jumped over the fence.

The assassin had crammed a note of white ream paper, into the mouth of Fajil Sajid Bhotto. It was written in black ink, and revealed the hate harbored by the killer, and a list of reasons. But the police never leaked the contents, and kept everything closed and tight, and after all these years much of the murder evidence remained swept under the rug.

Because I could not stop for Death,
He kindly stopped for me;
The carriage held but just ourselves
And Immortality.

We slowly drove, he knew no haste,
And I had put away
My labor, and my leisure too,
For his civility.

We passed the school where children played,
Their lessons scarcely done;
We passed the fields of gazing grain,
We passed the setting sun.

We paused before a house that seemed
A swelling of the ground;
The roof was scarcely visible,
The cornice but a mound.

Since then 'tis centuries; but each
Feels shorter than the day
I first surmised the horses' heads
Were toward eternity.
—By Emily Dickenson

"Imagination is more important, than knowledge."
—Albert Einstein

"In skating over thin ice our safety is in our speed"
—Ralph Waldo Emerson

Watering Cans

Some of those practicing sorrow came around the village cemetery in the evening. Sure there were plastic flowers. But there were real faces too, cut flowers in vases hugging the crypts and adorning the maze of above-ground tombs; and in the prelude of dusk, but still when the field of sunlight filled the burial ground, women came across the street with metal watering cans. It was nice for them too, because the caretaker always left a hank of red rubber hose with the spigot in working order, and there was no need to lug watering cans across the cobbles, and slosh water all over their dress. When the women were all done paying respects and filling the vases with water, they generally coiled the red hose, in big serpent-like loops over the white concrete. The brass nozzle always seemed to seep water, and the slab stayed wet around the coiled red rubber, until the morning sun evaporated everything away, and the whiteness returned, and the new day would start over again. That's the way things were in Cessole, Italy, in the summer of 1952.

Just up the cobble road was a market, and there was no front door, and their business was very satisfactory. Tight rows of hemp rope hung to form the front entrance, and it took quite a while around town to get use to the ropes hitting your head and brushing across the shoulder; after a while you learned to part the ropes with your hand and stoop slightly, just like the town people made way to enter the establishment.

Inside the roadside market, salamis hung from the rafters on big spikes. Most of the time the butchers coupled the salamis together at the skin's button, served with some kind of meat wrappers twine, in order to have two casings draped over a single spike.

They had them in all sizes and price, nice variety of seasoned skins, but they would not half-section any salami. You needed to buy the whole thing.

The women who tended the graves also supported the market, because they not only had genuine Milano, Genoa, Toscano, Napoli salamis, and during special holiday brought in links of Sopressa, but it was the best place in the village to bend an ear toward gossip. You could hear almost anything behind the ropes.

Behind the market was the river, winding of blue-green currents, quite shallow, not far across, and on the far side was the stand of Lombardy poplars. Tall and with soldier-like trunks and winding the valley floor behind the cemetery. It was clear the Lombardy were plantation stock, groves of trees lined out as whips. But now the woodland along the gurgling river, its lush green canopy of leaves on blue sky, and the rigid vertical lines of gray trunks rising from the meadowland, painted a picture like Monet himself was on the scene.

I crossed the planked bridge over the river and went up the gravel road that parted the grove of trees. The comprise of the roadbed was a swath of whiteness in the high sun, and its pebbled shoulder wound up through the rolling hills. Under the high shade of the forest, I averted my gaze back across the river to the village hillside cuddled with white masonry — a shift of four stone men had been working the cobbles on the road that rose to the church. They were pulling cobbles, husky rectangular stones, and setting them at level planes again. Over long time, the running of tractors had cupped the bed, and they were trying to take out some of the stone's curse.

Higher on the slopes, figures were picking wicker baskets of ripened grapes; you could see the human-like chain of basket people toiling the grapes to the cart's bed, where at the day's end would begin their crushing for the fermentation process. That's the way things were in Cessole, Italy, in the summer of 1958.

I headed up the road. It was all uphill to the farmhouse. The soles of your boots rose dust from the roadbed. The hot suns had done their work. High above the valley, the endless ridges swept along towards the Alps, and nearly every side of mountain had furrows over the crest, making a world that was just about all under cultivation. Those Italians believed in breaking ground with tillage, and they took the good with the bad. Their collective efforts of farming produced a giant mosaic pattern across the mountains, and just before sunset in the flat light, the details were accentuated and far in the distance peaks and ridgelines turned a dusty blue to gray scale along the border of Switzerland.

The roadbed was dimpled from the hooves of goats. The herdsmen had moved goat flocks that very morning to higher grazing of greener meadow in the mountains. The signature of their pointed tracks was all over the road.

Two kids emerged from over the bluff, whizzing down on Vespa scooters. They were farm boys, and both of their scooters were separate shades of blue. The putting of their motors made a soothing bath of combustion down the road. The boys sailed by me, smiling wide and putting a lot of grips on the bars, and they went down below and crossed over the bridge and out of sight.

That's the way things were in Cessole, Italy, in the summer of 1958. The place was in a time warp. It seemed the hands of Father Time had been arrested for decades. You could blink your eyes, and still see the German tanks gunning their deadly armor through hedgerows, the Panzer's tracks tearing up native land; the tank commander peering from the turret's hatch, feeling the titan power of mechanized armor, pressing the war machine towards its destiny of malice.

Running the imagination, much like a movie picture, you could still hear the high whining of steel pads, the German half-track speeding through the village past the market, beyond the cemetery, searching out another battle that would produce more body counts. Lashed inside the Hanomag half-track's tail, the stiff legs of two red and white Herefords, plundered in the farmer's barnyard by execution with a German Mauser's round just behind the ear, sailed along towards the butchering of prime cuts for the Nazi indulgence.

I went up through the white wooden door of the farmhouse, and up the stone stairs to the second floor. All the Italians were gathered around. The aroma of spices and stewing kettles on the gas fired range, filled the kitchen with the preludes of a home cooked meal. The white dinner plates were already set around the table, with the big afternoon meal on the range, and I was already smacking my lips. I hung my cap and flannel shirt on a row of wood pegs in the mud room, and reaching in my canvas knapsack, slid a fresh salami across the kitchen plank table.

The grandmother, who had been sweeping the kitchen with a corn broom, and clinching a straight smoke between her lips, waved her hand across the table at the salami, grinning through the whisk of gray smoke trailing by her eyes... and said something to me in Italian. There sure was a barrier in Northern Italy. From where I'd began my Italian journey in Milan, riding the tracks to Alessandria, changing trains toward Cessole, conversation in general had been full of mystery — not a single person in my path spoke English. All my business was conducted by hand signals and body language. I'd carried an Italian dictionary in my pack, but I found out if you flubbed around too long cross-referencing words, you risked missing your train. So then, I depended on street smarts, holding small flash cards with my destination.

I'd been overseas on the farm for two months. There was another on the books. I'd signed on through most of the growing season. Simple conversation was still a struggle. Never was a face encountered in Cessole that spoke English, and on the farm of eight workers, only the farmer's wife Maria spoke broken English. Most naturally, all the signs were Italian too.

A white sign was fixed to the farmhouse, with very beautiful split-shades of blue letters, hand painted by a local sign writer. It read: Cielo Blu Vigneto — Blue Sky Vineyard. Below the blue font, the sign writer had painted a gorgeous setting of a young girl picking grapes. The girl's face was caught in the school of impressionism, rosy flesh tones on her cheeks, flowing black hair, a child caught in innocence. Her hand on the white sign was reaching for a cluster of purple grapes. The painted sign was one of my favorite things about the farmhouse. It casted the scene in nostalgia. Walking up through the ankle high grass and looking upon the blue letters, was an experience that never waned in wonder. Returning home each day from the field's toil, was returning to your old friend in the sign. I'd seen many tourists taking the sign's portrait with film cameras, and there was something about it that never got old.

My adventure across the oceans to Italy, began on our farm in the Finger Lakes Region of New York. It was an old farm with ancient stone walls and looking past the grove of rock maples was the blue lake. We had a respectable vineyard of wine grapes, and another 35 acres of apples. It was a family operation. I was the fourth generation coming up the line. Growing fruit was in our blood.

My neighbor Giovanni Cellini, who was an old man, had been born in Biella, Italy. He nationalized to the United States as a ten-year old boy. As an old man he tended grape arbors around Lake Canandaigua. But now he was retired and dabbled in making Caprino della Valbrevenna from the milk of his four goats.

Giovanni subscribed to the Corriere della Sera, the oldest newspaper in Milan. He bought the Sunday edition, and the Italians sent him four at a time in a paper tube from the old country; a month's worth of news arrived in each batch.

That's when Giovanni spotted the add in the classified: Ricercato: Potatori esperti di vigneti, e gli vomini del fruitero. Cielo Blu Vigneto. Cessole, Italy 39-007894311.

The next day, driving by on the tractor, Giovanni's hand waved me down from his mailbox. "Look at this," exclaimed Giovanni clutching the paper. "The Blue Sky Vineyard is looking for a good pruner." He came closer, and raised his voice above the barking diesel, "I believe it will be an excellent opportunity. Speak to your family at once," he told me in his heavy accent.

My father made the call overseas. All my uncles had their ears glued near the receiver. My father was cutting a deal over the dial telephone with Luca Monteverdi, the owner of Cielo Blu Vigneto. I could see the story of my fate, in the cheerfulness of my uncle's faces. Both men had cut a deal in short order. It only took perhaps three minutes. It was all business talk. Both men talked like they were paying a million dollars a minute on the phone. Cielo Blu Vigneto made the finest wine. They'd won the Piedmont National wine tasting contest, three years running. I'd become the fall guy. My father threw out an offer — I'd work the whole summer with no paycheck, room and board, for exchange of what really went down inside the stone chamber that housed the wine press. A summer where all the steps of wine making would flow through my fingers, from pruning vines, to coaxing the Italians into revealing a few blends for vintage stock.

Sweetening the pot, my father offered Luca Monteverdi all sixteen years of our spray program, soil amendment charts, and new concepts of organic farming practice, a scientific file comprised from the minds at Syracuse University extension service. Luca bit hard and fast.

"Listen," said my father, cramming $500 in cash money into my shirt pocket, "what you can't remember, write it down in the yellow tablet." He handed me the yellow pad with blue lines, with a ball-point pen clipped to the sheaf's cover. "Just make sure you come back with the Italian's deepest secrets on wine making."

My Uncle Adolph had given me a ride to Idlewild Airport in the City. He suffered from feebleness of the chest, with bullet wounds from the war. Adolph dropped me off in the DeSoto, and the last thing he did was lay a twenty-spot on me, and said, "Have fun, Travis... it's a wonderful but short life. Make it count."

Working in Northern Italy was heaven. The idea of that yellow notebook had been sagacious thinking. We bonded as a family at first sight. You could feel the love across the kitchen table. I'd stay another two months, where knowledge was my paycheck.

The code of friendship has always been Trust. We trusted each other. Luca gave freely and with enthusiasm, many tips on making wine. He broke open the note pads, going back thirty years in time. He reasoned, with us on the other side of the world in 1958, sharing secrets would not hurt his business. I was allowed to make detailed sketches with measurements of the wine press's chamber, and many other inventions. In return, Luca Monteverdi was highly impressed with the records I'd brought from the university. In the summer of 1958 in Cessole, Italy, organic farming was looked upon by some as quack thinking. The spray booms were deep-seated in their minds; their rational was formed by dead bugs and grapes bearing immaculate skins. Period.

But Luca could see very clearly the lush landscape of the Piedmont's quilting of farms, was being plastered with pesticide. He'd seen in his very town, during the calendar's intervals for insect and fungus control, fleets of tractor-drawn mist blowers, coughing the deadly bellows of various pesticides. The very next season after I went back home, Luca Monteverdi would start the first trial plots with organic farming in the Cessole hills. The idea of building insect traps with lure, was alive in his mind.

The Italians blew away the farms of the Finger Lakes Region. There was no comparison. The demarcation was extreme as grade school, to academics of university level. The picture I've painted was without distortion: The Italians cultivate every square inch. I'd seen grape arbors, strung between the trunks of walnut trees. I'd seen crop furrows on terraced slopes so steep, even a ski racer would feel the rush at those grades.

Cielo Blu Vigneto was a lot more than about grapes. To tell you how it was — I never went near a grape plant for the first three weeks.

My second day on the farm, a flatbed truck pulled in from

someplace down south. It was a 1953 Gold Comet Reo with weathered paint, but the owner had provided new tires for the beast. The enamel lettering on the green door read — Angelini Vivaio. The flatbed was stacked with hazelnut trees. They were second-year whips, and they were not in leaf. A tarpaulin protected them from road winds. The guy driving the truck had the shiniest black hair you ever saw. He combed it straight back, and it glistened in the early morning sun. It looked like he rubbed down his head with olive oil.

Maria Monteverdi had come outdoors to inspect the trees. When she got close enough, I tapped her arm and said, "It looks like that guy has olive oil in his hair."

"It's true," she said. "I've seen it many times before."

I wasn't surprised. Those Italians were inventive and used everything in sight. While the truck driver was folding up the tarpaulin that had covered the nursery stock, I examined the trees. At twenty-four years old, I knew my plant material. On the farm in New York, kids started at the age of ten-years old. Planting whips was nothing new. We set them out every spring, across our orchard overlooking Lake Canandaigua.

I was sure glad they were not bare root. The trees were B&B dug, had nice straight trunks, and had good branching at a young age. If Luca had bought bare root trees, it would have been a tragic experience. The weather was too warm. We would have needed to rush the job. Many trees would have died come winter.

While the truck driver was coiling the lashing ropes, his back turned smoking a butt, I took my Queen Stag jackknife and cut the burlap over the root ball. Looking inside the window, I was relieved to see a wealth of fibrous feeder roots. The nursery had provided us with a good stock of trees. We stored the trees in the stone barn and doused down the roots with a barnyard hose.

The next day, planting commenced. Two hundred trees a day went into the ground. We were lining the trees across a high bluff, good exposure on perhaps sixteen hectares of scruffy meadow. It was all pick and shovel work. Four of us were assigned to the task. A town girl in the last year of high school, was on the planting crew. She had worked the farm over three summer vacations. For some reason, she liked swinging the pick.

We planted the hazelnuts at exactly six meters apart. It was ample spacing for the passing of tractors and harvest. Luca had provided a measuring stick, a peeled pole from the forest. The pole was weathered silver in colors, and light to the touch. It was stored with others in the barn, and was used specifically for orchard line out. The rest of the season they remained at rest in the rafter bays, piles in the somber lights with the spiders.

Planting the hazelnut whips, took many steps. The trees were shuttled to the high slopes by tractor drawn wagon. They were stood like soldiers in the field's edge under the forest's shade, to help arrest the desiccation of strong sun beams. We dug the holes in series of 50 trees.

Luca was adamant about soil preparation under the root balls. He wanted no stones in the vicinity, and a heaping grain shovel of rotted manure under each tree. From what I picked up in the broken language, the manure was a comprise of cattle, rabbits and horses.

During an afternoon of grey somber, low cloud banks were over the valley; still planting, I bade Luca at length about the possibility of burning the tree's tender roots with this potent blend of manures. I implored him by hand signals and facial expressions, cast into the planting holes. Luca directed his recitement in locution of phonics, swinging his arm horizontal across the planting field, his voice running in the musical tones of the Italian language.

"No problema," Luca told us with a beam of confidence. He gave us the thumbs-up, boasting his big Italian smile. His white teeth were embraced by a dark complexion. He then walked away with his springer spaniel dog and disappeared going across and over the bluff.

All whips need staking. We drove in the wood stakes with 3 lb. mason hammers. Then we cinched the stock with hose and wire, bracing them against the combing of gales.

Watering was another thing. It was not like down below, where the mourners of the crypts, could water flowers for the dead off the red rubber hose with watering cans. No place on the hillside of sixteen hectares, could water be found. No heads had been sunk. Drawing big gallons off the farmhouse, could jeopardize the well. Luca wanted no part of the risk. We transported tanks of water from the Bormida River. There was a communal donkey engine and pump with a suction hose, that ran from the river's pool. Many farms relied on the donkey engine. Some drew water for cattle troughs. A farmer had been seen tanking water to fill his collapsible swimming pool. But under no circumstances, were pesticide spray rigs allowed quenching of thirst from the river; get caught by the polizia, and the next day a judge would be throwing the book at you.

When our water tank was full, you knew it. You could only run second gear tops on the tractor's gear box, pulling that much weight back up the mountain.

Watering the trees was murder. It killed your back. Because of the rolling slopes in the hazelnuts, watering by hand was necessary. It seemed by gravity feed off the water tank, you could only get a few trees with flooded saucers. All the others were soaked with pails. It was hard to believe with all the technology in 1958, that three out of every five buckets on the farm, were constructed of wood.

Lugging and sloshing a wooden staved pail in the high orchard, tugged on your muscles. Numerous revolutions were made in a day's work, and it seemed we were always switching arms, in order to save some of ourselves. Those wooden buckets put it to you; the metal loop handles bit into your fingers. But we never jeopardized a tree's survival, on account of laziness. We'd hump a second pail up the slopes, pushing sweat beads, and make sure the saucer basins were flooded. We lost very few.

Those wooden buckets were something though. When we first broke them from the barn, they leaked like sieves. Their wood was dry, and the staves had shrunk. But the lugging of water had swelled the grain, and after the second day they were sound vessels and never leaked a drop.

Luca had been right about the manure mix too. At summer's end the hues of green leaves were out of this world, and the platoons of hazelnut whips were pushing succulent growth.

Other surprises loomed. They arrived in assortments. A big surprise was the Jonagold and Braeburn apples. A small grove of Red Delicious grew near the brook. The apples were set the size of peas. I'd bit a few in half, inspecting for worms. There was none. A spray of walnut trees reached for sunlight on the lee side of the barn. In the dappled shade, the grey trunks of the nut trees appeared rough and sheathed of furrowed cork. A scent of spice lingered in their shade.

The hazelnuts were Maria's private reserve. They existed for cooking needs. From the pantry in the secret shadows of nighttide's slumber, I'd raided the nuts on occasion. They were a vast temptation.

In my bedroom, hung five beautiful paintings. They were originals. The artist had succumbed a long time ago, a few years after the Japs needed to sign on the dotted line, because they had gotten blown up by the H-bomb. The artist was in the rest of eternal peace someplace below in the tombs near the gurgling river. But I have no idea if he was on the list of the woman who anointed the graves with watering cans.

For what the oil paintings lacked in size — they were about a foot square — they won back with the strokes of a master. They were all subject matter of village children, beautiful oil work, and so well done it proved impossible to have a favorite. It was very moving sleeping with the brush work of the dead Italian artist, and I admired his work each evening, before the arc light on the nightstand was killed.

But the biggest shock of surprise fell on a sun-splashed forenoon, when Marcia and Luca pulled me aside, and revealed on a few afternoons a week, my assignment would be child-sitting for their son Luca. He was nine years old. Luca was like a lot of American boys. He was full of piss and vinegar, and a tempest in a tea pot.

If there was one thing you could say about him, it was that he had his own mind. He would not listen. Luca was stubborn as a mule, too.

In Luca's imagination, he was a motorcycle stunt man. He'd seen it on a flyer in Alessandria. The poster had a motorcycle man sailing off a jump through a ring of fire. Luca raced his fixed-gear bicycle on the white cobbles of the rear courtyard. The boy had built a makeshift jump out of planks and a wooden soda crate.

He sailed a great distance for a little boy. I warned him at length to aid caution. He only laughed and pedaled in quick spurts around the circuit. His brown eyes were full of glee, but dark shadows of mischief were casted above the boy.

The bicycle track was comprised of three patios connected by walks and hemmed by gardens. From my sun chair, I could see glimpses of Luca speeding past the veil of plants. On a certain occasion, speeding in a rebellious streak, he crashed on purpose before my very eyes, steering his front wheel on the farmhouse. Afternoon sun flooded the patio's masonry, and it provided an immense hot box for sunbathing. You could feel the sensation deep in your bones. It seemed I was aware of many things on the wooden-slated sun lounge; and it went as far to sense the invisible veil of the heat wave beaming from the blue sky. Luca sprinted on the pedals in this heat wave of summer. His bicycle tires scuffed black marks on the brick paths, and I saw him run over a bed of flowers.

From the garden, a million colors surged. Black and yellow sunflowers towered above the summer perennials. Bluebell-like flowers, sprayed over the white cobbles. Sweet peas hung in green pods.

A lemon tree grew in my retreat of the patio. The branches fanned against the stucco of burnt umber masonry. For effects of old-world craftsmanship, the Italian mason built a stone ledge running the farmhouse. In the prominence of all these features, was a jet-black cat. His name was Casper. After all these years, penning this paragraph block, the shining of the black cat's fur is still extreme in my daydreams; the yellow lemons hanging plump off their stems against the orange hues of masonry; Casper standing on the stone ledge and stretching the chords of its back legs, his black spine flexing and cutting a silhouette against the sunbaked masonry. Soft purring rising from the cat's vocal cords, and the sensation of ghost phantoms of Hallow's night was only arrested by the yellow bright sun and blue sky.

High above in the farm's vineyard, far removed from the black cat with the turquoise eyes with yellow pupils, the honey bees had pollenated the blue grapes, and a marvelous setting of fruit had taken place.

Higher in the mountains, other farms were also in production. It was a common site to see farm tractors clipping past, their V-treaded tires singing a mechanical song, rising bellows of dust plumes. But in the hours past the afternoon siesta, it was rare indeed to catch a glimpse of a human figure. You could see abandoned barnyards, cows peering from barn windows, chickens scolding the atmosphere, and miles of grape arbors under high cultivation. Some farms had gasoline pumps. But to see an Italian in the high countryside, in the hours before the drums of night began marching, was a rare sighting.

I'd looked for somebody for a long time. I'd spent many an evening, hiking the dirt roads that spanned the crest. I'd put many a sunset to sleep in the mountains, washes of orange sunglow falling in the forest's black shadows. But I never saw anybody for weeks. You began to wonder. The first encounter was something. The high farm road across the mountain was dead still. No farm trucks. My full attention was riveted to tracks of creatures that crossed over the dirt lane. Both shoulders of the road were all chewed up. The trail came out of the orchard, crossed, and went up the slope into the forest. Fresh earth showed heavy movement. The creatures were making high use of the trail. The tracks were from hoofed animals. I stooped for closer inspection.

A man appeared. He was an old man, walking with a wooden cane. He came down the dirt road, walking slightly pigeon-toed; off his left flank the slopes dropped steep, and a fantastic view spilled out for the old man.

He'd seen me looking down. I rose from the road and brushed off my knees. It was a good thing I carried an Italian dictionary that translated inside my canvas pack. The old man had closed on me. With the enthusiasm of a gold star schoolboy, I thumbed the dictionary's pages. Finding my precise words, I pointed to the hoof marks, got down on all fours and exclaimed, "Selvaggio maiale? "I snorted loud through my nose, pawed the ground with my right hand, snorted again and said over, "Wild pigs?"

You never saw anybody laugh so hard. His face lit up like Christmas lights. He tried to look away over the fantastic view, as he was laughing so hard.

It's a hard thing to pin down — Italians don't laugh exactly like Americans. Their laughing is more sincere and from the heart. It's like most Italians in general, practiced dignity in their laughter. They shunned away from outbursts of laughter, if the only outcome was coming over the top on somebody and hurting somebody's feelings.

The old man had stopped laughing, but still wore a big grin. I looked down at the chewed-up trail and turned my hands up. Then I asked him off a foreign tongue — "What's up with this?"

"Cervol! Cervo!" exclaimed the old man, falling apart again in his bashfulness to strangers.

I pulled my Italian dictionary from the pocket of my blue jeans. Speed reading, I quickly found the plural noun in the foreign language.

"Deer tracks?" I asked him. You should have seen how small the hoof prints were. They were tiny. Maybe we'd got out wires crossed. They looked more like goat tracks. Those Italians must have some of the smallest deer known to mankind running around the northern mountains. I'd hate to see the look on an Italian's face, if they saw a monster buck hanging from a game pole, up in my stomping grounds of Steuben County.

The old man averted and headed back home. Looking up the road past the clump of lilacs, the old man's farmhouse reached against the sky. Longer shadows had grown in the forest. Shifts of wind were sweeping the wheat fields. Knowing the old man suffered feebleness in walking with pigeon-toes and cane, I followed him at distance to make certain he made it home. He never turned back. He never saw me. I saw him turn past the lilacs, go through the whitewash wooden gate, up the stairs and into the farmhouse.

I turned away and headed off the mountain. The shadows waxed a murky blackness under the tree trunks, and the crickets had begun singing their tune. The meadow larks were making their last sweep over the meadows. Looking from the panoramic bluff, you could see pieces of the village below in the valley, and the steeple and cross of Parrocchiale Nostra Signora Assunta piercing the sky. The old man's farm was not only the highest in all of Cessole, but it was the steepest. The slopes were so steep, the grape trellises were woven and terraced in all kinds of cultivation. Sleeping between the grape rows near the road, was a vintage Cletrac machine — a miniature track machine with chipped paint and rusted sheet metal skin. It was born in a factory before World War Two. It was a stout machine, a tiny powerhouse fitted with a spartan steering wheel, and a giant seat of metal. No kind of rubber tire tractor could navigate on the old man's slopes; that kind of thinking would be a tragic mistake. You might blow an axle shaft at best, and if things turned sour, tumble down the slopes and get killed in the process. All the gnarly pitches in the vineyard, bore the scars of grouser bars from the track machine. Glancing up the roadbed, a night light was burning in the old man's parlor.

I descended at a good clip in the fading light. A cool summer breeze came through the mountain forest. A distant owl hooted.

The first platoon of night stars had moored in the sky. Rounding the bend in the lower fields, a spectacular sight came suddenly into view; it was something that stuck with me through life: The Italians were burning a chicken coop.

I'd seen its destruction many times before. The sash was in ruins, with glass shards besprinkled about. So much decay had devoured the fascia boards, the birds flew freely in and out, nesting at leisure in the rafter tails.

The Italians had dismembered the coop with sledgehammers and axe blows. A furnace roar of combustion raced from the flames. A billow of a million sparks, rose in a frantic plume toward falling dusk. The Italians were shouting some kind of merry songs and taking pulls off a bottle. I could see their figures against the giant bed of coals, and the orange flames licking.

I huddled closer to the hedgerow for a better look. Parting the saplings with my big hands, I stuck my head through the whips. In the distance, their voices had become louder, and they were pitching wooden shingles into the blaze — a crackling crescendo roared in the flames. I was thinking about introducing myself out of the shadows and pressing them for a few pulls. But I was already over one hour late for supper, and I pulled out and marched double-time back to the farmhouse.

I had other companions in the high mountains. I became very fond of them. But all of them were dead. They were the green lizards. I'd seen them on several occasions. All of them had been cut in two, severed by the V-tread farm tires buzzing the dirt roads. I measured all of them at extreme length. Some had marvelously real sections from the front legs forward.

You could see their vivid green skin, their snout, the look in their eyes. Others only possessed anatomy of the tail section; their grim facial expressions flattened across the mountain road. They'd never made it across. They got squished in the crossing. A lot of times I'd thought about severing the good sections with a jack-knife, and joining two lizards, so the full picture came into view. But their deaths were many hours apart, and it was never feasible to practice that kind of roadside dissection.

I looked for green lizards, this way and that way. I turned over stones and logs. Parted meadow grass. Looked for them in the grapes. But I never saw a living and breathing green lizard. All of them were quite dead, and I'd seen a lot of them, sinking their claws out into the roadbed as they slipped away.

My summer was just about wrapped. Time had run out. I was down to a single day — the whole day of Sunday. Then I'd be gone. My flights were ticketed from Milan to Bruxells; there I would change planes and head back home across the Atlantic Ocean. I'll tell you something Mister, that Bruxells Airport was sure a strange place. You saw all kinds of mysterious and strange people from faraway places, and the hardest thing was trying to read their faces, because a lot of them were so serious with shifty eyes. On my flight into that foreign country from the United States, three tough looking characters from Burma, were sitting on a red bench with their feet kicked out. One of them had a banana-shaped scar running across his jawbone. Airport Customs was shaking down five guys from Yemen. The chap sitting next to me from Liverpool, told me he'd heard they got pinched for crossing the Red Sea with counterfeit papers made off a printing press in the basement.

But Italy was another thing. It was a great land, and after spending my summer tending her grounds with friendship from the village people, a large portion of my heart had converted to Italian.

Luca Monteverdi had given me my last three days off. He'd thanked me at length for my service. I'd worked myself to the bone; and he knew it.

My first day off was Friday. I spent the day packing and making certain my passport and travel papers were in order. I traveled all the way by foot to the village of Cessole, and inside the market with the hemp ropes for a front door, bought three large salamis to bring back across the ocean. I'd stuffed the salamis inside my duffle bag, hidden inside the pants leg of my dirty Levi's. Sometimes it's possible to trick Customs.

The afternoon of my second day, my taste for wine had gone too far. Luca Monteverdi, had given me four bottles of vintage wine to take back home. But I nearly killed a whole bottle by myself, while I sat by the Hi-Fi listening to Italian music. It really hit me. For a young man who seldom touched a drop, I had more than a glow. What notion had summoned me, no recollection exists. The only possible explanation — for memory I have none — is that the gayety of the wine's spirits had gotten hold of my reason. Nevertheless, somewhere after my fourth glass of wine, snapping my fingers to an Italian beat, I made a foolish decision under the influence, to venture down the winding stone stairs to the first floor. In the stairwell, everything had become supernatural. My footfalls seemed to be landing in space. The golden glow of the arc lamp in the landing, its rays casting on the pine board wall, painted fantasy into my reason — the sensation beckoned me forward in a false security.

Some kind of buzzing in the silence of night was reaching my ears. I tripped on the last stair and catapulted myself into thin air. I remember the shock of my head walloping into the masonry wall. I shouted a swear word back at the wall. My outburst had startled the grandmother from her mattress, who had been sleeping away her siesta. She gathered my senses at the scene and served as a human crutch to minister my needs. A brisk rubbing on my head, indicated swelling had been almost instantaneous. What an egg I gave myself. Without her auxiliaries, I would have been a helpless case. My equilibrium was shot. We made it to the bedroom. I crashed in a heap. A galaxy of stars from far away worlds, spun in my head. I heard and saw many things.

In short order, the grandmother shook me vigorously into a semi-trance. A steaming bowl of homemade soup was in my presence. She essayed me to have some of the broth. From what she tells me, I consumed the whole bowl. Then I passed out.

The next morning, a miracle had taken place in the night. I felt like a million bucks. I'm not sure if it was the chicken soup, or the bag of ice she placed on my head. My guardian angel must have been in the mix. Most of my lump was gone. All the stars in my head had drifted away. Imagine though, if I'd stumbled the other way. Catastrophe could have spelled on the stone stairs. A man could break his neck under those conditions. They would have sent my corpse to the morgue in Allesandria. If nobody ever sent for me, I might end up down where the local woman sprinkled flowers for the dead with watering cans.

Anyway, after that I quit all the sauce. Never touched the spirits for fifteen years. Oh sure, a Christmas beer or Thanksgiving drink was one thing. But four water glasses full to the brim, was out of the question. I'd proven my blood stream could not handle that much spirits of fermenting grapes in short order.

Birds sang outside the window. A clear day had broken. Sun was in the forecast. It was Sunday. My last day in Italy.

A singular want was on my mind. To visit church. I felt it would be respectable to show the Lord thanks, for my wonderful stay in the Italian farm country ... and permit my destiny to flourish, without mayhem on the flight of stairs.

There were three Christian churches in town. The people certainly had faith. There was Parracchiale Nostra Signora Assunta down in the village. Actually, it was one church on top of the other, the foundation winding and climbing around the village bluff. The towering church reminded many village people of a giant castle. There was a second church too, the Chiesa di Sant'Alessandro.

But because I was a farmer, living in the high country surrounded by farm, it was in my heart to show blind allegiance to the chapel in the mountains — Madonna della Neve. It was perhaps twenty-minutes walking from Cielo Blu Vigneto, a small chapel built on a scenic bluff in the higher mountains.

In those days, I had a wonderful mop of hair. So, in order to cover the mischief on my forehead, I simply tousled up the locks, fluffing the bangs over my swollen lump. My dress was clean work clothes, with respectable work boots. My orange-handle Felco #2 shears in a leather sheath, were fixed to my belt. My ascension to church would embark me across several hectares of our grape production, and it was inevitable I'd spot suckering or vine correction in passing.

It was a deep-seated experience, to never venture in orchards or the weaves of vines, without sharp hand pruners. I went out the farmhouse's back door up the slopes across the vine furrows, through the seed heads of the grain fields. The meadows had put out a phenomenal amount of growth. The surging stems were brushing against my ribcage, and I waded through the sea of shimmering blades. The going was all uphill. I craned my neck above the seed plumes, making a press towards the farm road. Swarms of grasshoppers lifted from the golden chaff. Passing through the neighbor's property, another grape grower, the farmer's observation had marked my presence in the moving grass; he quickly scurried across his white porch in the distance, trying to measure my countenance for trespass. Upon revelation — word had traveled the valley an American volunteer was present — the farmer just about dislodged his arm from socket, in his recognition to see me cutting his land. He gave me the welcome of a noble king. It was a great distance across the golden meadow to his porch, and the beaming of his smile was clear as day.

I arrived at church. The Italians were piling inside. The Madonna della Neve, held only a small portion of people. It was a cozy chapel with tight seating, and although the sun was shining bright outside, long shadows were falling inside, and gave a spectacular effect to the flambeaus on the altar, the flames waxing and waning from the caress of soft breeze across the open sash. All the Italians were wearing suits. Maybe fifty people were inside, and all of them dressed like that. They were very old suits, and all the older men's suits looked to have been around since the first World War. They were winter weight too, and these men, their white cuffs showing bold on the dark olive skin of the wrist, were in long sleeves with neckties. The heat was coming on from the valley, but none of the *nonnos* budged an inch. They remained rigid and proud. A grandfather next to me, sweat pouring down the veins of his temples, pulled a *fazzoletto* to pad down his brow. It was a blue handkerchief with white dots. After it was wicked with sweat beads, he stuffed it into his suit's pocket. I was seeing this from the back pew. Sitting in the front pews would be too pretentious. I afforded the whole front seating to the regulars.

The Italians had me hemmed in on both sides. A baby in a bassinet, was cradled in her mother's arms. There was a lot of commotion around the baby.

Then the priest entered the altar. All commotion was arrested. Silence cloaked the mountain chapel. Not even the baby made a peep. Then the older priest, speaking the dialect, began mass. All the parables went over my head. I fathomed nothing. Lip reading provided no clues. It was a deeply moving mass though, and all those times Uncle Adolph took me to New York City on holiday, the long hours both of us put into people watching on the Number Six Train running Lexington Avenue, paid off exceedingly in how I could read their faces. I read everything in sight and wheeled to measure that baby again. She had spit all over her cheeks and was teething a red rubber ring. She had pools of chestnut brown eyes, and they were looking at me from the corners. The mother was repeatedly kissing the baby's forehead, and her tiny toes were wiggling.

Behind the priest, was the statue of the Hail Mary. She was painted in the traditional color of baby blue, and her hand clutched the rosary. A set of old, time worn Christmas lights in tiny blue bulbs, wired in parallel conductors, was fastened to a semi-hoop around the Hail Mary's head.

The effect of blue electricity in the dark shadows of the church, shafts of pastel sun in the glow of morning light, presented an illusion of a radiant halo. It casted forth a powerful pictorial image of holiness. I could not take my eyes away — the twinkling blue lights brought about a devotion to her presence.

In this kind of mass, where all the words added up to a song of strange syllables, a person could say prayers for all their loved ones, to pass some of the time with usefulness. I prayed for all the family across the ocean on my farm, and said a silent Our Father for Luca, so he would be protected against smashing himself into the masonry on his bicycle. Prayer was offered for my best-friend Richie, the kid on the farm up the road from our place. I'd thought of him often over the summer, knowing he was pulling broad-backed trout from Lake Canandaigua with his level winding reel. Sitting on the wooden pew, its grain raised from the years of pilgrimage to the cross, I locked my fingers and said a devotion for Giovanni Cellini my Italian neighbor back home who got me hooked up in the first place. A dispatch had arrived in the chapel, crossing my mind, to offer my Communion host for vulcanizing Giovanni's soul. No timing could have been better.

He had died the past Monday. It had taken place sometime in the late afternoon. They had found him slumped in his rocking chair on the porch. There had been no response. My family had held back telegram. They deemed it needless worry. No clairvoyance on the penetration into his death, had entered the subconscious. Too, sad indeed, the funeral for Giovanni Cellini, was on the very afternoon too much red wine had spilled down my throat. I rubbed the lump on my head. Nobody ever felt better than me. That grandmother knew her potions of soup.

Fatigue from cradling the bassinet in her bosom had commenced the lady to pass the baby over the back pew to the grandmother. You never saw a baby with such fat calves. Tickling the baby's toes, I reached across and gently squeezed her calf muscles, and to my astonishment they were like steel. There was no question in my mind, she'd have plenty of power to work the high green miles of grapes in her youth, and possibly be a star on the running track.

The priest finished his gospel. His rendition of preaching the Bible, had mirrored idiomatic traits of many Italians. He was alive in colloquial street pantomime with saber-sharp hand gestures as the vehicle. He practiced vernacular gusto in the voice box from the pulpit. The priest brought back visions of a lady who'd sat next to me on the train out of Milan, an Italian who pushed so much hand motion into our broken language, she closely resembled a broadcast messenger making sign for the deaf-mutes on television. Her excited motions were nearly perpetual motion, and the only time she braked was to eat two cupcakes.

The basket-collection boy had slipped from the shadows. The basket had an extended length in the handle, fitted with green felt on the bottom. The youth shook down the assembly. Fumbling past my orange hand pruners on the right hip draw, digging in the pocket, a few American bills were extracted. I tossed two bucks in the basket. The kid froze up in marvel. He'd never seen American money. He looked at me with riveted specter. The basket collection boy delivered the money on the altar, his shoulders held back in proud achievement. The priest's eyes got bigger on foreign currency too.

It finally dawned on me. The baby had arrived at mass for purpose. That's why the old men had broken out winter weight suits. The mass would conclude with the tiny girl's baptism. The rite took place on the altar. Jesus nailed to the wooden cross, and the Hail Mary in the sea of blue lights was the primary witness. The crowd had pressed around the rites of holy water. Some of the old men in the outside ring of people, made an effort to stand on their toes to see more; but they lacked the agility at that age to attempt floor exercise. I measured the ceremony from the back pews. All the others had advanced tighter into a huddle. The vertical figures of Italians painted a piano keys scene of black and white habiliments. The priest was chanting in a rhymed meter. Outside, the green lizards were running for their lives between the blades of meadow grass.

I stayed long. The service had long ended. Small talk had gone on for many minutes in the church's rear. Flash film cameras were clicking. Many frames were taken. The baby produced more spit on her face. The grandmothers kept kissing her cheeks. They subconsciously rubbed their aging hands over the baby's soft skin, but could not reverse time, and failed at delivering themselves into the hands of youth.

At last, silence prevailed. The baptism people had gone up the corkscrew mountain road to the relative's house, where they would indulge on coffee and Italian pastry. Uncle Ignazio had picked up cannolis from Gilda's Bakery in the village. The mother of the baptized baby had made a wonderful Panforte Margherita, which was nice and firm under the knife cutting. But Zia Gianetta just about blew away the deepest willpower of the holdouts in the crowd, when she pulled back the tinfoil of her Ossi Dei Morti Biscotti. Leave it to the Italians to even mix their romanticism into cookie dough — the name of Ossi Dei Morti Biscotti translates to bones of the dead in Italian, cookies made for All Soul's Day. On this day, practicing old customs, the Italians went to the cemetery for paying respect to the dead, then reflected with a meal topped with the cookies. It would be safe betting that the woman down below with the watering cans near the red rubber hose, also baked Ossi Dei Morti Biscotti on All Soul's Day. They were like that. It's highly doubtful, however, they ever left any cookies behind in the cemetery for the dead, because they were a coveted treat, and that kind of practice would only leave crumbs behind from the sparrow birds.

I sat alone in the back pews. The baby had spit out its red rubber teether. It was on the floor next to the kneeling pad near my boots. The view of the altar was now wide open, with no heads in the way. I was glad the lady three pews forward, who had twisted her hair into a towering beehive, was long gone. Now I could see more of the charm.

The star-like galaxy of blue lights fanned the Hail Mary in the chapel's silence. It was very still, and some of the sun's rays coming through the window, fell across my face. Across the distance, I thanked Mary for my adventure in the far lands. A world, it seemed, living and breathing inside our planet. I could not estimate when or at what striking of hands, crossing into the time capsule took place. For the border crossing was invisible; and I was at ceiling inside a silver fuselage when we entered Italian air space. But we'd perforated into a demarcation of anachronisms, where the vice of modern civilization had faltered in finding victims for its marching jaws. The tranquil mountains and its inhabitants were a singular sanctuary of old-world customs, and its presence had moved me to the core. I'd be taking some of its treasured lessons of enlightenment, back over the sea between my rib's cartilage. My imagination was alive in colors, and the memories would be safe there, locked in the sinew.

I'd saved a backwards glance, going out for the Hail Mary. The only acknowledgement was spiritual. I remember a tingle going up my spine. Then I glided down the stairs under the zenith of blue sky. A grey vole scampered across the chapel's floor, nudged the red rubber teether, and scared himself to run back inside the woodworks.

I descended the corkscrew mountain road. There was fresh cut hay in the air. Bronze rays of the sun were sparkling off the Bormida River. Two victims had not been successful. A stone throws apart, two green lizards lay buckled in the road. Their beautiful green skin, iridescent in the forenoon's light, was a sad discovery to behold.

I cut across the soft shoulder and entered the meadow. Black and orange butterflies were hovering and darting in the green blades. Just then, below in the valley under the blue enameled sky, the revelation had returned — a German Tiger tank had shown its deadly armor. Imagination was alive in colors inside this time warp, and I tightened against the landscape. The silence of the morning was shattered under the bronzed rays casting the thronged forest, the tank creeping the steel hulk of its appetite for destruction, crushing pole size trees as match sticks. It's dappled snake-like camouflage poked its turret from the veiled woods, its waist gun coughing lead into the field's brush. The stentorian speech of the tank's main gun sailed explosive rounds on the high bluff. The belching echo of its orange flamed muzzle, was followed by inhuman whistling in the air. Through the thick and lush green curtain of forest, a pink glare flashed. Rushing forward in the tank's flank, a swarm of dark suited foes with sloping helmets, made a mad dash towards the slope's toe. Two Germans in the echelon, toppled like wood pins, stone dead as they pitched into the Italian till. These sights were painted very real in my mind, and I blinked my blue eyes twice.

Their comrades raced at what appeared twice their past ambition. They were men running a military press, and their payment was living to see the setting sun.

From the high slopes, the sputter of M-1 rifles became a steady roar. A machine gun kicked in. An American infantry company was dug into the stone choked crest. In the prominence of all these figures, the raging war machine under the tiny blue lights of Hail Mary, was my Uncle Adolf. My uncle who had driven me to Idlewild Airport, for my destiny into the network of Italian vineyards. My Uncle Adolf who had feebleness of the chest. The near fatal wound had been inflicted in a slanted gunfight, outnumbered two to one, all because they were trying to protect the Italians from the fascists. That attack of the German boots, backed by the Tiger tank with its big bore gun, would indeed pay out very dear prices.

Hanging back in the wake of destruction, a German sniper with a long-tubed scope, looked hard through the clear optics. He was hunting humans. The sniper's rifle rested on a fallen tree, its root ball blown clear from the bombardment. Pressing his eye on the scope tube, he hunted with the crosshairs, until he found a vulnerable victim on the stone-choked slopes. With enough of the American's boiler-works under exposure, the German sniper touched off a shot.

Uncle Adolf was dug in a foxhole, up to his brisket and dog tags. He'd circled his position with a ring of stone. He felt invincible, looking down from his nest of beetle rocks. But the fine reticle, had him dead and square. The German sniper went for a head shot; but the speeding bullet dropped in flight and took Pvt. Adolf through the left lung. It blew two chunks of ribs out his back. As seen in the movie film reels, the round sprayed a wealth of crimson blood against the foxhole's wall.

The concussion blew Adolf backwards. Still buckled in his chin strap, the helmet's weight snapped his head back against the foxhole's rim. His eyes glanced in disbelief at the heavens. Great brown clouds floated in the still sky above his position. With the beetle rocks digging into his back, Adolf could see soaring birds with white plumes against the brown sky. They sailed in silent circles of thermal air. He felt some of him slip away.

Adolf closed his eyes in the heat of panic and clutched the dog tags. He envisioned his name and birth date, embossed on the patina of silver tin. His fingers tried to wring a salvation from the metal beaded chain. Blood was all over his bracelet of fortune, pressing firm on his own chest in the desperate moves of self-preservation.

The medic took over. He placed an immaculate white dressing over the sucking chest wound. The gurgling chorus of oxygen and blood was put to rest. The medic's action was perilously close to the reaper's calling — Adolf was hanging by a thread.

Things turned around. A lanky kid from Bowling Green, Kentucky, got brave and belly-crawled up within range of the Tiger tank. He put a bazooka round into the bottom rollers at point-blank range. The German war machine blew a track. Then he dumped another armor-piercing rocket into the engine bay. The crew came out coughing from the blistering spews of black smoke. None were taken prisoner — as the crew came out the hatch like a row of frantic grey ants, a GI worked them over with a Thompson sub-machine gun.

The feverish pitch had waned across the battlefield, and way below in the valley, a string enemy soldiers was running into the forest. That's when a U.S. Army firebase, three clicks south-west, opened up with a salvo of walking artillery. The F.O. radio operator had been right on the money, and he hit the key and exclaimed, "Fire for effect, boys. You're right on 'um." The radio man watched the work of his radio transmission explode over the fleeing figures. He instantly felt powerful as God. "Pour it on 'um, boys, "his eyes bigger than wooden nickels.

Nothing ever made cannon cockers happier, as when they got dope on running enemy inside their zero. The battery worked the massive bolts in a fever pitch, ramming rounds home. The report of artillery boomed above the forest, the scathing shrapnel raining a world of hurt on the fleeting Krauts. Trinkets of leaves twirled from the green canopy, and Germans fell as if struck by lightning. This cove of dappled forest may have appeared to ethereal wanders, as a bloodbath debacle of terror stricken by a meteor field. The metal rain of field artillery had carved into the tree trunks, and the visage of dead soldiers were mirthless grey with mouths gaping in the cool blanket of shade.

This opened a chance for saving Uncle Adolph. They lashed him to a stretcher on a nimble jeep. A plastic intravenous bag dangled and fluttered in the slip stream. He was taken over hill and dale, moving with vigilance under the jeep's winding gears towards the 349th Mobil Field Hospital. After the surgeon closed his chest wound, Adolph was taken back across the ocean on a Navy ship and given an iron-framed bed inside Walter Reed Hospital.

When Adolph arrived at the hospital ward, the other men also hooked up on tubes, had shown vast interest in the new man. They prompted him at length about the Italian battlefront. But Adolph was not in talkative moods. His mind was on the bold newspaper print of the Washington Post. Under the veil of evergreen boughs in the Ardennes Forest, the Battle of the Bulge was in full swing. Uncle Adolph's buddies were in the foxholes. His unit had drawn cards for the front lines. He could picture many things from his hospital wing — upon the chatting of machine guns from the nests — upon the immaculate white snow and green forest — upon blood spattered across the snowflakes.

Four months later, after two painful surgeries, he was discharged. Against all doctor's orders, he lit a smoke. Some new kind of depression was around him. It was something like pellets of hail, coming and going with its painful burden. But it never went away. Adolph could not shake the melancholy of this unmerciful beast.

The crashing of the German's sniper bullet had stripped out

over twenty-five percent of Adolph's left lung. He could still run the mile under ten minutes. But he could not swim very far under water. His love for woman had not faltered from the incident. He married his sweetheart, Gracie Hendrix out of Rome, New York. They brought three children into the world. The Beast of Depression suddenly vanished. Adolph got back to cracking jokes at family affairs. He had a canine tooth made of genuine gold. That was part of the inside joke. When Adolph laughed, sparkling wide in precious metal, everybody laughed. His dental work was a propellant towards laughter. But Adolph still saw the battlefront, on certain nights in the blackness of his bedroom. It was a lot easier to kill Germans, pulling the trigger under the bedspread. Many Germans fell. Distant bands played patriotic tunes. The stars and stripes fluttered gallantly in his sleep. All sharp images of conflict, died in the breaking of daylight. He kept all the visions inside and private. No matter at what angle he was browbeaten by the curious, he never gave out extorted confessions about any of the blood shedding.

I went down through the high meadows. The fluttering of orange and black butterflies had grown to a heightened frenzy. The colored winged insects, traced out darting flight patterns above the field.

A huge contingent was performing before my very eyes. I could see their beautiful spots very clear, and the sheer construction of their wings. But this ephemeral frolic, was truly only understood by the aerial participants; many parts of the sky dance, were above the head of man's reason.

The visions of deadly war, the grumbling of war machines, had vanished. But a new revelation had dawned on my brain, and it was a poignant messenger: the Italians had been responsible in certain measure, for the crashing of that high-powered bullet through my Uncle Adolph's chest cavity. Many of the Italians, had become affiliates with the Germans during World War Two. That fact had never crossed my mind; standing in the high meadow looking across the blue river and the village of Cessole, I fought in earnest against having my love for Italians slip out into the squadron of butterflies.

I'd be flying out the next morning from Milan. The last thing I wanted, was all the homespun memories of Italians, to go down the tubes because of a recent history lesson. It took willpower to fight the sudden burst of anger.

But in the end, everything worked out fine. A lot of the good Italians would take care of the dirty work.

Nobody could blame everything on the Italians. Much of the problems, were incited by an evil figure, who was brought into this world as a little boy in the city of Dovia. He'd founded the nationalist band of Fascists, who dictated Italian lives through beatings, murder, and wrested exile into his own bloodlines. His name was Benito Mussolini and would go down in history books as one of the most notorious rascals to ever walk on Italian soils.

Like a lot of the wicked and evil, Benito Mussolini was full of himself. He lived for throwing out his chest under square shoulders, full of theatrics with a jutted jaw and clinched fist for the fotoreporters and basking in the chants of his blind followers —
"Il Duce! Il Duce! "

But Benito Mussolini was no hero. His craving for seizing power through conquest, only caused a fizzled collapse of the Italian Army. He proved to be a merciless coward on the battlefront, a bully behind the war machine when Mussolini's troops invaded Ethiopia, when he ordered the deadly muzzles of machine guns leveled against the sun-blackened tribesmen, who clutched spartan bow and arrows. Many of them, still in the state of astonishment, never had a chance to serve a feathered nock on the string. The survivors who escaped into the jungle at dead runs for their very lives, still stricken with fear, never returned out of the triple canopy jungle until long increments afterwards for the possession of corpses. As the imagination paints the picture, with those kind of heat waves dancing in the tropical slaughter grounds, the flies had commenced laying eggs; working at feverish pitches, the tribesmen dragged corpses and buried the dead, the stench of death hanging in the humid blanket.

When tested in World War Two, Mussolini could not get the job done. He failed miserably in Africa. Benito got so banged-up in his invasion of Greece, he needed a backup from the Germans to keep from getting creamed. He found out under the most malicious circumstances, that his game face was nothing but a stillborn quest, when he decided to bang heads with the United States infantry. His troops got pummeled; and after that even Adolf Hitler noted how disheveled and haggard Benito Mussolini suddenly appeared in public.

History books are full of those kinds of lessons. The pages go back a long way. A great deal can be learned by reading. But I got my history lessons of war from homespun knowledge — I grew up listening to my Uncle Adolph's gasping for air, his left lung bearing heavy scar tissue from the K-98 Mauser's round.

Adolph's battle wound was a metamorphosis of declining health over time. His gift had always been balancing figures. He kept the books on the farm square. He cut the payroll checks and deals over the telephone with the wholesale vendors. I can still see him in the farmhouse's office, crunching numbers over an old adding machine, pushing the ivory keys with black numerals.

I cut sharply down the meadows. My fingers raked the long stems of grass, as if grasping at straws to find solutions to the complicated problems of conflict. Numerous particles of chaff collected in my palm. They held no answers. My fingers released their message. I wove through the grape arbors and skirted the chicken coop, then began packing my suitcases.

On the 25th of April in 1945, Benito Mussolini and his mistress Clara Petacci, began packing their suitcases too. Their scheme was to escape into Switzerland, and fly undercover into Spain for refuge. But their timing was poor. None of the stars of Lady Luck lined up for them. Cutting around the shores of Lake Como, the snow-capped Alps of Switzerland looming in the zenith before their very eyes, they got pinched by the Italian underground in the village of Dongo. That blunder would cost both lovers their very lives.

At the time, Mussolini had already been reduced to a puppet leader, under the protection of the German liberators. Most Italians wanted him dead. They would get their wish.

To demonstrate the ruthlessness mindset of Mussolini, when he discovered his son-in-law, Galeazzo Ciano, was included in the fascists who sold out on him at the Fascists Grand Council, he ordered to have him executed. What kind of man would give the green light to have his daughter's husband rubbed out?

Clara Petacci's brother posed as a Spanish council, trying to make a power broker deal with the Italian underground, begging to spare their lives. But there was too much bad blood in the air. The underground was in no mood for sympathy. They would never have released Benito Mussolini and his hanger-on, for twenty million dollars. They wanted him dead.

That evening, I packed my suitcases in earnest. Because of all the souvenirs collected during my stay, I crammed everything into my suitcases mumbo-jumbo. Worrying about wrinkling clothes never crossed my mind. Fitting everything inside was my only concern.

After packing, I drew the water nice and hot. Then I sprawled out in the bathtub with a fine glass of wine. Nothing ever felt or tasted so good. I quickly reminded myself about the most unfortunate incident, when I tripped off the staircase with too many glasses of wine under the belt and walloped my head against the masonry. Hence, I cut my consumption to a single glass. It was nice wiggling your toes around under the lukewarm water, with a relaxing buzz going from the wine. Luck for me — the owners of Cielo Blu Vigneto supplied free mineral spirits for the room and board, and you always found a box near the tub. They advocated the spirits for relaxation, and because they wanted workers fresh in the morning.

That evening, a wonderful cool breeze enveloped from the high mountains. A colored quilt was procured from the chest. A window was cracked. During the night a galaxy of stars twinkled above the farmhouse; all through the blackness of night, I slept safe and sound. The next morning in the crack of dawn, Luca Monteverdi drove me to the airport. We crossed the bridge over the Bormida River in his Fiat automobile. Fog banks engulfed the river, and wisps were hanging around the village of Cessole. Somewhere on the other side of the forest that hugged the river, a rooster's voice called through the grey mask of fog. There was a certain urgency in his fluid shrill.

Benito and Clara spent their last night in the house of the DeMaria family, in the village of Mezzegra. It was the month of April, and the crisp cool air was in the night. But Benito could not sleep well. Dead men walking cannot sleep. In the midnight hour, it's easy to imagine Benito was peeking out under the Venetian blinds, looking for a chance to escape. But the Italian underground had him boxed in tight, armed sentries at all exists. Benito Mussolini was collapsed as a puppet leader, and all done pulling strings.

The next morning, Mussolini and Petacci were shot in cold blood. They executed them in the small village of Giulino di Mezzegra. After the gun smoke cleared the air, all fifteen members of Mussolini's henchmen, were also dead and spread like dead sparrows on the beds of stone.

Like the rub-out shooting of Osama bin Laden by Seal Team Six, where a certain code of vagueness remained in place who pulled the trigger, the man who carried out the executions was a partisan leader but used the nom de guerre of Colonnello Valerio — a phony name. His real name is lost in the clandestine spirit of the underground, but by conventional wisdom the man is thought to be Walter Audisio; however, other partisans who witnessed the hit, controversially alleged that Colonnello Valerio was none other than Luigi Longo.

But two things remained in place. Benito Mussolini lay in a pool of blood, already riddled with bullets. Two days later, Hitler and his wife Eva Braun pulled their own plug, and committed suicide. And in less than a week, the world had rid itself of two notorious villains.

My plane had climbed steadily in the night. We'd come out of Milan, through Bruxells with mechanical delay. While the wrench men made their overhauls outside the hanger, I sat still and studied the sea of faces. It seemed you always saw strange people in the Bruxells terminal. This time was no exception. I saw a guy wearing a yellow and orange turban, with a long narrow face; and he was smoking a white pipe with a high bowl and long narrow stem, puffing on the stem from his neck muscles; he had a very stern face, and never smiled, and all around his narrow and long face with a sloping Roman nose, was a cloud of grey smoke.

Now it was daylight. The airplane's engine had a healthy whine. I could see the ocean far below. We were over the middle. There was nothing but water. Craning my neck in the window glass, I could see the Flemish Cap. Out there in the stormy chop, you could not help but see and say a prayer for Billy Tyne's soul. It was the same waters, where the Andrea Gail pressed for home, her holdings teaming with dead swordfish packed with crushed ice.

Our plane went over Sable Island. Then after falling asleep, the jarring on the landing strip brought me around. I was back on the home grounds of the United States. Uncle Adolph was waiting for me in the terminal. We rode together in his old pickup truck.

It was a wonderful feeling when I handed over the notepad with blue lines, filled with information. Luca Monteverdi had been very generous with his knowledge. Over half my tablet was filled with useful information.

I crashed out again on the seat. The humming of the tires had put me to sleep. I think the plane ride had given me jet lag. It was very satisfactory sleeping on the Western seat cover, heavy knit like a horse blanket. I slept very sound. My dreams reached across the ocean to Italian meadows with colored butterflies.

The day of the impromptu funeral procession was the 29th of April 1945. There were no flowers. No tears were shed. Everybody was happy. They loaded the corpses of Mussolini, Petacci, and all the executed fascists, like the boned carcasses of pigs at the slaughterhouse. They heaped them as chucked cordwood, the bodies humped in a human pig pile.

Then in the dead of night, under a bath of silver stars, they rolled into Milan with the stack of corpses, and dumped them off the truck on the grounds in the old Piazzale Loreto. The truck operators got enormous satisfaction heaving off the dead. They sported mischievous grins, grabbing the ankles, the other underground men clasping both wrists, and with a glorious swinging motion, sailed the dead off onto the cobbles.

Much excitement filled the Piazzale Loreto. In the wash of daylight, shafts of orange sunbeam coming across the town square, the pile of corpses were noticed. The freedom fighters began cracking their knuckles, and were ready to seek revenge.

The roof of Esso gas station over the pumps, was nothing more than a trellis of iron works, wide open to the blue sky. After many of the town people got rid of their pent-up frustration by kicking the bodies, they dragged them across the cobbles to the gas station. The heads of the dead bodies bounced with a faint thud. A lifeless victim broke a tooth on the cobble stones. Then they were hoglashed with rope and dangled from the iron works by their ankles.

As part of the much-anticipated public horror show, they strung up Mussolini and his lover Petacci side by side, upside down with their arms lurching in space. This effect alone brought out the devil from a lot of people: hordes of the angry crowd gathered around the corpses, and while stoning them at short range, chimed with chants, "Down with the Fascists! "A great deal of them in celebration, had already taken long pulls on whisky bottles and from flasks of wine, and there was a lot of them under intoxication, that went hoarse and lost their voices.

By high noon, mayhem had taken over the Esso gas station. Abuse of the bodies went on hard and long. Many rocks were scattered on the pavement from the stoning of corpses. The memories of the partisans were pointed and bitter. They recalled with a vivid picture, their own loved ones being executed in the same town square by the Axis, then dangled from the same set of steel works over the filling station. They could still see the German soldiers cradling their deadly sub-machine guns, and with sinister sheens across their countenance, nearly choking on laughter watching their partisans get executed. This drove the revenge to a feverish pitch, and under the effects of alcohol, the reins of sanity had been severed.

The revenge was served cold. It lasted into late afternoon. To show just the kind of turnout the dead Mussolini had triggered, so many people had swarmed the Piazzale Loreto, that all the popcorn and candy bars inside the Esso gas station had been sold out.

Over at Ariosto's liquor store, every bottle of cheap wine had been sold, and the nips of hard whiskey had been riddled. Around the town square were many cornices, old stone staircases, and window sills with stout and wide stone ledges; in all these places, dead soldiers of wine bottles rested by the hundreds. Clear glass jugs twinkled, and those who killed them were exceedingly drunk. With the tempest of a good drunk in the press, came a vicious mean streak.

The crowd pulsed and lunged in madness. The screaming of the wild people had reached a furnace roar, and there was much name calling. Even the poliza were infatuated with the wild hysteria and turned their backs on the goading of corpses.

The old man finally got his chance at Benito Mussolini. He'd watched for hours inside the crowd, feeling the proudness and watching the young bloods welting the corpses. The young bucks were getting shots in for him. Their blows inflicted revenge for all partisans, the living and those who once lived.

But now it was his turn. The crowd parted. The old man moved forward with the assistance of his wood cane. Some flies were buzzing around Mussolini's head. Even in his decrepit state, the old man could see the ghastly film which had formed over Benito's eye. The old man spread his shoes apart for a better balance, for the feebleness of old age was all over him; and with a hand on his dress hat, he inverted the cane with his free hand, and tried walloping Mussolini's head with the cane's crook. But so much rheumatism was in his shoulders, that he could not land a solid blow. Just then, a young man in the press, Rocco Parini, came to the old man's assistance with a wooden soda crate. It was much easier for him off the wood slatted crate, a miniature platform where he could catch a balance. Rocco braced the old man's shoulders with genuine love, and the old man worked over Benito. It seemed the old man had enough, when after his cane struck dead square on Mussolini's nose bridge, he heard bones break. That crunching noise took away some of his resentment against what the fascists committed, but it was only short lived and superficial, because he then showered a profanity into the thin air around Benito's corpse, "Cagna sporca — purefazione ali' inferno." And he really meant the part about rotting in hell too. Then he sauntered back inside the swollen crowd, and many people were slapping him on the back.

A young woman who was very beautiful with long black hair, and wearing a lime green sweater, took over the old man's place. She had watched the Germans murder her father in cold blood. His hands were tied behind his back when they shot him. She'd watched the shooting go down while braced in terror on the vibrant green grass of the town square. The woman bore deep emotional scars, and now standing under the mutilated fascists, she had the opportunity to remove some pent-up hate on the dead.

She had brought medicine for Mussolini. In her hand was a fly swatter, and she began slapping his face. The sharp reports of skin being slapped, ran across the gas pumps. The forest green paddle of the fly swatter got little rest, for she'd turned it on Petacci, and was repeatedly slapping her cheeks. Any woman who made love to that kind of man, deserved no less. To end her abuse, she slapped both of Petacci's hands good a few times. Then she walked defiantly back inside the wild roar of the crowd and cooled her nerves with a smoke.

A brisk evening had fallen over the corpses. It was still spring. The angle of sun was still weak. Far up the road, heading up through Saint Bernard Pass in the tiny village of Astoia, the puddles were beginning to freeze on the side of the road. That's the way it was in the Alps in spring. A man had just slaughtered a goat. The sable black goat hung upside down off steel hock hooks, and the mysterious winds blew against and fluttered its black fur.

Down below in Milan, they were cutting the corpses loose. The same truck pulled around. The driver and his two accomplices were coming off a good drunk. The driver of the truck popped a few white pills of common aspirin. Looking at the corpses sober was another story; but not too much you know, because the hate in them would last a lifetime. The truck embarked across town with the pile of dead and dumped the bodies into a vacant factory.

The brisk night had put a good chill into the concrete floor, and Mussolini's corpse stayed nice and cool through the night. His decomposition state was arrested, and all the flies had flown away to other places. After two men dug his grave the next morning, they buried Benito Mussolini in the Musocco Cemetery on the north side of town.

Back at the Esso gas station, the last of light was falling. Everybody had gone home. The streets were empty of people. The gas station had packed it in for the day. The place was locked up, and the owner was home counting his wads of money. The only things left behind, were the severed short hanks of rope still fixed to the steel works, and many circles of blood which had dripped down on the cobbles. The blood had dried to a dark burgundy on the stone, and just about everybody in town would agree it was dirty blood in more ways than a singular definition.

A lady was mixing red hair dye in a pot. She did not want to be recognized. There were three ladies in all. Their husbands had been involved in the mayhem at the Esso gas station. The three ladies had refrained from attendance. They had stayed inside Rosalinda's place, and while fanning cards across the table for gin rummy, they cooked up a scheme. While they played their cards over the afternoon, every so often a tattletale would come inside, and spread more gossip about what they saw in the stoning of the corpses.

But now in the last threads of light, it was time to move out and get on with things. The lady who gave herself an over-red job on the head, toweled down her hair. She opened the front door and flung the rest of the hair dye in the vessel off the porch and across the bed of flowers. Then the lady began putting together her disguise around the chairs of the kitchen table. She was very nervous about being identified by the fascists, who were still seething about the abuse. The over-red lady wanted to gather many habiliments that were out of her personality, so she'd be in travestito coming out the front door and throw off many people as possible.

Rosalinda was a few doors down, looking out the window for clear sailing. Across the pinched lane, Carmela was cinching tight the laces on her herdsman boots. She knotted the bootlaces and watched through the curtain for Rosalinda's signal.

The over-red head wrapped a sky-blue babushka across her

head. She pulled it down to cover her temples and disguised the freckles. Red hair stuck out over her big ears. The bangs covered her brow. Dangling off her ears were extremely long gold earrings, much like you see on gypsies with the circus in town.

Rosalinda pulled the huge pot of water off the wood fired range. The water had come to a slow rolling boil. She hefted the simmering kettle with oven mittens, and carrying the steaming vessel off the porch, dumped it into her watering can. Then she went inside, and with a face drawn tight in nerves, jerked the light switch up and down three times. Carmela looking out the laced curtain, caught the signal. The over-redhead peeking out her cracked door, saw it too. It was time to move.

Three ladies came single file down the pinched lane, lugging watering cans. Some of the tepid water sloshed on Rosalinda's dress; in her free hand was a stout floor brush. The over-redhead had reported in an olive trench coat, searching further to mask her identity. All of them were in disguise. Carmela kept her hand cupped around her eye socket, shielding her countenance from the passing windows. All of them were in fear of being spotted by the fascists, because the Axis sympathizers might concentrate their resentment of them. They moved swiftly into the dusk with a gamble, hoping to dodge getting their houses fire-bombed down the road. The three ladies crossed the cobbles of Piazzale Loreto and scurried to the Esso gas station. A last glow of orange sun was setting behind the far mountains. A gang of arc lights came on across the town square. None of them said a word.

What a mess the angry crowd had done. There were spatters of all kinds of blood under the steel works of the filling station. The ladies anointed the wicked splashes of blood, sprinkling down on them with the watering cans. Rosalinda procured a squirt bottle of dish soap from her overcoat and squirted down the blood. Then she commenced to scrub her long-handled brush, working over the bed of concrete. Of the three women, Rosalinda had the widest shoulders, and was the woman who dwelled on zest.

Once down at Ariosto's liquor store, a man had pulled cuts on her when she wanted beer really bad, and she'd driven the heel of her hand so swift and hard between the man's shoulders, he instantly lost his breath and almost stumbled to the floor. It was common knowledge around town, and accepted by most men, that Rosalinda could most likely beat all the skinny men around town in wrestling match. A lot of men around that part of Milan thought she was half-crazy, which of course she was when pushed to the brink.

Rosalinda was really bearing on the brush now. Foam of red blood was beginning to flow from the cobbles. Under the steel where Benito Mussolini had been strung-up, was the most blood. Where the blood had dripped from his broken nose, a pool had formed bigger that a soccer ball. This was the biggest quest for the three evening stalkers, removing this evil blood. Rosalinda worked the bristled brush with the lightning speed of a curling star, the stiff bristles biting deep.

Rising phlegm in nervousness is one thing, but Rosalinda mustered a nice load of spit, and spitting down on Mussolini's blood, she barked into the echo chamber of the Esso gas station and said, "Good riddance — you dirty bastard! "Her voice ran clear and sharp, in the dead-stillness of dusk.

Under the ordinary living of her life, Rosalinda had a clean mouth. She refrained from swear words. The stiff-arming of the cuts man was a singular event. Rosalinda was deeply religious. She wore a hefty solid gold medal of the Lady of Fatima around her neck. Although they lived on a shoestring, she always dropped a few five-lira coins into the collection basket on Sunday. But during this pursuit teaming with vengeance, figured it best not thinking about the Lord on this kind of occurrence.

A short length of red rubber hose was snaked around the gasoline pumps. The owner of the Esso gas station always offered free water, for the topping of radiators, and cleaning of bug-stained windshields. Carmela and the over-redhead had cracked the spigot of the red rubber hose and refilled the watering cans. The stream of cold well water made a sounding noise against the metal cans. The over-redhead took a good swig off the hose. Carmela wet both hands, and splashed about her face, then killed the tap.

All the women now were in the second round of blood washing. Small channels of watered-down blood were seeping into the cracks, and a heavy stream of red water was streaming into the storm drain off the curb. The evidence of their husband's involvement disappeared with the river of blood.

Everything was back in order. The concrete slab glimmered from the dousing of watering cans, and a fresh smell filled the night. The red hose had been coiled. With the watering cans empty, their metal hoop handles creaking a chorus line, the three ladies hurried across the cobbles of the Piazzale Loreto.

Averting in the night, they gave one backwards glance to the Esso gas station. The reflection of water shimmered under the site of avenge. Caught in the skyline of the twinkling night, the silhouette of short ropes hung from the steel gallows, hangman's knots that had cinched around the ankles of the dead. The mortal woman stood in echelon on the town square, holding themselves exceedingly proud. A strange confidence was with them. The gang of arc lights of the Piazzale Loreto glowed into night, and the jubilance of the moment was caught on their faces. Rosalinda threw Carmela a wink of victory. Then the three women scurried across the white cobbles, and up the pinched lane towards home.

The three woman departed ways of their fighting force. As if on cue, they dutifully placed the watering cans on their porch, snug and hugging the wall.

The woman very cautiously turned their front doorknobs, very quietly in the night, and went inside. Rosalinda cracked her bedroom window. Her husband was under the covers. A wonderful stream of fresh air seeped inside on the spring night. Rosalinda took off her hefty gold medal of Fatima, and hung it like she had for years now, dangling off a wooden peg near her headboard. The medal heliographed in the soft yellow light from the nightstand.

Out on the front porches, the domed spouts of the watering cans, pointed triumphantly toward the banks of twinkling stars. Closing their eyes on the pillowcases in darkness, the three ladies let go of their feelings and drifted into a sound sleep, because the last of the dirty work had been completed.

Practicing Law

A fog bank had the Irish Sea socked in tight, and it was raining. Over on the Blackpool side, the Moonlight Maid had her beams lashed to the pier's head, riding thing out. The crew, four Brits and a Chinaman, were playing gin rummy below. It was in the hours of late breakfast, as everybody slept in, and as the men shuffled and played cards, they showed their fondness of eating home fries sprinkled down with vinegar and salt.

All five men knew the colour of the sea. It was blue slate of green hues as looking towards Ireland. There were white caps on the swells, and as the men stole sporadic glances through the port hole glass, there was a constant and methodical lapping on the heavy plated hull.

The tides were swelling on Buoy 1273 in the fishing grounds, and the tether chain of the red and white buoy was wrenching against the sea. Cod and pollack were feeding on the coarse sands, and schools of horse mackerel were so thick, the sea turned the colours of dark blue with green flecks from the procession, their sides flashing silver in the fathoms. The Chinaman who had recently obtained proper citizenship papers to the Union Jack, shuffled cards and dealt out more hands of gin rummy.

In a few hours, the schools of fish would be subjected to the otter trawl of huge nets, the Moonlight Maid winching in the sea's bounty. The Liverpool market was paying high on fish, and the Queen was exceedingly fond of oven seared cod, with the accessory of baked potatoes from County Louth. The potatoes were the commodity of an Irishman's sweat and blood.

Across the sea on the northern Emerald Isle, a solid five days of misty rain was winding down. Cloud breaks could be seen looking over the Mountains of Donegal. The rains had turned the village and countryside into a postcard you see around the tourist shops. The field stone walls were hemmed in by green pasture; white stucco cottages were encompassed with the greenest of grass. The rains had brought out a million shades of Kelly green, and it was hard for motorists to keep their eye on the road with this kind of coloured landscape.

The lawns in the village had surged; and there I was mowing Mister McClatchey's lawn. The bright sun had dried things out nicely, and I was making good time mowing and putting vivid stripes across the lawns. The flower bed along the house under the kitchen window, had been planted with blue delphiniums by Mrs. McClatchey, and the power of the blue colours against the white house caught in the fairy yellow sunshine, was enough to arrest people's attention. I'd seen several motorists stop for a second look, and a lady pushing a stroller was pointing for her baby at the flowers.

The heat had come on strong, and Mister McClatchey had invited me inside for a sarsaparilla on ice, with two slices of Irish soda bread with KilCullen's butter. It was always nice eating that kind of bread, because his wife was not stingy with the raisins.

Attorney Muireach McClatchey, handed me the beverage and sliced bread on a plate, then started massaging his forehead and said, "Son of a gun, those customers down in my law office are taking me over the coals. My phone never stops ringing. I was on the telephone yesterday for seven hours, but everyone was calling for free advice."

The both of us had been looking out the window across the backyard. Mrs. McClatchey had an oval bed of perennial flowers growing back there, planted between a boulder field, and with all the colours and bloom, I saw a hummingbird out of the corner of my eye. He was a green and ruby feathered fellow and darted around like film clips from a cinematograph movie.

"Would you like another glass?" asked Muireach.

"No thanks, Sir," I told him.

Then Attorney Muireach McClatchey went on with his story. He began rubbing his temples again and waived his hands across the pane window towards the flowers.

"This free advice stuff is for the birds. I could spend my life talking away on the house.

What a lot of us lawyers are looking for these days… is billable hours. Get the picture? Billable hours! Billable hours!" he revealed with a grin.

I said nothing. He was out of my league. I just listened and let the important things stick inside me. I knew someday I'd be a writer.

"It seems the older I get, it's almost impossible to find the kind of hours that pay. Everybody's my big buddy and wants to put soft touches on me for a free buck."

"I'm sorry Sir."

"Don't worry Son. Everything will come out in the wash. But I must be getting back to the office."

I went back outside eating my last piece of Irish soda bread. The bright sun was hard on my eyes. I fired the motor and began mowing. It was good knowing my labors were set in stone. I was paid six pounds a pop for mowing. There were two more customers waiting up the street. I could count my money sleeping in bed, and knew they were good for all of it.

But there would be other forms of collection in the following weeks, from the Ulster Defense Regiment. Just across the border in Londonderry, they had implied Marshal Law with a curfew an hour past dusk. The IRA had struck hard that day, and in ambush style had killed a RUC Constable by the name of Molly McGrath, mowing her down at the Foyle Bridge crossing. Bad blood was in the air, and the Ulster Defense Regiment would be out for pay back in the wee hours, and the collection would come through the motorized armor cars with 50 cal. Browning machine guns, in the forms of quarts of blood and body count.

Across the Irish Sea, the crew of the Moonlight Maid was counting the British pounds from their catch, and the Queen was seated around candlelight with fresh flounder and baked potatoes garnished with butter from the grounds of County Louth, but all of them were far enough away to wash their hands of any bloodshed.

A short story written in a single sitting, on March 2nd of 2018, the same day as Billy Graham's funeral. The story came to me in the last few days; and the rest arrived in sleep. I started in daybreak and finished up over the typewriter well into the blackness of night.

The Jews at Weizmann's in New York City, charge like hell. But they did the cleanest developing work and never ruined your negatives and produced prints of the highest quality.

So nobody minded paying the price. They were set up on 37th and 5th Avenue, and I always did business with the owner's son, Maxie Weizmann. The Jews offered a 7 ½% discount for cash money. On big orders, that could be a big chunk. So I always paid the Jews with a wad of bread. The New York City Jews were honest too, because no matter what the balance in dollars and cents, they always knocked off the cents and dropped to the lowest figure. They gave out free complementary dust rags for wiping your expensive lenses, and more than once Maxie placed a couple in my hand. No matter how many times you made the trip, there was always some kind of street adventure in the City, and a pleasure doing business with the Jews at Weizmann's.

— Stephen Deck

Christ Belongs to The Whole World

It was the morning rush hour. The crowd was coming up the stairs of Penn Station like ants on the 7th Avenue side, and a Jehovah Witness was having a hell of a time selling religion. I'd been watching him a good two minutes, and he'd sold nothing. The flyers were free, and there was not a taker.

"Good news of the Watch Tower," he was saying, "Good morning, good morning, good morning." The guy was waving those flyers into the sea of people, but nobody responded. Nobody ever acknowledged the guy was alive. The crowd streamed by the guy, like he was thin air.

The morning sun was falling across 7th Avenue, perched in a yellow ball above the East River, and there was a beautiful bite in the spring air. Because it was a beautiful day, and because I found the guy selling religion in a foreigner's voice so intriguing, I pulled behind one of those stainless steel stanchions, and was all ears.

The name of that dark-skinned guy selling religion, was Akeem. Everybody knew this, because he had a white plastic name plate on his shirt, like you see around a fast-food joint. He had on a hat something like the sailor's wear, but much more stylized of carmine silk with silver tapestry and fitting his slim skull like a glove.

I placed my styrofoam coffee cup on the stainless-steel pillar. They made a nice miniature table. There were 18 of these shiny steel pillars in all, fashioned in a semi-rectangle around the station. Those huge metal cylinders, were on the short side of history around New York City.

For instance, they weren't there on the spring morning of 1969, when four Marines lugging duffle bags, came up the very same stairs. They'd just cycled out from a notorious gunfight on the north side of the Perfume River, when the 6th NVA communists pulled a fast one during the Vietnam lunar New Year, and stormed Hue city. The four soldiers had coughed out brass shell casings all across the Truong Tien Bridge and had sacrificed many brothers of their 1st Marine Division, from enemy machine gun fire sweeping the bridge's span. Thinking back — it's really too bad those stainless- steel barriers were not anchored to the grey cement, wrapped and coiled with the American flag, because it would have been some kind of welcoming party, instead of the cold stares they got on the sidewalk of 7th Avenue.

Akeem had come prepared. He not only had Watch Tower pamphlets stacked on the steel pillar, but had piled very tall stacks of more religion, on the next two steel stanchions down the line. Akeem had arrived to sell religion alright, but there were still no takers.

I sipped my coffee and looked around. Six cabbies were nervously pacing the sidewalk, looking for customers. They were doing a hell of a lot better than Akeem. In less than a minute, all six yellow cabs had sped off into the rat race.

Akeem never lost any tempo in his sales pitch, his voice remaining sincere, and he had said, "Good morning, good morning, good morning," to more than a thousand street travelers. He was very persistent and kept on waving those printed flyers. Akeem was quite tall, and you could see his carmine silk hat with the silver tapestry, looming above the crowd.

Above my head and behind my back, a metal sign in memory of a dead man, was fixed at right angles to a light post. The man had been a black man. The sign read: Joe Lewis Plaza. Many nights of the fight game had gone the rounds next door, the thrill seekers packing Madison Square Garden. Behind and roosted above Joe Lewis' memory sign, was a tiny billboard. It included portrait pictures of two boxers. The black letters made a simple advertisement — Crawford vs Kahn. The time and date were listed, for those moved by seeing heads get rocked in the fight game. The signboards presented a timeless aura of boxing over the crowd, and standing below on 7th Avenue, I could feel a pinch of history and the arena bell still ringing inside The Garden.

Just then, twelve African refuges had begun streaming from the staircase. All of them were Fur people. They had escaped in deep fears from their village of Kailek, when the genocide got heated up in Darfur. They had seen many bad things. Many of their blood lines never made it to square one, because quite frankly, their heads had been separated from the torso by an axe blade, wielded by Janjaweed soldiers whose countenance was of crazy-eyes and shouting voices bent on revenge. A young mother inside the tribe of Fur people spilling out of Penn Station, coal black skin that glistened in the morning sun and went by the name of Ruba, was a living beholder of the horror-stricken scenes. Against her wailing cry for mercy, the Arab militiamen had tugged her four-year old daughter Yaya from her play box, dragged her son Jamal of eight years old by the heels, and tossed them bound by a veil of chicken wire into a bed of blazing cherry coals. The children had been burned alive as pawns.

And the cross-town morning rush throng thought they had things rough over on Lexington Avenue, riding in on the Number 6 Train in tight quarters. A great deal of them were put out, because with no available plastic seats, they were forced to stand and clutch the metal hand pipe and ride things out.

If only that kind of ride on steel tracks, had been available to the twelve shining black faces at Penn Station, measuring a man selling religion. The Fur people had struck out on their conquest for freedom, humping long miles for weeks on foot, striking across the desert region between Djibouti and northern Somalia; inside shifty clandestine rings of smugglers, the Fur people paid in money, rape, and set-up jobs, for the chance of slipping away off the Horn of Africa; crossing the Gulf of Aden in marginal crafts, they escaped into the war-torn shores of Yemen; enveloped in the barbaric charm of refugee camps, bolstered with compassion from the Regional Migrant Response Plan, including Interos, Danish Refuge Council, and Unicef, the Fur people were shifted into Saudi Arabian work camps, where most of them were paid wages for manual labors, waiting for embassy clearance into the United States. After all that suffering, forlorn wanderers who faced peril of rolling breakers in the Red Sea, ventured into the war-torn landscapes — here stood a dozen Fur people in the star-spangled sun of America.

Even in the streets of New York City, known as the melting pot, the Fur people stuck out like sore thumbs. Their visual astonishment in the sea of faces was driven by the colorful dress codes and beaded necklaces, culture of their native African roots.

Say, you never saw more happy faces, when the Fur people hit the sidewalk of Seventh Avenue, and saw Akeem giving out free paper. They'd only been state-side for a few weeks. Culture shock was still in place. They could not believe their eyes — free newspapers with no censorship. Paper was a rare item across Sudan. Any weight or color of paper — if you could get your hands on a few scraps — was a cherished item. Writing paper was used for penmanship in the native alphabet; artists scoffed it up for bringing out their medium. Any clean paper could be folded and compressed into makeshift bandages. In their exodus from the blood thirsty hands of counterinsurgent forces, dry paper was a treasured item while embarking across the desert sands of Djibouti, because as you can imagine in the lands of sunbaked sands were Mother Nature only provided grains of golden sands and thorny plant life, a dry sheet of paper would be very satisfactory and provide dignity when the sphincter muscles moved.

"Good morning! Good morning! Good morning!" Akeem was saying this with a beaming smile. His teeth gleamed white in happiness. He was quite certain some takers were coming his way and got ready to set the hook. He's sold enough religion, to well mark the spark in the African's eyes.

"Good news from the Watch Tower," exclaimed Akeem waiving a clutch of colorful pamphlets. He was anxiously waving them on, calling them towards his flyers stacked on the platoons of stainless-steel pillars.

It was a good thing Ruba had sharpened her skills, inside their refugee camps in Yemen. Kharaz was one of the biggest refugee camps in Yemen, and there was a daily class on learning the English language, taught by an overseas schoolteacher inside a white duck canvas tent. This class on reading and writing was run by a Unicef volunteer, a young lady who'd listened to her calling and signed for a two-year tour, leaving her stable teaching job in the village of Summer Hill, Illinois.

Sitting inside that sweltering tent, Ruba was already connecting dots. She had a world of confidence her dreams would come true. The black refugee on the run, knew she would need some language under her belt. The very first interjection she'd learned was good morning. Ruba was all over Akeem.

She broke from her people, and with open arms exclaimed in the native Fur tongue, "Avilakoa! Good morning!"

"Welcome my friend," cried out Akeem in delight. "Take some," giving all of them a heavy wad of papers. "Take enough. Give them to your friends."

The Fur people were gobbling up the Watch Tower papers. On the front cover was a colorful lithograph of Jesus, walking on water. He was in the act of salvation, rescuing seamen from the capsized fishing boats in the storming seas.

Akeem had become very giddy. He was almost to the point of being unglued. You never saw anybody so happy. The tribe of Fur people had taken away seventy-six flyers. Some people caught on fast, seeing the Fur people digging into the free papers, and thought they might be missing something; they fought their way in and took some for themselves. Akeem could not control himself. He kept on thinking how happy his boss would be in the Watch Tower meeting hall. Akeem had sold religion with over one-hundred free flyers, into a single wave of people.

I watched the Fur people move out. They were shoving those Watch Tower papers in their travel sacks, shopping bags, folds of their clothes; and pretty soon they were gone and disappeared into the crowd.

Akeem was riding high on his new success. So much indeed, he'd pulled away from the stream of rushing wayfarers, and took a breather.

I'd been watching all this from my improvised table, which in effect was a stainless-steel vehicle barrier. There are not as many smart cookies in New York City, as a person might think. Nearly all of them had answered my questions of what direction to take for my business meeting, and they bade me at length on special stops to disembark my train. They had been very helpful.

But every so often around the Big Apple, you see the work of a smart cookie. On top of my stainless pillar, shining bright, was a Liberty head nickel. I'd tried to slip it away discreetly and put it in my pocket. But some wise guy had fixed it tight with super glue. I scrutinized the coin. It was struck with a date. The portrait of Thomas Jefferson was embossed in the silver. I tested the glue's strength with my thumb. The nickel was not moving. It proved impossible to put in my pocket.

Akeem was rummaging in a small sack of oatmeal colored twill. He pulled out a vessel of glass. It twinkled amber in the sunbeam. From his front pocket, he procured a tablespoon. I saw him three times, fill the spoon with golden elixir, and slide it down his throat.

I'd sprung from my post and moved in for scrutiny. I needed to see what Akeem was doing. Passing the religious material, I brisked away a Watch Tower paper, and placed it inside my attache case. The rendering of Jesus walking on water was very well done, a wonderful illustration of anatomy, and I wanted to look it over on my train ride.

"Good morning my friend," I said, patting Akeem on the shoulder.

"Good morning! Good news from the Watch Tower," came back Akeem. He'd seen me take a flyer. I could see new numbers spinning in his head.

"I see you like honey," I told him.

"Yes indeed. Honey is wonderful for the voice box," replied Akeem.

I guess with all the sales pitches Akeem was making, he needed to keep on his vocal cords. Up close and intimate, his carmine hat was very vibrant in the sun; the silver tapestry twinkled in the spring rays of sun. Akeem's countenance was free of wrinkles, and his skin was pulled tight with the color tones of ripe nectarines. There was glitter of righteousness in his black eyes.

Akeem licked the spoon clean, wiped it cleaner with his tunic, and said holding out the silver spoon, "Want to try a jigger?"

"No thanks," I told him. "I just had two sugars in my coffee." The plain truth was, it had been maybe twenty years since I'd last put sugar in my coffee. I just didn't want to hurt his feelings, that's all.

"You should get on honey," bade Akeem. "It's an excellent source of energy for walking fast and brisk in New York City."

"I'll be trying some."

"Just don't buy any kind."

"What should I look for?"

"It's mandatory you only buy wildflower honey."

"You've got to be kidding."

Akeem became very serious with that statement. He took me the wrong way. Akeem thought I was telling, when I was only asking.

"Do you think I'd be kidding about honey?" he reported in a stern voice. "Practicing the sales of religion is a very serious business. I'm trying to steer you right." Some of the instantaneous anger had vanished from his face, and in the faint light of shadows from the skyscrapers, I could see the hurt all over him.

"Take it easy, Man," I told Akeem. "Calm down."

"I'm calm," he told me. "My voice box is soothed in the golden nectar."

"That's good."

"Most definitely. Having a voice with range that carries in a crowd, is always good."

"Where can I find this honey?"

"I've only found a singular place in the New York City, that sells this caliber of honey."

"Where? …Please tell me."

"Billy the Greek sells it down by 24th West and Fifth Avenue. You can't miss him — Billy pushes the honey out of a wooden cart near Madison Square Park. His street cart had wooden wheels, painted in bright yellow."

"Is that the small park down by the Eataly?"

"That's the place."

"Sounds terrific," I told Akeem. "My meeting is in that general direction. I'll be certain to track down Billy the Greek."

"I'm telling you, putting down that amber honey from the fields of wildflowers, is almost like passing through the golden gates of heaven." Akeem's face lit up. He was enormously pleased with his metaphors.

"Does Billy the Greek charge big bread?"

"Price is nothing. The effects are out of this world. It's only seven bucks a bottle."

"That's not too steep."

"Why go second rate?"

"Absolutely."

The morning rush hour was dying down. It was mid-morning. The sun had risen higher. The tiny film of frost on the beds of yellow daffodils had burned off. Two foot-patrol cops were around. A lot of the cabbies had pulled out in traffic and were working the crowds on the east side of Central Park.

I put out my hand and wished Akeem the best. "Thanks for the tip on honey, Man. Good luck on selling religion."

"God bless you Brother," said Akeem in sincere tones. "And be careful — I've seen many pickpockets in the crowd."

I averted and wheeled into the crowd. The street people were a good twenty deep across the walk. I shoved my Buxton wallet deep into my front pocket. The last thing I needed was getting worked over by pickpockets.

Charles Taze Russell, founder of the Watch Tower crowd, might have been slightly disappointed. The free papers from the Jehovah's Witnesses, had panned out very poor. None of the Fur people converted. A few of the jet-black Africans carrying the deepest emotional scars, had thought about flipping over. They had begun to wonder, questioning themselves, how any God could allow the ruthless slaughter and abuse of their defenseless innocents.

But then they recalled free will, and after they thought about that for a while, it would be hard to paint Muhammad into any kind of corner. The Fur people knew they would need to look deep inside themselves. Evil men had committed mortal sins against the tribesman. Muhammad had nothing to do with anything. They all decided to remain as Sunni Muslims. They were too scared to consider options. Things had been rough; but at least the Islamic prophet Muhammad had led them from the forlorn desert and brought them into the melting pot of New York City. None of them would dare risk that kind of freedom and start playing games with religion. Also, all twelve of the Fur people had been vaccinated against evil as small children, with the Five Pillars. The most poignant pillar for Ruba, was charity. When she got off the bus on the south-side of Washington Heights, she gave a dirty bum a chocolate bar, when she had only five bucks in her blue beaded purse. She knew there might be serious consequences if Muhammad caught her breaking rules, and all thoughts of flipping to the Watch Tower quickly relinquished.

As for myself, there would be no conversions. I was a disciple of the Roman Catholic Church. I 'd been blessed on the altar with Holy Water. My hands as a young boy, clutched a white burning candle during the procession of First Communion. My faith was riveted in allegiance to the Father, Son, and Holy Ghost. There would be no flipping.

But let me tell you Mister, I'm still plenty thankful I got that Watch Tower newspaper from Akeem. That very afternoon on the Number 6 Train, I'd taken my yellow handled Queen Trapper's jackknife, and skived off the colorful lithography of Jesus. The rest of the newspaper was very respectfully placed inside a paper recycle tub on the corner of Park Avenue and East 84th Street. To this very day, many years later, the colorful image of Jesus remains thumb-tacked over my writing station. Many artist's renderings of Jesus fill my collection, but even with the collection of mass cards handed out at the dead's funerals, my souvenir from Akeem remains a true favorite.

Weaving through the crowd, I gave a backwards glance to the sea of faces. Akeem was back in position on the stairs of Penn Station. He was a tall fellow, and his carmine silk hat over the dark copper skin, marked his figure well.

Akeem cupped his long slender fingers, and caught in the head rush of enthusiasm, he played a snappy tom-tom beat on the drum-like head of the stainless pillar. He closed his eyes tight against the external world and beat a jazzy rhythm into the stainless. Then he cleared his throat under the effects of wild honey from Billy the Greek and began selling religion.

"Good morning, good morning, good morning," sang his golden new voice with a burst of energy into the bustling crowd. "Good news from the Watch Tower," preached Akeem.

You need to give Akeem a lot of credit. He sure had plenty of perseverance. Most people would never take a shot in those odds for Jesus. The world had changed. The stainless-steel pillars in themselves, were a pitiful reminder of the hate infused across the planet, sunk hither and tither all around Times Square after the terrorist attack. There was danger of somebody snapping; there was a high ratio of quacks in the vicinity. You saw that smart cookie glue down a Liberty head nickel for kicks. I'd heard a few guys in the mix coming up the stairs, say they thought Akeem must be nuts. Taking one last look at Akeem selling religion, some married guy caught my eye trying to put the moves on a sultry number under half his age. But she shot him down so fast it wasn't even funny, when telling him she was not interested in fooling around with a guy like that with a bald head, and with the dark circles under his eyes. That foxy sex-kitten didn't pull any punches with that loser looking for adultery, and the guy seemed to age a few more notches from hearing the bad news.

If given sufficient time, the police can crack most cases. Inside information of the pickpockets had surfaced. They'd been alerted by radio from headquarters. But trying to spot those kind of angle men in a vast crowd, is a tough nut to crack. Those Manhattan pickpockets move like lightning. Even the most astute, had never felt a thing.

Feeling a bit nervous, one of the cops, a rookie named Billy Breedlove, had become wiredrawn under his blue uniform. He'd been schooled well at the police academy. He realized the pickpocket, if confronted, might reach for his gun. Thinking ahead, Pvt. Billy Breedlove slipped the leather thong over his automatic good and tight, seating the barrel in the black holster. His draw hand rode over the pistol's handgrip, and he looked deep into the crowd for those shifty hands.

Akeem was sure a marvel. He reminded you of one of those war guys, a medic who took a veil of lead and won the Medal of Honor, just because he wanted to save his buddies in a blazing gunfight. He could take the heat. He'd never wither.

In this kind of world, the way Akeem was hell bent on selling religion, the Lord would have a hard time painting him into the corner of shaky ground, and Charles Taze Russell would be enormously pleased with Akeem's drive for keeping his angles on religion coming fast off the printing press.

Pencil Box

It was him alright. I'd seen him many times before. He always started out by drawing the right eye. The guy set up with all the other artists, just inside Central Park where East 61st Street runs into the dead end of Fifth Avenue.

You will know the exact place, by the following instructions: The sidewalk runs north and south, just off Fifth Avenue under the shade trees. The walk is lined by park benches, long continuous rows of green benches and sound seating with stout iron legs. All the benches wear name plates. They are embellished in memory of those who once walked the earth.

The artist was the middle-aged man who had the voice box with the heavy foreign accent. He needed spectacles when drawing and wore loafers that looked like the brown leathers had not seen shoe polish in years. He always appeared presentable in an older button shirt of cotton with a collar, and the artist set up his easel necked to the green painted slats. He sat on a wooden stool just behind the assemblage. Throughout Central Park, there are virtually thousands of name plates on benches, each presented to the pangs of love inside the hearts of survivors. You could spend weeks taking dictation. But in this exact spot, on the eastern border of the sidewalk, under the dappled shade casted from the towering American Elms, are two name plates in specific. The first reads:

In celebration of our happy
Times in the park
Larry, Carol, Pete, and Lydia

And the second was simply inscribed: FOR ALL THE DREAMERS. Looking over the name plates, East 61st can be detected through the gauze of plant material. Casting a glance over your right shoulder, high over the tree canopy on the south-west side, you will see the huge red neon sign of the Essex house, looming against the skyline. Now you have found the exact location, where the artist with the peculiar format began his portraits with pencil marks of the singular right eye. That alone blew my mind.

It was a tail-end of August, a wonderful forenoon with a dead calm over the park, with angled sun beams coming down past the towering stand of tulip trees, when I first spotted the guy. He was working on some subject matter.

A little girl sat very still on the green bench. The artist, hunched forward and focused on the composition, pressed his attention to the girl, then darted and moved the pencil point with skill. The guy knew his stuff. He worked the eye with great detail. He was right on the money.

The little girl sat with both knees together, her hands clasped over the dress folds across her leg and looked with the most inno-cent casts toward the artist. She looked at him through the top of her eyes, her chin down in the parade rest position.

I sneaked in behind the artist. My sneakers offered no detection, creeping along the concrete slab. I scarcely drew breath, silently watching and making observation. I watched him draw the eye. His artist box was crammed with pencils of all hardness scales, stubs of charcoal, grey blending cones, and a jackknife with yellow handles and its blade sprung open. Fastened to the box's lid, was a Metro Card held fast with a huge paper clip. The guy must have ridden the subway to work.

I watched him very closely. He certainly wasn't making quick sketches of the kid's eye — the artist connected all parts which comprise the organ of vision, until there on the white paper, was a perfectly rendered eye in high detail jumping out at you. At this point in time, the eye had the power to capture all observers.

I inched closer. In my hand was a black zippered pouch. It was filled with drawing pencils, pastel sticks, charcoal stubs, and a nice soft gummed eraser. A wardrobe of drawing implements. I was a student at the world-famous training grounds for artists — the Art Students League of New York City. Some of the masters who revolved through its doors are James Bama, Winslow Homer, and Norman Rockwell. Actually, the list comprised hundreds of famous names.

We had been groomed extensively. All the landmarks were made known. For if the artist is not aware of these forms, the anchor points all across the human figure, it's impossible to connect and join the forms, and thus present their version of reality inside a frame.

But this guy used no landmarks. I scrutinized the drawing. There were no lightly drawn circles, as the planets revolve a universe, as to indicate the skull's projected circumference. No shapes were sketched. He hadn't even found the neck's pith, thus making direction the subject was looking. I saw no evidence of nothing. If he used landmarks — and nobody would ever know for certain — they were inside his head someplace.

There was only the eye; but still, he worked the orb to even higher perfection. The man arrested my attention. I watched retracted in clandestine, silently watching and observing, seeing if I could break his code.

This guy might not have known all the landmarks. But he was far from a quack. He was a professional artist in the very least, even though he left his mark out of the box.

The little girl sat in admiration. She had been drawn into the situation. Her mother had agreed to pay cash money. The artist had warned everybody, expect to sit a full hour. That way everybody would get a fair shake.

The little girl was still in admiration. She was hoping everything would come out good and studied her mother for some kind of answer. The mother paced in tight circuits on the walk, looking and reading, rubbing the cup of her chin with fingers. The artist, his head cocked, was placing a faint cast shadow on the upper eyelid, bringing forth the illusion of her eyelash. It was very convincing.

The little girl had some of the most beautiful blue eyes in our part of the world. And that was really saying something Mister, because just imagine all the people inside New York City with blue eyes. But the artist was working in monochromatic of lead. There were no colors. Her mother and a few close relatives would be the only in a crowd to bring out the blue eyes, while looking on the pencil drawing of black and white value.

The artist reached for a harder pencil in 3H. He twirled the pencil inside a red pencil sharpener. He spent some breath blowing off the sharpened tip. Then after taking a long hard look at the girl, the artist began making light whisk marks. He was working in the eyebrow above her right eye. All eyebrows follow the upper mass of the orbit. Below the flesh, is the bony supraorbital eminence. Rub your own skull and feel it for yourself. Here is where the artist had set his sights.

Just then, the little girl blew my cover. She put some of that innocent look on me. The artist picked up right away; he spun, and took off his glasses, and said to me, "Want to be next?"

"Oh, not now," I told him. "I'm a student at the Art Students League."

"Over on West Fifty-seventh Street?"

"That's the place."

"Why not be next anyway?"

"Not now," I said again. "I'm on my way over to the Metropolitan."

"I visit there myself for inspiration," confessed the artist.

"You are good," I told him. "But I never saw anybody start with a singular eye. Where did you learn?"

"Learning is a slow process. It takes one lifetime to get most of the way."

"But the eye... where did you get the idea?"

"It must have started in the old country. Maybe I taught myself. I can't remember when I started the eye business."

I never pushed him on what old country. I figured he must be from Morocco with Spanish blood lines. But that was a wild stab into thin air. He could have been from Madrid, just as easy.

I could feel my presence was bringing out friction on the artist. His bubble of concentration had been broken. He wasn't of the disposition to have people breathing down his neck while trying to focus. I gave him breathing room and blew the scene.

I checked time. The artist had been in production over twenty minutes. He still had plenty of time. I'd stop back when the full hour had been stricken. That way I could see the finished product and find out by the girl's expression what she thought of her rendered image.

I walked south in the park. The dogs had gone home to their apartments. People had taken their places. It was nearly noon. The thong was beginning to swell. I sauntered up past The Pond, weaving between the gardens on twisting walkways, under trees in and out of the sun, up the stairs and through the wall's opening, around the corner and sat on the bench. Next to me was Kim-Ly on the bench.

She painted people's names with vibrant watercolors, using tiny wedges of sponge as a brush. Kim-Ly had been a United States citizen for a few years. She was born and raised in Vietnam, up near the Roung Roung Valley on rice farm.

Kim-Ly made beautiful names in color. She used the shapes of sailboats, dragons, butterflies, peacocks, and many other symbols of our world, depending on the letter shapes that made your name. In the Vietnamese language, the name Kim-Ly transforms to — Golden Lion.

In homage to her people, she always signed her autograph on the art, and with a few quick swirls dabbed in Gouache gold, painted a scene of a crouched lion. It was a nice touch, and customers loved her work and the nature of the woman very much.

Kim-Ly's husband painted names too. He set up shop around the corner of West 59th Street, just about across from Harry's New York Bar on the sidewalk. That way the husband and wife had people coming and going.

Because I lived up on East 89th Street on the edge of Spanish

Harlem and needed to cut across Central Park in order to hit Columbus Circle and angle down to the Art Students League, I always made time in my travels to visit Kim-Ly. Even though she could barely speak broken English, we found ways to getting across by simple words and hand signals and became exceedingly warm street friends.

We sat on the bench. Everything would need to be cut short. Time had advanced — I had ten minutes, until the little girl was completed. We needed to make it short and sweet.

Along the road of Grand Army Plaza, you can always find horse-drawn carriages. They were there. A horse with a giant show plume of raspberry-colored feathers was eating oats from a pail. The chestnut was bridled and reined to a white carriage. The carriage driver groomed him over with a stiff brush. As it was the end of summer, and the bristles of the brush collected a good knot of hair, for it was near the time for the mammals to put on winter coats. The horseman tugged away the pail of oats, and he wrangled a full pail of water under the horse's snout. Its big lips curled back, and the horse made slurping noises while drinking water.

We had light conversation. I'm not sure if it was the timidness of Orientals, her nature, or if she liked me, but Kim-Ly was always smiling in our broken dialogue. The pattern of her nature exhibited these traits.

Across from our green bench was the monument of William Tecumseh Sherman. The statue loomed high above the wayfarers. Up and down the Grand Army Plaza and in close formal beds to the statue, were soldier rows of annual flowers holding spectacular colors. The army general would have been exceedingly proud of the military neatness of the grounds, and the fact all cigarette butts were policed in the area each morning by a colored fellow driving a motorized vacuum cart. That colored fellow darted in and around the plaza in the first cracks of dawn, dressed sharp in a green uniform, and took great pride in presenting an immaculate landscape.

I looked keenly towards the general. The gilded bronze of the statue threw off a high radiance in the August sun. Spearheading the scene, an allegorical figure of peace reached to the heavens. She was the forerunner of revealed truth, and her mantel of wings rose in heroic scale.

Prancing under a bit brace, a golden horse with its lips rolled back gasped for air. Perched high on its back riding a calvary saddle, was the army general. His general composure was ramrod straight on the gilded skin, and his cape fluttered frozen in time in the sculptor's wind.

I advanced my attention to General Sherman. A quote the commander once said came to mind. His voice ran clear as bells over the common, and the recollection of his words came across to the green bench: "War is cruelty. There is no use trying to reform it. The crueler it is, the sooner it will be over."

Kim-Ly knew all about war. And if you were tight enough in her circle and waited for the right mood, she might divulge some cruelties of war. She had leaked some to me.

But now her face was washed in cheerfulness. A customer had arrived with American money. The request was to paint the name Sophia. Dipping in some aqua marine paint, Kim-Ly started the S with a sea dragon sitting on white caps of the blue ocean. It was very effective. She painted the sign on her lap. I studied her face. No trace of war existed.

But I knew below the surface was hidden horror, invisible and emotional scars from the Vietnam War. She'd revealed horrific ordeals with confidential measure drawn on her mouth. The early morning an NVA company sauntered in and executed two water buffalo with well-placed rounds behind the ears, the village's Pot-Bellied pigs squealing in a bamboo corral and snorting from the gunfire, was blood-revenge payments for collaborating with the American sky soldiers. Her village had paid for a ratfink. Some of her stories had gone deeper, and drew more blood farther up the food chain, from the walking of gunfire that cut her village people to ribbons. Then they looted all their white rice and melted back into the green jungle.

Time was out. I gave Kim-Ly a peace sign and moved down the walk.

"See you tomorrow," she said with a sweet ring. Looking back, I think some of the reason she was always happy, was most likely because she had grasped true freedom.

I looked over the wall of Central Park at East 60th Street, and I could see the artist had risen to his feet. The mother and girl were huddled around the work. I sprinted towards the man who began things with a singular eye.

The artist had sold them on a cheap paper frame. They were worth the money, just for the sake of protecting the work. I looked inside the frame. Stunned is a good word to describe my comprehension. The drawing was absolutely beautiful. The best work I'd ever seen come out of Central Park. And I'd seen plenty.

The drawing was accurate, and lifelike. The thing that got me the most, was how he rendered the girl's flesh. His work reminded me of Lucas Cranach (1515-1586), with the subtle tones over the knowledge of anatomy. The artist had merely suggested some of the hair lines and her attire, but the face was highly detailed reality. You wanted to reach out and kiss the forehead. The mother did.

The artist had gone far enough to surpass his preliminary goals and brought out highlights and planes with black and white chalk. This effect alone had put the art over the top, and a vast crowd had circled around the scene in admiration. The artist got two more takers from that gathering.

"Hey man, I've got to tell you — that drawing is fantastic!"

"Thank you," said the artist. He looked at me with a grin over the top of his drawing glasses.

"I'm headed up to the Metropolitan," I told him.

"The forecast is rain for two days this week," informed the artist.

"I might go to the museum. The second floor is special to me."

I saw the opening for an angled question — "Back in the old country, did you have museums too?"

"Oh yes," he said with a beaming smile. "We had a real nice museum down in Barcelona. I was frequent there in the student years."

So that was it. I got lucky. It was not about being smart. I'd put together his skin tones, his speech rings through street smarts, and got lucky. He was a Spaniard after all.

I moved through the park and checked my watch. There was still forty-five minutes to kill. I was supposed to meet Amelie out front.

Near the south end of the Metropolitan Museum, I pulled over. There was a nice bench in the full sun. I was feeling sleepy. The sidewalk was plastered with vendors. One of the guys was selling throw rugs. Against his tent shelter, leaning on the back wall, was stout cardboard. It was of good measure.

"Hey Mack, mind if I borrow that piece of cardboard?" I asked.

"Take it for good."

"Oh, heavens no… not that. I just want to try taking a nap on cardboard."

"Go right ahead. Be my guest."

The cardboard was just about six feet long and wide enough for two. I rolled it up on the bench and patted it down. It fit the curved slats like a glove. I bunched up my Levi jacket, which had been tied around my waist, and made a nice pillow. My head faced north, towards the Harlem Mere. A pipe of wind was coming down 5th Avenue from that direction.

The cool air was very satisfactory for breathing. The sun had warmed the cardboard, which served as insulation, and the blanket of heat felt terrific. The small things of a hobo's life dawned on me. This was life. I stretched out, my head nestled on the jacket, and slept sound. It turned out to be a wonderful kind of experience. It never cost a penny.

A sharp tug came from my trousers. It was Amelie.

"Let's go sleepy head."

I rose out of a dream. Folding the cardboard, I leaned it against the vendor's tent stand and said, "Thanks Mack."

It was always good to see your girl. We held hands while walking. I leaned over and kissed Amelie on the lips. Then we ascended the long staircase and went inside the Metropolitan Museum.

The fee for art students was cut-rate, reduced to half price. But the standing policy of the Metropolitan is that the students may pay what they wish to donate. Sometimes I paid the discounted rate, which was about ten bucks. But since we visited so often, many times making the trip to study a singular painting, a lot of times we coughed up two bucks and called it close enough. Nevertheless, during a training grounds semester, it seemed I'd stopped in many times over, and the museum got a fair portion of our savings.

Amelie sat right next to me in Anatomy Drawing at the Art Students League. We became sweet on each other while sitting on old wooden chairs in the classroom. We had started out as pure friends, which was always the best way for finding love. But now things were escalating. We'd spent the last Sunday in Central Park, all afternoon and into the falling dusk, snuggling on a blanket and kissing.

Amelie was in the Art Students League for a continual four years of groom out in oil painting, and I would be long gone by then. Her lifelong dream was moving back to Luxeuil-les-Bains and supporting herself as a portrait painter of high caliber. We both knew that. As lovers we savored our love while we could, and let the sparks fly in a sphere of faithfulness. We both knew what we had and could feel the goose bumps.

Amelie and I walked the wide stairs inside. We both knew the exact route to our favorite oil painter, just as we knew the back of our hands. He lived on the second floor.

We walked up the stairs in the soft shadows in the bright sunlight past the pane windows, around the corner and past certain halls, under archways in the wall and security agents in button-down dress, weaving in and out of the mazed rooms, until we went around the last corner of the high domed room; and there in a back room, was our favorite oil painting in the whole wide Metropolitan — The Weeders by Jules Breton.

Exact numbers escape my thinking. Visits to those brush strokes of oils stricken on canvas had been perpetual. A long love affair. The painting brought an aura of mystery to the gallery, and its effects mesmerized a great field of viewers. There was this relationship of inspiration, and I never tired from climbing the stairs. The emotional resonance of Jules Breton's painting skills arrested my soul with the beautiful chords of pictorial language, and the visits brushed on religious experience.

This introduction to inspiration, went beyond and far exceeded the effects of opium. The fields of colored poppies growing and swaying in the native land of Ancient Greeks, could never hold any light to Breton's fields.

Through Amelie's eyes, this was more than wonderful art. It was blood lines to her native land — Jules Breton had painted The Weeders in a farm field near the village of Courrieres. This inspiration brought on a vast measuring stick inside Amelie, knowing her fellow countryman had left powerful and vivid marks in the art world. She never dreamed her brush strokes would have the historic flair of Breton's sable hairs, but it was something to shoot for, and she was certainly going to try.

It was in her last year of high school, in the village of Luxeuil-les-Bains, when she set her sights on the motivation which had been sparked by Jules Breton. She borrowed her father's Peugeot, a metallic blue 304 SLS, and drove to northern France. That evening, she arrived in the hunting grounds of Jules Breton — the farm district outside the village of Courrieres.

Most naturally, the farm peasants that served as figures for the original work, were all dead. Time had wheeled. But the farms were still there, and so were the farm workers. She scoured the French landscape for subject matter. This could be a daunting task, especially when looking for a scene that had grown in her mind and was a moving target in the landscape. But cresting a bluff of harrowed land on a crofter's farm, the Peugeot's tires rolling out a plume of powered dust, her dream was revealed with living figures. Seven farm workers were hoeing in the setting sun. They were fanned in the field's foreground, and an orange sun threw out a halo of radiance on the horizon. In her mind, she had just struck gold. Three of the women caught in the falling sun, had a violet glow under the field bonnets, and the magic of blue hour had enveloped the landscape.

Throwing the Peugeot in gear, she eagerly cut the distance. Bringing up her Leica 35mm camera, rolling the focus ring, cutting in the F-stops, she bracketed and fired away. Frozen in time was her subject matter, instigated by brush work from the dead artist.

Now all she needed was to sharpen skills. She tacked the photo to the leg of her wooden easel. It would be there when she flew back across the ocean, sharpened and calibrated in the measure of producing art in oils. She had no doubts the Art Students League would draws out these skills.

I saw The Weeders in other light. The scene brought me home to existence. There was strong pictorial communication. A cohesion of ideals. My lifetime had been an accompaniment of many farms. The scene of peasants in the fading twilight, dedicated in the labors of pulling weeds and thistles for a people's survival, paid a homage to all farmers.

Breton had once said, "Their faces are haloed by a pink transparency of their violet hoods, as if to venerate a fecundating star."

I could see that. But there were other themes and plots in the composition. Stories told in Breton's brush strokes. There was harmonized juxtaposition of the setting of an orange sun and the risen crescent moon, a passage for the viewer to harbor between day and night. It afforded a promise of days to come.

The placement of the figures, perfectly rendered with believable action, was not derived by chance. It was the plot of Breton's composition, part of the secret map which captures a masterpiece. In a clockwise sweep, the crouched figures rising in scale, the sole figure standing below the silver moon, sweeping the eye over the scene and back around the haloed sky, so the viewer's eye is captivated and finds it impossible to escape the scene. That Jules Breton had everybody nailed down, before he ever grabbed a brush.

Amelie and I walked back down the stairs. She looked far away. I wondered if she was back in the fields of northern France. I clasped her wrist as we went down the treads of stone.

"I'm meeting Veronica and Sally at Eugene's Place for drinks. They make nice stiff margaritas. Want to meet up with us?" hinted Amelie.

"No… I have another class this evening." I was in a pen and ink class two evenings a week. "I'll see you around the school tomorrow?"

"I'll be there." We hugged off, and she went out the door.

I darted down a looming passageway and headed to the sculpture wing. Roman and Greek statues adorned the wide chasm. I moved in earnest to the back museum. I walked past the display of stone figures, some missing heads or arms or both. In the far remoteness of the vaulted expanse, a figure was in action. The quack was back inside.

Almost nobody liked the guy. He was pompous. He was full of himself. The guy was close to being the biggest show off in New York City.

Most artists would find a singular pencil box sufficient. But not this guy — he surrounded himself with a wealth of art supplies, including two suitcases of pencils and drafting implements. The lids were open in the anti-aircraft position, and there were so many hundreds of pencils, all very tidy in furrowed rows of red felt. My first impression was that he was some kind of traveling art supply vendor, trying to make a fast buck.

The artist not only submitted an easel; he lugged in two aluminum easels and bridged with a huge piece of bristol board. All his implements were in impeccable order, and he even had a special tub for a handful of pencil sharpeners.

Behind the artist's easel, was a marble sarcophagus. Carved out of stone by Roman hands in about A.D. 220-230, the beautiful marble carving depicted Dionysus on a panther, surrounded by attendants of the four Seasons.

The scene is vested in Bacchic figures in tight order. The mood of secret rites in adoration of the gods, is characterized by body language that flirts with border-line orgy. The vast chunk of quarried marble was nearly seven feet in length and threw down a crushing weight across the floor. It was one hell of a block of stone, even by Roman standards.

It must be said — and it's given begrudgingly — that the artist had skill. He was a good draftsman. The rendering and shadow casts were accurate, and graduation scale of the graphite tones were in order. But the spontaneousness of fluid enchantment was lacking, his figures were rigid and lacked the spark of life. The whole sentiment was caught in the trapping of photographic quality. Everything looked a little too perfect. Suspension surfaced.

I went in for a closer look. The throng of museum dwellers had enveloped the drawing, and many were bringing praise. I inched my way through the crowd. Easing my way through the figures, I stuck my head past a few shoulders and took a good hard look.

"Hey! Not too close," boomed the showman. "That's a masterpiece."

I enveloped back into the crowd. But I saw everything. He'd left behind crucial evidence. The trail of deception was wide and clear. The proof was there alright, and he'd never be able to talk his way out.

All along the drawing's border, were the hash marks. I'd seen them wide and clear when I gave everything the evil eye. Very faint pencil lines. He'd tried to erase them, but in the late night, he had failed to notice everything. In the secret chamber of his apartment, he connected the hash marks on two-inch intervals, with other marks across the page. He made a grid section on his drawing, almost invisible, with a very hard 3H pencil. That way most of the trail would be vague and discreet.

The little devil. He'd entered the Metropolitan Museum with a film camera, most likely a 35mm on a tripod. He'd captured the marble sarcophagus, again most likely in sectionized shots, while he spliced the developed prints back together in the seclusion of his apartment's silence. He ran the panoramic capture through a roller copy machine. The photo's copy was then also scribed with grid lines in half-inch squares of black pen ink. He then gridded his drawing paper in faint lines of two-inch squares, as to gain almost lifelike proportion. What he had done for himself, was to produce the crutch of an adult sized coloring book.

The crowd lurched from the swell of figures. A jostle had occurred in their attention span; new faces moved forward. A redhead brushed me. She was tall and lanky. Her long red hair fell over a cowboy shirt. Tight boot-cut jeans hugged her rail legs. Her cowboy ropers were Alpaca white, embroidered with sage green thread. Her cowboy shirt was Big Sky blue. The redhead's girlfriend was slight in the pear shape, vaguely plump, but with such smooth fair skin and a beaming smile that revealed a lighter side, a wide range of strangers found themselves quite fond of her. In the prominence of all these circumstances, trends, and mixed feelings among the crowd, were the white pearlized button snaps on the redhead's cowboy shirt.

We had not to this point, made visual contact. I only listened.

"I can't believe my eyes," said the redhead.

"It's him alright," said her girlfriend.

"What a creep."

"I was hoping we'd never see him again."

"Excuse me young ladies," I interjected, "do you know that guy?"

"Know him?" said the plump one with a wide grin.

"We know him alright," said the redhead. "He's one of the biggest creeps I ever met." She pushed back her untucked cowboy shirt and jammed her thumbs behind a western belt buckle. It was a huge oval buckle of sterling silver, and a stylized V was engraved in the face. The redhead threw back her shoulders like she was ready for confrontation.

"How do you know him?" I asked.

The girlfriend with beautiful skin said, "He was in our drawing class at the National Academy of Design," with astonishment still in her eyes.

"What a loser," the redhead told me out loud. "He's got to be one of the world's biggest creeps."

"You would never believe what he told us," the girlfriend mentioned.

"What a trip," said red.

"What was it?"

"He told us inside the National Academy of Design, that he was the singles scull champion three years consecutive at Yale," said the girlfriend. She threw up both hands.

"Him?" I scoffed. "I doubt that very much. Look at his guns. His arms are so weak, I doubt he could lift a bale of hay." All of us took another take of his physique. "He'd be lucky to pull off a canoe ride, on a dead-still lake," I told them.

Red chimed back, "That's not all he told us."

"You would never believe what else he said," expressed her friend.

"Tell me."

"It's not nice to gossip."

"We better not say… it might get back to him."

"Who cares?" I added. "Tell me anyway." Looking at a guy like that, I could never guess he had so many angles. They would need to make a revelation.

"It's too bad there's no place to sit down. It's really far out," said the redhead.

"I'll take it standing. I don't care if it's laughing or crying material. If you tell me, I'll show you more shady things about that guy."

The redhead told the story. Come to find out, the phony artist expected everybody to believe, he was the spelling-bee champion at Yale University, including the master's degree people of the Ivy League school. That he'd blown everybody on the weeds in that contest and captured First Place.

The pencil man had caught the attention of two tourists. They moved closer, and one of the elderly ladies presented him a compliment — "Talk about talent."

"It takes years to develop this kind of talent," he crowed in flat tones. His eyes never acknowledged their sweet ovation. He avoided looking at them wholly. His focus remained on the drawing. For hours on end, he'd never left an area bigger than a farm egg, his pencil point buying time for public attention. The elderly ladies bristled back; even the tourists were beginning to see through him.

"Does that guy still attend the National Academy?"

"Oh no," said the redhead. "Have you ever heard of Billy Preston?"

"Never."

"He was a revolving instructor at the National Academy. Mister Preston was a fantastic illustrator, and he taught a poster class in gouache."

"It's a nice medium," I confessed. "That look still has its place in the world. No computer can touch the human inspiration, laid down by human hands in the spectrum of gouache. It's got its own special look."

"Anyway," said the girlfriend, "Mister Wonderful asked Billy Preston to critique his skill in gouache. Mister Preston had said, 'Your colors are all washed out, and your composition skills are poor.' He was devastated and huffed out of the class. I can still hear him slamming his metal locker in the hallway. Nobody's seen him since."

"Speaking of that," said the redhead, "we've got to split."

"Me too." My next class was in two hours, but I was getting hungry. "Before you go, check the hash marks on his drawing. He's using the grid system at night and giving everybody a snow job by day."

The girls gave a quick swing of the pencil drawing. The redhead went in for a quick read, swung around and threw her eyes to the heavens, and gave me the thumb down. They filed away between the crowd and down the hall.

I'd turned to leave, clutching my pencil bag, when just then the security guard's voice boomed.

"Hey! What's the matter with you! There's no food allowed in the museum."

But it was too late. The creep had spilled a huge tub of buttered popcorn across the floor. The yellow kernels had spewed a great distance, a wide fan that spilled across the open pores of floor tiles.

Three Russians had wandered through the sea of popcorn. They had been so amazed at the presentation of genuine art, enlightened by the Roman's sculpture, they had never noticed the side show man pushing pencils. Nearly spellbound in immersed concentration, throwing gestures around with sweeping arms, they had wandered through the popcorn, and traipsing a trail of buttered footprints.

The security guard hit his side band of his radio, and said, "Send a couple of janitors to south wing of Floor One. We got trouble. Some goof-goof spilled buttered popcorn all over the place." He thought for a second, then added, "While you're at it, get ahold of the park rangers, and call the city police. This guy needs an escort job."

The three Russians were shuffling in a tight circle around a stone nude. Their footprints resembled a cattle yard. They'd left an awful mess behind.

"Listen my friends," said the security guard to the Russians, "it's not your fault, but you've got butter all over your shoes. Why not take a seat, and it will be a pleasure for us to clean your shoes."

Three janitors arrived pushing hot water tubs fixed with wringers and mops. The security guard snapped his fingers and reported, "Let's give these guys a hand with cleaning their shoes. The soles are plastered with butter from goof-goof over there."

"We can do," said the older Russian. "We can do no problems."

"Are you sure?"

"Yes, we've been through much more. This is nothing," said the younger Russian.

They'd been through a lot more. If that wasn't saying something. The abuse of dictatorship lingered, even in the years after the Iron Curtain was lifted.

The older Russian remembered. He remembered what it was like inside the Communist Bloc. He had vivid recollection from his father's story, when Lavrenti Beria tried using his role as head of secret police to establish his supreme rule, and how the communist government secretly tried him in a kangaroo court and gave him an execution number. He remembered as a young boy, the last years of the Machine Tractor Stations, when the communists held a monopolized grasp on all farm machines and told farmers when and on what grounds they could fire motors.

So then, this cleaning shoes was nothing. Absolutely nothing.

The three Russians were lined out on a stone seating slab. A young Russian put his shopping bag on the slab. The last thing he wanted was butter stains on his new dress shirt. Twirling around in the discotheque nightclub with butter on your new shirt, would be a tragic experience in front of beautiful women. He wanted no part of not being able to impress women.

"Day mne zubochistku," said the older Russian.

One of the younger Russians took a tiny cardboard box from his shirt pocket. He asked, "Skol'ko?"

"Day mne tri," said the older Russian.

The younger Russian passed the three toothpicks around. The old Russian put a toothpick between his canines.

"Snimay svyol obuv'," said the elder. He clapped his hands and spun his trigger fingers in circles — take off your shoes.

Two of the janitors were slopping out the mops of hot water. They had erected orange cones. Foot traffic was halted in the spill area. The janitors worked feverishly, as they were trying to arrest the butter's seepage. Butter stains on mortar joints, would not sit well with the board of directors. One of the two bent down and scrubbed the grey mortar with a stiff brush. He really gave it a world of elbow grease.

The third janitor walked to the three Russians. He produced a clean white cloth from his back pocket of blue trousers and swashed the wet rag with a spout of Mister Clean. He splashed ample amounts into the rag and handed it to the older Russian.

Holding the rag, the Russian looked at the picture of the bald guy on the cleaner bottle, and said, "Good stuff."

And then the Russians began to clean their shoes. They wiped the soles many times over.

All the shoes were passed to the older Russian, and he dug out the cracks with toothpicks. The security guard was enormously pleased. Those Russians knew how to work and were sure thorough in the task.

"What's da matter with dis guy?" asked the Russian looking over the artist's way.

"Who knows," said security.

"Dis guy brings enough food for an Army. What a giant tub of popcorn for a single man."

The park ranger and two precinct police were rounding up the guy. The ranger did most of the talking. The city police were there for physical presence.

"You smuggled food into the Metropolitan Museum? You were selfish enough to take chance with the world's greatest talents ever known?" remarked the park ranger.

"I need to keep my energy up, and produce art," said pencil man.

"The only thing you produced," said a city cop, "was a one-way ride out of here."

The police escorted pencil man out the main entrance on Fifth Avenue. The artist lugged the two easels and suitcases. A cop obliged by toting a metal box loaded with gear.

The two elderly ladies who had paid him complements on the drawing, were resting their swollen calves on a bench. They needed to rest before hitting the pavement. Both of them had just popped. It was hard swallowing aspirin with no water.

"Look!" said one of them, "it's the guy full of himself." The police were taking him out the front door.

"They're giving him the business," exclaimed her friend.

"It's about time somebody did," said the other blue hair. She gave her feet a brisk rub down, then the old ladies followed the cops to see what would happen.

Soon order returned. The floors had evaporated. The orange cones had been lifted. The mop heads had been wrung out, and hung by their tousled heads between wooden pegs, deep in the catacombs of the janitors' room. The giddy nervousness of the crowd had ceased; the assembly pressed the circuit in merriment of wonder; the security guards stood at their posts in composure, producing nods to the crowd, and keeping an eye for the masquerades of folly.

Several days had passed. I was back in the old haunts. The sun was in press of descend. September had arrived. I pressed the Wein Walkway in Central Park. I gave a casual glance to the wave of pedestrians along Fifth Avenue, scanning the sea of faces for Kim-Ly. But she had packed it in for the day with her husband. They would be boiling rice soon in a pot on the home range.

But the artist who began every portrait with the singular eye, was still at his post. He was a stickler, and you could count on his presence like clockwork. I watched him closely in the musk of falling gloom. Long shadows were advanced in the urban forest. The march of fall had arrested the leaves of those shallow rooted, and the birch across the park had begun their golden spattering.

He heaved the wooden easel across his shoulder, grabbed his satchel bags, and headed up East 61st Street toward the river. You saw the Metro Card in the pencil box. The artist could only afford to ride the tracks, began and ended his days underground down below in the tunnel complex, and rode the Number 6 Train from a platform in Spanish Harlem.

Darkness had fallen. I pulled over and sat. Behind my back on the green slats of the park bench, cut into the metal plate, were the four most satisfying words in the lexicon of the perpetual visionaries — DEDICATED TO THE DREAMERS.

People moving by were only forms. Arc lights in gangs of cool white globes, spewed rays into the blackness. Looking to the south-west through the lattice of limbs, caught high against the cityscape's night, was the red neon sign of the Essex House. The sign itself brought charm and reeled back the years for the city, and it was very romantic to be sitting in retreat with the element of nostalgia. In the City That Never Sleeps, the sanctuary of Central Park, was close as anybody would ever find to a world of penetralia. I rocked back and took in the scenes.

It was September. On certain nights of any September, the moon washed Central Park. It was there. I sat on the bench for dreamers and looked high between the V-crotch of the sycamore; and there caught in the sky just east of the Plaza Hotel, was the crescent moon.

I thought things over on the bench. Striking a match, I lit a straight smoke. I blew the smoke into the night. It was too bad there were no mosquitoes around, because the cigarette smoke is very satisfactory for warding off certain bugs. I streamed a jet of smoke towards the moon. It hung around in the atmosphere like veils of miniature clouds.

Many forms and figures crossed my mind. Countenances formed in the night. Their faces were caught in the moonlight. They were people who crossed my path that day. It had been a remarkable day. The characters and figures were all out of fiction novels. They'd played convincing parts.

Amelie and her friends were still at Eugene's Place. They were like that. All of them loved chitchat, and they would stay inside the bar until they were almost touching a good drunk... then they would leave. A waft of French perfume drifted through the elm groves under the moonlight. I blew out smoke and averted next to me on the empty bench in the dark shadows.

Kim-Ly crossed my mind. I recalled her stories. After brushing with death in the Tet Offensive, she escaped through Hanoi on crooked papers, good counterfeits that spilled from a printing press for those willing to pay the price gouging. She met her husband Tommy-Lee, while working the docks in Staten Island.

If they sold 30 hand painted signs in a day around Central Park, that was a good day. The signs sold for $5 a piece; and that money cut all the way, because there was no extra charge no matter how many letters formed your name, and Kim-Ly gave you extra with the hand painted symbol of her crouched gold lion in the bottom right corner.

They bought their own paper and paints. They lived in hostel-type commune living with five other Vietnamese families. They painted signs seven days a week, and as you might expect, there was never any agenda or days off, because those weekends were the two best days for ringing up sales pitches on the tourists. But there were never any complaints because they were now involved in a new kind of world, where they were allowed freedom of being small-time proprietors for cash money, with no worries of getting a stiff arm from the communist dictators.

The artist who started out with a single eye was really something though. He sure could draw. Do you think he picked it up in school? They don't teach those kinds of things around. Maybe he picked it up around the streets. Maybe he taught himself. He sure was something though. He worked and drew like a machine. He never stopped. It must have been his calling. You could see it in him. Do you think he had mixed blood? The Strait of Gibraltar is not that far across. They had wooden boats. The Spaniards liked sex too. They could have crossed on smooth seas to Kingdom of Morroco and got hot on each other. They tell me on certain streets you can find sultry bars in Casablanca. I heard they have women who rub the inside of your legs under the table in the saloons. In these kind of places with the flow of booze and the low lights and those kinds of seduction, you never knew what could happen. He might have had mixed blood lines from across the strait, because may times figures with hoods came back across in wooden boats after nine months, to show what lovers had made in the Casablanca night. He never told me though; I'd asked him about the single eye more than once; but he always dodged the question. It was really something though how he captured a portrait. He worked all week over the easel for a living. I saw him eat lard sandwiches on white bread on the job. Nobody ever accused him of being a cheat. He started with blank white paper. He drew from life. You could watch the whole process develop wide and clear. It was clear as day. The guy was really good, and he was worth every nickel of the fifty bucks he charged for a portrait. Many people tacked on a tip with a fin. They were more than happy to shell out cash money for the real thing.

It's a good thing Mister Pencil Man never tried charging though. He would have starved.

People would have only paid to get rid of him. Wasn't it awful the way he talked to those elderly ladies though? They were only trying to be nice.

He sure was a storyteller. He told all kinds. Just about all of them were told in falsehood. Most people saw right through him. The redhead in the tight jeans born and raised in Austin, Texas, and her girlfriend with the luxurious skin and kind voice, looked through him too. The pencil man never won any spelling bee at Yale. He never even attended. Red's friend down in the National Academy's front office, snooped around. They pulled his entrance request letter and resume. He attended Rawlings Community College in Percy. His grade average was 3.0. He just about got by with the skin of his teeth. I could tell just by the way he was, he never rolled in words.

It would have been impossible for him to be a scull champion, carving effortlessly in the pulse of current. He looked more like Olive Oil. He would have a hard time with paddle boats in Central Park. That guy was a weakling and lacked the coordination for knifing oaks with any kind of synchronization. He would have just gone in circles and made a lot of splashing.

I still feel sorry for the Russians. What bad luck they had, running into a guy that smuggled a monstrous tub of buttered popcorn into the Metropolitan, and spilled the whole thing while trying to cram handfuls into that thin-lipped mouth. Did you know the older Russian, had just bought the Clark walking shoes two weeks before? He was still breaking them in, and they were his pride and joy.

Those Russians were sure good sports though. They did all their own dirty work. Those toothpicks and white rags got everything. They cleaned their shoes real nice. They'd been through more. The old guy still remembered the Kremlin telling his father when the tractor would be fired up and driven out of the Machine Tractor Station. But still; wasn't it awful though what a mess that creep made with the buttered popcorn? You should have seen the look on the security guard's face. He almost popped a gasket. His face was red as a beet.

It would have been one thing, if pencil man had come clean. He should have come clean to the people, left all the grid lines on the drawing, been man enough to admit he was just working between known points to capture the marble sarcophagus. But his head was too big. He lived for being a showboat. He made the illusion he was drawing from life.

But after the crowd saw him spill buttered popcorn on the floor, and it was revealed that his masquerade was a cheat, and thus, painted himself into all those shady corners, he proved to be nothing more than a copycat.

Could somebody please tell me where men like that come from in the first place?

The Clacker Man

I heard the accordions coming across the courtyard, and then the drums and brass, and they came around the corner of the church. The white stucco of the church hurt your eyes in the field of yellow sun, and the colours of the Portuguese band were bold in the day and against the blue sky. They were dressed in folk lore costumes of the old country, reds, green, habiliments of black, and all of them were full of energy and boasting of pride. The band moved by and took its place near a foot of the stage, and behind stretched a long double row of dancers. They were paired up man and woman, man and woman, and girls with boys. All the women had old world patterns of embroidery on scarfs over their heads, and all the men had black felt hats like you might see around a bull fight.

Seared terra firma of the town arcade comprised a dance floor, and a huge sea of national figures formed a human ring around the music makers. The dancers entered the ring, still holding in a double line. Much of the crowd was applauding wild, but the bellowing notes of accordions and brass horns drowned their enthusiasm into that of a pantomime movie.

An older man in costume was in the prominence of the dancers, and he danced with all kinds of zest and energy — in both of
his hands were clackers to get the music's beat. He pushed on them
with his fingers, twisting around, holding the clackers high over
his head. His face was very stern. He pushed out some sweat, but
not too much you know. His daughter was sweating heavy, and she
was breathing hard after the second number. The older man, her
father, jumped around like a human rattlesnake. All the dancers
cut a big circle, going this way and then that way, and the crowd
could actually feel the music swelling against them. Around the
dancers was a huge crowd, maybe ten people deep, and in the back
row a woman had fainted from heat stroke. The policia were working her, shoving the crowd back, and a man with a pitcher of water
poured it over her head on the bed of hot white cobbles. The woman
was mumbling something, and the policia man was snapping his
fingers in front of her face and telling her something into the ear.
There was no response. She was out cold.

The band played on regardless, and when the music slowed
the dancers went into a crouch, and when the accordions opened
up again the dancers jumped up wild and began more twisting
around. You could tell the older man was really into everything,
sailing high, and he was more serious than ever and pushing the
beat from his clackers. At the next music break his daughter went
for water, and beads of sweat were all over her face. The older man
was sweating too, but refused to drink, and only cinched up the
wide black dress-band around his waist. The bellows of the accordions filled again, the drums were beating like a deep tom-tom,
and all of a sudden, the dancers went back jumping around like
connected to strings on a puppet show. But it was the real thing,
and when the daughter signaled that she might need a break, you

could see the temper building in the older man's face, as if some of his pride had been affected.

It was very hot. The heat was getting to the kids on the floor. You could see it in their steps. They lacked endurance at this age. They were sweating profusely from the baby fat around their cheeks. Some of the boys looked up to the older man for guidance and put on stiff upper lips and threw out their chins, pressing out the last number.

The older man poured on the gas. His fingers drove the clackers, dancing on the toes of his black herdsman boots, and his daughter took one last gulp and joined in. He wanted her full enthusiasm, putting out dance moves with the gusto of an insomniac, because the next Festa of Fatima would be another year away, and she would have all kinds of time for resting.

The simple questions of the tattered man had been knife thrusts to him. They asserted a society that probes pitilessly at secrets until all is apparent. His late companion's chance persistency made him feel that he could not keep his crime concealed in his bosom. It was sure to be brought plain by one of those arrows which cloud the air and are constantly pricking, discovering, proclaiming those things which are willed to be forever hidden. He admitted that he could not defend himself against this agency. It was not within the power of vigilance.

—Stephen Crane
The Red Badge of Courage

The Three Chinamen

The ginkgo leaves fell early that year. It was early fall. There had been no killing frost. But the ginkgo trees, survivors of the prehistoric age, were dropping their leaves. Their yellow fan shaped leaves, with a shape and romantic flair of the orient, were spattered on the walk along West 110th Street. The bright yellow ginkgo leaves showed bold on the grey cement. It had been a night lacking dew, and the bright yellow fans laid flawlessly beautiful and delicate in the concrete jungle. They were not like rain matted leaves, wrinkled and trampled. They displayed such an unusual sight of perfection, nature's works of art, it seemed exceedingly close to a sin against those who trodden the deep veined yellow fans of foliage.

Three Chinamen walked in the night. They came down out of the West Side's shadows and crossed down into Morningside Park. They descended the steep, winding staircase in the night. A big Chinaman was out in front. He puffed on a straight smoke, and the smoke's head glowed an orange burn in the park's blackness. It was very still and silent. None of them spoke. The two

Chinamen walking point were carrying tin pales; the D-shaped handles creaked in the dead silence, and the empty buckets swung to and fro in the night; the third Chinaman carried a six-foot aluminum ladder, as procured for pruning duty in the orchard. The Chinamen reached the last stone rung of the staircase and headed across Morningside Park.

There's a spectacular drop, from the high street plateau of The Cathedral of Saint John the Devine, down the winding shifts of stairs of Morningside Park to the park's table land and green grass.

From the towering faces of apartment blocks along Morningside Drive, looking down across the road and down winding stairs, and observing the Chinamen, those affected by the fear of heights would get those funny feelings in their belly. It was a long way down. It could remind you of Barcelona, Madrid, and the high village towns around Lake Como in northern Italy, where masonry and the landscape dwarfed the sea of human figures, and had panoramic bluffs falling to the steep pitches.

The three Chinamen came down West 110th Street, and marched right across the yellow ginkgo leaves. They had big feet and wore big boots. The big guy out front noticed the yellow ginkgo leaves were something like Chinese lanterns in the night. The spatter of bright yellow leaves marked and manifested the sidewalk as a walking trail. He used the leaves as guide-on in through the black shapes of night. The three Chinamen walked very silent and soft in the darkness, and the ginkgo leaves gave to their foot falls.

It was an hour and one half before daybreak. They had enough of time. The lead Chinaman clipped his smoke on the light post. He crushed the butt and gave it a flick in the shrubs. The three figures, circled the west bank of the Harlem Meer, climbed the huge ledge outcrops in the night, hugged the ledge's face on a thin trail well known to the men, and angled into the North Woods. Here, the blackness multiplied by two folds. They navigated by memory. Below in the Harlem Meer, a lone bullfrog croaked in the night. A spatter of stars filled the night sky. Some of them twinkled. The bullfrog switched to a lower tone of singular croaks. His voice carried across the pond.

The three Chinamen descended into a naturalized grove of crabapple trees. They had struck the landing zone. They flicked on their battery-power headlamps and set up shop. The crabapple trees grew on the bluff, but at the same time in a sunken hollow, and their movements were blocked by the dished landscape and the wealth of deciduous shrubs on their flanks. They were completely out of sight from any throng of wanderers in the night.

But their action did not escape detection. An old lady inside the apartment complex on Central Park West who occupied the 12th floor and faced the park, arrested her attention to the three flickering lights in the North Woods. She could see them flashing between the tree trunks. She had been talking to her cat Samantha on the windowsill. She had been living alone now for over 20 years since her husband's sudden death, and often had conversations with the cat, and other times with and into the dead silence.

She studied the lights. She figured they were nightcrawler pickers. Her guess had been wrong. The three Chinamen were collecting ripe crabapples for the making of crabapple jelly in Mason jars.

The Chinamen never had any doubts picking crabapples in the park was legal. The grounds keepers had seen them picking fruit many times over, and never raised questions. In the spring of the year, Chinamen by the droves picked yellow dandelions in broad daylight for wine making. Central Park had provided a harvest horn for years.

But the Chinamen, nevertheless, wanted to pick in secret. The last thing they wanted, was to give other Chinamen the heads up. None of the other jam and jelly makers, had spotted or noticed the ripe fruit. The crabapples that fall had a marvelous set of fruit, bright red and firm crabapples, and with such abundance they resembled the count of grapes. Red clusters hung everyplace. It was easy picking. They were not going to raise any flags and chance having lights go off in other Chinaman's heads.

They picked steady and fast, with light beams zeroed on the prize. The third Chinaman worked the high ground off the ladder. They worked at filling the pails. They had lugged in a total of five pails; the ladder guy could only handle a singular pail. They were careful not to take too many stems and clutter of twigs or leaves. Twigs were a tragic mistake in the making of jelly. Even after the passing through a sieve, the bitterness of the crushed twigs could be tasted in the product. Blackness still cloaked the park. Off in the distance along Fifth Avenue, you could hear the gunning of trucks from the newspaper men, racing south in downtown towards the newsstands.

Across the Harlem Meer, a Crown Victoria was parked with its lights off, the window cracked, the motor running. A security guard was slumped against the steering wheel, deep in a paid sleep. The cool night air seeped into his lungs. This was not his first rodeo on the clock, and he knew where and for how long he could push the night train envelope.

Down inside Central Park, spread out across the carpet in the Superintendent's Office at the 79th Street Yard, were two other security guards. But they were not sleeping. They were wide awake, with fast heart beats. They had been short on words. The windows of the office were steamed. They could hear the electric clock ticking. Neither of them had never said anything about being in love. The woman buckled her bra strap. The man jumped up and fixed his trousers. He bent down and kissed her lips. They felt very moist on the kiss, and there were drops of sweat beads on the sides of her mouth box. They quickly finished getting dressed and fired the patrol car. They wanted to make certain their movements were documented by security cameras in the patrol circuit.

A yellow wafer of sun rose over the Hudson River. Dawn had broken. The sky was French blue. Puffs of white clouds were banked high above the blue. The Chinamen came across and out of Central Park. Wine red crabapples spilled from their silver pails. The Chinamen lugged the pails of ripe fruit, passed the brinks of Malcom X Boulevard, and the Chinamen's boots again fell over the spatter of yellow fanned ginkgo leaves on the grey sidewalk. Five blue jays were hopping and yelling on the common, working the blades of green grass. The wafer of yellow sun was salient in all these features and colors.

The Three Chinamen cleaned the crabapples inside their apartment flat, while listening to Fantasia type rock music on the box radio. They played it quite loud and snappy for that hour of the morning, and while cutting the stems back with pinking shears, they cooked sunny side eggs in olive oil on the iron skillet. On their plates in preparation for the sunny eggs with black coffee laced with sugar cubes, was a raisin scone on everybody's plate. They simmered down the crabapples in a large kettle pot and listened to the radio station playing their Fantasia. The year was a big crop of crabapples that fall, and there were plenty of unpicked candidates in the park. They would be up at it, until the trees were picked clean, and that left behind was on the way out for the birds.

The crabapples began a slow roll in the kettle. Tiny bubbles were finding their way to the surface. It would be a long process, before the pulp was sieved down, the sugar and Certo pectin added, and poured into Mason jars. The big Chinaman fired a straight smoke and watched the heads of steam come off the kettle.

But they had plenty of time to kill. The three Chinamen had been working the moving racket for Max the Greek out of Corona, Queens. He paid them by the job and by check. But the Russians had to cut into the Chinamen's turf. They offered to work cheaper, and even brought along a younger helper for free. The Russians were driven and worked exceedingly fast while speaking the native tongue and made Max the Greek a lot of money. Max favored the Russians, and the Chinamen were down to three days a week. In the beginning, the three apple pickers were not happy with the payment by check from Max the Greek Movers. But now with him showing just about blind allegiance to the Russians, and winter on the doorstep with heavy snows when the moving business fell, they had Max the Greek over the barrel with a layoff. Collecting unemployment was a good way to spend the winter, because the unemployment check covered the rent, and they made beautiful cash money while shoveling snow. On a big dumping last winter, cleaning walks and shoveling out buried cars, the three of them grossed out fourteen hundred bucks in three days. Consequently, they always had plenty of money to get by, and what most people would call endless free time.

That afternoon, the big Chinaman and his skinny friend, bent heavy half-inch galvanized mesh. They formed a stout cage. It measured perhaps in size of three suitcases, and they lashed the box's ends with a good grade of mechanic wire. To the cage they fastened a carabiner as used in mountain climbing, and from there on a tether ran out a 50' length of brown hemp rope.

They had fabricated a trap of similar design, three days prior. That trap had been set out two nights ago under the cover of blackness and had been working around the clock. On this very night, the three Chinamen would go in for a look.

They made preparatory the night before. The battery-powered lights passed the test. A long handle fisherman's net was placed against the door. They neatly folded a tan canvas tarpaulin into a square package. The big Chinaman put a roll of heavy twine in his pocket, as seen on construction sites for level lines. In the refrigerator was a white pail fixed with a tight fitted snap lid. It was crammed full of fish heads. They secured them from a friend who worked a fish market out of China Town. They would need the severed heads with bulging eyes, for re-baiting of the cage traps.

The alarm clock began its mechanical song. The Chinamen quickly dressed. This time they would be taking no chances. It was three hours before light. They were breaking the rules this time around and were not gambling with getting pinched. They all wore brimmed hats and long sleeves. The skinny guy grabbed the fisherman's net going out the door, and others lugged the fish heads, various gear, and yellow battery lantern capable of floating in water.

They came out of 115th West and crossed the high road along the plateau, and knifed down into Morningside Park, descending the long flight of stairs. They had been in the brown stone stairs many times for the free apples. But this time they would not be working the frames of trees. Their plot was underwater, and all of them donned knee-high rubber boots. The boots were lined with soft foam, and it was very satisfactory to feel the snug warmth against your shins in the cool autumn night. The Chinamen reached the break where the staircase spilled into the park, but this time instead of heading towards the yellow ginkgo leaves, they wheeled hard left into the night. The big Chinaman came down through the forest, down the steep bank, and slipped into the pond.

He walked very slow, as to not slosh the water. He could feel his soles sinking in the mud. The two other Chinamen kept guard, hunkered down in the shadows behind a park bench. The arc lights were here and there across the park, and they could easily spot an intruder from a great distance.

The big Chinaman found the marking stick. He'd cupped his battery-powered light in his hand, and only let thin threads of light escape past his fingers. He swept the surface with needles of light, until he found the marker. The skinny guy had skinned the bark off a forked stick with his jackknife and anchored the tether line to the stick. He drew the tether line above the surface and walked hand over hand toward the trap. The brown hemp rope shed water, and the fat drops pattered on the pond's surface.

His boot stubbed the trap. He released a wash of yellow light past his fingers. A beam of light filled the night. A school of pin minnows treaded water around his boots. He heaved the heavy trap from the pond. His actions were slow and deliberate. The boots were inches from taking on water. Caught in the light, eight turtles clawed at the galvanized mesh. The three Chinamen had struck Chinamen's gold. They had just been blessed, with plenty of stock for turtle soup.

The turtle trappers played their cards on both ends. If they got skunked, they would re-bait and set with fish heads. But they had scored on a fat catch, so they would pull the trap.

The big Chinaman lugged the trap from the pond. He carried the trap as a man totes a large case of eggs, the cage resting on his belly, his arms outspread around the catch. The skinny guy paid in the hemp rope, coiling it around his arm, while his buddy made the way to shore. Trapping in the night could bring trouble. They wanted no part of pandemonium.

Option number two immediately came into play. The two Chinamen on the shore opened the square of tan canvas tarpaulin and prepared the ball of twine for serving. The big Chinaman abruptly skidded the cage trap on the sidewalk. His teeth gleamed in the night.

"Nice catch," he said.

"You're not kidding," exclaimed the skinny Chinaman. "Look at the size of those two buggers in the back."

The three Chinamen quickly engulfed the turtle trap with the canvas tarpaulin. They took care to fold the corners and smooth the canvas snug around the cage. The twine was very satisfactory for keeping the tan tarpaulin in neat order; when completed, it looked more like a giant suitcase. The big Chinaman half-hitched a shank of rope in the mesh, as to form a useful handle. The big Chinaman spun and ascended the stairs. The rest followed. They ran black in the night. Turning on lights would bring needless attention. The skinny Chinaman averted over his shoulder and scanned the distant blocks above the East River. A faint wash of the new day was rising in the earth's revolution. He thought he heard a squirrel rustling in the high nest of the forest. They climbed in the charcoal grey curtain.

They came out of the park on Morningside Drive. The big Chinaman was walking point. The guy who had carried the ladder on the crabapple run, took up slack. As he came through the opening in the wall's masonry of brownstone, he was arrested by a sight in the skyline: seven crosses from the seven gables, and an angel blowing the warning call of a trumpet, looked down at the

Chinaman from the roof line of Saint John the Devine Church. The symbols of religion showed bold against the high zenith of machine grey sky.

A sudden wash of emotion fell over him: vigilant revelation summoned the figure with higher calling. He felt very sharply in the hot flashes of guilt coming across him. It had everything to do with taking the turtles.

The Chinaman looked at the silhouette of crosses. He felt an urgent need to say something. He said it out loud in tones of the confessional box.

"Oh Lord, I'm sorry for my sins," confessed the Chinaman. "Please forgive us and watch over my friends."

It was very still on the street. The big Chinaman heard every syllable.

"Sorry about what?" asked the big Chinaman.

"Taking the turtles."

"Don't start that stuff on us," barked the big Chinaman. "We're low on money and just about starving. Keep your mouth shut and keep moving."

The three Chinamen went up the walk single file. They didn't get very far, when one of the crosses gave them a subtle goading. A set of headlights pierced the grey veil on West 113th Street, and the din of tires came down between the buildings. It was a police cruiser out on patrol.

The police officer came around the corner, pulled in the middle of Morningside Drive with the motor running and headlights beaming; the driver's window rolled down by electrics, and the police officer questioned —

"What's in the box?"

"It's Lucky Chinese Bamboo," said the big Chinaman.

"Where are you going?" the police officer wanted to know.

"We're going to our apartment," said the turtle trapper. "It's just up the road on Columbia property." The turtles had begun a commotion in the cage. Muffled metallic vibrations erupted. But the running motor blocked the police officer's perception of fine hearing. Turtle scratching went on under the tarpaulin.

"How come so much bamboo?" the officer wanted to know.

"We sell it down on Canal Street," lied the big guy. "Do you want a root stock for free?"

"Oh no… not that stuff. My wife had some for years in a pot. It grew like weeds. Thanks anyway," said the officer waving his hand.

The policeman was pulling out, when he noticed the skinny guy holding a fish net.

"Hey… what's the business with the fish net?"

"Oh officer," said the skinny guy, "the net is very useful when buying Lucky Chinese Bamboo wholesale. Often times the root stock is sunk in the huge water tubs, and the net can fish out the product with great speed."

"Have a nice day," offered the policeman. He pulled down Morningside Drive, and the Chinaman saw the vivid glow of red brake lights, when the cruiser shot up West 115th Street towards the university.

High above the scene, the outline of the heralding angel showed bold against the powder grey sky.

The three Chinamen went double-time up the walk, crossed the road, and disappeared into the alcove of Block 44 on Morningside Drive. They walked under the stone arch, where high above was chiseled with an arched format — CATHEDRAL.

Roger the doorman was at his post. He recognized the Chinamen, as they had previous acquaintance.

The Chinamen had been residents for less than a month, but Roger was quick on faces and recalling traits.

"What's in the cage?" asked Roger.

"Lucky Chinese Bamboo," said the big Chinaman.

"What's it good for?"

"It's simple to grow in pots. Want some?" offered the big Chinaman.

"Sure," said Roger, "why not?"

"No problem," they told Roger, "we'll give you some tomorrow after the bundle is sorted."

"I'll get a vase ready and pick out a good place by the window," said Roger.

"Good idea," the skinny Chinaman told him.

The three Chinamen took the elevator to the top floor. They had been living huge. Under normal conditions, the three Chinamen lived in a marginal flat up in Flushing, Queens. But the big Chinaman's uncle, Professor Billy Chen, taught English at Colombia University. The seventh year had rolled around, and Professor Billy had decided to take a six-month sabbatical in Peking. The professor had been fond of photography for years. He shot a box camera of the old school — a Linholf Master Technika 4x5. With relatives in the heart of Peking, which provided a sound base for his adventure, Professor Billy Chen would make excursions to the far villages and chains of mountains and see what could be caught on film.

Meanwhile, the three Chinamen were nothing more than house-sitters. Their rent was free. All electricity and phone bills were paid by automatic withdrawal from Professor Billy's bank account. Their only obligation was to run the vacuum cleaner every few days, make certain the pipes didn't freeze or break, and feed the two parakeets — Wilbur and Petunia.

The big Chinaman put his key into the lock, spun the tumbler with a loud click, and went inside. The other rogues followed. Rays of sun came through the balcony door. The skinny Chinaman threw off the cover on the bird cage and sprinkled a handful of bird seed down through the meshed dome. The birds went into an immediate feeding frenzy, and twirped songs of joy.

Dead silence filled the apartment. Purls of heat from cast iron radiators — satisfactory in the Autumn's morning chill — murmured invisible waves of replenish.

It was sure some apartment. The imagination of Professor Billy Chen reached the limits of indefinite decorum. His taste was like his photos, spanning the spectrum with wide interest. The apartment embodied the charm of former era, where craftsmanship was the heart of life. The rooms were laid in hardwood floors of finishes that accentuated the grains, and fine furniture of antiquity appointed the chambers. Oriental rugs cloaked the floors, and tapestry hung in the master bedroom. The professor had a trained eye for color and effects. He burned only certain scents in candle wax. The linen closet held a collection of well-made pillow cases and embroidered bed covers, and bath towels were quality terry with high napping.

In this apartment too, was a wide spattering of table lamps with colored shades, sconces, and an electric candelabrum, and the rays of stained glass streamed off a ruddier light pattern around the chambers, and in vespertine the fantastic colors beamed a cozy warmth to the inhabitants. The proclamation the three Chinamen were living grand, beyond the wildest dreams, would be sheer understatement across the board.

In the beginning, the three Chinamen put on the tinhorn. They bought second hand Izod shirts from the Goodwill Store in Washington Heights. Two of them purchased dress hats as seen on Kid Rock. But everybody in the community saw through them right away. Their vocabulary did not match the campus scene, and their mannerisms were not in line with social refinements of higher education. None of them owned an automobile. The soles of their tennis shoes were half worn. They were just part-time movers, who moonlighted as house watchers.

So then, after a few days, they went back to normal activity, street clothes, and hung their laundry of white T-shirts and socks on the balcony until Roger the doorman informed them no clotheslines were allowed in visible sight on the premises. This was the Cathedral Building, not the dude ranch out on the plains. It was a place where sidewalks out front were meticulously sprayed down each morning, the janitor laying down fans of nozzle water across the concrete slabs, and the house sitters would need to keep in check with rules and make attempts at practicing etiquette.

The first six weeks on the Sixth Floor of Block 44, were absolutely golden. The Chinamen were stoked. They could finally live in a world of charm and dignity. But then came the bad news.

Professor Billy Chen had called long distance from Peking. It was late afternoon New York City time, and the three Chinamen had been playing Rummy cards on the kitchen table.

The phone startled them, as Billy's number was known only in small circles — *ringgggggging… ringgggggging*. The big Chinaman jumped up and grabbed the white receiver.

"Hey guys," said Professor Billy Chen from across the world, "we've got trouble."

"What's wrong?" asked the big Chinaman with his head down and ears spiked.

"My relatives over in Jackson Heights had an apartment fire," informed Professor Billy.

"It's not Hop?" asked the big Chinaman shaking his head.

"That's them," filled in the professor. "They will need to stay over my place for a few days. Put them up in the study room on the floor."

"No problem," said the big Chinaman.

But it was a big problem. The three Chinamen who got burned out, were perhaps the laziest Chinamen in New York City. Hop and Hong were brothers; their cousin Chang was just as bad. They had naturalized into the big Apple, from the Kirin Province of China. Their reputation was well known. None of the good Chinamen liked them. The hard-working Chinamen along Canal Street worked long hours and seven days a week, and they had no use for those three men. They were too lazy.

Lazy is one thing, but cheap is another, and sometimes both go hand and hand. All three of them were cheap skates. Hong smoked like a chimney, but never bought. He was always mooching smokes. If they couldn't put the soft touch on somebody for a free cigarette, they were fond of picking up clips on the street. They had one of those red metal machines for rolling your own smokes, and they always thought they were quite sharp, because all the tobacco from all those mixed brands, most times made a puff that was out of this world.

But the worst thing about those three cheap Chinamen, was that they were stingy on food. They thought nothing of living for days on nothing more than Skippy peanut butter and crackers. They liked buying those extra-big boxes of saltine crackers and were very frugal with thin spreads of peanut butter.

The thing that bothered the big Chinaman the most, was that Chang had huge spaces between his teeth, with a big mouth and wide thin lips, and when he talked there were big wedges of peanut butter and cracker crumbs between his teeth, and white crumbs all over his breast. His gracious smile took some of the ignorance away, but in the long run he was still a slob.

The big Chinaman walked over to the stove and struck a match. Blue flames danced from the gas orifice. He put water in a huge kettle and began a steaming roll. It was time to give the turtles the coup de grace.

He looked out the window. It was a long way down. A vast flock of black birds angled past the window, swooped down through the forest, and landed in the ballpark of Morningside Park. It appeared there must be over a thousand birds. The big Chinaman could see the black feathered masses working the stand of crabgrass for seeds. It must have been a prolific year for seeds, and the birds held their position for long spans of time.

Steam rose from the kettle. The big Chinaman tossed in the turtle meat, assorted vegetables, and dashes of several herbs. He cut the turtle soup to a simmer. Chunks of Golden Yukon potatoes tumbled in the stock. He slid the dome lid back over the kettle pot and went back working turtle shells. They had split the upper and lower shell plates with a hand-held grinder, fitted with a metal cutting disc. It was dangerous work, because one slip with the whirling steel, could slash your wrist wide open. But this was not their first turtle mission, and all eight turtles had been sectioned. When you cut turtle shells with an electric grinder, the reek of burned bone rises off the blade.

It's a fusty kind of smell, and the skinny Chinaman opened the kitchen window a good six inches. The belly plates on the turtles were good for nothing, but they sometimes saved a few shells for conversation pieces or ashtrays.

Finishing scraping the turtle shell with his jade handled

jackknife, the big Chinaman looked again into the steaming kettle. The meat was turning white in the stock. Everything was going as planned. The big Chinaman poured a few jiggers of beer in the soup, then he investigated down the hall. He cracked the study's door and peeked inside the makeshift bedroom. The three lazy Chinamen were sound asleep on very thin mattresses over the floor. All of them brought pillows, and Hop was huddled inside a heaped quilt. His mop of black hair and big ears were under the blackness of covers. A tiny air passage was evident near his head. The big Chinaman saw Hong wiggling his toes a few times and heard him make a singular moan. He closed the door very slowly, and he went back to tending soup.

It was nothing for the three lazy Chinamen to sleep into lunch time. They never had much pressing. There were many things the good Chinamen could say against the three loafers, but the one thing they could never say against them, was that they were not clean. Because time itself was a mere accessory to them they showered three times a day. This caused a great ordeal in Professor Chen's apartment, because there were always damp towels hung on pegs, and water spattered on the black and white tiles around the tub.

Hop, Hung, and Chang began most days in the forenoon, down in Morningside Park. Chang lived under the illusion he was a fantastic trumpet player. He played every fair-weather day on a bench in the park. It was a good place to practice. The notes of brass carried beautiful in the park. It was its own amphitheater. But the trouble laid in the fact Chang would have trouble carrying a note in a wheelbarrow, although he could occasionally purse his lips and make nice music. He was making ground on pushing the brass plungers, and the squirrels scampered at the report of horn, racing up the bark and harkening down on him from the high limbs in wonder.

Hop and Hong liked calisthenics. It cost nothing. They needed no equipment. Membership to the gymnasium was not necessary. The two brothers worked themselves with upper butterfly moves, as often seen in military training camps. They religiously spent free time to build tone. Their bellies were flat. All this activity pushed out beads of sweat and brought on hunger, and the three loafers liked to finish with hot showers in Professor Billy's pad, and then snack on peanut butter and saltine crackers. They were exceptionally fond of black tea, and always seemed to have bags steeping. Many afternoons when he needed a fix, Hong stuck his head out the window to make one of his home-made smokes made on the red machine. Hong knew Professor Billy was exceedingly particular and could smell smoke on the curtains a month later. He wanted no part of burning bridges on free rent.

Good news had come. The big Chinaman was very happy. Professor Billy Chen had called again long distance from the Orient. The kitchen fire in Jackson Heights was only minor. The lazy Chinamen had started fire by toasting English muffins, while past bills had been stacked next to the toaster oven. Smoke damage had been the biggest obstacle. The landlord had assured Professor Chen, his three relatives could move back in on the following Tuesday by noon. This news broke cheerful smiles across the three Chinamen on house watching duty. It would be a big load off everybody's mind when they cycled out.

The turtle soup became ready at three bells straight up. All of them were starving from the 5:00 AM departure for their turtle trapping. Mid-afternoon would be a swell time and close enough for dinner. The skinny Chinaman had just returned from a package store run. He'd bought a big six-pack of IPA beer with an Irish trademark. It was hard to picture Chinaman drinking Irish beer, but three green beer bottles were on the white oak table. The medullary rays of the wood, amber tinted golden grains, brought out nostalgia against the three green glass bottles. The Chinaman who had a guilt complex under the tooting angel and field of crosses, had boiled pure white rice. He allowed the pot to steam off to obtain fluffy rice. The big Chinaman had begun ladling the turtle soup into big bowls of chinaware.

The three lazy Chinamen were down in Morningside Park. Hop and Hong were conducting knee squats with deep palm lunges to the turf, as seen with pitchers in preparation for World Series baseball. Chang was back at blowing the trumpet. He'd found an antique music stand of stainless steel along the tree belt. Fastened to the holder clips was sheet music. But it was exclusive singular varnish of masquerade — Chang could not read music. It was only a clever maneuver to put a snow job on the wayfarers of the park. He occasionally flipped a page of music to create illusion, but the real truth was he could not distinguish from a G-clef and a double flat note symbol.

"Brother," said the big Chinaman, "this soup is out of this world."

"You're not kidding," said the skinny Chinaman.

The guilty Chinaman ate in silence. But like the others, he brought the soup into his mouth production style, and savored every bite of the turtle meat. He had come to terms with his conscious. Turtle soup was not available in the supermarkets. He remembered the turtle soup his grandmother made in the cast iron kettle. He finished off the bowl and took a slug of beer.

The voluminous kettle held many days hot of meals. The three bowls hardly put a dent in the vessel. They would be eating hardy turtle soup into next week.

"Make sure nobody gives away soup to the free loaders," warned the big Chinaman.

"Hong said he wanted to try some," said the skinny Chinaman.

"Never mind Hong Kong," said the big Chinaman. "If I catch him in the goods, it will be curtains."

Then the big Chinaman reached in his pocket and produced a Mason jar. He held it in plain sight. The seal had been broken. The big Chinaman had been doing his homework. The light bulb went off that morning. He immediately began detective work. A trip inside the pantry had revealed thievery. Foul play had been discovered in the batch of Mason Jars. Sun rays angled past the window and into the crabapple jelly in glass. Tints of tangerine crimson showed in the jars. The big Chinaman knew from hard labor, that they made 27 jars of jelly. They were working on the first jar in the refrigerator. But the count was at 26 Mason jars. Math never lied. One of the crabapple jellies was missing.

The big Chinaman had rummaged through the kitchen. Nothing. He double checked all cabinets and drawers and the cluttered countertop. Nothing.

He pressed his gut feeling into the moocher's bedroom. After a short investigation, he found evidence: Hong had hidden the half-eaten Mason jar in the foot compartment of his sleeping bag. The big Chinaman had felt the bulging glass, when padding down the folds of bedding. A stainless butter knife was on the nightstand. Across the blade was circumstantial evidence — a smear of crabapple jelly laid across the steel. He had them cold. They would pay dearly for pulling stunts with their labor.

The big Chinaman twirled the Mason jar in his fingers. "See this?" he said to his friends. This evidence was inside Hong's sleeping bag."

"The lazy bones practiced five-finger discount on our pre-serves," remarked the skinny Chinaman.

"That's it," revealed the big guy.

"That will be the day I let those bums start jonesing on my crabapple jelly," said the Chinaman with the guilt complex. He mopped his soup bowl with white bread. It was very satisfactory to get the last morsel in your mouth, because the thickest gravy and bone stock was on the bottom. He licked his fingers clean and patted down with a napkin.

Suddenly, footfalls filled the staircase. The three loafers were returning from Morningside Park. The knob turned and here they came.

Hong was the first through the door; the big Chinaman riveted him to the wall in a chokehold. Hong tightened like a deer in head-lights. Jacking him around the collar he said in anger, "Listen you punk, steal anything again, and I'll break you in two."

Hong buckled at the knees. His feet tread in thin air. A vein of sweat was running from his back hair.

"Listen," said Hong in panic, "cool it… I'll give you two bucks for the jelly."

"Two bucks — are you nuts? Cheap jelly costs three bucks in the Dollar Store," countered the big Chinaman. His big hand was right on Hong's throat. "I'd never sell you any for eight bucks a Mason jar. You creeps are not good enough for our jelly."

"Take it easy," said Hong with bitterness, "you're crushing my smokes with your body."

The big Chinaman let him go. Hong pushed his hair back straight. He reached a hand into his jacket and extruded a huge bag of clips. Through the clear plastic, it appeared there were over 200 street clips in the bag. Hong blew inside the bag, and shook it vigorously around, as if to instill the possession of life back inside the stubbed smokes. That evening the three Chinamen gutted out the tobacco from the street clips with a razor blade, and rolled up some smokes on their Bugler cigarette rolling machine. They were cheapskates and loved a free smoke from the gutter.

No event of celebration was in sight. It was not Chinese New Year. Thanksgiving was two months out. Christmas never entered their mind. But in a rare experience, the three Chinamen had decided to let go of a few bucks and treat themselves. They had pooled their pocket money and splurged on a block of Vermont sharp cheddar. Top shelf cheese. Chang was still shaking off giddiness, smiling wide across that big mouth with those thin lips, that they finally had mustered enough nerve to spend some money. Hop sliced off thick slices of the cheese. The chums immediately made tiny sandwiches on saltine crackers. The sharpness of the cheese excited their senses of hunger.

"What a sandwich!" swelled Hop.

"Talk about living," gushed Hong in happiness.

Chang was on his third sandwich. The Vermont cheese was getting all wedged in the big gaps between his teeth. He needed to pull the cheese chunks out with his fingers, and it was common for him to pop cheese back into his mouth for another go around. It had been said many times that Chang could win a corn on the cob eating contest through a chain link fence.

A loud knock came through the door. It was the big Chinaman with a big knuckle rapping. He opened the door clutching the half-eaten Mason jar of crabapple jelly.

"Here," he said to the cheapskates, "it's on the house." He handed the jelly to Chang. He smiled wide. The big Chinaman could not believe all the cheese stuck in Chang's teeth, and all the cracker crumbs on the floor. It seemed Chang's wide teeth, destroyed everything in sight.

"Thank you!" chimed Hop.

"No problem," said the big Chinaman. He closed the door and listened behind the door. He could hear Hong giving free advice about spreading frugal coats of crabapple jelly over cheese sand-wiches. A rattle of silverware came from behind the door.

The big Chinaman's act had nothing to do with kindness. He knew the free loaders ate with dirty utensils. The last thing he wanted was some kind of germ bugs. They could keep the stolen jelly and roll the dice on their own watch.

The night wind blew. It came down out of the north-west from the farm country of Upper State New York, combing the trees of Morningside Park and raking the rows of apartments. The three Chinamen finished off the Irish IPA beer. Green bottles were all over the white oak table. The turtle soup was in the calico kettle inside the refrigerator. It held at least three full meals for the three Chinamen. Red flags were already flying; the big Chinaman took a fresh paint stick from the cupboard and stuck it straight into the soup; he thus marked the level line with a ball point pen. He wiped the wood with a paper towel and placed the paint stick on the refrigerator's top for future reference. All trust had been obliter-ated. He would be taking another measure of soup in the morning.

All the inhabitants were in bed. All the lights were out. The wind rasped the window screens. Gusts could be heard racing up the alleys. Everybody was sleeping except Hong. He could not sleep thinking of turtle soup. He licked his chops in the night. Temptation grew. He formed a plan — Hong would move when he was certain the others were far away in dream world.

It was past midnight. The big Chinaman was deep in sleep.

Hong made his move in slippers and night garments. He snuck into the kitchen on pins and needles. Nervousness was about his countenance. Very, very nervous, because he knew what would happen if he was caught. It was a world of black behind the masonry. Streetlights had absolutely no effects on the sixth floor. Hong opened the refrigerator. Yellow lights captured the fright on his face. His mouth was wide open, and he listened with awe through his ear canal. Hong lifted the lid… silently… silently… and in his mind marked the congealed soup line on the kettle. He quickly spooned a bowl full; and in the next breath, he drew tap water and filled the void. Hong stirred the cold soup. The level quickly came back into its original state. Hong knew the consequences — the big Chinaman would give him a first-class thumping for pilfer of turtle stock. But those raised in the ghetto hamlets of Kirin Province, knew all the tricks, because everybody in the margins of poverty needed the steal to survive. With his tracks covered, Hong quickly heated the turtle soup on the range, and then sneaked down in the living room. He knew Hop had a good nose. A commotion in the night would be a tragic experience. Hong would much rather ride out his escapade in victory. He ate the turtle soup with a big spoon on the sofa in complete silence. A quick wash in the kitchen sink took all evidence of foul play down the drain. Hong burped once, then went back inside his quarters, where he sunk into the soundest kind of sleep. His conscious was clear, because lessons learned on the hard scrabble streets of Kirin Province, stay with men a long time. He passed a long stream of gas, caressed the pillow, and slept sound with no interruptions till late morning.

Isochronous sentiments, however, were not present in all the inhabitants. In a far bedroom, the product of guilt was still working the complexed Chinaman. His subconscious would not let him sleep. He tossed and turned to find shelter from the storm. He could not calibrate any certain position that would reward that simplistic comfort. His mind was going too fast. He listened to the howling gusts; some place in the night cans were rattling a dance on pavement. Somewhere into the marching night, he enveloped in deep sleep.

Dawn broke clear. The wind had slackened. Mysterious fluttering worked the tree canopy in Morningside Park. The confessor walked into the bathroom with bare feet. He looked out the window, and the twinkling rays of sun streaming through the tree limbs hurt his eyes. The Chinaman noted the wind had slackened, and the sky was a crystalline blue. He could see the sun beaming over the East River beyond the skyline, but he could not see the river itself. He knew about those things through assimilation. Farther down the river out of sight, the tugboats were working the pearled water. The wake lapped the pier docks. The Chinaman was up a long time, before he realized he was supposed to be feeling guilty about dead turtles. He went out through the door on the balcony for fresh air. A new and fresh reminder was next to the iron railing on a wooden stool. A turtle shell rested on the seat. Somebody had stubbed out a cigarette in the hollow shell. The night winds had scoured away all the flecks of ash. But a burn mark was circumscribed into the white rough cartilage plate. In attempts to rid himself of a sudden flash of ill feeling, he took the turtle shell in his hand and sailed it off the balcony with the motion little boys used when skipping flat shale rocks across the lake. The turtle shell sailed far out in space, and he could see it spinning and getting smaller, gliding through the forest of Morningside Park and ricochet off a big trunked sycamore tree, sailing down into a bed of Baltic ivy. The turtle shell had stayed there on the forest floor over two seasons, until the mice and rodents had gnawed the shell into the remains of oblivion.

With some of the remorse shed, the Chinaman stung by a heavy conscious, went inside and dressed for a street walk. The Otis whirled down in the elevator shaft. He heard the cable drives vex. Roger the doorman was not around. It was far too early for him to be on post. The emotional wreck went out under the Cathedral archway of the Block 44, and he trudged down Morningside Drive. He was on a mission of faith and sauntered down the walk toward his offhand confessional box.

A few blocks down at the West 113th Street crossing, he threw his head back on the shoulders, wincing from the collection of images. They were still there. The seven crosses cut the sky, and the angel was still in the steep pitches of the church steeple.

But on this particular visit for the Chinaman, there was living and breathing emphasis on the scene: a priest in the black habiliments of religious order looked at the Chinaman from the premise. His white collar showed bold against the black garments, the figures silhouetted against the granite blocks of Saint John the Devine Church.

The priest extended a round house wave with a beaming smile of silent ovation. The Chinaman returned a precent in a cordial hand signal, high five sweeping thin air, offering the universal sign of friendliness in mankind. Relief enveloped the Chinaman. He entertained the thought that his confession with the purging of burden, might not be a bad idea. But the squelching was short lived — the priest whirled and went through the oaken door into the vestibule.

So much for support. He would need to decipher terms on his own accord. These were strange grounds, and he felt a little wobbly in the legs.

The Chinaman knew nothing of the Roman Catholic Church. He was born and raised on his knees as Buddhist. He could not tell the different between John and Matthew. He had no idea where Pontius Pilate fit into the testament. He silently wondered if the Angel of Trumpet was a leading figure in the church.

So, the Chinaman called it close enough; he'd seen others bless themselves in public; then he swung a few circles around his forehead with his trigger finger. It would need to be close enough. He mulled all the excuses he could invent in his mind for eating turtles from captivity. The man knew he would need to be short on storytelling, because from the seven gables of the seven crosses, they could see sharp and clear the turtle pond in Morningside Park. He knew the power of the Holy Ghost could see all things.

The Chinaman was grasping at straws in his defense, but he never got very far, because he remembered out of the blue, the seventh Commandment of not to steal. He felt he'd run into a brick wall and was cornered in stalemate. Nevertheless, he had a very devout conversation with the angel blowing the horn, just in case they had some pull inside the church. His repertoire was serious and from the heart, and he spoke for several minutes, occasionally offering his open arms to the heavens. But there was no response. He'd heard no revelations. Everything was stone quiet, and although he expected something in earnest, he felt nothing. The Chinaman gave himself one last semi-classical blessing of the forehead, the kind of business you see on the fringes of religion and walked across the street to have a talk with his other god. Maybe Buddha would see other angles.

The Chinaman felt more on home grounds. He'd been with Buddha a long time. He felt he could really open up and spill his guts in this confession. This time all the stops would be pulled. The

Chinaman looked over the wall of Morningside Park, and began collecting lines of logic. Many colorful ideas came to mind.

He remembered the lessons of religion Uncle Amos gave him in 1982 on the poor side of Brooklyn. Amos was very strict on religion, and the uncle instructed the boy he would have few character flaws in life, if he could find faith.

The Chinaman knew from the lessons, that Gautama often lived as a hermit in the forest. The lone figure practiced yoga. The Chinaman recalled from Uncle Amos's lore, Buddha once discovered a lovely spot on the riverbed, where he sat under the cool shade of a sacred fig tree, and the revelation of faith came to him.

The Chinaman hopped up on the wall and assumed the yoga position. He faced east towards the rising sun. The ball had changed from orange to a yellow wafer. The sun was framed on a blue city sky. He took on the celestial forms of yoga in stern seriousness. He was all about obeisance. Speaking to Buddha was serious business. He would not chance taking anything too lightly. His lips were pursed and jaw jutted. Above his head was the dappled shade of the forest, its leaves a million flecks of color from the advance of autumn. The Chinaman was certain he was near holy perfection, because the park trees were as close as anybody would ever strike to finding the Bo Tree in New York City. He figured if his action was pleasing to Buddha, that he might be granted mercy.

The Chinaman closed his eyes on the wall and drifted into a world of meditation. All his thoughts embraced the thought train of passiveness. A sudden calm enveloped him on the wall.

The turtle trapper came level with Buddha in his first phase — he admitted to Buddha that under no circumstances, would he stop eating turtles. He liked them too much. But he came clean with an oath to his teacher, he would curb his appetite on killing turtles from Morningside Park or the Harlem Meer. The Chinaman had plenty of hot spots along the Hudson River and East River's coves, where they could fill steel drums to the brink with big ornery snapping turtles like clockwork. And that was without mentioning their hunting grounds in the Adirondack Region, where they could set out giant Mustard hooks baited with chicken livers, and horse in the saw-shelled beasts with hides like rhinos and vice jaws that could cut bones in two.

The Chinaman was also quick to remind Buddha of his finer attributes. Many people liked him, he said. He sold comic books. He told Buddha about how many friends he'd made from selling funnies at a fair price. Everybody involved knew they were those one-time friends a man stumbles upon with life in general, then never cross paths again.

At least it was something. Bridges had been spanned. Having that many friends was sensational. He remembered their faces and recalled their genuine smiles, happy with their new comic books. The Chinaman saw this as a bolster towards humanity. He grooved on distant drums and could see star spangled banners in the parade. He stayed that way a long time on the wall with eyes closed and holding back breaths, but Buddha had remained silent and distant. No salient angels had jutted understanding. After a while the drums died, and even in the meditation nobody ever came forward and put a token pin on his lapel. Absolutely nothing happened. He snapped out of meditation, when he heard a hermit thrush twirping in the deciduous bank of shrubs below.

The Chinaman felt arrested with his task. Awareness told him there was no room for debate — the Four Noble Truths were on the table. The Chinaman knew suffering played a vast role in man's existence. He was fully aware that suffering is fueled by desire for things; and that we become slaves to these lifeless objects. Uncle Amos had taught the boy desire for possessions prevent us from the acquisition of knowledge and understanding. Amos schooled the boy, that only by destroying all evil desire, the chains of sorrow can at last be shed.

The Chinaman acknowledged his hands were tied. There was no need to finish the book of Noble Truth. The first few lines had him pinched. He'd caused his own sorrow, with the desire for too much turtle meat from Morningside Pond. With the revelation of truth, the Chinaman leaped off the walk and cleared the gutter line, landing flat feet on the street. The roadbed was dead. No traffic moved. He walked slowly to the yellow lines, the bounds of intermediate between the powers. Now all of them could commence in three-way conversation.

He felt between a rock and a hard place. On one side the giant stones of Saint John the Devine Church loomed, where he was outgunned eight to one, with the figures along the gables who knew exactly the number of saints inside the church. Gut feeling told him he was facing insurmountable odds. The Ten Commandments had him so pinned down, it wasn't even funny. He threw his hands up in mid-air and surrendered.

He took a reading on the other side. He found no wiggle room. The Chinaman knew Buddha didn't fool around, and they hadn't even gotten to the Nobel Eightfold Path. Once he began down that path, the Chinaman realized he would be fortunate to escape with his hide.

The Chinaman, driven by frustration of the extreme, jumped around on the yellow lines as if whacked by lightning, and exclaimed out loud with his trigger finger to the heavens, "Hey guys… let's cut the funny stuff! I'm really not that bad of a guy."

He looked around for some kind of answer. Perhaps a verdict of supernatural wisdom would descent. He presently expected and wished for a pair of grey doves, the holy sign of perpetual peace, to circle above his presence and land beside his feet. But the only grey feathers he saw, was a flock of nuisance pigeons nestled near the trumpet angel; their cooing of soft putts pierced the morning silence. The only conclusion he could form, was that the Maker was not sold on his confession for the lust of turtle meat.

The Chinaman did not believe in pagan gods. But he was high on superstition and believed in good luck. He'd exhausted all options. None of the Gods had gone this way or that.

He clutched the string of blue Mardi Gras beads around his neck. His fingers went up and down the beads with the motion of those who practice the rosary. He got the blue beads from a hot number at a New Year's Eve party two years back. He'd kept them in place all that time around his neck, because it was the first time in years a babe made a pass. The hot number actually asked him if he wanted to give her a quick screw. The Chinaman was so dumbfounded, he nervously laughed in her face. The last thing those hot Chink numbers in short skirts on that side of town want is some guy slow on the draw when it's time for action. So she dumped him fast. But he kept the string of beads anyhow, because it was the closest he'd come to a score in a long time.

The Chinaman squeezed the blue beads. He knew in his heart they were completely useless against the power who reigns beyond the galaxy. He believed that Buddha could disintegrate the Mardi Gras beads in the snap of fingers. The Chinaman cultivated absolutely no doubt, he was painted into a very tight corner.

The Chinaman had no knowledge, the angel he'd been having discreet conversation with over the last two days, was the

Angel of Gabriel. The archangel whose primary role was the messenger of God to man. The same angel who made revelation to Daniel in the bible. But the Chinaman never knew who he was dealing with.

The Chinaman delicately massaged the blue beads and twirled them in his fingers. He looked up at the angel clutching its trumpet, holding fast to his blue beads, and asked one last favor. He spoke to Gabriel in the most sincere tones a man could muster, and asked if it might ever be possible that if another hot number came along with those kind of offers, that if he could un-twist his tongue and make him say the right things, so he could get someplace later on in the bedroom. The Chinaman blessed his forehead three times over, and reminded Gabriel one last time, that if he could manage to pull some strings, he'd be forever grateful. Then he simply spun on the yellow lines and began walking the street. He started whistling Dixie. The Chinaman had come clean on his own terms and was feeling a lot lighter about everything. He hit the curb line and looked around the gutter for some cigarette clips, when he noticed the priest looking at him through the black bars of ornamental iron.

"Everything going well, my son?" The priest had been watching him for quite some time. He'd come back out to cultivate the tea roses, and the priest had been measuring the Chinaman while putting down labor in the soils.

"Not too bad," said the Chinaman with a straight face.

"We're always here if you need us," the priest offered. "There's no off hours in the calling, so just ring the buzzer." The priest leaned on a long handles cultivator that had three hooked tines. Behind the priest, school children were walking the school yard connected to the church. They were all parochial kids. Some of them were still cut out by nuns. The girls wore white blouses and jumpers. The boys had on white shirts with blue ties. All of them had the initials S.J. embroidered on the shirt collar.

"I'll keep the offer in mind," the Chinaman told the priest.

"You seemed deep in tribulation back on the sidewalk under the shade tree."

"I was," admitted the Chinaman.

"We have a confession at 3:00 PM this afternoon. Why not stop by for a few words of salvation?"

"Jesus, not this time around Father," said the Chinaman pulling on his ear. "I feel like I've been through the ringer already."

"I've taken thousands through the box," proclaimed the priest.

"I'll do my homework and think about coming back soon."

"No problem my son... have a good day."

"You too Father," said the Chinaman with a nod. Then he moved very brisk and with a lighter step down towards Professor Billy Chen's apartment. The Chinaman crossed West 114th Street with a burst of energy, and then turned under the porte-cochere of the Block 44. Roger was on post behind the concierge's desk. It was Roger's business to give everybody the once over as they came up the flanks into the premise. The chance of thievery, a prologue of gang violence from the 70s brought on this mind set. If trespass was detected, Roger quickly contacted the Campus Police, as just about all real estate for 20 blocks was owned by Columbia University. And if the Campus Police couldn't shut things down, they got on the horn and brought on the power of the New York City Police Department, assigned to that precinct.

But Roger recognized the Chinaman right off the bat. Roger might not know all the names on those six floors, but he had all the faces and personal traits in his mind.

Roger smiled. The Chinaman gave a wink. No words were spoken between the men. The Chinaman pushed the brass button for the 6th floor, walked through the elevator door, and rode her up. He was by all stretches of imagination, done for now about any guilt complex brought on with turtle soup.

It was a slow day for all six Chinamen. The lazy freeloaders were full of apprehension with the slight breeze and cold temperatures. They blew off their training regiments in Morningside Park. All returned to bed after black tea and crackers.

The three lazy Chinamen knew a wealth of facts that were almost useless in society. They spent many daylight hours in front of the television set, and thus, could recite almost verbatim the names of all the hit stars in the soap operas. They dial surfed from one episode to the next.

They were strong on home movies too. Hop had a collection of The Three Stooges. There were over twenty of them in the collection. The three lazy Chinamen had watched them so many times, the movie casings showed wear. It was a funny thing too, because the three guys on the movie set and three glued to the screen, both could bring on the laughs.

Another love — and especially Chang who was addicted — was watching King Kong at the movie house. They watched the newspapers like old ladies looking for bonus coupons and scoured the movie box for a run with King Kong.

They were especially fond of the Japanese versions of King Kong, and once rode the Number 6 Train transfer into Brooklyn seven nights consecutive, when the Bing Theater was running the big ape with free popcorn.

The big Chinaman and his two companions also stayed indoors. They devoted the day for house clean and vacuum. Nobody knew exactly if Professor Billy Chen would bring a surprise visit on them from the Orient.

Later that afternoon, they broke out the turtle soup. They ate the soup in front of the lazy Chinamen. Chang was rubbing his jowls with the want for a hot bowl of soup. But the three turtle trappers were not worried about contra bonus mores, and ate the hot soup in enormously good spirits and laughter. The Chinaman who once harbored guilt, now clean with repent, heaped up a second bowl and patted the gravy away from his mouth with white bread. Hop sent Hong up to Cusumano's Market on West 123rd Street with seven bucks in singles. He traveled by bicycle. It was the kind of bicycle you see chained to posts in New York City, a tarnished frame set with bald tires and fitted with a steel basket up on the bars. The bicycle traveled at a good clip of speed on account of the baldie white walls, but they were prone to blowouts. A good half-hour later, Hong returned with a full over pound of Mother Goose liverwurst in skin casing, and two-quart cans of porridge. The three Chinamen could play games too. They sat around a card table next to the other three still seated at the kitchen table. Chang made liverwurst sandwiches on crackers. Hop heated the porridge in a Corning Ware pot. The soup was fortified with bison meat. Hop made sure he made it hurt, when he boasted how delicious the porridge tasted with wild meat, and that he never ran into liverwurst that good with the nice bite in the after taste.

The big Chinaman measured them. Crumbs of crackers were sprinkled about the card table. The soup was seeping out between Chang's front teeth. The big Chinaman laughed inside, when he pictured the three pinned in baby bibs. Hop licked the bowl clean. It's a good thing he never found out about Hop stealing turtle soup in the midnight hour. It was bad enough they got caught red handed with hot jelly. Stealing turtle soup would have put the big Chinaman over the top, and because he never knew his strength, you never knew what might happen when he blew a cork and let the temper fly.

The Chinamen stayed the whole day indoors. Professor Billy's apartment was back in order. The three lazy Chinamen killed a couple of Three Stooges comedy numbers. Hop found a new part in one of the movies.

All of them retired early. The radiator's heat against the autumn chill, had taken a great deal of vitality from the men. The household slept sound, but the sandman's work was cut short before sunrise.

The skinny Chinaman wiggled his toes under the covers. He thought about Vicky. She was his new girlfriend. Vicky was the big Chinaman's old girlfriend. The skinny Chinaman never told the big Chinaman. Vicky liked the skinny Chinaman. He was affectionate toward Vicky, especially after the third date when she popped her brassiere straps on her own accord. After that the skinny Chinaman had a one-track mind. The big Chinaman was the one who broke off everything. But he still loved Vicky deep inside. The skinny Chinaman was worried about hurting his friend's feelings. They spoke in secret by telephone. Everybody involved in the past and present had run their fingers around the dial. Vicky had called her ex on two occasions. She wanted to return personal items that were given when they were sweet on each other. The big Chinaman kept his feelings inside. The skinny Chinaman never said a word. Once revealed and the big Chinaman was filled in, the incident would play out as the most painful love triangle any of them had ever experienced.

The big Chinaman woke near midnight to pass urine. He listened to the weather forecast on the waves of AM radio. The forecast was going to take a dive on the following evening. He went over quick math in his head. His hands filled an empty soda bottle with tap water, and tightened the red cap. He took his large L.L. Bean rucksack from the pegs and leaned it against the wall. Then he went back to sleep by set alarm.

Night engulfed the sleepers. The big Chinaman was on his feet. He shook his buddy who had been stricken by guilt.

"What's up?" he questioned coming out of a deep sleep.

"The weatherman predicts a deep frost for tomorrow night," he told him. "We must move now. It's our last chance to harvest more crabapples."

The three pickers packed gear and got ready. Then the big Chinaman walked down and entered the bedroom of the lazy Chinamen. Hong was snoring. He threw a flashlight beam into Chang's face, drilled his boot into the ribcage with a side blow, and barked out loud, "Xing-lai! Wake up!"

Chang squinted from the beam. Wedges of cheese were between his teeth. "What are you doing? Are you crazy?"

"Never mind the funny stuff, Mister Funny Boy," he told Chang. "We caught you cold stealing jelly." Payback time had come in the night and out of the blue. The big Chinaman had dictated his action by long thought in advance. "Get dressed," he ordered across the bedroom, "it's time for you lazy bums to pick the apples back that went down your throats."

The six went out into the night. The big Chinaman led the way. He shouldered the big empty rucksack. The three lazy Chinamen lugged two five-gallon pails apiece. The metal hoop handle of Hop's bucket squeaked in the dark. They descended the stone stairs of Morningside Park. Walking slack was the guilty Chinaman wrangling the aluminum ladder. Out in the fresh air of the night shifts, away from false security of the apartment block, some of the pre-monitions were coming back. He knew back in the night the angel was watching every move he made. A new edge creeped over his disposition. He changed shoulders on the ladder and tried to vanquish some of his feelings.

The Harlem Meer was dead quiet. Nothing moving. The bullfrogs had dived below into the mud flats. A good deal of the waterfowl had pulled out and began the fall migration across the sky. A flock of Mergansers seen around days before, were in formation along the Maryland brackish tidal sloughs.

The crabapple picking was extremely productive. Red fruit hung every place in the night. This time around, the apple pickers had the human machine of twelve hands. That number of fingers jacked production with so much speed, they had picked out within the hour.

Chang liked picking. He had never picked. In the beginning, he thought Chang could eat one for three in the pail. He tried. It was a poor endeavor. He found the fruit was tart and hard. They lacked sweetness. Chang had a sweet tooth. But the biggest drawback was the crabapples got speared by his front teeth. They hung from his gums like tiny Christmas balls. He needed to pick them off, or chomp down and break them in two. After a few attempts, he spit a wad of pulped fruit on the grass and went back to business.

While picking, the big Chinaman had thought once of Vicky. He tried putting her away. Small snippets of her would not go away. Vicky drifted inside the skinny Chinaman's imagination — he'd momentarily froze and stopped picking apples in the night and saw her black bangs and brown eyes. Vicky was not that far away. She had a rental one-bedroom place on Lexington Avenue not far from the corner of East 107th Street. Why sure you know the place.

She lived right above Joey Cantilino's Barber Shop. See that? Why sure you've been by a million times before — it's the place where all the white and Spanish kids sit on the front stoop, lined up for a buzz cut or one of those two-stage jobs you see around.

Vicky had thought of both Chinamen in tossing sleep. She was having mixed feelings. Vicky had been introduced to a guy who broke stock in the market. His name was Gary. He was handsome and dashing. Gary had asked for her number. Vicky put him off. Things were going too fast. She thought perhaps it might be best to jam on the brakes, and let her true feeling rise and come forward.

The six men went single file out of Central Park, passing between the stone blocks of Warrior's Gate. They could see across the road, and down the long aisle of Adam Clayton Powell Boulevard. The boulevard was dead at that hour.

Their bounty had been a plentiful harvest. They'd picked enough of crabapples for a winter's supply of preserves. The big Chinaman carried over sixty pounds of crabapples on his back. The rucksack was full to the brim chord, and he placed the thump line around his forehead. Arc lights were still above the footpaths of Central Park. Thin shrouds of fog vapor were hugging the Meer's water. From the wisping bank entered a singular duck, his paddling feet left behind a V-wake on the glass.

The guilty Chinaman rubbed his hand on the brown stone of Warrior's Gate. He'd seen a new conviction. Warrior's Gate had sparked the images in his mind. What they formed, was a perfect defense. He was exceedingly glad it had come to him, for now he had several new angles to unfold on the Angel of Gabriel.

He averted east down the sidewalk. He could see his first line of defense: the wall opening of Farmer's Gate was just down the lane. The gap in the wall spilled across the road into Malcolm X

Boulevard. The angel would have a hard time wiggling out of this one. A vision had come back to the skinny Chinaman.

This preface had happened the summer before. But because the skinny Chinaman was in the circle of turtles, it had come to him through the grapevine. He knew the whole store too well.

Evidently, she knew. Positively she did. The oddities of the odd, the novelties of the novel, and the ignorance of the ignorant, all are part of this story. The facts indicated the ignorance some will practice in order to obtain their needs by breaking the law. She knew all day long.

She had got pinched on the hot sidewalk of Malcolm X Boulevard. It was broad daylight. It was summer and New York City was under the heat wave. The park ranger in green uniform had grabbed the Cambodian lady by the arm and arrested her motion. She had been pushing a shopping cart full of turtles. There were one hundred six turtles in the cart. Thirty-two of them were already dead from heat stroke and suffocation.

The shopping cart had been covered with a green tarpaulin, served with stout lashing on the sides. But an observant pedestrian noticed all the feet squirming, when a passing bus fluttered the tarp's cover. The officials were notified. The park ranger had instructed the lady to avert her destination and start pushing back towards the Harlem Meer. In this kind of heat wave, turtles would need quenching in the pond very soon. Their shells had already begun to take on heat.

The turtle trapping ordeal had started the day before. The Cambodian set up her illegal operation on the south shore of Harlem Meer, in the fringe of cattail beds. She had learned many tricks in Cambodia, when they were starving to death. She chopped out a small lagoon in the cattails, swinging a machete sidearm from the hip, slashing at the reeds. A nice hiding place was born. The pond's bottom tapered into gravel beds. The schools of bluegills liked to fin over the gravel beds, and the sun angling through the water brought out the orange and blue scale plates on the fish. It was here she planted a giant cage trap, baited with chicken carcasses. This was a huge exchange, because the Cambodian lady liked chicken soup homemade from the carcass — but she liked turtle soup much better, and it was the kind of soup that stuck to your ribs in the winter.

The park ranger had marched her to the pond's shore. She looked very grave. It had just began sinking inside, that she had been apprehended. The summer heat had perhaps slowed her reactions. She could see down the road, and the consequences were appearing like sign in a high-speed chase along the highway. The sun angled through her hair, and it was very evident that the brown shafts had been altered with hair dye.

Inside the shopping cart was a fishnet, that consisted of telescopic nature. It was a very useful tool in this type of clandestine operation. The big hoop net comprised of three sections, secured by jam nuts and push pins.

"Open the net to full extension," ordered the park ranger. He snapped his fingers many times in the air.

The Cambodian lady quickly and expertly brought out the net. She socked the sections home in seconds. It was a sound net, and the handle of stippled aluminum was very rigid and could heft plenty of weight.

"Give me the net," instructed the park ranger. "You load the net, and I'll send 'um back out."

The Cambodian loaded turtles into the net. They were good size turtles. She used both hands, always skidding the shells across her belly, the wild claws raking thin air. They tried for five turtles every net load.

They put back in seventy-four turtles. One of the victims went belly up; its feet worked back and forth in feeble attempts to stay alive. The park ranger scooped it from the pond and flipped the net over on the grass bank. The turtle's legs went in a circuit a few more times, slow and then slower, until the turtle was dead. Slits showed over its eyes.

"Put in back in the cart," he told the lady. Now thirty-three turtles laid dead in the tumbled pile of victims.

"Tarp it over and let's get moving."

Several of the curious had gathered. They wanted to know all kinds of questions. Two boys were looking into the shopping cart at dead turtles. The youngest boy reached through the cage and tugged a foot. The soft pads gave when the boy squeezed. His action aroused nothing. The painted turtle was stone dead. The yellow markings showed bold under the blue sky.

"Keep quiet. Get going. This is confidential park business," the ranger barked. "Get away. Get going. Clear the way!"

Just then, a woman of perhaps thirty years, an over blonde with loose curls set up in a hair iron, stuck her semi-classical face past the crowd. She was dressed in a high-end running suit in salmon pink, and sported top dollar running shoes in burgundy silk-like cloth, adorned with silver glitter. That kind of outfit not counting the sneakers, would run an easy five hundred bucks, and was only exclusively available at Pierre Pascal, a chic designer clothing store in the garment district of New York City. The kind of people you saw there were Cindy Crawford. On certain occasions, Ivanka Trump had been seen browsing.

She had a terrible reputation. Not many people liked the woman.

Now that she recently had been turned into an instantaneous trust fund baby, even more disliked her. She was rude. She was spoiled and pompous. She'd never worked for anything, never suffered, and appreciated almost nothing except the limelight. Her only friend was Pauline, a hanger-on to grandpa, who after the old timer croaked, would leave her a bundle and set up Pauline as another member of his T.F.B. club.

The trust fund baby opened her big mouth in that round semi-classical face, and started screaming across Central Park, "Seize her! Arrest her! Take that woman to the nearest jail! Arrest her!" Her face flushed to beet red; and around her neck was an enormous gold necklace, the kind you see on movie stars and news anchors. The lady took off her Pierre Pascal running jacket and stomped it on the pockmarked sidewalk in a temper tantrum. The wild stampede of her sneakers had scuffed a hole right through and ruined the jacket. "Remove this anarchy from my world at once!" she ranted into the heat wave.

"Holy Christ lady…take it easy," the park ranger told her in a calm voice. "Everything is under control." Everybody in the assembly could see the turtle trapper was under apprehension, and the trust fund baby must have been staging a publicity stunt.

A local cruiser on NYPD pulled up on the walk. The park ranger asked for assistance in breaking the crowd. While the police officer disbanded the crowd, many of them looking for new gossip, the park ranger led the Cambodian lady under the grove of dawn redwoods and out to the bustle of Malcolm X Boulevard.

The park ranger had a very important tactical decision to make. Thirty-three dead turtles in the Brooklyn landfill would do no good. It would not be a humane quality in the end. Their lives would show no purpose. He let her take the victims. But he rung her up on the arrest ticket for all 106 turtles. The park ranger felt he'd made the right move, for the Lord would not approve of waste. The woman disappeared into the congested background of Malcolm X Boulevard.

The judge went easy on her, or so that as far as the book would allow. If it would have been an entrepreneur selling shells and meat on the black market, he would have thrown the book at them. They would have paid an easy $125 per turtle, and they would have paid square before being set free.

But the judge was smart enough to read between the lines. He could see her life history in front of his eyes on immigration papers. It was also, however, because circuit Judge Cuatro Sanjurjo knew and remembered his roots.

Cuatro was Americanized. He was born in the United States. But he remembered the stories from his grandfather Don Sanjurjo, about the family history around the streets of Madrid. Don Sanjurjo had once lived in a white stucco, six-unit row house on the el gueto, on a cobble street out front, and a dirt alley with trash cans hugging the back porch. They lived a lot on soups of gazpacho, but you know, living on cucumber and tomato soup cannot cut it forever. So right off the bat, Judge Sanjurjo could see into the Columbian lady's world, standing now before him with her head down for getting pinched on turtles.

It was a common practice for Don Sanjurjo and a wide selection of the neighborhood, to buy dead bulls after their blood had been spilled in the bullfight. That kind of fresh meat for people on the edge went a long way for eight pesetas a pound.

There are many things one needs to know about bullfighting. This heritage of blood and sword is cloaked in mysterious lore. Some of the things nobody thought about were that you never saw blonde men with blue eyes in the bull rings of Spain. Those colors were not around, because it was not in the gene pool. Light blue eyes would always be squinting in the beating sun. All the cuadrilla had brown eyes. The same cast was in the matador's eye sockets. Wild chestnut eyes. Even the madrilenos, those gypsy kids hired on to pull on the bull's tail, had eyes that sparkled with excitement and the rush of danger through the pools of brown.

Some of the worst sticking happened in the nocturnals of mid-week fighting. They always saved the best bulls, and the youngest climbing stars of Madrid, for the matinee bullfights on the weekend, when they were assured of a full gate. That's when people seemed to get the most from their money, and the cleanest kills.

The nocturnals were a different story. The brown eyes took on vague information in the gangs of artificials. The arc lights were murder in the picador's eyes, whirling around on horseback in the blinding lights, their boots in the box-stirrups driving hard into the night. It was the same things for the major league baseball players in a playoff series, when for a few innings they needed to face the setting sun, then play into the night shifts, with the eyes trying to redress the effects of night vision in the sea of floodlights.

There are many things to know when buying dead bulls. It seemed you always just about got bad sticking in the nocturnals. The hind quarters were all jabbed up, and the picadors coming on with plenty of gas with bad sticking on account of those blinding lights, had the prime cuts on the back straps all gouged up. Don't think for a minute that the cuadrilla with all the throwing of the red fletched banderillas never did any damage, because five darts under a bull's hide can congeal a terrible waste of meat in the blood clots. So then, you could still buy from the nocturnals, but you needed a sharp eye, and keep a lot of the money in your pocket and bid low.

Across the street from Don Sanjurjo's house, looking across the plaza laid in white cobbles, you could see the circumference of the bull arena looming. After the main event, after the crowds dispersed, the mules dragged the dead bulls from the arena past and through the twin planken doors, plowing furrows in the orche soils; and when they hit the plaza the mule chains made a clink-clink-clink sound across the white stones, and it was common to see alley dogs hot on the blood trail.

The poor stood around with axes and herdsmen's knives, rubbing the coins in their pockets, waiting to see what their money could buy. The prices were extremely low, and nobody ever weighed a bull. It was all by calculated guess on the low side. And the operators never charged for the guts, heads and horns, and it was standard practice to deduct the weight of the first leg-joint to the hoof, which was considered waste. But little was waste in the el gueto, and the bull's hoofs were seen much like the delicacy of pig's feet. Another inside bonus held close to the chest by buyers including Grandpa Don Sanjurjo, was that bull's brisket smoked for hours inside homemade smoking chambers over smoldering wood, fell apart in your mouth. A favorite pastime on hot summer nights — and don't forget just about every day was a Sunday for the poor who could not find work — was searing up brisket and drinking red wine. Grandpa Don had filled Cuatro's head with a story of one sweltering evening, the fire's smoke cutting back the mosquitos, when everything went a little too far, and they tied on a good buzz. It was the gayety of the gay, and maybe too much you know, because his friend Pablo Santana had a good glow and was pulling scalding brisket so fast off the grill and putting it down, he'd burned his lips and mouth so bad, that he needed to refrain from oral sex for almost a full month.

Nobody knew if the story was true. It was told many, many times over. Cuatro told it around the school yard in Brooklyn, and as far as storytelling went, it was a giant hit for boys coming into puberty. None of them knew what end was up but laughed like seasoned professionals.

So then, Judge Cuatro Sanjurjo had more than a good idea what was going on. Staying in touch with the roots of his family tree, let him know about everything. Cuatro was also fond of verse memorizing in blocks of poetry, and had read many times over by William Carlos Williams —

> *"My surface is myself.*
> *Under which*
> *To witness, youth is*
> *buried. Roots?*
> *Everybody has roots."*

The courtroom was jammed with hard-left activists, and they were out for blood. You could see it in their eyes, the ugly glare of predisposition weighing heavily; and in the back of their minds, they were already spinning the nomenclature of pet names for the dead turtles. They amounted to some of the narrowest minded people on earth.

But Judge Cuatro Sanjurjo would have none of it, because he'd been on circuit for over twenty years, and he'd seen his share of sad faces and crying jags from the face put-on people, looking to swing a verdict by staging effects of emotional rescue. He could see through them like glass.

Judge Cuatro Sanjurjo went as easy on the Cambodian as the black robe's oath would give. But in the same breath, he knew his sentence must also impose a lesson. The lady needed more Americanization. He slapped her with a fine of six hundred dollars for the first major offense of turtle trapping. Payments on installments were acceptable. The Cambodian lady paid her fines by cash money in person. At thirty dollars a month, she had walked over to the courthouse house on twenty separate occasions and shelled out the green bills. Four months shy into her second year of payments, she was paid in full.

The guilty Chinaman, lugging his pail of crabapples and shouldering the aluminum ladder, followed the other five Chinamen up West 110th Street. With the story of the Cambodian turtle poacher fresh in his mind, he was just about on cloud nine. He was enormously pleased on this new state of cleverness, for he'd just hooked up with an accomplice in turtle trapping. It showed a pattern. Maybe those religious guys up around the crest of Morningside Park, and the Gabriel the Angel, would listen with a little more heart this time around.

The Chinaman was so thrilled he'd almost certainly stumbled on his own perfect defense, he thumped his skinny ribcage with a cupped fist. He instantly felt strong as King Kong.

But all the inside angles in the world, would never tell anybody the true hardships the Cambodian turtle trapper had endured. Not the guilty Chinaman with an inside scoop on the grape vine of turtle trapping, the shallow money queen who became an instantaneous trust fund baby after somebody loaded checked out, the contingent of hard-left animal activists pointing fingers with cat fur clung to their slacks, or Judge Cuatro Sanjurjo who was staring dead blank at her immigration papers stamped 1977. None of them had a clue.

They were some of the most blood spilling bastards on the earth. They had hurt her bad. All of them were more ruthless than any fleet of Vikings, because they executed their own people. They practiced autogenocide. Their name was Khmer Rouge, and the regime of rebels was led by Pol Pot. The security apparatus of the Khmer Rouge was called Santebal, and the head thug calling the shots was Comrade Duch. It would be safe to proclaim, that the nearly three million people that were killed by his orders, considered him the first cousin of Satan. Their goal was to indoctrinate all farmers into the field of agrarian socialism, a desire infatuated by the communist traits of Maoism and Stalinism.

Once upon a time, Tuol Sleng was an ordinary high school. A place where Cambodian children could be enlightened. But Comrade Duch seized the school and turned its walls into an interrogation prison. The Tuol Sleng Centre was coined another name in history — the horror house of S-21.

Over sixteen thousand people passed through S-21. But eyewitnesses of the hideous murders had confessed, that only seven of them are known to survive.

The Cambodian lady's family got caught in the meat grinder. The Santebal showed up at sunrise in the tiny hamlet of Kampong Spen Province. Chickens scattered in all directions around the village, clucking wild, terrified from the rebel's trucks barreling in and slinging caked mud. Brandishing AK-47's and holstering ugly tempers, the Khmer Rouge rebels savagely forced the village people on their knees, begging for mercy.

The Khmer Rouge nearly completely obliterated her nucleus of family and relatives. She knew for certain twenty-eight of them had been exterminated.

Her brother Chakara was on the list. The case-hardened rebels force ran the entire village for three miles Navy Seal style, just for the fun of watching people suffer. Whoever dropped out in the tropical heat waves got a punch in the face and a rifle butt across ribs with the order, "Roksaa kar phalsa btau r! — Keep moving!" At the junction of Route 5, they loaded up the innocents for questioning, and trucked them to Phnom Penh. During the interrogation inside Tuol Sleng Centre, her brother was found guilty of wearing eyeglasses and reading foreign books. Those two items would cost him his very life.

Along with the thousands of others, Chakara was executed on the mud flats of Choeung Ek. The communist dictators of Khmer Rouge in order to save bullets, executed the victims with pickaxes. The screams filled the forest outside Phnom Penh. Those still squirming on the ground in fetal position, fallen from the blows of swinging steel, were clubbed with herdsman clubs fashioned from the forest. Many of them hemorrhaging from the teeth, died a very slow death. The sea of corpses, with rigor mortis set in their grey death, were shoved like rodents into mass graves. Some guy who smoked cigars and drove the old bulldozer, shoved dirt over the graves.

It's a good thing the Cambodian lady was a good liar. She had to tell the communists with a straight face she had no confidence in the Catholic Church. Because if you got caught with a crucifix, your fly infested carcass would be with the others in the bone pile. She manufactured sentence blocks that she worshipped Comrade Duch and would love to set example by following his wish. That kind of falsehood told with the glee of zest, sold the communists. They spared her life, for seemingly ulterior motives — it was impossible to read into the logic of radicalized fanatics, who wore sarcastic grins during interrogation.

The Cambodian lady's reform went well. She paid her fines for turtle trapping on a regular basis. She often thought of the over-blonde in the salmon pink running suit form Pierre Pascal, who bore public insults on her in front of the park ranger. Thinking of her was like a private joke. If the Khmer Rouge ever laid eyes on a piece like that, the salmon pink running suit and the burgundy running shoes adorned with silver glitter and topped off with that semi-classical face, there would have been the sperm of over twenty separate men inside her before two sunrises. And because she worshipped money and gave up faith a long time back which would have given her hope and love, she would have cracked. Caught in the hot flashes of hysteria inside S-21, the communists would have goaded her with excruciating torture, then marched her down the row of mad executioners where the spartan blows of pickaxes struck home. If only the over-blonde in loose curls knew about torture. Then that spoiled trust fund baby in pink would have known the true meaning of anarchy, and kept her big shallow mouth shut around New York City.

The flashback of her day in court for turtle trapping, played on her too. She could still see the angry faces and ugly scowls of the hard-left animal activists; those in the front three rows ready to string her up. She felt pity on them. They operated on one-track minds, focused on the thong of morning dog walkers in Central Park. If only they had lived under dictatorship in places like Kompong Xiem, they would have known something. The activists would have very little worry about cats and dogs, because there was few around. People had eaten most of them. The Khmer Rouge had virtually forced the complete population of Cambodia into social mobilization of agrarian socialism, where over one million people died in the experiment. When your ribs and cheek bones have become focal points, anything that moved became fair game. That included dogs and cats in a stew pot.

Judge Cuatro Sanjurjo's influence on the Cambodian lady went extremely well. She became Americanized. She had bought a genuine New York State fishing license and had taken up fishing in the Hudson River. Several giant carp were caught on corn. She was immensely proud of the two striped bass she'd caught that spring, live-lining herring from the banks — rapacious linesiders that tipped the scale over thirty pounds. She proudly pushed them on ice inside her shopping cart, up and over the sidewalks, all the way across the West Side to her stomping grounds of Malcolm X Boulevard.

Living in the United States was grand. But the most appreciation the Cambodian lady got out of living in New York City, was that she could practice her faith in broad daylight. A world where she could become a Christian again in the holy sphere of worship, and not forced to pray behind dark curtains.

Every Sunday morning, the Cambodian lady came through the brown stone of Farmer's Gate into Central Park, a lone figure dressed in her Sunday best of a white canvas smock. She liked pressing along the pond, watching the bluegills finning in the shallows. Then the lone figure sauntered east, angling toward 230 East 90th Street, where she passed through the ornamental iron gate and up the stone stairs past the heavy doors into Our Lady of Good Council Church.

She never missed a Sabbath morning mass, not even her first winter long ago still on U.S. Visa papers, when the city got walloped with sixteen inches, and after trudging in along the snow drifted walks, she was one of the seven figures for mass.

There were many things, strangers learned from the Cambodian.

Short street conversation with big meaning. They could find out about Pan Ron, the lovely woman who got executed because she had talent in song writing and singing. As the story went down, the Khmer Rouge tricked her into belting out a tune, and then killed her in cold blood.

New Yorkers scratched their heads, after finding out of 2,680 monks who once held down eight monasteries, only 70 monks were still exchanging oxygen after the dust settled. The rest were executed for devoting a lifetime to kneel and pray before Buddha.

But none of the strangers, and few others, knew the Cambodian lady's deepest secret. In the flashing seconds of time before the Khmer Rouge pounced on her brother Chakara, both of them still inside the hut, he had lobbed underhand, his string of rosary beads to his sister. The white pearl beads and silver crucifix twirled in flight, the hank of beads coming out of coil; her hand clutched the beads tight. The rebels were still advancing the hut with angry muzzles streaming forward, when she stuffed the white rosary into a sunken earthen vault. Hot for blood, the rosary went without detection.

Now, after all these years, the Cambodian lady clutched the white rosary with the silver cross. It was all that was left. Most everything else was dead. She grasped the white beads, and often inside Our Lady of Good Council Church, dedicated the decades to the twenty-eight of her executed family, and the soul of her brother Chakara. Like she told everybody that crossed her path, living in the United States was grand.

The six Chinamen humped crabapples up West 110th Street. The yellow ginkgo leaves still were there. They were spattered across the walk, the yellow fans of leaves resting on the dove grey cement. Oblivious to the spray of color on the grey pathway, the six figures humped red apples, each man in his own world, the new day breaking, the pickers moving toward homeward bound.

Hop, Hong, and Chang were completely exhausted. They were famished too. None of them could remember, when they worked straight for over two hours. Beads of sweat ran down Hop's forehead. He'd been lugging two 5-gallon buckets full of red apples. Lagging behind his comrades, he skidded the galvanized buckets to rest, and quickly brought out a fold of waxed paper from his pocket. Inside was ten saltine crackers spread with peanut butter and jam. He divided the crackers between Hong and Chang, after he ate six in a row for himself. Nothing ever tasted so good. None of them had eaten T-bone in years. Their mindset was on crackers and cheap stuff. They offered nothing to the other three Chinamen. The snack seemed to afford Chang with a good boost of energy, and he accelerated up the walk with bursts of energy.

The big Chinaman was thinking far ahead. He'd spoken to his uncle Professor Billy Chen in recent days. The professor revealed it would be another four months abroad. His photo shoots were going well in the lower villages of the Greater Khingan Mountains. That pushed the free living in the Cathedral Building just about into March. They would be living high most of the winter. In accessory, he'd got another call from the lazy Chinaman's landlord. The smoke damage had been repaired. Fresh paint and new carpet were installed. In a few more days, the freeloaders would be out on their ears. Things were looking ahead for the big Chinaman.

The skinny Chinaman was thinking of Vicky. Nothing but Vicky, Vicky, Vicky. The revolutions never ceased. He could see her face. Touch her soft skin. Taste Vicky's lips. Remember the long kisses. The skinny Chinaman was certain he'd found something special. It was too bad, in the next two weeks he'd get the axe and have a broken heart, all because of a smooth talker who broke stocks.

The guilty Chinaman plodded along. The aluminum ladder was biting his shoulder. He was licking his chops. The story of the Cambodian turtle trapper resonated well. He had drummed up positive proof, others too had committed wrongful acts. The Cambodian lady had exceeded him by great numbers, in the offense of procuring live turtles from the Harlem Meer. He felt his defense might hold up.

Other ideas surfaced. In the last faint wisps of fog, another angle came to him. The evidence was some 270 million years old, a living descendant from the prehistoric age. Ginkgo trees have been traced to fossil remains in shale stone. Scattered about the north end of Central Park, stooped in the early dawn, were figures of women. Two here, one there, a lone figure over there by the bicycle path on the grass island. Some of the women were Vietnamese. Other pairs were Chinese. A lone Tibetan, very old with character road maps across her face, hunkered under the ginkgo trees. All of them were picking nuts. Gathering the fall harvest was in their blood. It went back many generations. Picking was second nature. They knew all the lore and tales about them. The white pulp itself is poison. Even gorging on the nuts can have bad side effects. Some believe the ginkgo nuts have the magic of love potion. Why sure the men of the house were popping a few for aphrodisiac. Didn't you know that? I'm surprised you never heard about them. But what really called the women to the forest for picking, was sprinkling the white kernels into a vegetarian dish known as Buddha's Delight. At their age, they considered it good as sex.

The women picked diligently. They reminded the casual observer of robins in search of worms. They pecked around, moving in quest. In the fairy light of the new dawn, their canvas totes were already packed to the brim. The woman had procured small carts for giving the sacks of nuts a ride home. The carts were the size of suitcase buggies seen racing around airline terminals.

The guilty Chinaman averted over his shoulder and watched six Vietnamese ladies come through Warrior's Gate. They marched in single file. They moved with purpose. Their canvas sacks, teaming with white nuts, were cinched with pull cords. The six ladies moved with a good clip of speed across the street. Two of the pickers came into view. One of the women pulled the cart backwards. She felt steady in that position and experienced more power in pulling. They followed the clan of six Vietnamese up Adam Clayton Powell Boulevard.

The old Tibetan lady had picked out too. The harvest horn of her white canvas sack, served with Spruce green piping, was rounded with the white ginkgo nuts with yellow markings in the pith pockets. The old lady straightened, as if to offer a symbolic salute to the rising sun. She was in absolutely no rush to go anyplace. Living was everything. On the banks of the Harlem Meer, grew a naturalized bed of Japanese Anemone, commonly known as Windflower. Their ruby pink brackets stood soldier still in the cracks of dawn. Their yellow stamens showed bold against the colored petals. A ruby throated hummingbird appeared in the garden; his wings beat at supersonic speed. The green on the bird's plume marked sharp against the rose-pink flowers. The hummingbird pressed its long beak past the yellow stamens, collecting nature's nectar. The old Tibetan watched with glee. She felt a wash of some kind of supernatural excitement.

Nobody ever found out if she had premonition. She could have experienced fate. Maybe she was enjoying still beating the odds of numbers. Nevertheless, on the seventh day of the next Chinese New Year, she was dead.

It was a hell of a thing alright. The old lady had gone full circle. As a young woman at the height of her child-bearing age, she escaped over the towering Himalaya Mountains from Tibet to Nepal. Her escape covered over thirty days on the run. Inside-out people had printed papers for her in Nepal. She paid dearly. A jet liner whisked her to the United States. She lived a happy life of freedom, not shackled by the chains of oppression, and being told what to think. But her wish was to return to the old country after death. Three days after she died, they ran her corpse through Swidonovich Crematory up in the Bronx and flew her remains back to Tibet in a copper urn.

Relatives gathered at the airport and escorted her ashes back to Shensa Dzong. She was born in the village. That was a long time ago. It was before China pounced on Tibet. Along a small brook in the village grew a bed of orange Oriental poppies. The bright orange poppies possessed the vice of man's fix, known as opium. They were stunningly beautiful flowers. They sifted the old lady's ashes into the flower beds. It was a very satisfying experience. They cultivated the old lady into the soil with hoes. It was truly refreshing to know that every summer when the poppies bloomed, the old lady would be around them and never go away, much like the eternal birds and bees.

The six Chinamen pressed west toward Morningside Park. The big Chinaman was still walking point. The three lazy Chinamen closed on his heels. Hop offered to carry the heavy backpack and give the big Chinaman a break. Hong tried telling jokes. Chang traded step for step with the big Chinaman, walking at his side and smiling up at the big man, rubbing his shoulder as if all of them were locked in the bonds of indelible friendship. But none of it was genuine and from the heart. It was only a butter-up job. The big Chinaman had promised them beforehand, if the free loaders picked well, if they helped in the canning process of preserves… he'd give them four jars of crabapple jelly to take home. The lazy Chinamen were only making certain the big Chinaman lived up to his word.

The thought of homemade preserves, almost put Hop and Hong and Chang over the top. They'd been living on cheap jam for too long. Life was too short. They moved very rapid and with purpose after the big Chinaman made the promise. They had clipped coupons like it was going out of style for original Skippy chunky peanut butter and four-boxes to a customer on genuine Saltine crackers.

They hoarded so much free newspapers from the recycle tubs along the walk, they had enough coupons for 20 boxes of the real thing on Saltine crackers. Talk about living. They could hardly contain anticipation. The thought of eating plates of top-shelf Saltines with homemade jelly and genuine Skippy peanut butter, was almost too much for them. Their dreams ran wild with imagination into the morning.

The guilty Chinaman was feeling swell. Gee, you should have seen him clasp his fingers and crack his knuckles. Say, his confidence was all over him. In his own mind, he'd just manufactured another bullet-proof line of defense. He doubted very seriously that none of those big-time religious guys on the knoll would be able to wiggle out on this one. The woman harvesting out ginkgo nuts was only living off the land. It was the Creator's plan for man to harvest from the world. Apples and oranges and ginkgo nuts, turtles and chickens and bushels of eared corn, must have been on the Lord's list. The guilty Chinaman clicked his heels. He rubbed his hands very brisk, with the serum of bliss. He wondered with his ego sailing high in the clouds, that perhaps his deeds would be likened to the next Perry Mason. He was certain now, that with one eye opened, he could successfully pass any kind of bar exam.

Off in the distance, the six Chinamen could see the forest of Morningside Park. Just then, a sudden wash of emotion fell over the guilty Chinaman. Out of the blue he felt very fragile and small. He realized that angel guy blowing the horn must be watching him. He moved up behind the face of a building. Nothing subdued. He darted behind a tree trunk. None of the sensation vanished. He understood then, the angel on the roof could see through buildings, and had the vision of Superman. He threw in the cards. He tossed up his hands. The guilty Chinaman knew then he was at the mercy of what kind of verdict the big rollers on hill wanted to dish out. His logic seemed to go out an invisible window.

The Chinaman streamed ahead. Orange rays of Indian summer sun splashed across Morningside Park. A man in the outfield of the ball diamond was twisting himself in some kind of yoga move. He seemed to be worshipping thin air.

Chang looked over to his old bench. The bench was still there. He could see himself playing horn on the green bench. He made plans on the spot, during that afternoon after taking a good morning power nap, he'd descend into Morningside Park and let a few notes rip.

The six men began to ascend the stone stairs. The big Chinaman held his position. The others followed. Off the flight of stairs in the dappled shade, three cats were stalking on the ledge outcrops. They hunted with silent steps over the green beds of ivy, and the cat closest to the Chinaman, a white cat with black spots, looked at Hop through his puzzled blue eyes. The cat looked wild with matted fur. All the cats appeared to have sickness. The wild streaks had returned back inside of them. They looked like red foxes you see around, confused in the last stages of rabies. All of them were feral cats, and they lived in the ledges of Morningside Park.

They were ruthless killers, cold blood thirsty cats. They had racked up a notorious body count in the park. Since the May rains had started pushing flowers, they had killed 26 fledging doves, 48 chipmunks, scores of songbirds, and 6 baby cotton tail rabbits. They walked around like they owned the place, because they did, and had no natural enemy that could take them out. All the dogs were on the leash law. White men had exterminated the bald eagles long ago. The three cats killed at will and without mercy. It would be very safe to proclaim they enjoyed every second.

The guilty Chinaman paused on the stairs. He looked hard on one of the cats, a silver-grey male spread in the duff. The cat was guarding a fresh kill. The victim was a hermit thrush, its head gnawed and severed. In the stealth of feline moves, crouched and poised, the silver-grey cat had leaped from the ledges, and pounced on the docile bird that was feeding on spilled popcorn. There was no struggle. The bird had been caught in the hot flashes of panic and took its medicine. The claws had sunk deep. A trail of brown feathers was scattered down the slope highlighting the murder scene.

It was a crying shame alright. In life, the hermit thrush was a beautiful bird. He often perched in the forest, its tell-tale sign of its reddish tail in flickered movement, singing its clear, ethereal notes across Morningside Park. Many found likeness of the hermit thrush's song notes to a flutelike sensation. But now the noble bird was dead, the splotched breast plumes fluttering in the breeze, a prize of the feral cat. And the truth of the matter was that very little of the bird's flesh would ever serve a purpose, because it was killed for mere fun.

The feral cats were past reform. It would be best to give them euthanasia. The animal activists that tried stringing up the Cambodian turtle trapper might tell you different. But they were dead wrong. They missed the frontpage column in the Chicago Times, where the feral cat still driven by wild streaks was adopted into a loving home, but clawed out Regina Blackwelder's right eye. She lost her sight on the morning in her playpen, four days after her 2nd birthday. And it was sure an awful thing because the little girl would need to spend the rest of her life half-blind, all because the activists could not get hold of their emotions and used Regina Blackwelder as a pawn so the feral cats could escape the gas chamber.

In the new dismal sadness, the guilty Chinaman tried dodging bullets. He reminded Buddha that he never killed for sport. He collected food for survival. He had the red apples in the bucket as proof. He looked up the staircase. Time was running out. Looking up through the forest limbs, he could see the outline of the angel guy blowing the horn. He went up the stairs at a good clip.

The guilty Chinaman was completely at ease. He'd tried every angle known to mankind on the religious guys. He'd pulled all the plugs, twisted logic this way and that way. A strange calm was all over him, because he had come clean, and in confessing he had spilled his heart. There was nothing else to try. He'd taken all his medicine standing up like a man. In his back pocket was the virtue of fortitude, just in case things got rough up on the hill.

The guilty Chinaman mulled things over. He prepared for his last chance to mend fences. He reminded the religious guys he was really a good guy. He worked hard and lived humble. He never stole money, never had brushes with the law. That at the very core was a simple man who always reported first to the religious guys. He'd never strayed from his faith. The guilty Chinaman's only hope was that the big guys on the hill would give back some love.

They would. They possessed supernatural understanding. The Eternal Powers knew and saw everything. They could see light years ahead. Everything had been written in the tablets long ago. They could see through the guilty Chinaman's soul. It was crystal clear. He would pass all the tests. The Lord had seen plenty of worse examples — men who sold their souls on the insider's racket of forecasting profits on the New York Stock Exchange, surfaced as evidence. All the religious guys truly loved him. His action of faith had saved him. The guilty Chinaman already had a free ride into the pearly gates.

But he never had any way of knowing these things. The guilty Chinaman lacked the power of seeing into the future. He couldn't fathom what those guys were thinking on the other side of the mirror. He climbed the stairs. The aluminum ladder clinked on his shoulder. The bucket of red apples tugged on his hand. He still was just a soldier of faith, plodding along.

All the Chinamen went over the crest of Morningside Park, and passed single file through the break in the wall. The intersection of West 113th Street and Morningside Drive was dead still. Nothing moving. No traffic. The priest was not present in the church window. All the circumstances were in place for a simplehearted conservation with the Lord.

The other five Chinamen went up the road. Hop, Hong, and Chang were still on the big Chinaman's heels, working him for the four free jars of jelly. The guilty Chinaman had stayed behind. The looming presence of Saint John the Devine Church dwarfed the

Chinaman. All the seven crosses and Gabriel the angel was in place.

The guilty Chinaman had spun in his tracks and looked across the bluff of New York City. The sun had climbed. The guilty Chinaman blessed his forehead in proper fashion, not rushing, touching his fingers to form the cross. He felt the warmth of his fingers making the holy round across his visage.

The guilty Chinaman faced the orange wafer of sun. In the sun's beam, a flock of black birds disembarked toward the outskirts. The Chinaman drew a last breath and promised the religious guys no matter how much saliva ran under his tongue, he would refrain from any more turtle trapping in the public sector, because he knew the angel of Gabriel could see through skyscrapers and around corners, and that Buddha could disintegrate his blue Mardi Gras beads with the blink of an eye.

The jackass was lying in the road. He was paralyzed. His spine had been severed by gunfire. He had been moving. His lungs were filling with blood. Some of the blood ran out his nostrils on the cobble blocks.

It was smashing. They chose revenge. The only more cheerful than the Jews were the Poles, and then the Russians themselves. The Jews remembered from their dreams how the screaming of their people standing nude in the chamber seemed muffled, but not the terror. The Poles accounted that their people attacked on horses, some of them pure white, were crucified by German machine guns and cannon fire. The battlefield was simply littered with dead horses and Poles crumpled in all the figures of death. The Russians were still in the flashes of bad blood because of everything getting wholesale slaughter from Moscow to the border line and everything blown up and in the rubble heaps.

So when the Russians got the Germans in their U-shaped ambush, which is the deadliest of all ambushes of the ground forces, the Russian commander said to his men, "Remember what they did to our people, and the German's sperm inside our women without their permission. When we get inside, shoot anything that moves."

A German was looking through a blown-out window framed by red brick and seemed to be waving something. A block headed Russian pulled up and shot him through his forehead. The blood ran down over his eye socket and dripped off his high cheek bone and seeped into the pulverized masonry fragments. His camaraderie jumped up over the rubble with a white flag. The Red army captured 90,000 Germans. They death marched them back to Siberia. They worked them to the bone in freezing cold with no night blankets. Less than 5,000 ever made it back alive to the native soil. The payments of revenge can be served with the bluntest kind of tool.

—Stephen Deck,
written the morning of 9/11 in the year 2014

Field of Dreams

I had stopped by the side of the road to pick berries. Nice fresh strawberries. They grew in a boxed field of banked loam in the full sun. Figures were picking and straight out from me was a lady in a white sun hat picking into a cardboard box.

But before I even read the picking rates nailed to the farm wagon, the farmer was trying to push sweet peas on me. There were two farmers under the deep shade canopy leaning on the farm wagon, and it was the skinny one with a few gaps in his teeth doing the talking. The other man was husky and the silent kind. They both had on ballcaps; those cheap polyester hats they picked up for free someplace along the line. The same kind of hats you can see lined up down the bar of the VFW club on Sunday afternoon with the Red Sox on the set and brown bottles down the bar and the farmers talking field talk. Even with the heavy shade the hat made for the skinny farmer, I could see his eyes had BB pupils from squinting down on the field sun.

"How much for U-pick by the quart?" I asked them.

"Listen," the skinny farmer said right off the bat, "I can give you one heck of a deal on sweet peas."

"I've come for berries."

"Hey, listen Sonny, you don't understand." He put a hand on my shoulder and spun me a half-turn to face across the road. There was another field in full flush and even a city slicker could tell the foliage was different. "That field of sweet peas is ready now Sonny and in two days they will get tough on me."

"How much?" I asked.

"I'll give you one heck of a deal," said the skinny farmer who had started walking in nervous circles.

"Well how much?"

"Just a deal," he said. "You go fill the box and then we'll talk price."

Those river bottom farmers. You can never figure that bunch. They have a chance all summer to practice their lines around the roadside stands and at the same time fill the box with cash money. The two characters I stumbled upon were stuffing it into a green ceramic cookie jar that had its front casted into a bullfrog.

"I'm heading out into the strawberry patch," I told them. The serious farmer who smiled when his buddy came out with a line, gave me two woven baskets.

"Any place in the field is good picking, but head toward the middle and then back to the woods line for the best."

It was mid-morning and very still and getting there. Birds were still singing in the high silver maples along the river. It had not come on yet. I walked the cart road for speed and then cut up a row towards the woods. There were no footprints in the dry loam. The picking should be good around here. I bent over and spread open the plants. Sure enough, the plants were plastered with bright red strawberries. I had just started picking with both hands when the skinny farmer shouted across the field.

"Hey there Sonny! These aren't the kind of berries that jump into your basket — you have to pick this variety!" I could hear them both laughing across the field and could not hold back myself.

The strawberry field was necked to a thin band of woods and through the break in the background was a farm pond with spending yellow flowers of lily pads and it was there, a man in a wood rowboat was casting plugs. I hunched over and watched the man fish. He cast a red and white swimmer plug. It gurgled on the mirror waters next to the pads. When he retrieved the lure to the tippets, drops fell from the treble hooks and spattered the surface.

All the women had picked out. The field was empty. I picked alone and along and filled the second basket. You could feel it coming on soon. I could hear more chatter and the farmers were talking alright. They were telling the last lady customer something. But the distance was too great and what was being said I was missing. I moved at once, both baskets in hands, cutting over maybe twenty rows until things got clearer. I could not believe what they were trying to feed her.

"You've got to be kidding," she said with a grin. The lady was sitting behind the wheel in her boxy green Volvo wagon.

"It's the best you ever tasted," the skinny one was telling her. "Honest — I would not trade roasted squirrel for anything."

"Only the hind quarters though," the serious farmer added.

"I'm not sure about that dish for me," she told the farmers with a smile. She slipped it into gear and putted off down the lane.

I was sure. The serious farmer said it was so and that was enough. But I'd heard more other days before down the road from the other farmers. They'd all lived and farmed and suffered through the Great Depression and I was certain they ate their share of wild game for the price of a 2¢ long rifle bullet.

By the time I reached deep for a few bills for the berries, their money pot had bills from all angles sticking out over the rim. They kept the change separate, in a cigar box. They cashed me out and then we started on the peas.

After they knew I was serious about the sweet peas, they made up a solid price off the top of their heads. But only by the quart. The price on the big cardboard box for U-pick was always open for moods and dickering. I told them, no matter how good the peas were, that many would be too much. So then, we settled on a dollar for every quart. You could hump them as high as you wanted. I crossed the road and began picking. It was easy picking. The peas were hanging everyplace. The thought crossed my mind for the big box, but what are you going to do with that many pods of sweet peas?

It was coming on strong now. My hat brim pulled in the sweat. Some ran off my nose. For some reason I thought of Billy Tyne out of the blue, how in his last moments he hits the sideband and warns the rest of the fishing fleet from doomed seas of the Flemish Cap: *It's commin' on boys, and it's comin' on strong.* I capped off my basket and moved back across the blacktop. You could feel the heat rising.

We cashed out and I put the full baskets on the truck's seat. I made a nest around the baskets with my old sweatshirt. Farm roads can pitch a basket in a heap. The skinny farmer just couldn't get enough. He moved from the shade and across the sun splashed grass and back into the cover under the huge sugar maple. That shade had kept my truck from baking out. He needed to tell me about the stand specials coming soon. That the heads of cabbage were well formed and just about ready.

"You eat golabki?" he wanted to know.

"Sure."

"That's good. Come back in two weeks and we'll have plenty of cabbage leaves so you can roll some up," he told me.

I could see the heat was getting the best of the farmers. It's not like they could take it like young men. You could see the white of their T-shirts, casted over by dust plumes, were sopping heavy with sweat. That the silent farmer was already sitting on the wagon's bed and brought a blue hanky to his forehead.

"You come back anytime Sonny," said the skinny farmer full of jokes. It was funny though, all of a sudden in the heat he looked kind of serious.

"Don't worry and keep working on those new berries that jump. That's what I'm looking for," I told him in jest.

I pulled out in the heat. A huge plume of dust rose from the cart path. I could see it in my mirror rising. It came on strong. I wicked some burning sweat from my eyes and ate a pea pod cold. But for the life of me, I couldn't figure where two guys would get the notion for roasting squirrels in that kind of heat. It fit the day though, and all I could think of was a campfire in the deep woods banked with coals and giving heat to the blackened skillet.

A short story written in a single sitting, in the morning of 4th of July.

It's based around a true story on Wally Hibbard's farm. He died a few years back in his early 90s. The farmer was so active in the white church by the blue pond with the yellow lily pads, a lot of town kids going by on bicycles called it the Wally Hibbard Church. We dedicate this short story to Wally Hibbard, who could both tell good jokes and spill out his heart with the spirit of life.

Angel came down from Heaven yesterday
She stayed with me just long enough to rescue me
And she told me a story yesterday
About the sweet love between the moon and deep blue sea.

—ANGEL

BY JIMI HENDRIX

Ivy

The stylus of time was stricken. The miners were dead. The mines had closed, after the veins went dry of silver. The miners were below the ground in Lone Tree Cemetery. Above the cemetery on jagged crests of the mountain, was the ski tows. The big storm had pulled out; high in the bath of lemon-yellow sun against the Cobalt blue sky, the wink of colours was a constant stream on the white belts among the evergreen forest. Frolickers caught in the hysteria, darted and raced to slash the virgin carpets.

She was just a kid. Her countenance was that of perhaps eight years. Maybe nine. The ski instructor had pawned her off on me. She arrived in my world out of the blue.

I'd been digging my poles through the line, working through the Bunny Ears run, trying to work higher into the steeper and gnarly stuff.

I wanted desperately to attend the madman revel on the mountain — upon laughing hysterical — upon singing madman songs of Anacreon, songs we had learned under the indulgence of Chian wines inside the Brown Dog Pub with my seven comrades along the wooden bar — upon shouting into the mountain's echo chamber and cutting powder.

From the corner of my eye behind the ski goggles, I could see the ski instructor working my flank. Eight kids were nesting around her. All of them were girls.

"Would you mind watching over her on the lift?" She asked the question with jabbing her pole baskets on the snow.

"No problem," I said from behind the rose-colored goggles. "My pleasure."

When you see a woman like that on the slopes, dashing in a red quilted jump suit, tight figure, brazen skin from sun beams coming off the snow fields, high cheekbones and a marvelous smile drenched in heavy accents — they were almost always from Austria.

"You ski out of Innsbruck as a kid?"

"I was born in Saint Anton," she told me. "We grew up in the mountain, and we skied to grade school on cross county gear. It's a good life."

So that was it — she was Austrian alright. Those kinds of packages stick out in general, let alone captured on white snow. She was very beautiful, and I could have sworn there was suddenly a scent of perfume in the air.

Pushing love envelopes was out of the question. Those kind of Austrian hot numbers always packed a man. Schemes had crossed my mind. I sure would've loved to try. But it seemed you always bumped into them in the tavern, both of them still in red ski instructor gear, drinking drafts and singing with all the cheer in the world, holding hands and kissing.

Thinking about women at this point, would be tragedy. I was supposed to watch out for the kid. Not chasing European tail all over the mountain. She sure was beautiful though. Her lips were worked over in gloss stick, and I had to fight from looking.

The kid shot out from her ski class with quick jabs on the poles. She glided on the staging platform. I was right on her shotgun, watching like a hawk. The lift attendant bumped down the rheostat lever, and the giant bull wheel slowed to a crawl. You could hear the vibrations building in the gear train, and metallic songs were rising on the suspension cable.

We stood side by side for loading. No love had taken place. We felt nothing. That would happen later. Under our skis and just below the powder dust, a red line was painted in the decking. It signified the heart of the loading area. We were right on the money. The kid stood stiff as those mannequins you see around Park Avenue, and she was bracing with the ski poles. The chair lift came in behind. They always arrived quicker than expected. I was glad to see the blue foam over the wood slats. That kind of foam always felt like a heating pad against the dead of winter.

The lift attendant rocked back the chair and eased her down as to not wallop our legs. I'd already formed a plan. I'd be taking no chances. My left hand was resting between her shoulder blades; when I saw the lift clip her thighs, my big hand sucked her ski parka back into the rest; with lightning speed, my ski glove shoved back her breastbone, and lowered the safety bar which enveloped the child. All doom had been arrested, and we sailed out into space.

"Keep your feet on the rest," I told the kid.

She listened. We climbed swiftly over the ski run. It was a good way down. All the colours of the world were darting and zipping across the ski trail. We had a bird's eye view of everything, and you could hear the skis making those squinching sounds over the packed powder.

Making conversation was like pulling teeth. She was zipped up tight. I hit her with all the angles.

"Beautiful weather, Huh?" I offered.

"Yes," she said.

"Are you on school vacation?" I wondered.

"Not this week," she answered in monotone.

"What terrific ski conditions," I said with enthusiasm.

"Sure," she flatly answered.

The little girl looked dutifully ahead under a white ski helmet, from behind ski goggles of dark green lenses. It was a bluebird day, and the bright Colorado sun twinkled the snow field as if cast with millions of cut diamonds, and you needed that kind of protection against squinting. She held the black grips of her ski poles in the vertical, kind of like a ski racer in the starting block for a giant slalom competition. She used the gap between the poles as a buckhorn gun sight, slightly hunched and rigid, keeping the train of her thoughts and focus up the ski run.

We covered the span of two towers in silence. Our lips remained sealed. We listened to dins on the tower heads, sounds when the chairlift arm ran across the gang pulleys.

Suddenly and out of the blue, magic words were spilled. Actually, I was talking more to myself than anybody, when I said, "I woke up in the cracks of dawn. Mellow yellow sun was filtering through the aspen grove. I'd crossed the foot bridge over the river, and it was exhilarating to watch the rapids sweeping past the ice frozen boulders. I'd flushed a red cardinal from the willow thicket, and as the creature perched and worked the berry patch, it was very special to behold its vivid redness on the virgin white snow."

"Cool!" she exclaimed. "I'm an early bird too!" It was as the secret combination had been tumbled. She opened like a faucet. I would hear before our departure, a great deal of her life's history.

"What time you rise?"

"First light," she said proudly.

"What do you do at those hours?" I needed to know.

"Not much," she said with a smile. "Maybe pack my school bags. Maybe go over my ski gear."

"Your parents get up early too?"

"Hee! Hee!" she giggled. "My parents are really nice, but they're like corn balls when it comes to getting up early," she told me. "They like sleeping in."

"What time do they get up?"

"On weekdays they're not too bad. But on weekends… they sleep in late."

"How late?"

She leaned over and said behind her mitten, "They sleep in till about 9:30 AM on Saturday." She spoke in terms of embarrassment, as if she'd just revealed some kind of venial sin. "That's too late," she revealed with a big grin. I saw her wiggle a bit closer to me on the chair.

A vision formed across my mind. Her parents appeared as nerds. Adventure seekers rise with dawn. So, I asked her the question, "Are your parents something like semi-nerds?"

"Not really," she said in astonishment. "True — they play board games on the kitchen table, and play Bingo with the old timers," she admitted. "But my dad plays afternoon golf once in a blue moon." She leaned over and whispered, "They're more like couch potatoes."

The chair took us swiftly up the mountain. Glancing down across our ski gear, it was noticed her skis were engraved. They read in white letters on the blue skis — Ivy _______________.

Since we were breaking ice, hitting it off and getting deeper into metaphysics, I figured it was worth taking a shot and get personal.

"Well Ivy, at least you're with the early birds." I pronounced her name Evy, and not like the green trails of ivy that clings to the brick apartment blocks along 89th Street of the Upper East Side. I'm not sure if that was the correct pronunciation, or if she was just being polite, but she never let on to me, so I stayed with the same phonics.

"Not anymore," she revealed.

"Why not?"

"Because I'm grounded," she said looking at me square.

"Grounded?"

"Yea, my parents say I'm too much of an early bird," Ivy told me. "I'm not allowed to get out of bed anymore on weekends… till 7:30 AM."

"What about slipping out of the covers, and tip-toe about the bedroom?"

"Nope," reported Ivy. "I'd love to," she admitted. "But if I got caught, they'd ground me longer." Her facial expressions were blocked behind her big green goggles. It was impossible to read her eyes. I got my information from body language and rings in her voice box. They revealed mischief.

"Just the other morning, I was thinking about sneaking down into my garage, and looking at my bicycle," she confessed. "But then I changed my mind. I didn't want to get pinched, have them get mad at me, and ground me longer under the covers."

Just then we saw a kamikaze pilot coming down the slope. He was a real schussboomer. The guy was way over his head. We spotted him near Tower 7, and he was really moving; his red skis were pointed straight down the mountain, and he was yelling something. He never turned once. On a beginner's run like Bunny Ears, the snow makers shaved and cut the slope flat with tracked machines. It's flat and worked over.

But just as luck would play out for the K-pilot, he hit the only two moguls on the run; they were necked into Tower 7, where the snow cats could not get in tight. He hit the humps wide open — upon looking like a straw man on skis — upon throwing himself airborne — upon landing and lurching like connected to electric voltage — upon sailing down the mountain on his suicide run of madness.

He dragged his ski poles behind, and the baskets shot out twin rooster tails of snow plumes. But the concussion from the mogul field, had jarred loose his blue toque and goggles. The fairy yellow sun spilled across his blue hat on the slope. Several novices wildly averted, their skis spitting out powder in hopes of not running over his gear.

Renior once said, "White doesn't exist in nature. You admit there is a sky above the snow; the sky is blue, so the blue must appear on the snow."

Ivy and I took in the view. The sky was cerulean blue, and over the ridge by Society Circle the sun was twinkling silver. We watched the guy sailing past on the snow field of blue hues, and he was throwing his weight around trying to slacken speed. The man was bald as a cue ball on the top plate and had grown a spectacular comb-over. Under normal practice with hair dope, the guy combed everything over in a full turban cut. But now in the blasting winds from his joy ride, that patch of brown mane was fluttering in the air stream.

"Holy cow," exclaimed Ivy.

"You're not kidding," I agreed with the kid.

"Now I've seen everything," said Ivy from behind the choppy bangs.

"That guy is really far out," I told her.

The daredevil barreled down right under the lift, and when looking down we could see his chrome dome. His face tightened in protest. He tried an ultra- high-speed snowplow, right rudder; and he turned alright; but he ran out of groomer, plowing into a sea of drifted powder, and poindextered himself into space. Whoom! A giant powder puff erupted out of bounds. The man screamed into space. He missed the snow fence by slivers. The crash drove him under the white blanket, and his planted face had risen from the powder puff with the trappings of flakes.

"Oh brother," exclaimed Ivy.

Two red figures pulled up on the ridge line. They were ski patrol. Their red parkas with the white cross, stood out bold on the blue sky. The taller figure bent over and gathered the man's hat and ski goggles. We could see him in the distance tap the goggles against his poles, and snow spewed from the lens chamber. His partner quickly carved turns down to the stricken agent of calamity. Her talents were rare in the technique, and she carved sweeping turns that kicked out sprays of powder. She approached the man who was sitting on the snow and looked down on him through blue aviators.

"Are you alright?" she asked with deep concern.

"I'm fine." The crash victim was still seated in black snow pants, rocked back on his arms.

"Are you sure? It looked like you took a real clobbering."

"I feel alright," he confessed. "Most of the stars in my head are gone." The crash victim was now standing, missing a ski, and shaking his arm around in exercise motion. His face was glistening from melted snow, and tiny droplets formed on his brow.

The lift suddenly arrested. It stopped cold and our chairlift bobbed a few times. Some beginners much have stumbled in the loading station below, and the attendant killed everything. This afforded us a world of crystal clarity, and we could hear everything below clear as bells.

"Better let us check you out," she warned. "You seem to be limping."

"I think my ankle got twisted," he admitted. The other Ski Patrol glided down and tossed the guy his hat. He covered up his bald spot right away.

"Better slow down next time," warned the Ski Patrol guy. "You were out of control. This is a beginner's run. We saw you crash."

"I'm no beginner," countered the snow-covered heap. "I'm on my way to becoming an expert."

"No kidding?" said the female patrol, grinning wide.

"How many years have you been on skis?" asked the other patrol. He had the guy's goggles strung around his neck.

"This is my fifth time on skis," bragged the guy. "But I'm a cross-over from water skis. I can cut up glass on Tupper Lake like nothing. You should see me — going around the lake and making fancy turns on one ski is nothing. I'll catch on real quick to snow."

"We can see that," said the female ski patrol. Her eyebrows arched in astonishment. She found it was hard to look him in the eye.

I measured the guy from the chairlift. He was wearing a cream cable-knit Norwegian sweater. A goat skin wine flask was draped across his chest. The crash must have dislodged the screw cork — bright purple stains had seeped into the sweater's yarn. You could see flecks of wine across the snow too, and it reminded us of blood. The evidence did not sit well in the crash victim's corner — he'd been consuming alcoholic beverages on the ski slopes. Why sure he was popped. The cross-over guy from the lake, must have been guzzling and taking pulls on the ski lift.

Maybe that's the reason he had been full of false courage. He sure came down with a world of confidence; but it was the booze that was pushing him.

The Ski Patrol braced the guy, as he hobbled out back on the groomers. He'd put back on his blue toque and screwed tight the cap of his leather wine flask. They unfastened his singular ski and plunked him down on a brown army blanket.

The lift bumped back to speed. That kamikaze pilot quickly vanished from thoughts. We ascended the mountain, and again began the conversations of our world:

"Was that guy drinking?" asked Ivy. She'd picked up on him too. I was exceedingly proud of her vision.

"He was half popped," I told her.

"Why do people drink?" asked Ivy.

"Mostly to be happy."

The temperature that morning was not climbing. The sun was bright yellow; but there was a sting on the mountain. I clapped my mittens and squinched my fingers to get blood moving. The cold snap with no winds, invigorated the theme. It made you feel alive. I looked over at Ivy — her complexion had taken on the beaming circlets of rosy cheeks, and the foundations of her youth spilled out across the land.

"Was the guy suffering from sadness?" questioned Ivy.

"Listen little buddy… it's something like this. A few chocolate bars from the Wonka Candy Factory, can be a good thing. But start eating them by the bag, and the pounds will start creeping. You might explode the bathroom scale."

Ivy busted out with laughter. She did not try to cover her mouth. Her laughing spilled across the mountain stillness.

"Same thing with the booze. A few beers or highball never

killed anybody. But when you start pushing the envelope with the sauce, eventually you crash and burn."

"The guy looked happy to me," whispered Ivy across the lift. "He was even joking with the Ski Patrol." She seemed to lose her lightheartedness and looked out through the silent forest.

Happy is one thing. But being gay on the gaiety of cheap wine is another. Nobody could prove nothing though. He could have gotten the feebleness in his legs from practicing ski moves over his head or had a monkey fix from the indulgence of spirits. He was a stranger, nobody knew him and let alone had ever seen him, and a spray of wild opinion about the K-pilot was all across the ski slopes. The gossip had reached the ski lodge almost instantaneously, and a murmur was in the crowd a drunk had crashed over on Bunny Ears. A woman with faux white earmuffs that looked like rabbit fur, was heard to exclaim over by the soda-jerk counter, the guy must be a nut.

Down in the infirmary, the Ski Patrol was putting more of that two-plus-two together. His blue toque was embossed with Coors. He had ruined his expensive Norwegian sweater by dumping wine all over himself, and he reeked of liquor. While having his ankle served with white gauze, the guy had been singing broken numbers of a jazz number. There are times when the observant fill in between the lines and paying attention to detail carries more weight than confession. The Ski Patrol threw each other a wink. They had drawn conclusions.

"I'm glad my parents don't drink or smoke," Ivy told me.

"That's really great kid," I cheered. "They sound like good role models."

"If only they stopped sleeping so late," added Ivy.

"Oh well…" I answered.

"I'd sure like to know what they're doing behind that bedroom door," said Ivy with bewilderment.

"I have no idea," I told her with raised eyebrows under my rose-colored lenses. "Absolutely none."

Out of the blue, high on the ridgeline of the stone-faced Rockies, an explosion rocked the landscape. Kaboom! Both of us averted hard right towards to zenith. Because of the maze of mountain divides and bold outcrop faces, it was hard to pinpoint the effects of the first detonation — Ivy spotted it first.

"Look!" she exclaimed in astonishment.

Erupting from the crested buttes under a fairy blue sky, a big spray of snow plumes feathered across the mountain. The Ski Patrol was working the avalanche shoots with artillery. The cannon was Army surplus and had once fought in war. The charge was right on the money. The results were both instantaneous and with power to detain all viewers in sheer astonishment.

The avalanche began in the chute pockets; a monstrous wave of driven snow, began gobbling up the mountain face; when the thunderous sea of snow hit the tree line, it walked through the forest with the likes of linebackers pummeling lightweights; groves of lodgepole pines were sheared and snapped like stick matches, and evergreens tumbled in the slide as toothpicks tossed by a Thor giant.

"Look!" I tugged on Ivy and pointed for her to look upon the wild blue yonder, caught in a bath of tangerine sun. Many tiny specks of colour were nested. All of them were basking in the rays as mountain goats loafing in the sun. They were the transponder people. The cannon cockers had caught their attention, and the figures were absorbed with the colossal might from their birds-eye view, solemn witnesses of the avalanche.

The transponder people were still wearing game faces, for their quest was searching out sheer rushes and plunging out of bounds with homing devices tucked into their packs — the tragic beeps might give them enough breathing room for their buddies to claw and dig them out, before all vanquished and then suffocated in the frozen chamber of eternal death.

"Are those specs of color people?" Ivy wanted to know.

"They are transponder people. They like to get hopped up on adrenaline. Those kind of bushwhackers push the limits out of bounds. It can be a dangerous commodity. That's how daredevils operate."

"I want to go up there," said Ivy. "I like adrenaline."

"Were you born in the Rocky Mountains?" I inquired.

"No… not me," she admitted. "We came here from back east."

"Where abouts?" I needed to know.

"Oklahoma City," revealed Ivy.

"Was the move about work?"

"Not really," filled in Ivy. "My parents said it was about getting away from everything.

"Many people think around those lines," I uncovered. "This valley was voted the best small town in America."

"I guess they started to think about moving before I was born." Ivy beamed wide in her knowledge.

"It must have been the seed of their dreams," I said.

"Maybe so… but I heard them talking through the bedroom door one night. They were talking about a bomb and a guy named Timothy ________________. I can never remember his last name," said Ivy wiping her nose with a mitten. "I don't understand too much about the story, but that's part of why we moved. From what I understand, the United States government hunted him down."

"You live in heaven now," I said changing tone.

"I love it here," confessed Ivy. "We just moved to town. For the first three years we lived down valley in a ranching community. The cowboys were nice. But we finally found a place in Telluride," said Ivy in the chords of cheerfulness.

"How's school?"

"Great!" she beamed. "I have a lot of friends, and that's where I met my best friend."

"What's her name?"

"Her name is Victoria," gushed Ivy. "She's two chairs back." The kid turned around and waived her black mitten into space.

"It must be great having a best friend so soon," I confessed.

"Nothing could be better than Rocky Mountain living," she exclaimed. "Especially with my best friend Victoria. We talk every night before bed on the telephone. When the snow melts in spring, we're going to sign up for dance lessons," said Ivy pumping her poles.

"What kind of dancing?" I wondered.

"I'm not sure," admitted Ivy. "Our moms will help us with that kind of stuff."

Our conversation suddenly ended. We had reached the crest of Bunny Ears. People were spilling off the lift, and down the unloading ramp. Ivy tightened; her mind raced against falling.

We pinched our last words. There was a hollowness in departure. Our visit had been quite satisfactory. I raised the safety bar. A metallic report summoned. Ivy stiffened more; she raised her ski baskets at the sky.

"It was really nice talking Ivy." My voice rang in tones as those reserved for a little sister.

"Maybe we'll see each other again on the ski trails," said Ivy.

"That would be great."

"I'll most likely be on Bunny Ears."

"Listen kid — don't fight your element. God made you an early bird. It's not wise to go against the grain."

"Don't worry," said Ivy. "The early bird gets the worm." She spoke in bursts of a child's energy.

We glided down the ramp. The tangerine sun glistened on the snow. Ivy banked right and waited for her ski instructor.

"It was nice meeting you Sir," Ivy ended.

It felt as though stars had aligned, and rare chords struck in a new friendship. It would have been swell to make a few runs with the kid. We could have ended the runs with hot chocolate. Maybe she could have told me more curious things about her world, and I could have given her a few conditioning tips learned when I raced bicycles on my Pinarello fitted out with Campanolo groups of Super Record in friction shifting.

I dug in my baskets and skated with long strides on the skis. You needed to climb a slight hump to reach Twin Peaks lift. I began climbing the rise, skirting the pine grove in herringbone fashion. A soft breeze worked the canopy. Thistledown of snow dust trinkled into the air.

I looked at the blue sky. There were big- puffed clouds. With the snows blown in the back country, blanket of tangerine sun working the summit chutes, everything had turned around in big favor for the transponder people.

I looked down through the pine forest. Below on the beginner's slope, a promenade of colors advanced. The ski school had been set in motion. Ivy was in the prominence of those figures. I reached over and hugged a lodgepole pine and pressed my cheek into the coarse bark. Astringent whiffs of pine needles accentuated the setting, and I dug my fingers into the bark furrows. I was completely integrated now, and I took a good hard look down where the pine forest spilled into the slope's toe. I waited until Ivy hit the sunlight place on the slope. She was bracketed between a cluster of dark green needles, and I watched her carve a beautiful stem christie in the powder.

Below in the valley was the village. The river was still there. A trail ran across the foot bridge over the gurgling river and wound through the solemn row houses into town. The white clapboards of Town Hall made sharp contrast against the landscape. A pinnacle of the church pierced the sky, and on the Sabbath certain inhabitants thumbed through the prayer books inside, and on other occasions a priest administered the necessary sacraments. A big American flag flew on a high silver pole, fluttering its red and white and blue over the scene.

High above the town, chains of snow-covered peaks loomed in the mountains. In the early morning of days still to be stricken, the adventure seekers would shoulder packs fixed with thump-lines, and ascend to the alpine tabernacles, where they could flirt with those obsessions of thrill seekers on the fall line.

A surge of confidence had suddenly pearled in the yellow sun wash across the village, because it was plain now after growing out of the groundings and being able to sign on dotted lines, the little girl could then be an interpreter of the remedies sacred to the mind of thrill seekers, high in the mountains where tangerine sun streamed through the green boughs of firs.

The short story Ivy is contrived of fantasy and exists only in the author's imagination. But the story was inspired by an actual event in the Telluride mountains, when the ski instructor placed a little girl in my care on the Chondola chairlift. As she reads the paragraph blocks, she will know who she is.

Stephen Deck — the author.

When the Subject Matter Caught Up with Everything

CHAPTER ONE

It was a gigantic platform. All steel and brawn. She could take almost everything. The oil drill platform sat in the Gulf of Mexico. She stood up on high piles driven into the sea's floor. On a clear day, you could see Dry Tortugas through looking glasses. There were spans of long weather, where every day was like that. Some were not. On the rough days she could really take it. The chop and seas could not move her. She never budged.

It was a professional operation. We drilled through the ocean floor, and extruded millions of dollars in real money. We counted it by barrels of black gold. High counts of drums put exceedingly big smiles on the owner's faces.

Some thought of us oil drillers as mercenaries. We worked for weeks straight on the platform's steel for big money. Some of them said we'd sell our soul for money. There were a few on the steel island, splintered fringe that would fit that criterion.

Jimmy the Greek worked the platform. He monitored the drill's speed. You could see him counting dollars in his eyes. Jimmy picked up all his calisthenics on the platform and claimed he could push out seven miles a day. Nobody doubted him. He ran around in circles and clover-leaf patters for hours on the off time. He ran in all kinds of weather, day and night. Somebody said he got the distance by one of those measuring wheels, with a build in clacker to record feet. Jimmy the Greek had pushed it around on two separate occasions to measure distance. Nobody doubted him. He was hungry for the buck, and never messed up on figures.

That oil drilling platform could really take it. She was built like a tank. Her steel pilings driven into the sea's floor, were webbed with a fortress of H-beams peened with massive rivets. The storm had swept across the angry sea a hundred clicks west of Dry Tortugas. It was a class-4 hurricane, running under the handle of Valerie. We got the news on short wave. The weather forecasters said she meant business. They evacuated us just in time. They rode us in on a sea-going 50' tugboat with twin 350hp Caterpillars. She had one hell of a beam on her and remind you of a husky bulldog in the water. She could buck the seas like nothing, and you'd be surprised what a nice plane she put out wide open.

Nobody knew what the blow did to the platform. Valerie ran in the blow and brought about twenty-foot seas. The wild sea was wind riven and breakers with gale forces of white foam in the caps sailed as driven snow. Nobody wanted to look into the hurricane's vice when she was at the dinner table. We'd run the other way, headed north into Oklahoma; the move played into our hands too because she clobbered the seashore, and blew big channels up the beach, and turned over big boats like Match Box toys. The tidal sluices ran so fast and hard, 35 pigs in separate crates on a flatbed semi-truck, drowned swimming around behind the wooden slats and squealing like mad; when the sea dropped, all of them were in the position of sleeping on their sides in the wooden pens, and the fairy queer light that was falling through the broken cloud bank, really brought out the pink hues on their hides.

It's a good thing we ran fast and far from the blow. We were hunkered down across the Oklahoma border, over in Stephens County. She couldn't hurt us there. Valerie was too far away. Say, the winds were gusting a strong 40 mph outside. Say, we could hear everything rattling around out in the night winds. But we were thankful to have found refuge behind the mortar joints, because down in south Texas that Valerie was giving them a hell of a spanking alright. Pandemonium had struck. Airplane jet liners thrown around like aluminum beer cans, trees broken like stick matches, and hundreds of miles with blown electric wires lacing the streets, dead and with no usefulness in the hot flashes of paranoia.

We sat on long green benches in the train station. You could hear the limbs of sassafras trees brushing the copper gutters with zeal of angry winds. There were fourteen figures running from Valerie. Five of us alone were from the oil platform. Tommy and I were on a green bench, our brown duffle bags stuffed and leaning on the seat slats. Across from us were three Greeks. Jimmy was with them. We stuck together as oil drillers.

Down the way on another bench, were three Negros. They were not the yellow-skin toned Negros you see around the Golden State of the NBA. They were not even the medium skin kind of Negros, like the blacks who broadcast and report round ball on television.

These Negros were the blackest of the black. Their skin shined from the blackness.

They were cotton pickers too, running from Valerie off the cotton fields of Mississippi way. Two of the Negros were men, and between them on the green bench was a Negro woman. These blacks were not like the blacks you see around New York City, not like the blacks you find around Boston. They refused to make eye contact with white people. You could stomp your boots in the train station or snap your fingers, and they would still not look. They looked straight ahead, as if they were possessed with X-ray vision and could look through walls. And with all the suffering they endured, all the downtrodden history of prosecution from white men since slave boats, maybe through their faith and years of praying that they could actually see that far.

I looked at the Negro lady. She wore a long dress of coffee material like you might see in a curtain shop. White tuffs of cotton plume were stuck to her hem line. They must have been picking when Valerie came knocking. The Negro on the right had his left arm over her shoulder. The tallest Negro was smoking a corn cob pipe. I watched him mix Half & Half pipe tobacco with a few pinches of Cherry Blend in his palm, and stuff it into his pipe. His hands had lighter valleys of skin in the cracks from years of hard labor. The Negro struck a match off his leather sole and put fire to the bowl. The aroma was very satisfactory. The grey bank of smoke climbed into the rafter tails and hung in cloud formation for considerable length of time.

Six young men had been watching the Negro smoke. They had been staring at him smoking, since the match had been stricken. None of the Negros had batted an eyelash. They looked straight ahead into the yellow pine wall boards. I'd been measuring the six of them for some time. As a writer, I was curious about all of them.

They were studied at length. They told me plenty. They were down the far end of the train station, on a green bench near the tall silver radiators. The fins threw off a toasty heat against the blow. The train station was intimate quarters, cozy and provided with sound windows, with yellow pine rafters running the open ceiling, and sound really traveled where you could hear every word and read their faces and body language.

They were like a lot of young men you see around, climbing voices, telling their weekend to the thong of strangers. My ears were perked for the decipher of subject matter. But I learned as much from the jostle of their body parts, nervous habits and twitching, the rhyme and motion of fellowship, as what had come out of their mouths.

They told me a great deal, and we'd never struck a word of conversation. A lot of what they said stuck with me. All of them were English and Creative Writing majors. Four of them were Princeton boys. The other two were Columbia University material. I measured their smarts from across the room. All of them were bright boys, and exceedingly polished in manner. They came from good stock of breeding and refinement, and you could feel the weight of their knowledge across the room. But all of them were green, first year freshmen, and they had plenty to learn.

I measured them at great length. The new broad of thinking minority was before my eye. Would any of them pick up enough to nail down the Pulitzer Prize? How many of them along with the contingent of their classmates, would pan out to be best-selling authors? Was there a storyteller in the folds who'd rolled in enough of words to pen a novel, to virtually stun book critics of the New York Times? Would they have skills to climb inside best seller lists. Time would tell my friends.

Three or four of them struck me like they should have been in navy blue sport jackets, with a monogram school tie. They weren't though. One of the kids from Columbia, a redhead with bushy hair, was wearing a green and black checked wool shirt, like you see on lumberjacks in northern Maine. But he never wielded an axe in his life or bucked a saw log. He'd hardly put out any manual labors in all his years, and the thought of becoming a journeyman never crossed his mind. But he was a 3.75 GPA man, a real book worm, the future stock of scribes — he revealed these attributes from a raspy voice box, beaming the excitement across his companions.

I drew an immediate liking to them. There was a quality about them — a certain role of character which would shape man's destiny. They sure had a lot to learn though.

All four of the Princeton students, were embellished with the trappings and regalia of the school. The tallest and slender lad, pushing near six feet four, was wearing a blue and white pin stripe shirt, decked out with orange and black Princeton cufflinks. They were almost bling style; big square clasps with the school's colors, and he'd paid a bloody fortune for the set.

The other three Princeton boys were also on the cutting edge of vogue. The kid seated next to the redhead, was sporting a number three buzz job, and wearing a ballcap that boasted a P sewn on the crest. The hat was fashioned from fabric which resembled a zebra's hide, and the effects stood out against the assembly. With nervous twitches he was adjusting his brim to find new angles against the arc lights, and I got a good look at his electric taper, and it was a number three buzz alright.

His buddy had a white Princeton T-shirt, with Roman black letters. Simple and elegant.

Around his neck was a silver woven chain, the size and luster you see on movie stars.

The last Princeton student was wearing a dove grey baseball hat, with the school's trademark orange and black shield. Embroidered on the scroll work above the brim, were the Latin letters: DEA SUB NUMINE VIGET — Under the protection of God she flourishes.

I pulled a sandwich from my pocket. It was wrapped in waxed paper, a one-day old sandwich, a water roll laid thick with ham and cheese. I'd picked it up inside Purifoy's Market in Sugar Land, Texas. That sandwich maker guy sure was generous. I don't know if he was getting the heebie-jeebies, because the blow was already pelting the clapboards with sand plumes, or if he thought Valerie might take the whole market anyhow, but he sure laid it on thick. He sliced the cheddar cheese off the block, thicker than your shoe soles. Nice ham stuck out all around, and the guy really jazzed on the mayonnaise. Only thing though, the roll was getting a bit dry, and the crumbs made you wheeze a bit when she was going down. I could have cared less though, because all of us were hungry, and nobody worried too much about manners or sharing food. Everybody had the chance to stock up back south before the blow rolled up her sleeves.

I'd just taken my first bite against the storm. It was out of this world. I looked over, and the Greeks were eating too. But not too much you know. They only brought a quart of black olives. Trying to save a buck, they refused to pay for pitted variety.

Alexander Metaxas had opened the olives. He secured them with a giant wooden spoon. None of the Greeks had anything that resembled a bowl. They ate from their hands. Alexander dumped a nice load of black olives into Nikos Venizelos's hand. Then with the wooden spoon, he plopped more to Joannes Plastras — aka

Jimmy the Greek. Joannes accepted them with both hands joined and cupped; some juice spilled on the floor.

The Greeks spit the olive pits into their hands. Their lips almost kissed their fingers as they spit out seeds, and they kept on eating the yellow-green pulp in silence. They moved through the jarred fruit like machines. With a team reaction bonded on the oil platform, Jimmy the Greek dumped his pits into Vinizelos's hand, and likewise, Nikos discarded the stony seeds into Alexander Metaxas's big hand. Then Alexander walked over and dumped them through the red dome of the trash can against the brick wall.

The Greeks had gone through two servings of black olives, when Jimmy the Greek held up his hand like a traffic cop, wielding the international sign he'd had enough.

After a short spell, Alexander Metaxas pulled a tin of oiled sea sardines. He put the crank arm into the tiny silver tab and zipped open the lid. All the Greeks used their fingers for taking sardines, and they put the silver fish tail-first down the hatch.

"Bring any pie," said Jimmy the Greek.

"Pie," I said, aroused. "Don't talk about those kinds of things blast you Jimmy!" A man on the run has no time for packing a pie. It would spell certain misery inside your canvas tote. Jimmy the Greek got me thinking about blueberry pie though. Caught in the hot flashes of pie, dreamfully, I thought about a slice of blueberry pie with the purple juices running across a white China plate. The thought instigated a watering sensation behind my chapped lips.

The Negro lady had risen, and she walked slowly toward the canteen's window. At this very narrow passage, nothing more than the dimensions of the bank teller's window, she paused and counted coins. The electric arc light from a green dome, illuminated her forehead; her raven black complexion threw off a highlight as seen around a Cadillac's chrome bumper. I was mesmerized by the sight, the coffee-colored dress, jungle black skin of tribal roots, and the sheening skin off her skull plate's plane. Falling all around the figure, was a veil of yellow light from the electric light fixture.

The canteen's window slid open. The glimpse of a white counter man in spectacles filled the opening. The Negro lady bought a bottle of Moxie. The attendant cracked off the cap with a bottle opener. They were having some kind of discrete conversation. The white man gave the Negro lady three bags of oyster crackers. He'd put them on a white paper plate. No money was exchanged. He gave her crackers on the house. Everybody picked up on the move.

Then the Negro lady sat down between her men. They all swigged off the same bottle of Moxie. The Negros were eating the crackers in pacific lights, content with ease of mind, nursing the tiny bags of crackers. Just then out of the blue next to the silver radiator, the Princeton boy in the white school T-shirt and movie star chain, walked to the counter window, and procured a sheaf of napkins from the stainless dispenser. He then sauntered to the Negros, angelic in form, and lodged the white napkins in the Negro lady's hand.

She clinched the napkins. She beamed exceedingly. The Princeton boy, bowing ever so slightly, gushed and seemed caught in his own graciousness towards mankind's euphoria. But silence prevailed; nobody in the room had said nothing to this point. Nevertheless, a clarion call against racism had just sounded against the assembly. The sensation was short lived, and in a flash of time everybody was back into their own worlds.

My sandwich was going down against hunger. The ham and knife-cut yellow cheese tasted fantastic, and a rife of dry crumbs had sifted across my trousers. I'd just taken a big bite, the mayonnaise running over my lips, when Alexander Metaxas leaned over between us, and whispered some free advice for us oil men:

"I bet in a writing contest... those Princeton boys could blow those Columbia cats into the weeds."

I'd felt the sensation of being struck by a bolt of silver lining — "Ahuggh! Ahuggh!" — coughing on the dry crumbs in my throat. My whole presence froze up, and I was flabbergasted by the comment.

I could scarcely believe my ears. Blue collar Greeks critiquing the best writing schools in the United States? I was just about speechless. Especially since over the last months on several occasions, the Greeks had gotten stuck on the double-meaning of words inside Marvel comic books, and bade me at length to get them straightened out inside the funny pages.

I was certain inside the hallowed training grounds, both universities would groom out their writers to maximum extreme. Their writing professors — the best known around higher circles — would leave nothing to chance. All the English rules would be instilled into their meter. Lessons from the master's frequency response as seen on printed pages, would be cast into revealed lights. The students would learn from the dead.

Just then, the college boys opened up with school dialogue. They commenced in pinched conversation, but then became loud and then louder, until the whole assembly could overhear their reveal.

"Our language professors conduct forum, where the Development of English is explored. It's fantastic," said the Princeton kid with the number three buzz job. "The focus is directed to the Indo-European family of languages, and students are not only expected to fully grasp the sister tongues of Teutonic, but be aware of all eight sub-families, including Armenian and the Albanian tongue spoken on the Balken Peninsula." He rolled back his shoulders, like a proud rooster.

His fellow classmate with the white T-shirt and silver chain, took over in the train station's chamber. "Exposure is provided to the students, how the sweeping change came about in consonant sounds, enforced by rules of Teutonic. Those rules knocked out syllables in the inflection of word forms," pointing the eraser of a yellow pencil at the scholars. "Focus became fixed on root syllables in Teutonic — those syllables deprived of accent, were weakened in pronunciation over time by slurring of sounds together, and eventually those vowels and consonant sounds withered and disappeared." The Princeton kid twirled his silver chain in confidence, basking in his wealth of knowledge.

The Columbia kid with the green and black lumberman's shirt, butted in and went to bat for the school. "Our new pupil base of creative writers, were brought around to fathom, the living-breathing growth of our English language, was by all accounts, a very costly advance." He paused and looked over at the Negros. They were still looking straight ahead and had finished the oyster crackers. The guy behind the canteen window, had his ear cocked towards the college boy's conversation.

Then the Columbia kid continued, "That's because inflection forms of words, were allowed to flourish and exhale their new pronunciation, from victories of marauding wars. The payment of these refreshed nouns and verbs going forward, thriving on victor's tongues, was extruded from millions of lives, and the conquered ground seeped in bloodshed of the dead's phonics." The Columbia kid cracked his knuckles, took a read across the faces of those Princeton boys, then unzipped the green and black checkered shirt, and tossed it over the green wooden bench — the radiators were really spewing out heat, and the train station was a cozy retreat against the blow.

Eager to participate, the second Columbia student chimed in. He began by pulling a yellow-lined paper from his travel case, that had been filled with his writing in blue ink. He spread the yellow paper on his lap, and exclaimed:

"The title of my paper is The World's Stamp Collection." Then he began to recite the following words off the yellow paper.

We are a cosmopolitan people. The building blocks of our English language, are much like a hard-bound collection of World Postage Stamps, jacketed in rhinoceros hide. Our words like the postage marks of distant lands, have been assimilated from around the continents. Henceforth, while spinning the metal globe inside our Butler Library, focus on these particular landmarks — upon Spain contributing words like indigo, vanilla, alligator — upon Italy inspiring the need for crescendo, balcony, catacombs — upon Scandinavia with schooner, skipper, sloop — upon Mexico with chocolate, coyote — upon our Native American Indians with moccasin, tobacco, racoon — and upon the Danes providing us with the very beautiful word of sky.

Then the boy said, "That's about as far as I've gotten so far." Then he folded it in half and placed it cautiously inside his travel case.

"I feel it's going to be a great paper, but I realize it's going to need some subject matter to grab the reader."

"Ahh… subject matter," said one of the Princeton boys. "I'm having the same problems."

"You're not the only one," reported the other Princeton boy sporting the blue and white pin stripe shirt, buttoned down with the orange and black cufflinks of bling proportions. His buddy next to him on the green bench, tugged on the ballcap with the sewn-on letter P and zebra stripes, and nodded his head in agreement.

"I'm in the same boat," said the Columbia kid with the green and black lumberman's shirt. "Just the other day, I ventured to the top floor of the Empire State Building, trying to spark imagination. I figured a novel story might be looming across the sea of skyscrapers."

"What happened?" questioned the Princeton Boy with the black number three buzz job.

"Well…" said the eager Columbia student, "I'm scared silly of heights. I got knocked kneed and shaky around the edges and needed to descend. Looking down on the backs of grey pigeons soaring in the blue zenith, was not for me."

His other classmate admitted, "The other night in the jet blackness, I was trying to dig up some subject matter. Everybody else in John Jay was sleeping, and there was a nice breeze coming through the window off Amsterdam Avenue. I thought a great deal."

"Anything come around?" asked the lumberjack kid.

"The only thing that came around, was that Columbia P&S student — Ashley Frontenac. I spotted her on campus up near 168th Street, and she's got a package that doesn't quit. Her high cheekbones with those cute dimples really stayed with me, and I thought about kissing her long into the night, with the cool night shifts about my bedroom."

"Sounds like subject matter to me," said a Princeton boy. Then he tapped the thick soles of his brown wingtips on the floor and exclaimed, "I hung around the water bubbler up in Nassau Hall for a good hour, hoping to hear a sliver of a sentence that stung. Something that stuck inside. But it's hard to pan out rare conversation, in a body of students. The most interesting subject matter was the custodian, who pushed a six-foot dust mop around the foyer of Nassau. The grey mop cut a huge swath, and the custodian moving through the figures was reminiscent of a wing pushing a hockey puck past a defense."

"No worries," said his classmate. "We've still got over three years of scholastics at Princeton. I'm sure some magic insight will come into play, and that we'll put a handle of subject matter."

"Talk about smart kids," said Alexander Metaxas.

"They sure are bright fellows," added Nikos Venizelos.

"I'm proud of them."

"I'm certain they will seize their opportunity."

"I'd give anything for my son to attend that caliber of education," informed Tommy.

"I can see my daughter at Columbia," said Alexander. He looked dreamingly in space. There was a soft pinging in the silver radiator behind the assembly.

"I'd never send my kids there," scoffed Jimmy the Greek.

"Why not?" asked Nikos. There was no surprise on his face.

"Because I work too hard for my money."

"That's the whole thing," said Alexander. "Can't you see it? Do you want our kids to work like dogs? The grime of oil is buried deep in our pores. We work like animals, separated from our family for a great deal of time."

"It's great money," boasted Jimmy the Greek. "I like everything about the platform. It pays great."

So that was it. Everybody knew it anyway. Jimmy loved money too much, to send his kids into the Ivy League. He'd rather spend it on himself.

"I'm steering them towards trade school. It's free, and they make a good buck with their hands." Jimmy waved his hand across our side of the assembly, as if to give away free information.

The Negro puffing the pipe never reacted. He drew in and out on the black stem, cradling the yellow corncob in his palm. Grey wafts of smoke pearled to the rafters. The Negro lady never averted to the crowd. The singular glance she devoted to the college boys was furtive and shy. But she'd listened intently on the vocabulary of sentence blocks. She clenched her waist in apprehension, her slender fingers cupping the coffee-colored dress. The third Negro gazed straight ahead, and his hand was caressing the tension from her shoulder blades. None of them said a bow peep.

Higher education had crossed their minds only in a dream. They made very little money. These hard working Negros lived in a small house of white clapboards on the side of a blue brook, with a roof often patched with tar paper. The farm Negros realized their kids' only chance into the Ivy League, was a scholarship from a college board. Their kids were bright, were church raised, but the Negros were not certain of what collective grades on report cards would be their children's salvation.

In the silent harbors of the train station, a recital of an old mantra danced in all the Negro's heads, because their manual labors had vulcanized the term "cotton picker" deep in their black clay and spirit. The three Negros sat hunched as those taking in a ball game, and a cultivation of pride fell over the black figures from an amber glow spilling from the arc light. There was an undisguisable passion between the black farm hands and white farmer; and deep pride from hoeing the rows of cotton had steeped into their blood.

I studied the college writing students. They sure were a polite group of gentlemen. You saw the Princeton boy with the white T-shirt and movie star silver chain, pitch in and help that Negro lady. They had the keenest skills in grammar, were bright boys, and had prescribed themselves into the finest schools of the land.

But no amount of their parent's money, or the watchful eyes of devoted writing professors, could do anything for the boys, in regards of having any subject matter come their way. It was the singular lesson never offered in any classroom and could never be bought with any amounts of money. The English professors could hold Forums around the clock, and until they were blue in the face, but the colors of subject matter could not be taught. Writers have traveled a thousand miles to write a single sentence, and the boys would need to find these things out between the lines of street conversation, reading faces in a crowd of strangers, digging and panning until they found something that sticks, and what makes a story tick.

I said a short prayer for the boys under my breath: "Hail Mary, full of grace, may your guidance be with the boys. They are brilliant boys, a brood of well-oiled Romantics, the next wave of novel savants for penning out award-winning short stories. They are polished in grammar, but young men with plenty to learn, and need your guidance for subject matter now more than ever. Amen."

SUBJECT MATTER:
Six pelicans were huddled from Valerie under a belly-up rowboat on the white sands of Corpus Christi. The wood hull had been pitched against beetle boulders of a breaker wall, its blue belly to the ominous grey sky. Below in their nest of salvation, the six pelicans peeked from behind a fan of wing feathers, a spray of quills to their breast plumes from the rife of pelting sands. In the prominence of the effects, the howl of winds playing flute-like notes, was the cream-orange beaks of the pelicans in the queer bleak light.

SUBJECT MATTER:
Down in the far-off jungle of the Amazon, axe choppers had fallen a mighty Brazilian Rosewood for the black market. A rail thin native in a straw hat, hastily skidded out the log behind a mule.

Two days later the smuggled logs sailed out of Rio de Janeiro, and later that year after changing hands a few times and seasoned on stickers, the Rosewood was milled and shaped into a wonderful violin, crafted inside an instrument shop tucked into the masonry of a side alley over in Campobasso, Italy.

SUBJECT MATTER:

Twenty-seven feet of snow had fallen in Valdez the prior winter. It had been a memorable event. The Black Sheep saloon on the wharf, had them coming three over the bar on several occasions. That summer, the same bartender for the long and hard winter, was making stiff Martinis for the tourists with light conversation. The worst offenders who'd been running from cabin fever in the snows, had signed on for rehabilitation at the local Alcoholics Anonymous meeting.

SUBJECT MATTER:

July 25th, 1876. Black Elk as a thirteen-year-old boy, had been swimming in the Little Bighorn River with other young bucks. Montana summer had finally come to the prairie, and a bath of yellow sun fell across the surface. Black Elk stood in the river and feeling the grains of sand being stripped from under his toes, cupped his hands over the long raven locks and looked into the clear, brown water, colored from the pebble stones on the bottom; and there finning and holding rigid on the bottom were the cutthroat trout. He'd slipped under and swam along the brown pebbles to see the big trout; and when he broke the surface for air, water shedding off his copper back, he could see dust plumes rising from the beating hoofs of horses, and the flashing sabers of Custer's troops hell bent on the murder of Indians.

SUBJECT MATTER:

There had been some proof, that three out of four Personal Egress Air Packs had been activated. Was time available for Christa McAuliffe to know what it was about… or did she black out from the G-forces inside the space rocket.

Nevertheless, her best friend had been confronted by a distant foreboding, an angelic revelation, that Christa had gone back to her old way, and said the Act of Contrition just before the rocket fuel was ignited. All those in her inner circle, knew this was not stretching the truth.

This piece of information proved to be quite a relief, when the six pallbearers lugged the casket from the black hearse across the cemetery. All the mourners in black habiliments huddled around the tombs, drew a great strength from the reveal, and held themselves rigid and composed as a priest spattered holy water on the fresh dug grave.

Just down the road, a flag snapped on a pole outside the local V. F. W. club. Embossed in fine needlepoint was the inscription of Christa's land — "Live Free or Die"

Two double-toots of the giant whistle filled the train station. The Hartland Flyer was barreling down the tracks in the blow. The hurricane's vice could not budge the flashing silver streak, for her iron bulk was massive and mighty, and she shed the perpendicular sheets of rain into a slip stream of vapor.

All the travelers in the red brick station boarded. The Negros got cuts in the line. All the travelers that pulled in on the train, wore countenances of a game face. Our faces became serious too. Running from the hurricane was on everybody's mind. The college boys behind the Negros broke for the front cars — no permanent bonds had been formed in the train station. The boys wanted the glass behind the locomotive driver, as this kind of wide view would let their imagination run wild across the landscape, and feel they were in a world of adventure.

The Hartland Flyer ran the black night into Oklahoma City. Valerie had not foisted her violence this far north, and all options were open. We saw the three Negros board a yellow taxi on the meter. The cabbie informed the Negro on tobacco, there would be no pipe smoking in the cab. He knocked the bowl against his heel; red embers spilled by the gutter. Tommy and I changed trains and rode the spur track to Chicago.

Meanwhile, the three Greeks had boarded Lufthansa airlines, bound for Athens. Alexander Metaxas and Nikos Venizelos were legitimate Greeks. That is, they held full citizenship to Greece. Both men still lived in the city of their birth. But Joannes Plastras, aka Jimmy the Greek, played his cards on both sides — he held dual citizenship between the United States and Greece.

Alexander Metaxas had married his high school sweetheart, Cadie Angelopous. Nikos Venizelos had felt the pangs of love very early in his youth, and proposed marriage to Junia Pipes when they were still eighteen.

But Joannes Plastras was never married. He lived in a beautiful twin A-frame on Lake Superior, and his girlfriend Tessa had been under that roof for over fifteen years. They had three kids. Joannes had worked the oil platform since high school.

On the contract papers for the oil company, there was a small box. If you checked the small box with the ink pen, all your paycheck got wired directly to the wife and kids. We never met a family man on the oil rig, that never made the check mark. Like all of us men who drilled for black gold, Joannes had checked the white box with the black ink pen on the work papers. But Joannes had written in a stipulation — he wanted two hundred dollars a week for his own use.

That's the kind of guy Jimmy the Greek was. He had no use for money marooned at sea. His family could have used that kind of dough. But he loved money so much, he always needed to have it around him. He was so deeply in love with money, he ironed one-hundred-dollar bills, and inserted them standing up in his back pocket on free time. It gave him immense happiness, strutting around the oil platform with pressed money, showing off green bills. He'd used the same attention-grabbing kind of scheme in distant cities, to attract strange woman.

Joannes Plastras traveled to Greece many times, on his thirty-day furlough. He exclaimed a huge love for his native land and told the family it was absolutely necessary for him to experience his roots every so often. He also told Tessa, the opportunity existed for him to make big money in Greece, working very hard. And all of this was true, because may times Joannes had returned to the United States with a huge wad of money, counting out to thousands of dollars, when exchanged out of drachma currency. But it was cheap money, the kind most Greeks would never dream of taking behind their back and closed doors.

Like all Greeks, the three in the airplane loved the ocean. It was in their blood. They were all seamen at heart, and were struck by the medieval tales of adventure, when the Greek sailors had spanked across the blue sea at a great rate, knifing the oars of wooden warships into battle.

The three Greeks had implored Lufthansa airlines for window seats. They loved being glued to the windows, their eyes darting and reading, looking at wonder to the ocean below. It seemed the pilots always used Barcelona as a navigational landmark, the steady drone of the jet engines spewing out its vapor trail; they connected invisible dots with dead reckoning of air compass over Sardinia, pressed onward with navigation toward Sicily. On a clear day, looking south form the silver fuselage, you could see a needle point of Tunisia on the wee horizon. Gazing down from below the white clouds, the Mediterranean Sea painted a quilted pattern on blue-grey seas, tinted by the sun beams and hemmed in tight by the jagged seacoast.

But when the silver fuselage dipped below altitude, the details of the blue sea came alive with riddled swells. A white foam ran in the chop, and portions of the surface were marked with angry hatching. The sights were almost too much for Alexander Metaxas's love for the sea. He squirmed closer to the fuselage and looked past the window for a deeper sensation. Visibility was clear out a good league, and the white hulls of fishing boats were specks on the blue sea. Looking sharply down past the wing, Alexander saw the token wake of a cruise ship, the arrow-like hull pressing towards the boot of Italy.

The plane began its descent, and the sea's effects past the window, so quickly, became a sharp picture of rolling breakers with crashing of spray on the nests of black beetle rocks. Two men could now be distinguished on the stern of a purse-seine boat, and it appeared that men were paying out a net. Just then, the jet sinking above a breaker wall, Alexander glanced over the cove and saw the flashing silver of tiny fish jumping — big fish below were hunting the sardines.

With their work boots back on native land, the two Greeks with citizenship, closed the journey by heading home. Nikos Venizelos lived with his wife and kids in Galaxidhion. From his mortar house on the steep hillside in the other cluster of houses, he could see wide and clear out across the Gulf of Corinth. This experience was a spectacular way to spend a lifetime, raising a broad and being blessed with that kind of panorama of Neptune's main. For the thirty days of furlough, Nikos Venizelos never lifted a finger. He spent every day as quality time, long hours with his family: at night the complete family gathered on the porch in the fallen blackness, sky gazing for shooting stars streaming over the Corinth, and looking down at the magic show of lights across the bay in hamlet windows, the spatter of electric twinkle running the night.

Alexander Metaxas also lived on the seacoast. His people went back six generations in the town of Yithion. Alexander's yellow cement house was perched high on a crag against the Taygetus Mountains; and if you thought the pitch was steep around Venizelos's place, the cliff faces here were enough to make grown men shake with fear.

The view from Metaxas's hearth, was much like that panorama from Alexander's place, but overlooking the Gulf of Laconia, a wide expanse of ocean spiked with the penchant of high-seas adventure. Here in the palette of blue shades, the sea could be dead calm with the orange ball of sun rising, and platoons of white and grey sea birds gliding the thermal currents; then late in the afternoon with tides shifting and tables turning, a snarl of high combers could rise, enveloping the fishing fleet still on the grounds. Make no miscalculations — her complexion was masked in mystery, and plenty of seafarers paid the deadly price, when swallowed into her merciless fathoms. All mistakes were extruded in the extreme, and many of the men had fought in vain, only to be swirled by the underwater tomb where no exchange of oxygen exists.

Looking from the veranda of Metaxas's yellow house, squinting down below the Bahama blue sky, was the island of Kithira.

Hugging the horizon, the sliver body of land encompassed by the sea, appeared to have been patted down by a gigantic spatula from Neptune himself. It was between this far island and the main, that Alexander and his family observed these strange effects which have been painted.

But there were many wonders to cherish while experiencing life around the Metaxas place, where the sea afforded the dwellers with many facets of its splendor. In many ways, the daily passage of the sea, the rising and falling of tides, the smacks weighed with fish and spanking the chop toward port, was like pages of the Bible; the Greeks knew all the parables of their sailors who rode the main's chop, going back to the tablets of AD.

All this history tempered by courageousness of their dead, brought a spiritual connection to the ocean, a reverence that bit into their souls while reading seas from the mountain. The thought a Man had been spiked on a cross to die for their sins, in the days Greek skippers were pitching sails, was too much to shake. The swelling of the sea was in their veins. Their forefathers had died for the sensation of casting nets against the sea's peril.

And meanwhile, Joannes Plastras was still pacing inside a concourse of the airport in Athens. He anxiously awaited a jumper flight to a distant island. He was already counting dollars in his head.

Joannes Plastras's roots were from Crete. He was a native son. He was born there on the island; but at two years of age Joannes had skipped town with his family for the United States. Many of the Plastras clan followed. Like many Greeks of that generation, they dreamed of coming to America.

One thing was certain — Joannes Plastras had bade his two oil men in the strictest terms, never ever mention his nickname Jimmy the Greek overseas. Leaking this out in the native land, would be a tragic mistake. Some of the old men might look down at him. Jimmy the Greek would not ring well in the native tongue. Greeks would laugh in your face.

Joannes had returned a few times before to the island. He recognized nothing about Crete. But he located his old town of Ano Viannos and had discovered three distant cousins and a decrepit grandmother on his father's side.

And after a few visits, Joannes was still full of wonder, and his pride swelled being from the same linage. His long-lost relatives filled him in on parts of his family tree, he never knew existed. Old gloss photographs provided much of the picture; and he thumbed them over many times making sure the faces of the dead were absorbed. He stayed at his third-cousin's place, and looked out the kitchen window upon the street, measuring the press of wayfarers for countenance and traditions of the culture. The idea came to Joannes Plastras many times over, to move back permanently to his people.

It was common practice for old men to sit around the narrow passage of cobbles, telling stories drawn tight on the shade casted side of masonry walls to escape heat. There was nothing like it for Joannes, while he sat with the men and almost instantly they became his father figures. He even bought a short-sleeve button shirt in the local cut and picked up a Greek sailor hat to fit in with the guys. The old Greeks were amazed what Joannes revealed about the United States. They had a hard time believing gasoline was so abundant. But they were set back hearing about abortion clinics. Joannes also picked up useful information. The Greeks told him of the choice spots for fishing, and what tides brought the greatest abundance. Joannes also discovered an addictive love for Corinth raisins. You could buy them in 5 lb. sacks of fine-mesh burlap at Pappageorge's Market, and he gorged on them each day. He dumped them in by the handfuls, letting vast numbers fall into his big mouth.

But after a while, both sides got sick of each other. The old men had deep conversations that were way over his head, and those Greeks played some kind of foreign card games with strange rules. So, after a while, Joannes stopped coming to Crete altogether, and began island hopping.

CHAPTER TWO

The smacks had done exceedingly well that day. They ran into a giant school of sardines on the out-going tides, under an orange ball of sun on a flat sea of shimmering blue. The catch had come on suddenly from the deep blue, but the fleet was packed in close within shouting distance, and all of them made a killing. High pitches of the Greek's excitement filled the sea, as the mates pulled hand over hand on the bulging nets.

The smacks wood hulls were squatted with millions of sardines flopping their silver sides and beating their tails. These kind of holds in an open boat can be dangerous business. Many of the crew measured with both eyes the eight inches of gunwale to the sea, and a high-strung mate of *Little Cupid* kept saying, "Holy Smokes! We're running heavy."

The fleet pressed its white sails toward port. The crew's inevitability measured the distant beachhead. Behind the smacks in the fleet's wake, seagulls were diving on the sardines which had gone belly up on the sea.

And meanwhile, laid flat of her back in Santorini Hospital, widow Jenesis Constabtinides was fitted with oxygen tubes into her nostrils, fighting walking pneumonia. The doctor recently jacked her up to 5 liters of air. Jenesis was coughing on her own infection. The nurse had her running on double IV's. This kind of feebleness of the chest, would be very hard for somebody her age to shake. She had just celebrated her 87th birthday two weeks prior.

Joannes Plastras held her hand. He squeezed her hand a little tighter, to raise a reaction. There was no response. She looked trance-like at the walls, but her eyes sparkled toward Joannes, and she appeared in a very calm state.

They had met five years back, while Joannes was island hopping. She put the moves on him. They both had been inside a roadside hotel in Imerovigli, which was also licensed with a full bar. Jenesis had been sipping a glass of Vinsanto, at a small round table by the window. She'd noticed Joannes coming under the white arcade into the barroom, his vitality caught in the amber beam of wall lamps. It would have been hard for her to miss the cut of a man in his mid-forties, chiseled and toned, with that kind of swooping black hair. Through the waiter, she bought him a beer across the bar.

Jenesis had been married to a man from Bueno Aires. His name had been Benito Faustino Sarmiento. He was a horse breeder out of the world-class racetrack in San Isidro. His stock had won the Kentucky Derby. All of his skins brought the biggest kind of money. They say he was worth twenty million.

They had crossed paths in Santorini, when Benito and his hangers-on were on holiday. It was an exceedingly fast-moving love affair — Benito had quickly proposed marriage with a blue 3 carat diamond. Gushing in the hot flashes of love, Jenesis accepting while Benito was on his knees over the cliffs at sunset on Fira. But in honor of her father, Dititri Constantinides, and the pride of her Greek heritage, she refused to take his last name.

The couple bounced back and forth, between his villa in Argentina, and their whitewash accommodations with the blue dome roof, snuggled into the breathtaking view from Imerovigli's steep face.

But two years before Joannes whisked into town off the ferry boat, her husband had died of a massive heart attack in bed. They buried him a short distance from San Isidro racetrack, so in their minds, Benito could always hear the driving beat of horse's hoofs in eternal rest.

Jenesis and Joannes never kidded each other. They were adults. This was not school yard love, carried about in the innocence of youth. Jenesis was pushing forty years over her man. It was a lot more about curing loneliness. Jenesis knew that besides a bottle of tranquilizers from her physician, there was not many cures. So, she paid Joannes big money to be her gigolo.

They tried to keep everything covered. Hardly anybody knew what went on behind the bedroom doors, under the blue roofing tiles, a stone throw from the Greek church that towered above on the bluff. They sold off Joannes as a nephew from a distant aunt. Nobody on the island of Santorini ever doubted anything, because the last name of Plastras was well known on the island, and their people had always brought about a strong standing.

There was affection between them. Joannes showed he had feelings. He played the part of a distant nephew in public on the white cobbles of the island. But because Joannes loved money so much, he could never give Jenesis more than a sliver of his heart, and their affair was something like you see around a movie production set.

Jenesis was looking poor in the hospital bed. Compromise was all over her countenance. Her fingernails had turned blue, and her complexion had taken on the ghastly hue of marching death. Things had turned so quickly. True — the week before she was on two liters of oxygen with a home bottle. She had showed good color, and signs of pep. The thoughts then crossed her mind about having sex with Joannes. But because her breathing was shallow, and that Joannes moved around like a wild rabbit under the sheets, she pushed away that kind of thinking. Jenesis knew that kind of love making would take a terrible toll on her respiratory system, and she'd never be able to catch her breath.

The doctor entered Jenisis Constantinides's room. With a flick of the wrist and soft voice, he asked Joannes and the custodian who had been dusting the venetian blinds, to oblige him and leave the room.

Things had begun to escalate. The monitor in the nursing station, was beeping its warning signs. Joannes ran his fingers through her hair, sweeping back against the scalp. Then he retreated to the waiting room down the yellow tile floor. Seated in the captain's chair, he rubbed the wad of cash in his right front pocket. It felt so good to rub that kind of money through the trousers' fabric — Jenesis had squared up the day he got into town, with the full payment of ten-thousand dollars for his side of the bought affection. Joannes could hardly wait for returning to Lake Superior, where he could show Tessa the wonderful clip of money he'd brought back from overseas.

Things in Room 227 were turning bleak. Jenesis was failing. The doctor had tried a few medical moves, that had no effects on her general health.

The tall Greek priest in black habiliments and a long grey beard, came down the yellow tile — a nurse had called along to the rectory, for administration of last rites. The priest focused on his calling and paid no attention to Joannes in the lobby chair. Clutching the Bible, his black vestments swung in his cadence, and the priest went down the hall and disappeared into her room.

It was a short visit. Joannes could hear the priest's chants down the hall. Then there was a silence when he anointed her forehead from the vial of Holy spirits. The doctor raised her eyelid and beamed a flashlight across her pupil. There was no reaction. No pulse was detected. She was flat on her back and pronounced dead. The doctor stayed behind and snapped the white sheets in a tidy fashion over her corpse.

The Greek priest passed Joannes in the waiting room, and waved some kind of sign over him, as if to cover him with corporal blessings from the spirits. Joannes sat rigid in the chair, feeling something, closing his eyes tight for a few seconds; then he snapped out of everything and heard the leather soles of the Greek priest clomping down the yellow tile floor and around the corner.

Two days later on a cloud-pitched forenoon, they lugged Jenesis' casket up the stairs into the Greek Orthodox Church of Luke. As the six men were rounding the stone stairs with the wooden box, behind their black figures were the steep faces of the town's cliff, and banks of marbled clouds were drifting past the chain of islands. The speeding clouds marked by charcoal and orange tinge with white puffy rims, were pierced by a pinwheel of sun beams from the high zenith. These needle shafts were highly marked in the sky and fell below on the sea where white sails were cutting across the blue chop. Somebody shut the big doors behind the brightness, so darkness and symbolism of death invested the church.

A man was handing out mass cards in the vestibule of the church, small cards with Jenesis Constantinides printed on the back, with the dates of her birth and death. Below was a verse of Greek poetry, once taught to school children. A colored lithograph of St. Achilles adorned the front. In life as body and flesh, St. Achilles had preached the gospel from town to town, leading the people from the dark path of paganism into the light of Christ. He had inherited a huge fortune along the line, but because his creed was showing mercy on the weak and defenseless, he gave away money to the poor widows, and Christians who had fallen on tough times. This piece of historical insight would serve as a prologue for words revealed a bit further into the mass.

Many candles on sconces were flickering, and the flame waxing and waning danced a pattern on the walls. The six men rolled the casket now resting on a wheeled cradle, towards the altar. A song of grief was belting from the gold pipes of the church organ — a tiny Greek lady was pushing like mad on the keys. Taking a headcount of relatives, including distant grandchildren who had not visited her in the last ten years but cried the hardest when informed of their inheritance money, and people Jenesis considered family like her hairdresser, the butcher, and two mailmen, 157 were in attendance. The rest of the pews were crammed with town's people. The deceased was well respected and loved, and a few of the oldest could remember her baptism in the same church.

Like all Greek funerals, it was a long but moving ceremony. The funeral mass pushed way beyond two hours of steady chanting and prayers. The Greek priest waved a brass vessel spewing smoke around the altar and wound down Jenesis Constantinides's funeral mass.

The six bearers were making good steam up the aisle towards the rear. The Greek priest followed with three altar boys.

Just then, Ajax Zografos who was seated at the pew's end and measuring the face of the altar boys, reached over and touched the elbow of the Greek priest, arresting his attention. Ajax was perhaps the highest profile attorney on the island. He'd been in and out of Greek courts for years; he knew all the legal ropes. He'd taken cases all the way to Athens. Ajax Zografos was also Jenesis Constantinides's lawyer.

"Father, did you hit the jackpot," Ajax told the Greek priest.

"Pos einai afto?" questioned the priest. The closest altar boy was eavesdropping.

"Jenesis Constantinides left your church seven million dollars from the will."

"Echete na astieveste," said the priest frozen in his tracks. The altar boy's eyes had gotten very large, and he cocked his head at an angle toward Ajax Zografos.

"I wouldn't kid about something like that," Ajax told him.

The old man who had been giving out mass cards, had opened the big doors wide, and kicked down the pawl stops — a bath of light came up the aisle.

The best part of the revelation for Ajax Zografos, was seeing the look on the priest's face in the new light. You could see his mind racing a million miles an hour.

The procession began moving again. Joannes Plastras came out with the first wave of family. After all, distant nephews from the United States deserved some kind of cuts. Joannes had been seen walking with a very old lady in a black sweater, rubbing her shoulder blades as they shuffled out the church.

A vast number of mourners ringed Jenesis Constantinides's tomb. The sexton had dug a respectable grave, and you could see by all the stones in the till, it had been tough digging. The sea of black figures stood very still on the green grass. The Greek priest, still full of excitement from all of Ajax's good news, was fighting all of his emotions of astonishment, and put all his pent-up energy into the graveside sermon. His voice rang sharp and clear across the cemetery, words casted with hope for the broken hearted.

The mourners departed in a single wave of black habiliments. The black hearse car and procession of motor cars moved up the cemetery lane, and out through the stone pillars. Joannes had stayed behind.

He stood alone over the grave. A flood of colored flowers hugged the open charnel. Joannes blessed his forehead and said a very short prayer. He clutched the money clip in the grey vest over his heart and wiped a shallow tear of grief from his cheek.

Then with the edge of his boot, he kicked a sliver of gravel over the grave, because he wanted to get everything covered as soon as possible. A metallic clinking rose from the casket. The last anybody ever saw of him, was going sideways up through the tombstones, under the olive trees, and disappearing himself into the crowd.

Old Man Winter

Nick had been thinking about it for a long time. He'd been looking forward with a great deal of zest. He'd been waiting for everything to happen. Things had begun to come around. There had been some promise in the air. Grey ominous clouds had hovered over the lake. Snow squalls had been prominent the past Sabbath. The white crystals of hoar frost had come in the night — the oak leaves in the forest sounded a deep crunching under footfalls. Margins of winter had flirted with man. Powder dust of snows had settled in the woods. Puddles along the foot path, had begun to freeze at the edges.

But Nick could not grasp his wish. There had been lapses in weather. Cooperation had been slow in coming around. The silver platter for his wish, were cold snaps at large. Red needles of thermometers were hedging. They had not dived. But Nick knew it would come. He'd seen glimpses and parts while making circuit of the lake. Mother Nature would not let him down. He would get his chance.

Nick came down through the orchard. The ground was frozen solid. A dusting of fresh snow was sprinkled in the orchard duff; the cups of brown milkweeds, rattled in the soft breeze. Long blades of lush green meadow grass, so far immune to the sting of frost, lay hither and tither under the fanned limbs of fruit bearers.

Three bright Braeburn apples, lay dropped in the duff. Their red skins showed exceedingly bold on the white snow dust. Nick reached down, and picked the cold red apple, placing it in the slash pocket of his green and black mackinaw. Then he slipped back in his white deerskin mittens.

From a long thong of leather, Nick's hockey skates bounced on his back. Nick did not believe in the Bauer thing. He only skated on CCM. The blades of his skates clattered on the shoulder of his green wools and blowing out a stream of vapor in the cold air, Nick descended through the pine forest. Soft breeze was raking in the canopy. A platoon of chickadees was singing in the crowns of green needles. The black-capped birds with white cheeks brought notes across the forest — fee-bee…fee-bee.

Nick looked down through the pine forest. He could see the long sliver of lake, the grey ice beyond the stand of trunks with husked bark. In the scent of the evergreens, Nick's dream had come true. Four days, and four nights of cold snaps, had formed a sheet glass of ice. The silver platter had finally come. Nick could at last cinch up his laces and cut the ice.

Nick parted the brush curtain of choke cherries along the shore and stepped free on the ice. The ice was plenty thick enough to hold men. It was over five inches thick, crystal clear ice where Nick could look clear to the bottom. Nick jumped up and down in his pack boots. There was no response. He could see very clear by deep cracks where the ice flexed, just how thick and safe the ice was. In the distance, and running across the lake, Nick could hear the sonar sounds of ice making expansion — Thathumm! Thathumm!

Nick went back through the veil of brush and sat on the pine needles. He kicked off his packs. It was wonderful to feel the Woodsman socks on his feet; grey wool socks with a red cable knit collar. They were very special socks, because they were a Christmas present from his girlfriend Rachel.

It was a bitter-sweet experience. Rachel had bought Nick those socks, the Christmas before. She had a tragic accident that summer, while moving briskly on roller blades. Her head had struck the pavement at a great speed. After she went black, she never did come back on this side. In a deep coma of an ICU ward, where the monitor had provided poor results, the family had elected to let her slip away in dignity.

Nick brushed the dead pine needles from the Woodsman socks. Then he slipped his feet into the hockey skates, very slowly tugging and pulling one at a time, banging his heels on the pine floor to set things snug. He always felt warm and safe in those grey wool socks, because it felt like Rachel was with him in their world of love.

Nick reached in his green and black mackinaw jacket and pulled out the red Braeburn. The apple was firm, with a perfect skin. Nick bit into the apple. It was a very satisfactory apple, and Nick was very happy sitting alone, with the chants of chickadees singing in the canopy.

He ate and chewed very slowly. It was special eating a free apple, in the dead of winter. He knew the apple would give him a special energy on the ice. Nick worked around the apple, chewing off chunks, then chucked the core on the floor of brown pine needles. It tumbled quite a few times; and when it came to rest, a singular chickadee fluttered down, and pecked away at the seeds.

Nick tugged and cinched the laces of his CCM skates. He started down low, then worked the white laces, topping off with a few hitches. Nick loved the big box toes of his CCM's, and how the skates hugged his feet. His figure rose slowly from the seat on the brown needles, and Nick stretched out all his joints under the cathedral of pines.

A grey baclava was pulled from his pack. Nick had procured it from a commissary store on an Air Force base. Fighter pilots sometimes used them under their flight helmets. The grey hood was sewn out of some kind of napped cotton; and when Nick slipped it over his head, a wonderful warmth came to him.

Then Nick slipped on his helmet, with leather padding as once seen in criterium bicycle racing. It was a very old helmet. Nick had worn it in the old days. He'd been a Category racer. He did not especially like riding criterium, sprinting around tight circuits in a big city. He'd been a road racer by heart, riding 120 kilometers in the undulation of country roads. But the coach had pressed all the team into some criterium, so they would be well rounded and have snap in the pedal stroke. The coach always knew what was best for his riders.

Nick knew that skating alone in this kind of temperature, could be a dangerous business. There were only two cottages on the lake. The stove pipes were dead. The tourists had all departed for the land of snowbirds. Nick was all alone.

He knew that a fall on the ice, catching a blade in a rifle crack of the ice, could be a tragic mistake. He could very easily crack a skull and break a rib. If he blacked out on the ice bed, it might be all over. He might never come to. Rachel was no longer around to check on him. Nick knew if he never came around, when the black of night enveloped the lake, stars twinkling bright, the pack of coyotes would rip apart his flesh, and have a field day on him.

Nick fed the strap of his chin buckle and cinched everything down. Then he walked on the blades like a stilt man down through the pine forest, across the pinched shoreline back through the brush, and set foot on the ice.

He dug in his skates and headed north up the ice. It was adventure at its very best. Brother, you never seen ice like that in a long time. It was like pane glass. Around the shore, say twenty yards out near the shoals, you could see everything sharp and clear on the bottom. It reminded Nick of a giant cinematograph film, skating along and seeing the bars of gravel, the faces of rocks, old tree stumps, and the weeds close to shore, all under the beautiful ice.

The lake stretched for three miles long and was one-half mile at the widest berth. There was not a skate mark on the place. Nick had seen only deer tracks on the trail. The lake was devoid of all wayfarers. It was a ghost wilderness. Nick was all alone. This escalated his cheerfulness, to the highest degree. Adventure pulsed in his veins. He truly felt alive and on top of the world, as he carved up the lake ice in his CCM hockey skates.

Nick never ventured far from shore. He remembered what his father had schooled him about as a little boy, that a pocket of rotten ice may be lurking in water over your head.

Besides, near the shore through the glass-clear ice, you could see like magic to the bottom.

Making full circuits of the lake, never appealed to Nick. He liked skating up the lake, maybe, eight hundred yards, looping around in a power turn on the razor edges, about-face with swooping down long carving motions, working the legs and hearing the skates cut — krump — krump — krump. He liked sensing the craftsmanship in the stainless blades, slicing off grey shavings across the ice bed. After a few orbits, the scarring of the grey ice, made a guide-on for Nick to follow. He saw it as a giant criterium track on ice.

Nick knew his old coach would be happy with that kind of thinking.

Nick's favorite part of his wilderness training ground, was skating that cove up the north end, carving quick turns around the jagged shoreline. A big beaver lodge of chewed saplings and packed with dun-colored mud, formed a dome above the ice. Nick always could picture the beavers sitting below in the lodge and wondered what other positions they might take. He always looked for the beavers swimming under the ice too, but never could catch them in the act. The beavers were smart, and had gone nocturnal as night swimmers, because man tried to kill them for their pelts for quite some time now.

Over four days and four nights, Nick's dream lived. The weather had held steadfast. Every night hovered at zero. No storms in sight. The lake was a rink of glass, as if caressed nightly by Frank Zamboni, scooting around on his ice machine under the twinkled zenith of star banks.

Every day, for four days, Nick returned. He laced up in the same general vicinity under the pine forest. By no compass of imagination, did his enthusiasm wane — in fact, it *grew* nightly. His mind raced with fancies for the next day on blades, while castle-building under nightfall. Under the hand-sewn quilt, warmth seeping into his bones from the bite of winter adventure, Nick dreamed of magical circuits with his blades cutting the grey glass. He traveled with supernatural ease in his nighttime visions.

On the second forenoon, a peculiar revelation had dawned on Nick. There were no ice shavings from the day before, where his skates had carved and kicked out frozen skives across the ice. It had been a morning of flat queer light, traces of faint sun trying to break from behind the grey sky blanket; and Nick noticed the grey ice had healed, looking down from the cool shadows of the pine forest.

He quickly pressed to the ice in his packs, enthralled with his discovery. The deep strokes of his skates were still present, but the shavings of grey curlicues had vanished; the thought crossed Nick's mind they'd been smelted by the faint sun rays and had transfused back in company of the ice bed.

Each night, Nick ate well. He knew the needs of energy would be great on the lake. T-bone steaks were grilled on the iron skillet. Baked potatoes were smothered with farm butter. He boiled spaghetti noodles on the gas range, made the way when all of them were bicycle racers with little money — a plate of pasta garnished with olive oil, black pepper, and table salt. Nick popped Ibuprofen tablets too, because he wanted to shake the pain in his muscle groups by daybreak.

Before hitting the feathers, Nick always placed his CCM's by the wood stove, and laid out his Woodsman socks on the chair back, caught in the tepid heat of the banked fire. Saltine crackers were spread with chunky peanut butter and strawberry jam, wrapped in wax paper. His white deerskin mittens, old leather helmet, and his day pack, were all accounted for and gathered on the rocking chair. Then Nick drifted in sleep. In his sleep he practiced fancy moves on the ice and passed imaginary pucks to imaginary friends down the frozen lake.

On the third day Nick brought a treat for his bird friends. He procured a few pounds of beef suet from Ricardo's Butcher Shop. He's seen Ricardo with his own eyes, slice the white pasted insulation from the cow's rump on the meat hook. Around the kitchen table, Nick pressed in bird seeds, some boxed raisins, and a few dried cranberries. His fingertips became encrusted with the lard. A small section of big mesh screen was snipped out from the junk heap in the tool shed.

At the lake, Nick rummaged a baseball-sized stone from the shoreline, an improvised hammer from the toolbox of wilderness; and reaching in his pocket, tugged out an 8-penny box nail, and whacked everything home with the rock on a towering pine tree.

That afternoon, Nick was bushed from hours of continuous skating. He'd found a great deal of confidence that day, gunning it around in a giant figure-eight around the beaver cove, having exhausted all kinds of energy into the ice. Nick departed the lake, and coming up through the curtain of brush, beheld a spectacle of colours in the green forest: The Downy woodpecker was pecking on the suet cage. His red head against the bird's white back, was caught in the rays of sun. The bird jabbed its beak with a machine-like motion, until Nick inched forward to read the red feathers, then fluttered away in the cathedral of pines.

Nick's fourth day on the ice was casted in splendor. It was a bluebird day. An orange wafer of sun burned bright in the sky. Cumulus clouds traced with purple edges, patrolled the horizon. Nick could feel the sun's beam across his countenance, and the orange rays basked across his nape. The world of the lake was in deep silence — nevertheless, the ice pack had needs for flexing muscles, and rifle-like cracks broke the tranquility. The concussion of ice breaking sounded off the mountain face, and against the horizon a flock of black crows dotted the sky.

Nick put on his blue aviators and skated the glass ice in the orange ray of splendor, under the fairy blue sky. There was never anything quite like that sensation, the skating along the pine forest that hugged the shore, the green mantel of a million needle clusters towering above Nick. Trees that spread their roots under the stone choked bank and sipped from the lakebed. It gave perspective to things, and Nick felt a very small carving and cutting along the sentry soldiers of pines.

In that very day of mighty splendor, Nick was arrested with curiosity. The bright yellow sun was beaming through the clear, semi-blue ice in the shallows; and gliding with his skates above, Nick could look down with the effects of a giant aquarium. The golden stones below the ice, and beds of gravel where bluegills finned in summer, looked like you could reach out and touch them. Spectrums of wild colors, needle-thin rays of orange and blue were fanning above green faces of the weed beds.

Cruising the sheet of glass... Nick thought he saw something on a piece of driftwood below the ice. He wheeled around, the blades shooting a dusting of ice crystals. Dropping to his knees, Nick removed his blue aviators, cupped the white deerskin mittens around his eyes, and pressed his face very near the ice for a good look.

He'd seen something alright. There were two figures clinging to the silver-grey driftwood. He pushed his eyebrows closer to the ice bed and scrutinized the underwater world. Two salamanders were sleeping on the log. Both of them had their eyes closed tight. They were spread out prone, with their tiny claws dug into the log. They appeared to be in never-never land. Nick pounded the ice with his right mitten and measured the black salamanders. Nothing happened. They remained in the sleeping position. The salamanders must have come out of deep sleep in the mud, when they sensed the sun beam in the shallows. Nick pounded both fists on the ice, banging the white deerskins in a drum-like beat. Watching in the sheet of ice — Oh! Looking so very close — Nick saw a salamander blink its eye. The mittens came down with another burst, and spurred out from hibernating sleep, the two salamanders departed from the sun basked log, and swam very quickly with their tails wiggling into the beds of mud.

Nick sat on the ice and ate all his Saltine crackers at once. The peanut butter and jam tasted very satisfactory. Nick could not hold himself to one. He ate all ten crackers, wiped his mouth with the mackinaw's sleeve, and began counting out another few laps.

There's an old saying, "Smell the roses while you can." Nick was glad he'd followed the passage. Bluebird days could be a rare presentation, in the dead of winter. A dead calm had come across the ice, with an orange sun falling. Nick took one last circuit of the ice, hearing the chants of the skates cutting. A swarm of black crows pulled off the ice in the far distance, and the scavengers held up in the oak grove on a high ridge above the lake. The trunks of the trees were silhouetted in black against the rays of setting sun; and the crows were crazy yelling in the dead stillness. Their bellies were full. The carrion crows had been feeding on a deer carcass on the ice, taken down by the night predators. The deer had made a crucial mistake, a hoofed animal testing the ice. Fitted with deep claws and foot pads like sandpaper, the night stalkers had cut the deer to ribbons.

Nick came off the ice. He was bushed. It was a good tiredness though, and he could taste a beer going down his throat. Nick parted the brush and plunked down on the bed of brown needles. Taking off CCM's that fit your feet, could be big work against tired legs. Nick dug the sterns of the stainless blades into the pine duff, having made a human-lever. It was good to wiggle his toes around again and slip them inside the felt packs.

Nick heard something on the tree bark. High in the pine tree, a pair of nuthatches, were working down toward the suet cage. The white breasted nuthatch was a curious bird. They came down trees headfirst. They were born to be daredevils, throwing a beak towards gravity. Shafts of nearly holy light were falling in the grove, filtered sunbath from the setting sun; the steel blue plumes of the bird's back, the white belly and beady eyes, were caught in prominence of the sensation. The brace of hatches, nervous little fellows always on the move, filled their bellies quickly on the white suet ladened with seeds and fluttered off through the pine forest.

Nick swung the leather long-thong over his shoulder and humped it up the slope through the pine forest. It would be his last encounter on the lake ice, for things to come. He followed the deer trail over the bluff, skirted the orchard of stark frames, and stoked the stove inside his cabin.

That night, under a stiff blow out of the south-west, all the fires of his combustible passion for gliding the lake ice, had been vanquished. A wind driven blanket of heavy, wet snow fell by night; the white mask coagulated like iron when the temperature dived. Pine boughs in the grove by the lake, snapped like toothpicks, a thunderclap popping in the gloom of night. The suet cage was plastered tight, sealed by the cap of crust. The woodpeckers on the following day, would riddle the congealed snow with their beaks like machine gun fire, and open the feeding station.

But the lake ice had took a real mucking. Over a foot of snow had blanketed the ice. The glass sheet of ice was doomed. It would be a prelude for disaster. Nick's world could not recover.

Two days of rain followed, where fog banks hugged the ice field at daybreak. All kinds of weather, showed on the scene. One day would usher in a huge melting, where slush ran in gutters of the village. Then the next three diving way below zero. Sleet peppered the landscape — the limbs of the Braeburn orchard, bowed and glistened from the weight.

Nick waited a good month, but nothing happened. Mother

Nature had not dealt the cards, where her hands could render the perfections of glass ice. Nick tried daily repertoire of calisthenics and fanned himself with dumbbells. But it was not the same, for sheer adventure always beckoned on the ice.

A Canadian deep freeze had descended from the north, and for five days the temperatures quivered in the negative numbers. Nick had gone to the lake for investigation. But it was a forlorn experience. Looking down at the pockmarked ice, a million tiny craters made Nick think of the moon, after a barrage from the meteor fields.

Nick pressed back home. He cut through the orchard, crunching across the glazed snow. The last few Braeburns had dropped and had been pecked by the songbirds. On the bluff looking through the fruit trees, was Belden's Farm. Outside the white-washed cow barn, was a steaming heap of cow manure. It was the only thing Nick had seen in God's world, that was not frozen solid. Spontaneous fermentation had taken place inside the huge mound, a chestnut brown pile with shafts of golden hay chaffs. Grey wafts of vapor were rising against winter's grip. It was a very intimate scene, because Nick knew the boy inside the barn. He could see his bright red toque, passing by the spartan windows of the cow parlor. The schoolboy depended on forking cow plops for spending money. It was a meager pay at best; but the young boy was thrilled of the authority handed to him when taking on the position, and the job had basically gone to his head. Nick could hear him in the barn, the thin metallic tines clanging along, and the heavy sounds of cows clomping on the stout plank stables. Even the cows seemed sad from the weather. A row of them had their big heads out the open-air windows, looking placidly over the bleak fields. They had been rebelling against leaving the barn for days, mulling around rather than getting cut-up on the crusted snow.

The boy in his red toque, came out against the whitewash barn, dressed in an old sweater and country boots, pushing a heaped wheelbarrow. He dumped it on the manure pile and went back inside the parlor. Nick could see steam coming from the cow's nostrils. A few of them chimed in, and scolded Nick across the barnyard — "Moooo! Moooo!"

Nick's last episode on the ice, was two weeks later. A late winter thaw had come to Derby. He hiked around the whole lake. All the wide-open expanses where the sun could beat on them, were barren of snow. The brook on the north end, was roaring into the lake. The rushing currents from its swollen banks, had exposed a pool of water. A thin ribbon of water hugged the west bank along the mountain. There were many ominous holes in the ice, and in one of them by the reeds, Nick had seen the head of a beaver surface. He was a big, fat blanket beaver, and waddling into the woods, began gnawing on a black birch trunk.

Nick packed it in. He knew he was done. There were always still chances the ice could recover with a fantastic sheet, but Nick was not counting on anything this far into the game. He figured if gambling was going to play into the picture, why he'd go down to the smoke shop and rub shoulders with a bookie, and put a wad of bread on the skins, when they were running steeplechase down at Austin's aqueduct.

Nick began putting things away. He rubbed the black leathers of his beloved CCM hockey skates, with a nice coat of Sno-Seal beeswax. His fingers ran Vaseline up the skate blades, as to prevent any rust in the off season. His old bicycle helmet was given similar treatment. Then he washed his Woodsman socks from Rachel, with mild soap in cool waters by hand. When they dried by the fire on the wood folding rack, he rolled them up and put them by the skates. A mothball was placed inside each sock too, because moths could bring havoc to wool socks.

Then Nick waited for spring. He prayed to himself under a colorful lithograph of the Hail Mary on the wall, that something would happen soon and get back with his exercise program, because the way he'd been slugging down beer and freely cutting wedges of Vermont cheese on Saltine crackers, Nick was almost certain his physician was going to prescribe a bottle of pills that would knock down his cholesterol levels.

—A short story completed on February 22nd of 2019. I started this story on about February 9th, which drove a wedge in my novel Tales in the Mountains, which was on page 57. I knew if Old Man Winter was not nailed down when the percolation was fresh in my mind, it might slip away. Like every short story I've ever written, it was a blast to write and came to me like a front row seat in the movie house, all the color and vivid confrontations flashing in my mind, a pictorial language perhaps only seen by a true writer.

The commands to make way had the ring of a great importance in them. The men were going forward to the heart of the din. They were to confront the eager rush of enemy. They felt the pride of their onward movement when the remainder of the army seemed trying to dribble down the road. They tumbled teams about with fine feeling that it was no matter so long as their column got to the front in time. This importance made their faces grave and stern. And the backs of the officers were very rigid.

As the youth looked at them the black weight of his woe returned to him. He felt that he was regarding a procession of chosen beings. The separation was great to him as if they had marched with weapons of flame and banners of sunlight. He could never be like them. He could have wept in his longings.

—Stephen Crane
The Red Badge of Courage

Dolly Dagger

CHAPTER ONE

It had been just about one hundred years now, since any of the smugglers had gone over the notch. History caught up with them. All of them were dead.

The setting rays of a summer sun were fanning Smuggler's Notch in the Green Mountains. Glistening beams of light caressed the trunks of yellow birch, falling down the tree trunks and casting highlights in the bark scrolls. The groves of balsam fir spilled off the ridgeline, their vivid blue-green needles against the fairy blue zenith. To the west past Johnson, a fireball of orange hung over the village horizon.

Way below off the other mountain face, descending the twisty road from Smuggler's Notch, a man below in the village of Stowe, was ordering a single doughnut in a doughnut shop. This particular man had worked exceedingly hard for his doughnut, and he'd paid very dear for his treat. More than most people would ever know.

The man's name was Merle Long. He was an asphalt man. He had been like that, since he came home from the war. Merle was a native of Stowe, Vermont. His people went back six generations.

I stood behind him. He did not know I was standing there, nor did he know anything about me. I'd never seen him before. His name and past history were a mystery. The man was ordering his doughnut.

"Give me a maple frosting doughnut," he said.

"You must really like those doughnuts," said the counter lady. It was clear he was a regular.

I stood behind this man in line and studied him at full length. He was fumbling in his pockets for money. The guard hairs on his neck had turned silver, and he needed a haircut. He wore a company ballcap that his boss had given him; on the small adjustment strap riding above his silver scruff hairs, was embroidered in tiny letters: Ranger Asphalt Company.

The man wore navy blue suspenders, over a long sleeve red shirt. Although he carried a good forty extra pounds from the past ten years of Vermont winters, he still looked rugged. His red shirt in the heat wave, gave him an aura of a red badge of courage.

But it was his boots that arrested my attention. It would be impossible to divulge what hue of split cowhides when they sold. Now they were scuffed and banged, the tongues recipients of diesel sprays from misting the drop box and hand implements, and the toe boxes were frosted in black asphalt. The black top on his boots, shimmered under the belt of setting sun past the windows near the flower box. His work boots were a walking testimony, a shrine really, of the time frames he'd spent on the paving crew.

The soles were caked with black asphalt too. All the resins from the paving jobs, made walking heavy for him. It lifted the man and made him look taller.

I studied the man more. I listened in depth to his voice. In none of his speech tones, was any remorse and bitterness detected. He seemed like a very happy fellow. The black frames of his eyeglasses were tilted from the back. He looked like a week-to-week man; and I would bet a lot of dough on it too.

The attendant put the maple frosted doughnut in a bag. He folded it down three times, then creased the seam.

As the man averted, a long and ugly scar bore down his cheek. Where the jagged scar ingressed into his eye orbit, there was none. He was missing the eye. There was no mincing the injury. The asphalt man had elected not to go with a glass eye. The black rims of his glasses framed the face. The shape of the glasses took away some of the nastiness of the scar. It was very clear, however, the man had once suffered. Very few would know, just how much he did.

The man gave me a quick nod. His good eye made a quick reaction to the floor. His scar and missing eye had made him like that around strangers. I obliged him. There was a small spark in his eye. The man carried his doughnut in the bag, like a man wading in the lake. He carried the small brown bag in that position, all the way to his Ford pickup truck. Then he fired the motor and wheeled out. He stepped on the gas smartly toward the north on Route 100.

That summer, the roadbed of Route 100 was his sugar daddy. Ranger Asphalt Paving had landed the resurface job on the road. The scarifying began from Route 89 and ran into Stowe village. With that kind of huge contract, came along with long days and mandatory overtime. For Merle Long and his paving crew, this spelled out big fat paychecks, greenbacks a lot of the boys would salt away in tin boxes for winter. All of them were all over that kind of money. Looking at all those dollar signs on the green checks each week of summer, brought them sincere happiness. For blue collar men with no college educations, just being around those kinds of figures almost put them over the top. For a lack of a better term, a great deal of them got money hungry. There were no Roman letters of guilt burned into anybody's brow; Thanksgiving week brought about with golden turkey, and layoff slip for the asphalt men.

Merle Long motored up Route 100. The hands of time were 8:00 PM straight up. He had banked twelve hours that day. Merle went through his daily routine, eating his maple frosted doughnut on the move. He took bites between the bumps. He'd gotten his sweet tooth as a young boy, eating cups of shaved ice drenched with maple syrup. His lust for the flavor never waned.

Merle passed a fleet of Ranger's construction equipment, parked on the scuffed-out shoulder for the night — a Caterpillar bulldozer had punched out a temporary parking area for the iron. Johnny Terejko, head mechanic for Ranger Asphalt Company, was under the yellow bonnet of a Champion road grader. Merle could see him wrenching from his good eye. From inside the cab of the blue Ford, he gave him three toots. Johnny was doing a stunt man act, balancing on the rear tires, an oily rag dangling from each back pocket of his dark blue trousers. He gave a backwards wave, never averting his attention from the engine bay. Above in the sky below a procession of white clouds, the first of the evening stars had appeared.

Rebelliously, Johnny stabbed the throttle linkage under the grader's bonnet, and a huge coughing bellow of black smoke, filled the air with a tower of raven pother that drove back the mosquito swarms.

Merle drove through the village of Stowe, creeping along. The tourists appeared to be on a real buying spree. Many people with city faces were carrying all kinds of bags. They had a hard time fitting in. Even the transplants who lived in the village for years, still stuck out like sore thumbs. They had arrived in town with their treasure chests. Their money clashed with sharp demarcation against the nature of native Vermonters, and certain establishments were stricken in the hue of these altercations. In the prominence of these historical buildings, a red old house with weathered side shingles sat on the hill, with a clothesline strung across the porch with the wash and clasped by wood pins, and a boy on the stoop with bare feet and a round belly with no shirt, waived at Merle. The boy did not smile, and he watched the truck go out of site.

The blue Ford came around the turn on Mountain Road, putting out first gear, the old girl puffing a tiny stream of grey-blue smoke. The valve guides on Merle's Ford had been getting tired since ... had it really been three years now?

Merle Long glanced up the Little River. She was running with a purling current for the hot spell; the white fields of sun baked stones speckled up the banks, and the rapid's tail spilled into a golden sand floor of the river; the pool dropped to ten feet, and minnows were finning in the shallows; near the bridge abutment the current turned a dark ominous green, and veins of the shale buttress stood on end; way above in the S-turn of the Little River, was a leaning tree with stout limbs, that always seemed fit for a Tarzan swing; but there was no rope and only a cove of limbs over the water; near the ten foot hole of the green current, there was a gang of school boys swimming, slapping the water, and horsing around; some kid with a chiseled face down there, let out a scream of summer; he banged his skinny ribcage with both fists, and chanted a King Kong bellow up the river.

Merle was still stopped dead before the bridge. His yellow turn signal worked the traffic. But there was no break in the stream of traffic off the mountain, and a well-respected blonde in a white summer dress, drove by sitting high in her dark blue LR4.

Out on the front porch of The Stowe Inn, were many figures. Merle could see for certain from his singular eye, three ladies in straw summer hats. Come to find out, there was a big blowout for Tango dancing in a ballroom all weekend in the Stowe village. The Stowe Inn had sold right out. A no vacancy sign hung defiantly out front. Two guys in front of their wives, were practicing Tango moves on the porch.

One of the guys was a little too serious in the drama, and maybe a little too gay in the hard liquor; and the last time around he almost spun himself in orbit and careened off the white railing. His wife sat him down right away on the rocker, and she looked mad alright.

A break opened in traffic. Merle shot across. He went up the lane to Richie Spreda's blacksmith shop. Richie had been repairing the mowing deck on Merle's lawn tractor, a 1971 Wheel Horse. The deck was resting on the steel work bench, outside in the flat light of summer dusk. Fresh welds adorned a new gusset plate, and the welds had been highly laced with an electric grinder disc.

Merle bent down in the queer light. He inspected the welds. A bug was buzzing around his ear. The welds were perfect rosary welds, with no porosity holes and botched up slag, just what he expected.

Like many times in the past, Richie's shop was wide open. The barn style doors threw themselves open to the elements. The window in the above studio were cranked open. Merle could see a goose-neck lamp glowing on the work bench. Shadows were building between the floor tools.

Merle investigated behind the shop. Down under the forest's cool shade on the riverbank, the water of the river below spilling over the stone beds. A hibachi grill was glowing red coals near the plank table. A fork rested on a soiled paper plate. A bottle of ketchup was at attention on the green plank table. But no Richie around.

"Richie!" shouted Merle. There was no reply. He shouted again into the blacksmith shop. There was no reply. The assemblage of machines stood a rigid attention on their pedestals, for the next calling of service.

Merle shelled a twenty spot from his well-worn wallet, and placed the bill on the table, pinned down by a red brick. A cedar waxwing watched from above in the sanctuary of maple limbs. The beautiful bird was preparing for sleep.

Merle opened the tailgate, and heaved the mower deck, with the moves of a man well-schooled in lifting. He'd dug the chute into his thigh muscle, using the power in his arms, and threw the metal housing into the Ford.

He looped up towards Smuggler's Notch, the last glow of orange in the black shadows of the balsam firs, took Mayo Farm Road around, and cut over the rise by the old Parker barn. His running lights disappeared into the second growth timber, and all above Smuggler's Notch a galaxy of stars was twinkling in the blackness.

The blue Ford pulled in on the stone driveway. Amber arc lights shone inside the quaint red farmhouse. Merle went inside home.

"Hello, my Honey," said his wife, Dolly.

Carrying his tin black lunch pail, he walked across the wooden floor in his crusty tar boots, and said kissing Dolly on the forehead, "I love you Baby. I'll always love you."

And she knew in her heart he meant it too. They'd been together since sixteen. The spark went off then, and never waned away.

"How was your day?" asked Dolly. She'd already summed his answer.

"Man, what a day!" exclaimed Merle. "We really put down some material today. There's nothing like putting down asphalt in a heat wave. The steam roller men sure had a field day in the hot sun, and our seams came together like magic."

They sat for supper. Conversation was light, and happy, and went forward. Steam lifted from the Shepherd's Pie. Two ears of butter and sugar were on the dinner plate. Merle laced an ear with the pepper shaker, then worked the ear like an electric typewriter.

Dolly would have loved to ask him, if he'd ever tire from his job. He was on the high end of sixty. He was in excellent shape, except for the occasional pain in the bad eye socket, and many superficial afflictions. But she knew it would kill him to quit.

Merle was an asphalt man. It was in his bloodstream. There was nothing he didn't like about the job. He was addicted to the smell of asphalt, the pungent sweet smell about the paving scene. He got especially excited when the power auger in the drop box, started bringing in material and the black nuggets of glistening tar being drawn down under. He loved to watch the tri-axle jockeys backing up, the bell on the back hub sounding, "Ding ... ding ... ding ... ," as the trucker backed toward the drop zone; and every summer it seemed there was a kid on the crew fresh out of high school, who let the job go to his head with all the testosterone flowing around the big horsepower of all the iron; and just as the truck was backing, the smoke streaming from the twin chrome stacks, the kid would jump in view of the driver's door mirror, and start twirling his arms State Trooper style for directing traffic, and barking in his changing voice into a man, "Back her up! Back her up!" and the kid would be dead serious and keep waving his hands with the truck driver backing with no attention to the kid and bringing the load home to the paver's bump station.

But everybody on the crew sure loved the green boys, the new brood rising, because they knew he was of their flesh and clay.

Looking back through the mirror of time, Merle Long could see his face. It did not look like himself these days. He hardly recognized himself, handsome with both eyes gleaming with wonder. He could see himself through the high school kid on the crew just as well, that long ago summer when he came on with Ranger Asphalt Company.

Merle Long still wore his brass buckle, he purchased forty-seven years back, with his first week's pay from the mail order house. The well-worn buckle was embossed with a Barber Greene 879 paver, a track machine with tank-like steering. Ranger was running an 879 Barber the year Merle signed on, a beauty of a beast painted in dark green. In those days the tail men, gauged the asphalt by hand and measuring stick, with a giant wheel of spoked iron. It was more art than science. Back in the barn at Ranger's yard, were two SA 41 Barber Greene, just in case they got in trouble on a paving run and needed backup. And brother, more than once in a jam, they sent the Rogers 40-ton lowboy in a pinch, so the SA 41 could finish off the fight.

Back then too, Ollie Woods and Morty Strong, were both running Autocar dump trucks. Ollie was running a DC 87 with flat-topped fenders, decked with a Gallon body that was embellished with three asphalt chutes. There will never be anything again, like the raw spartan power of an Autocar on the construction site. Say, they could take a beating, and the driver needed to know how to drive too, because the 5+4 shifter, known as the rock crusher, needed a good ear and skill, to move the hulk forward. Morty and

Ollie had the skill. But they were dead now, buried in Stowe village cemetery.

All this collection of memory, the millions of hours on Merle's punch clock, had conformed and forged the man, and by very nature was how he defined himself. He could not fathom no longer being part of the paving crew, because he would be in strange territory and out of his element, where he would be grasping for new identities in thin air. This did not sit well with him. He liked his current definition of being his kind of man.

But in spite of these things, he loved Dolly more. He wondered often lately — and it sure felt that way after all these years together — that if people saw them as one. It sure seemed that way. That the procession of their lives through time, had transfigured them into the perpetual hands of a clock: that synchronicity had evolved in the form of flesh.

Merle polished off two plates of Shepherd's Pie. They had consumed the bowl of strawberries for desert, with scoops of vanilla ice cream. There was plenty of reasons, Merle Long carried extra weight.

The couple retired almost immediately. Merle took a hot shower; then they were off to bed. Four thirty in the morning comes fast. Asphalt men need their sleep.

Dolly killed the light on the nightstand. Merle put his head across her belly. He found that position very satisfactory. Although he never made fortunes to afford a hunting camp, and got his eye gouged out as a young man, Merle Long still considered himself the most fortunate man in the world. He had passion in those black steaming nuggets of road material, and he had the love of his life. He was a blessed man. He reasoned by living in faith, he had entered Paradise.

Within his wife Dolly, were many deep meanings. It was sure a story worth telling, and very few people in the village of Stowe knew its nature. Its content had never been divulged to the paving crew. Merle had discovered this story in the print of a magazine. He had been horizontal at that time and hooked to intravenous feeding in a hospital bed.

The year had been 1970. The magazine article covered Jimi Hendrix, focusing on some of his recording in the Electric Lady Studio.

Merle's eyes went to certain cut in the story — Dolly Dagger. He was stunned, that Jimi Hendrix and himself, shared the same birthday, November 27th. Merle liked that date, because his birthday a few years had coincided on Thanksgiving Day. He wondered if Jimi had done the turkey thing too.

Like a lot of Jimi's songs, the magazine revealed, Dolly Dagger was inspired by Jimi's girlfriend Devon Wilson. It's a true story. He instantly felt a brotherly bond. Jimi had been celebrating his birthday on November 27th of 1969. Mick Jagger of the Rolling Stones was present, and accidently pricked his finger. He'd asked through those world-famous lips and mouth box, "Does anybody have a Band-Aid?" in that British accent.

Devon rushed to Mick and told him, "That won't be necessary."

Then she grabbed his wrist and sucked the blood from his finger. So when Jimi wrote Dolly Dagger, he drew on his birthday party and penned, "She drinks her blood from a jagged edge."

Merle grooved on that. He was extremely moved that his girlfriend Dolly was in the bold print of the song's title. Merle checked his watch from the hospital bed. Dolly was due any minute. He could use her more than ever. The surgeons had just gone in for the second time. He could feel himself slipping toward some edge, and the bad demons were already in his head. He would need great assistance, to reach convalescence. His girlfriend climbing the stairs of the hospital, would prove with flying colors she would be his Dolly Dagger.

CHAPTER TWO

It was an early spring morning, when Merle rode the magic bus out of Stowe village. It was a fateful ride, that would almost cost him his life. He looked through the bus window, the green swollen buds of sugar maples, sprinkling the village with life. He could envision the dark ominous jungle in his eyes. In his mind, he was already having deep conservation within his soul. Mister, those zips were going to pay. He'd just been drafted. There was no turning around. He was going to Vietnam.

Merle Long could shoot running deer through the boiler works. His vision was still 20-20. In the past hour, under the tower bell of the white church in Stowe village, he'd kissed Dolly's lips. He'd wished it had been more passionate kissing. But there was much serious emotion in the embrace, hedged in with the regimentation of their game faces, as if the couple were kissing on prayers. Standing in the bus clutching the pipe rail, the bus lurching and climbing over the mountain pass, Merle was certain he could kill running communists with a clear conscience. His novel of love had been reduced to letter writing.

His life with Dolly, his rookie year with the Ranger boys on asphalt, was all too valuable. He would fight his way back.

But the Vietnam War, was not the kind of war you see in the movie house. Guerrilla warfare, jungle tactics, riding slicks into search and destroy missions, all provided savage bursts of contact. Especially up in I Corps, when the enemy was a fierce combatant like the 325th NVA Division. But contact was a short movie clip, over soon with only wafts of gun powder about, where Merle and his platoon found it almost impossible to get running dinks in their gun sights.

Merle sure respected the NVA. They were not moonlight soldiers, like the farmers down south who cultivated rice one day and killed Americans the next. No sirree Mister, the NVA were the real thing. They'd been at it a long time and had sent the French limping off the battlefield. They were pure jungle fighters.

On the other hand, the NVA feared the leathernecks. They knew from costly experience, going head on with Merle's company of the 3rd Marine Division, would be a tragic mistake. They would pay with BC on the jungle floor. So, the NVA orchestrated the fight with curted ambush, letting the Ak47s sling a little lead, then dee-dee and melt back into their jungle. Many times the faces of leathernecks had been struck with wonder, after combing the area after contact, and discovered the telltale signs of troughs from dead man's boots dragged across the jungle floor, the fronds of bamboo laced with blood trails ... but no bodies.

But then in the breaking dawn of that May morning, only a few clicks from the DMZ, the boots on the ground would come face to face in a real gunfight. When it was over, both sides would be sorry they messed with the other.

Late in the afternoon of the day before contact, they'd chopped out a bivouac area, and set up an NDP. High above the jar heads swinging machetes, a small, single-engine Piper Cub was buzzing the blue. The boonierat Marines peered through the triple canopy jungle, knowing well the Green Man was sitting next to the pilot. The Piper was very high in the sky, and at that altitude the engine's prop whine was out of reach to the human ear; the tiny metal bird presented a supernatural effect and inched across the sky. Sweat burning his eyes, Merle watched the airplane and said in his Vermonter twang, "You can bet your last dollar boys, that Green Man is fixin' to throw us into the meat grinder."

Just then, RO Perry Jones, spiked the volume knob on his Prick-25, connected over to battalion net, and listened very closely.

"Rover Dover Red Fox Leader, this is Jolly Green Giant, over," said the Marine commander from the plane's cockpit.

"Jolly Green Giant, that's a copy from the fox people. We've skipped the red rope on the comic book and have set up our November Delta Papa. Over," said radio operator Jones.

"Flip over to your Charlie Charlie," said the Green Man.

Company Commander Cpt. Wendall Oakley, hit the handset button and said, "Whiskey Oscar on net."

"Listen up," said the Green Man getting to the point, "we've got good intel, that the NVA is almost on your doorstep. A LRRP platoon from Marine Recon, confirmed heavy movement on a red-ball at coordinates" — he gave the exact spot on the topographic map in code, just in case the little people had hacked into their frequency. "I want you company on that objective by 15:30 hours on tomorrow afternoon. Any questions?"

"We could use a backup company," flatly said Company Commander Oakley, "and perhaps ..."

"Don't give me any bullshit," cut the Green Man into the conversation. "This is a Marine's war, Sonny, and I fully expect your

Marines to put a world of hurt on the little people, by tomorrow's sunset. Get the picture?"

"Yes Sir," exclaimed Cpt. Oakley.

"Don't worry boys, we set up a mobile firebase this very afternoon — Mustang Sally. There's a whole battery of Marine dime-nickel boys, just itching for some hot coordinates. We've got F-4 fast movers on station. Gunships of the Cobra people are awaiting my call. I've got your back covered, so let's get moving at first light." Then the radio went silent, and the Piper Cub pulled a huge swath into the fairy blue sky and went out of sight above the green tropical forest.

"Why that stupid prick," said RO Jones, in reference to the Green Man. He said it looking directly at Vinnie Palladino, M-60 machine gunner for the 2nd platoon, out of Queens, New York. "What's he think — this is my first GD firefight?" Jonesy cut off the Prick-25, quickly folded the antenna before he caught a sniper round, and continued, "I've been in contact with Mustang Sally all afternoon. They've got our NDP marked with a nice fat thumb tack. Their guns are fixed 400 meters west of our bedroom. I'm already two steps in front of the Green Man," said RO Perry Jones with a straight face.

That part of the story was true. Mustang Sally had pre-zeroed their guns on a forlorn hillside just inside a north fix of the DMZ. Fast mover pilots from altitude, had recorded the hits. They were right on the money. Firebase Mustang Sally had Red Fox Leader, covered with a fleet of 105 howitzers. The deadly blued muzzles, aimed into the far zenith. The firebase was kept on alert through the night. It would prove to be a well thought advance.

It was SOP for Bravo Company, to establish the FO listening post, within running distance from the resting rifle company, a three-man team with an M-60 machine gun. But in the very last threads of inky dusk, the listening post would move with a slight shift, just in case the NVA had their number. That's how Company Commander Oakley operated.

Following orders, the three Marines repositioned while night vision was still in order and set out the claymores along a pinched clearing near a tiny stream. They hooked the claymore mines in series to the clacker, so everything would blow at once.

They had placed the deadly muzzle of the M-60 across the log, peering from behind, and Vinnie Palladino pulled back the receiver bolt and loaded up. A long glistening snake of brass cartridges fanned across the jungle floor. Assistant machine gunner, Pvt. Terry Ford from Cody, Wyoming, linked up a second bandolier, his hands caressing the big brass rounds as if they were gold. PFC Floyd Leatherwood from the south of Moss Point, Mississippi, cradled his M-16. The whites of his eyes were like two moons in the gun encampment's black shadows. All three peered into the night, half-sipping breaths in their terror.

In the last rays of light, Merle Long had read Dolly's last love letter, three times over. He imagined himself kissing the inside of her wrist. He wanted her very bad. Then he folded the letter, placed it very carefully back inside the plastic bag, and fixed it with the rubber band. Merle always kept all his love letters in his fatigue's pouch pocket, riding high on his chest. Merle slipped under his poncho as a blanket, and spread out on the jungle floor, drifted away into deep sleep. Merle slept very sound, knowing all around him was the brothers of the Corps.

He was sure glad when his draft card arrived, he'd volunteered for Parris Island. The Marines gave him the sensation of being almost invincible.

The NVA began a trumpet note of tooting in the first rays of light. Roosting birds of exotic colors, fluttered in the high limbs. The music filled the triple canopy jungle, and the three men in the listening post were suddenly filled with goose bumps up the back. Merle sprung from his poncho, like a man pricked with thorns.

The Green Man had guessed wrong. The NVA had pulled a one-up during the night. They had creeped in under blackness, both the 324th NVA Division, and their compeers of the 325th NVA Division. The Marines would be in for one hell of a fight. The little people had them outnumbered five to one.

None of the listening post made it back alive. Floyd saw them coming first. He saw the pith helmets bobbing in the jungle, flashes of the little people in the lattice of foliage. Then Vinnie and Terry saw them too; glimpses of many figures running. Floyd had the clacker. He knew he must wait. He knew exactly Floyd must not waste anything. He watched with big eyes while the NVA were skipping across the stream — upon first three zips in the clearing — upon then a good ten little people gliding across the stream — upon entering the mine's kill zone.

Floyd hit the clacker three times. He hit the metal clacker, like a black man who once threw dice in a back alley of Biloxi, Mississippi. But this time Floyd was not gambling, because he remained cool and detonated the claymores at the precise second. "Whoom!- whoom! — whoom!- Kaboom!" Zips fell like cordwood, spilled from a wheelbarrow. Floyd sent them on a one-way ticket into the happy hunting ground.

The gook who had been crossing the brook, mortally wounded, started reaching across the sunlight floor. Vinnie lit him up with a burst of five fat rounds.

Then he started spraying down the trail head with lead. In the beginning it was easy shooting. The listening post had the edge of surprise. Vinnie racked them up. "Link up! Link up!" he was yelling to Ford.

Terry Ford was working feverishly in the veil of bullets, just like the redneck cowboy he was. He was not afraid to die. He linked up two more full belts. The thought crossed his mind, to quench the barrel of the Pig with his canteen water. But he would not live that long.

The NVA was swarming now. The little people were closing on them fast. Some of them were hopped up on white packets of amphetamines. Floyd, cool as ever, plinked running victims through the chest. He gave most of them two rounds; but high on drugs, the dead men walking still kept running.

Vinnie Palladino never felt it coming. He took a round in the forehead. Ford took over and began coughing lead. He streamed a gallant peppering of machine gun fire across the pinched clearing; and as the NVA showed themselves free of the jungle, Terry laced them up; they fell and stumbled like men in a cinematographic film, where the projection men had bumped the knob to high speed.

"Floyd! Run Man!" shouted Terry Ford. "I'll catch up."

See Floyd run. He ran very fast. Terry Ford would be doing no running. He'd caught a good burst in the right lung. No medic could save him.

Just before Terry died, he ran his fingers through the dog tags and found the gold crucifix, and said in his last breath, "I love you Ma."

Terry Ford died exactly, six days before his nineteenth birthday.

Merle could see Floyd. He looked terrified. His rifle was missing. Floyd was running in the hot flashes of panic and was beginning to believe in the magic of dice, when two AK-47 rounds bit into his back. Merle saw them come out the front side. Floyd stumbled and buckled inside the perimeter, then toppled over dead. He'd crashed to the ground with his palms down, and crimson blood seeped from his mouth.

Merle reached out with a single hand from behind the tree and dragged Floyd back in next to him. Something in Floyd's death always stayed with him. It was the way morning sun shone on Floyd's tight black curls across his head, still very lifelike on the warm corpse. Floyd saw the image many times over, and it had come back to him on the paving run up Route 100. The memory was still alive.

Just about the time Floyd had tripped the claymore field, radio man Perry Jones was on the horn. He'd begged the firebase with a frantic plea, "Mustang Sally, we're getting overrun with zips. Salvo six on our comic book. Fire mission on the gun's fix," shouted Jones into the handset. "The fox people are in Tango trouble, over."

"We're all over it, Red Fox Leader. Rounds out. Mustang Sally over on your ears."

A supersonic whistling came over the Marines position. A shrill followed by instantaneous explosions. "Kraboom! Boom! Boom! ... Boom! Boom! Kraboom!" Sheets of mud sprayed from the pinched clearing, and rains of leaves were trickling from the canopy. A pink explosion sprayed color into morning light.

"Fire for effect," screamed Jones. The veins on his neck rose in excitement. "You're right on the money!" Monstrous eruptions were heaving the jungle. Deeper in the green jungle, Perry saw a violent flash of tangerine beyond the trees.

Deer season had finally come for Merle Long. He'd been waiting a long time. Now it would be payback time, for Vinnie, Terry, and Floyd.

He'd done this for years. Merle had shot several running deer up in Stetson Hollow. Bucks running in white snow on the mountain's face. He was brought up in the old school of poor Vermonters: kill your deer and rabbit with one shot; there's no money around to waste bullets.

This is how Merle Long killed men. One shot, one kill. All American soldiers in Vietnam, used the big-holed peep sight for jungle shooting. They only flipped up to the small peep, for long range shooting, like across rice paddies.

Merle was in familiar territory. He was flipped down. You could find running men real fast in the big peep. He lay out prone position behind the tree. He locked his cheek on the black plastic comb and looked above the M-16's barrel. There was no problem finding targets. Three platoons of the 325th NVA Division had breached the perimeter. Taking dead aim through the peep sight, he started dropping enemy soldiers "Bang! Bang! ... Bang!" Three hit the ground. Merle kept shooting, and all the other Marines were shooting too. The chatter of automatic weapons was constant. Merle had racked up a confirmed 8 KIA. He could see their bodies wide and clear. He'd caught one of them trying to crawl away, up on his elbows, wincing pain all over his face, his canvas shirt all soaked in blood. Merle put the front blade just behind his shoulder and shot him deer fashion. The NVA never moved another muscle.

Merle would never repeat anything in public, even around card tables. None of it was ever told to sweet Dolly. Besides a Catholic priest in a black robe inside a confessional box, the only ears that ever heard a confession from Merle about killing men, was his fellow Marines.

Merle saw him. But he saw Merle first. The NVA had seen him ducking behind the tree. Now the little man from North Vietnam was ready. He'd been waiting for Merle to peek back around.

Merle saw him there right away. The NVA had brush sticking from his helmet and was crouched down, trying to camouflage himself. But he still looked like a man with brush sticking from his helmet, and the camouflage was more about effects than anything.

The NVA regular was down on a knee and shouldering something that looked like a spartan bazooka that had lost considerable weight. The NVA had the crosshairs on Merle's position. He saw the faint back-blast of smoke out the tube, and the last thing he remembered was the orange flame burst and the RPG rooster tailing toward his position.

There was an enormous explosion in his immediate vicinity — Kaboom! A rocket propelled grenade had sent its candy bag of shrapnel across the shooting gallery. A piece of Jimi Hendrix's jagged edge, hot flinging steel, caught Merle in the mouth box, and traveled up his face to the eye socket. The cheek was torn open, and the jungle was drinking his blood. Reeling in the states of shock, Merle looked at his own blood on the jungle fatigues, and the pool of crimson on the soil; and that's when he saw his other eyeball near a patch of wildflowers. The iris and pupil were looking off in another direction, and Merle could see the white ball with the red sinew of optic nerves. He looked away, and with the motions of a little boy, he tried cupping the back of his hand into the wound. Then the shock really came into play, and he began to black out.

The Cobra gunships had been pounding Bravo's position, with mixed effects. They were having an awful time finding running dinks under the triple canopy jungle.

But when the fast movers came with the napalm, another story came into play: burning men on fire ran berserk into the openings, and the bird's Mini-Guns cut them to ribbons. The 3rd Marines had repulsed the attack, but at a very dear price.

Medic Cody Hunter was all over Merle. He was a Navy corpsman, assigned to the Marine rifle company. He began the IV drips and jabbed him with a good blast of morphine. Two Marine grunts lugged him onto a canvas stretcher. He was on his back in his boots. He looked up at the blue sky with one eye. A circle of Marines was reading his face. A lot of their faces were stricken with the blank stare of combat. He wondered if he was dreaming. One of the soul brothers, offered him a hit off a Kool. He sucked in a nice hit and blew out a stream of battleship grey smoke. The taste of menthol stayed in his mouth. Then he heard the beautiful sounds of a slick hovering over the LZ, the rotor wash chopping the jungle with rushes of wind, and the steel skinned bird touching down for the Medivac.

Because of the horrendous number of WIAs, they air shuttled all the wounded to Mustang Sally, then flew Chinook loads of bleeding soldiers to the Naval Support Activity Hospital in Da Nang.

While on the ground in Da Nang, many macabre fellows came to visit Merle. They were all drug induced from morphine. Ghostly figures that appeared in thin air.

NSA was a busy place. A great deal of the medics were green, and all the stretcher bearers had no experience when their boots first landed. When the tail of the Chinook hit the ground, those stretcher bearers ran with all the world's energy up the ramp. A lot of them wore white T-shirts, and came back down the ramp still trotting, moving with speed lugging the victims.

In the staging area outside the NSA surgery wing, were maybe 50 wooden sawhorses in a tin building. Two sawhorses for every stretcher. The stretcher stalls were a constant revolution of pain. Some slipped away and died in their suffering. Others were shuttled inside with the surgeons. Inside the tin building, the stretcher bearers sprayed water. They used the force of hose water, to wash away the mud and grime from wounds, flush the bugs, and men's intestines hanging from cavities, that had been contaminated with jungle litter. What they had going, was a human car wash.

The stretcher bearers became very proficient in their task. Their thumbs served as adjustable spigots. For instance, on cavity wounds or the jagged edges of blown legs, the gentle stream of water was implored on the site. But on places like lower legs and dirty feet with jungle rot, they scoured deep with heavy spurting of water. Their visage became stoic through experience, and the water men had hardened themselves considerably against the hideous wounds. They moved about as factory workers on the assembly line. It seemed their socks were always wet. The pools of water under the sawhorses, were tinged with red.

After they put Merle between two sawhorses, after collecting his thoughts and looking around, he did not feel sorry for himself anymore. He could see other soldiers were sucking up a lot more pain. An Army kid had his left leg blown off at the knee. Three sawhorses down the line, a soldier was missing both legs at the thigh, and his right arm to the elbow. Another Marine from his unit, had taken a lead pill in the guts. He was screaming bloody murder. Merle was beginning to think of his wounds as superficial. Nevertheless, the Vermonter knew he was messed up for life.

The battle surgeons gave Merle very little table time. Other victims were pressing with higher priority. There were pecking orders under the tin roof. The scalpel men were working at feverish pitches, long shifts under the gun. Surgery nurses handed over tools, and kept their eyes glued on life support gauges. The blood speckled surgeons curbed their nervousness with steady hands, knowing they had taken silent oaths in medical school, to give every patient the fighting chance to exchange oxygen.

The surgeon squirted a syringe of something into Merle's wound. Then they sewed up his face. A nurse was holding his hand. Merle could not feel her from behind the curtain of anesthesia. A large white compress, immaculate as thistledown snow, was placed over the hollow socket, where an eye once functioned.

The surgeon signed an immediate order, for Merle's airlift to the United States. Several of his motor orbits had been tasseled. They understood that time was in the essence, for the plastic men to go to work. They didn't want any Frankenstein stuff on their hands and knew Merle's best chance was to give the plastic men plenty of elbow room in the states.

"Give these orders to the Recovery Station," said the head surgeon to the stretcher bearer peeking through the door. "I want him air lifted out on the next ride to the World."

"Yes Sir," said the stretcher bearer. Two of them scurried inside the surgery bay, grabbed the wooden handles, and lugged Merle in their classic trot to the Recovery Station.

In the crack of dawn that next morning, they carried Merle onto the airfield. A C-141 transport was warming its engines.

On the horizon above the silver fuselage, a communion of bronze rays was glowing against the fairy blue sky. The tranquil scene from the colors of heaven, gave the fellowship of wounded soldiers, a full measure of peacefulness; a lot of them craned their necks off the stretcher to behold the image of rising sun.

But Merle could not embrace the spectacle. His missing eye was facing the phenomenon. His brain waves were only sending some kind of pattern with twinkling blue and silver stars, in the blackness behind the white compress bandage. None of the spiritual insight could enter his soul.

It was during this time, compromised from seeing the aura because of drawing bad luck numbers in a shootout, when the ghastly figure gave Merle a surprise visit.

Merle cringed, when a scene of horror filled his brain. The drugs were in play. Hallucinations were in his head, and a very convincing image was before his singular eye: a German dirigible loomed in the sky. The flying Zeppelin was long and very warlike in its military hue of skin. Seated below in the dirigible's giant balloon, was a ghastly figure. He was dressed in a German war uniform. An ominous swastika in black vehicle, was painted on the stern's sheathing. A miniature propeller in proportion to the monstrous flying machine, beat its revolution in the high space. The mischievous figure was fumbling with the controls and appeared to be moving forward with dead reckoning. These effects were very realistic under the drugs.

Merle raised his arm off the stretcher, and pointing into the sky, exclaimed, "Zeppelin." The nurse in his vicinity heard him. But because of the C-141 firing power plant, and the commotion of those stretcher bearers moving about hither and tither, she had been distorted in perception.

"Led Zeppelin?" asked the nurse. "Why you Vermonter rock star," she joked. The nurse tickled his belly and flipped him over on his back.

The host of orange sun, streamed across his face. He could feel the warm rays on his visage. It was a very satisfactory kind of warmth. The cringe of his teeth went lax. All the tension in his face waned, and the nurse could swear she saw him wearing a smirk.

The wounded were ready to embark. The magnificent stretcher

bearers loaded the casualties. The flying hospital lifted toward Freedom Town. Thirty-six wounded soldiers were in the C-141's belly, strapped down tight and looking scared. The methodical whine of the airplane's engine, put Merle to sleep. He slept all the way home. Just before drifting off, his conscious was burdened with guilt, for leaving his fellow Marines on the front lines. But he came to terms that in this condition, and flying at these kinds of altitudes, everything was out of his hands. He had been informed the plastic men were waiting for him back in the World. The Leathernecks would need to fight their own way out.

In a second bay of the airplane, behind the closed curtains, were the caskets. Against the far wall, was the casket of Pvt. Floyd Leatherwood. The sad news had already been delivered in person, by a fellow Marine in dress blues. His mother, Vandelyn Leatherwood, had cried in hysteria. She'd collapsed against the porch's post, and nearly fell off the stoop. The Marine with the dress blues, sat with her on the white bench, for a great length of time. Vandelyn was crying hard in a mother's sorrow. The Marine's brass was in a high buff, in the flat light of Mississippi. His black shoes were spit-shined to perfection. A hanging basket of fuchsia flowers, streamed down across the scene of sorrow.

The Marine stayed with her, sitting very close to the sobbing woman. But after a long while he needed to leave, because he had other obligation a bit farther up the coastline, with the official letters of three other dead soldiers in his suitcase.

CHAPTER THREE

Dolly topped the flight of stairs. She wheeled and proceeded down the hallway of Walter Reed Hospital. She had traveled exceedingly light. In her hand was a complimentary paper bag provided in shopping centers, with a hemp rope handle. Inside this brown paper bag, were Merle's clothes. It was time for him to go home.

Inside the hospital, the plastic men had knocked out Merle twice. They had treated the re-crowning of his zygomatic arch, and the complex skin grafting of his face, as two separate knife jobs. The plastic men took great pride in their work. They made intricate stitches, and even cut him behind the ear, manufacturing a small face lift for the sagging cheek.

Dolly walked down the tiled hallway. There were no circles under her eyes. The floor nurses had comforted her over the last weeks, long distance over telephone receivers. The nurses had picked up on the Vermonter's accent right off the bat. A bond had formed through telephone conversation.

Dolly stopped in at the nursing station. All the nurses averted from their tasks and looked her way.

"May I help you?" obliged RN Maybellene.

"Maybellene?"

"Dolly?" came back RN Maybellene, "I could recall that voice a mile off."

Two nurses walked Dolly to Merle's room. They had small time woman's talk. "He's doing quite well, and his spirits are high," said Maybellene.

Merle had been dozing. The magazine was wide open on the bedspread, turned to Jimi Hendrix's gloss photo. Dolly tiptoed inside, closed the magazine, and removed a plastic fork from the covers. Very silently, she hunkered down and embraced her man, whispering, "It's time to go home baby."

Merle looked at Dolly through his eye. There were still sparks; the most emotional kind. He could still feel the pitter-patter in his heart. Merle glanced down at Dolly's naked ring finger. He knew right away, as he'd rehearsed many nights under the jungle canopy, he'd be getting down to business very soon and tying knots. He wanted very much, for both of them to hear church bells ringing in the village of Stowe.

Dolly laid out Merle's clothes. A well-worn cowboy shirt, green cotton with pearlized snaps. Levi blue jeans, already served with his favorite belt with the Barber Greene 879 brass buckle. His Justin roper boots.

But Merle had other ideas. Two days before, he'd sent out his jungle fatigues to the hospital laundry and requested a starch job with ironed pleats. He'd cleaned his combat boots, best he could, with a bar of Ivory soap. His 3rd Marine ball cap, hung on a peg near his bed.

Merle could hear the distant bands playing in his head. Their pitch and chords were of patriotic tunes. Kettle drums beat in the distance. Confetti clouds were fluttering from the sky. A sea of jubilant faces lined the parades across small town America. He could feel the pats across his back. In the prominence of all the home coming, was the figures of little boys and girls, waving the stars and stripes from the flag's wooden stick. The throng of crowds gushed in their patriotic cheerfulness, for the ticket punchers of freedom.

It was hospital protocol, for all discharged patients to leave the premise by wheelchair. Merle slipped into his jungle fatigues. His uniform felt to him as a second skin. He was very proud of his uniform, because he remembered the old timers of his clay and spirit, who embarked in the likeness of the thread and color. His fellow Marines who took an awful mauling on the beachheads of Iwo Jima, in the same uniform.

Dolly knocked off the wheelchair's brake and pushed Merle past the nursing station. All the nurses kept their heads down pushing pencils across their medical charts, because they did not know exactly how to break things off. Dolly wheeled Merle into the Otis elevator. Merle felt part of his stomach falling in the rapid descent of the steel cables. The Vermonters could hear some kind of mechanical commotion in the elevator shaft.

The bright sun was very hard on Merle's eye. He tilted the ball cap with the red shield of the 3rd Marine Division, flatter over his brow. Ten years later, he would still remember how wonderful the breeze of freedom, felt going down his lungs.

He watched the wind flutter the heads of State Fair zinnias. The colorful flowers stripped away some of the hard edge from the concrete jungle. Merle was certain that he never saw more beautiful flowers, than sprays of wildflowers that grew in the dark green jungles where he had been hunting men. He had remembered those jungle flowers of iridescent fuchsia, that climbed on a vine and had faces large as pie plates.

A bright yellow taxi with white wall tires pulled along the curb. A Greek with a razor thin face was the cabbie.

"The train station," said Dolly.

Merle stood on his own from the wheelchair. The couple sat on the vinyl back seat of the yellow taxi. A nursing assistant, provided valet service of the wheelchair, pushing it briskly back inside Walter Reed Hospital.

Merle quickly saw the sea of faces, in the metropolis of

Washington, DC. Huge crowds of wayfarers were conducting their agenda. But there were no parades, and all the patriotic tunes had died someplace in the maze of brick masonry, pinched alleys with mud puddles where the alley cats roamed.

Conversation in the taxicab was short. Nobody's mouth had opened. Merle listened to the taxi meter's ticking. His ears were highly tuned to foreign and suspicious noises, and his senses were still on edge from people trying to kill him.

The Greek wheeled the yellow taxi into the train station depot. Without averting his head, the Greek said, "Twenty bucks even."

Merle handed over a wad of cash. The Greek counted the money. There was an extra three bucks. The Greek never acknowledged the tip. He never paid Merle any eye contact. The cabbie with his thin razor face, reached over and killed the taxi meter.

Merle slammed the taxi door shut. The muffled noise of the yellow door closing was as close as you'd ever hear to the sound of NVA motors sailing out of the tubes.

Whoofit! Whoofit! Whoofit! Merle tensed up from the involuntary reactions of his jungle tour. He'd seen what could happen when the NVA began walking motor rounds.

Merle did not like the concrete jungle. It was hard on your joints. There was no give. It was not like the Nam, where a man's boots sank into the mud, the lug soles clawing for traction; where the sensation of creeping along the jungle floor, was like walking on cotton batting, sneaking about on the beds of leaf mold with fingers caressing the safety switch. Sure, up in I Corps the chances of getting killed were high, and you needed to wade rivers with the currents fluttering your fatigues; but your boots dried out in the sun, and at least there were no smart cookie cabbies around.

Just then, Merle saw old familiar faces. Two fellow Marines

were crossing in the bustle. Merle had spotted the white summer hats, and white belts drawn tight against the blue uniforms, and he could see the sparks in their eyes across the lane. The two jar heads were fast stepping now, because they recognized their colors of a red shield with the black and yellow star on Merle's hat. All three of them were nexus fighters of the 3rd Marine Division.

"Welcome Home!" said the biggest of the big Marines. He removed his white hat in respect to the soldier's sacrifice and squeezed him with a giant bear hug. There was 11-Bravo talk and body language conducted small traits that were only privately shared in the circuits of Semper Fidelis.

Merle measured the two Marines. Idealism was sailing high in their smiles. The biggest of the big Marines, had a scar on his face too. But it was a superficial scar across his chin, picked up when he locked horns with another linebacker in the Palo Alto High School Championship.

Thus far, neither of them in their blue slacks with the red piping stripes, had ever been baptized in combat.

The big Marine who still had a buzz cut with the colors of a towhead still in grade school, who still had a youthful appearance with no frown marks stricken to his brow, had revealed he'd just cycled through his MOS training. His place in the rifle company, would be the M-60 machine gunner. The Gunnery Sergeant had groomed him well, much like giving lessons to his own son, because the case-hardened Marine instructor knew the machine gun carried a tremendous weight in a fire fight.

"Brother, you should see how I laced up those paper targets," said the big Marine. "There's really nothing like running brass belts through the *Pig*. I reached out and gave that paper bullseye a real spanking at 800 yards."

Aaaahhh ... paper targets. Merle knew all about that rifle range stuff; and none of it was close to the real thing, when Charlie was spraying your position with AK-47 clips.

In no shape or form, did Merle lead on about Vinnie Palladino and Terry Ford. The deaths of his machine gun team on that fateful May morning, was a tender subject. The two green Marines would find plenty of subject matter inside their pages of active duty.

Merle and Dolly crossed the boulevard toward the train station. Three bums were curled up and sleeping away, conked out over the sidewalk grating. Warm air from the catacombs was rising around the hobos. Merle dug into his pockets and sprinkled their beggar's cups with pocket change.

Merle had a spring in his step, his future looking much brighter now, when trouble arrived from the parking stalls. A VW bus was gobbling parking time. A red flag of Violation was standing straight up in the parking meter's window.

The hippie van was a traveling billboard of colors. The heads had painted it with paint brushes. They had covered the back windows with homemade curtains. Many stickers of rock bands were plastered on the bus's glass — upon Janis Joplin — upon Pink Floyd — upon Steppenwolf — upon the Grateful Dead with the skull and lightning bolt logo.

But Merle's eyes went to the hand painted letters on the bus's nose: Make Love Not War. Those words painted in white letters on the patriot blue, were cupped around the peace sign.

Two hippies jaywalked across the boulevard. They walked like they owned the place and angled toward the VW bus. The girl hippie wore a colored Gypsy dress, and leather sandals with long thongs lashed around her calves. Her legs had not seen a razor blade in months. In her black curls, spiraling to the waist, was a yellow daisy.

The hippie boyfriend was wearing elephant bell bottoms, with a handkerchief of the American flag, tied above his knee. He'd taken his jackknife and tasseled the hemline, so the colors of red, white, and blue were tattered across the edge. The visual effect was a statement against current politics. His long blonde hair was tied into a ponytail, with a piece of rawhide.

The confrontation took place along the colorful sheet metal of the VW bus. Merle never saw it coming. He knew very little about hippies. He'd only seen the long hairs with their love beads, over the last year or so, on television screens when they were on R&R in the Nam.

They had brought smiles across his hard face from war, and he dwelled on the conclusion they were a fun-loving tribe. But on this morning of his convalescence, in broad daylight of the Capital district, he would discover their ugly side.

The girl hippie came right at him. No words were minced. She let him have it both barrels.

"You baby killer!" shouted the hippie. A very awful side of her character flaws had suddenly appeared from behind the yellow dandelion.

She curled back her lips and said, "Look at all the innocents you just got killed at Kent State."

Caught in shock, Merle braced himself against the psychedelic colors of the magic bus. Before he could think of something to come back with, she hawked up a lunger and spit in his face. "Take that you dirty bastard." Both hippies backed up a few steps, in order to measure the expression on Merle's face, while bubbles of spit were dripping down his scared cheek. The boyfriend had broken a grin under his blonde bangs and rode both thumbs in the jean's slash pockets.

Dolly lost it. She dropped the paper bag with Merle's clothes on the bustling sidewalk and gave the hippie chick a stiff-arm across the chops. "You dirty burnout Queen," barked Dolly, "you're close to an ambulance ride on the house."

"Like totally unrighteous," chimed in the boyfriend. "Like you cats are bad trips, Man. What a bummer." His eyes were glazed over, like he was stoned on grass.

"You tramps look like you've done a few too many acid trips," said Dolly. "Make tracks or I'll call the screws." Dolly gave the acid head another shove, banging her head against the VW bus skin.

Just then, a rush of figures came sprinting to the rescue. They were iron workers, who from above over the scene, had witnessed everything. They had seen her spit in the soldier's face. The iron worker foreman, Terry Pastrana, was also quick to recognize the soldier's red hat. It was very clear to him, squatting down on the steel I-beam, that he was a brother of the 3rd Marine Division.

Terry Pastrana did all the talking. He kept it short and sweet. They were on the union time clock. Many of the other iron workers were arrested in curiosity, high on the webs of steel. Terry Pastrana was ripped with toned muscles, and wore a white tank top, with black denim pants and steel toe boots. Around his neck, dangled a very pricy gold chain and medallion of the Blessed Fatima. On his right shoulder, was a tattoo of a bulldog, arced with the block letters: 1st Marine Division. Below the ferocious dog, was inscribed — First to Fight.

Terry Pastrana, grabbed the boyish hippie, and heaved the skinny young fellow into the hippie van, much like he was a straw scarecrow of the Wizard of Oz.

Two hop heads that had been talking to the hash pipe inside the hippie den, stuck their heads clear for investigation. Terry Pastrana got hit with a shotgun-like hit of gray smoke plume. He reached back through the veil of narcotic smoke and gave the ponytailed hippie a wicked backhand across the mouth. Dolly swore she heard something pop. Blood seeped from the hippie's lip.

Terry Pastrana grabbed him by the throat and issued a stern warning: "Your dirty bitch spits in another soldier's face again, and I'll flatten both of you like a GD steam roller."

With that, the three iron workers ran back up the ladder, across the scaffolds, and began peening rivets like nothing ever happened. Terry Pastrana peeked over the edge of the H-beam, cupped his hands and shouted to Merle, "Great job soldier. We love ya, Man."

With that, Dolly blew a silent kiss off her palm towards the iron men. Then she wiped the spit off Merle's face with a tissue napkin, gave him a few love licks across the cheek, and pressed her lips tight against the jagged edge. Merle knew then he had a Dolly Dagger and would never let her go. The couple held hands walking past the brass standpipe, down the stairs past the turnstile, and boarded the train for the Green Mountains.

Merle felt very vulnerable on the train ride home. Many riders stole glances of him, but nobody said anything. Nobody offered a smile. It seemed the public in general had been brainwashed by the media, drew too tight of conclusion from Walter Cronkite's opinion, and read too many slanted columns in the New York Times. The soldiers who died on the jungle floor, and those who beat the calendar's X marks and made it back home, regardless of whether you were dead or alive, stood in the long shadows of present historical significance, as shameful pawns.

All of Merle's hopes for a homecoming, went up in smoke. He realized in the village of Stowe, and the sleepy hollows through the Green Mountains, there would be very few Marines to protect him. From old faces still alive in his memory, he could only count on one hand the Parris Island people in Stowe, Vermont.

He remembered the New Year's Eve of 1968, when he took Dolly to the party inside the VFW of Enosburg Falls. There had been two old Marines at the bar. They kept their backs toward the country and western band. They were sipping amber tinted drafts. They were very tight-lipped about war.

There were a few other Marines up the lane, World War I veterans buried in the village cemetery, under the shade of the ancient sugar maples, very old gnarly trees. They had assaulted Meuse-Argone, sat on the same bar stools of the VFW as old timers, but kept the details of potting Germans a dead secret they took into the grave. In the fall of the year, the maples spattered yellow and orange leaves around the tombstones and gave home-spun significance to the village scene. In the Vermont winters, the fanning limbs of the giant trees, stood at attention under the grey skies for the dead soldiers. But all this was a distant satisfaction, many miles from seeing old faces in familiar places.

Merle would need to fight his way back into society. He knew quite well, his best and perhaps only viable cards, were his Dolly Dagger, and the long black ribbons of pavement he could put down with Ranger Asphalt Company. Some of his true friends of the paving crew, had mailed him pen pal letters to Vietnam. It was the truest kind of airmail available — the letters came in canvas sacks on the chopper slicks, along with the wooden crates of fresh ammunition. It was good knowing, at least there would be a tiny sliver of community love awaiting him in the village of Stowe.

The train sailed up the tracks north bound. The conductor had just blown the whistle at a dangerous crossing. Merle had a window seat. He could see the flashes of colors from spray bombs, from ghetto graffito in the poorest neighborhoods. A few blacks were on the flat roofs of a tenement house, spread out on lawn chairs and drinking cans of beer.

"Are you all right?"

"I'm doing fine. Everything is all right."

"No, I mean really."

"Well ... it's hard getting use to one eye. My world was much better and fuller with both eyes. And I guess the other thing — before what just happened to me on the streets of the Capital — it's much better in the first threads of daylight. That's when I get the soundest sleep. Sleeping in the blackness of night in the hospital bed, it was hard to let go until the wee hours. My mind was still racing from the calamity of war."

"Did you squeeze the call button?"

"No, I never squeezed. The problems were the kind no medicine tablets could fix. Only time could heal me."

Merle reached in his pocket. The plastic men had given him two separate tubes of salve ointments, that held some kind of special healing quality for his jagged edge. He unscrewed the white caps and anointed his scar tissue. Very slowly over the next few hours, the white cream sunk deeper into his skin pores.

Dolly snuggled tight against her man's chest. Merle felt a flush of love tingles rising. He kissed her neck and squeezed her hand tight. He realized what he clutched in his arms, would be the very best kind of medicine for his healing.

Merle closed his eyes and drifted into a cove of relaxation. He rehearsed many times over, the steps he would be taking in the white church. He bounced back and forth, the two top picks for his best man. The wedding vows flowed off Dolly's lips, and it was a beautiful thing in the silence of the church. Merle pictured carrying his bride across the threshold, her white laced dress sweeping across the rock maple floors.

The train raced toward night. All of a sudden inside the train car, a flashback appeared inside Merle's head.

It was the warm corpse of Floyd Leatherwood, face down on the jungle floor. Two bullet holes in his back, were ringed in coagulated blood around the circlets of brown threads. As always, the sheen of Floyd's hair was in prominence of the death experience. Soft rays of eloquent sunbeam, streamed down through the jungle canopy, and illuminated the tight curls of a black man, who once threw dice in the back alleys of Biloxi, Mississippi.

Merle realized that he would need a lot more work in the future. He pressed his shoulders against the seat, and closing his eye while listening to the constant chatter of iron train wheels, he tried counting white sheep in the green grass of home.

CHAPTER FOUR

It was a hot summer night. It was dead still. No winds had come into play. It was a very clear night. All the constellations were marked in the blackness. Stars abound. Orion twinkled, facing Taurus the bull. Tucked into the balsam firs, were the Great Horned owls. In the first threads of night, the owls had been full of conservation. They hooted long and loud in the night, and melodious songs spilled across the mountain faces. But now in the dead silent veil of midnight, they remained still and hushed, roosted inside the cover of fir boughs.

Below in the village of Stowe, a galaxy of stars speckled the sky above a farmhouse. Three cows were bedded in the timothy grass, chewing their cuds in the starlight. The farmhouse windows were cracked open in the sleeping quarters. A man and a woman were sleeping. The Shepherd's Pie had sat well with them. The man was sixty-four years old. He found with putting on the years, it was nice sleeping in with his wife. It had been forty-six years, since he got his eye blown out. There would be no sleeping in today. There was black asphalt beckoning to be put down. Merle and Dolly Long slept very soundly. The scent of fresh cut hay seeped in through the cracked windows, and this homespun charm of country living had cast them into a sound sleep.

Outside in the barnyard, dew drops had formed on the windshield of the blue Ford pickup. Down in Selvin Knight's barn, a big red rooster had fluttered down from his night perch, and was pecking around and clearing his throat, in order to open his beak and begin the cackling war cry across the village of Stowe.

The alarm went off. It was a windup clock, and after a while the sonic bell went dead. Merle rose from the covers and shook out his old bones. After starting the coffee grounds on the range, he went out the screen door in his bathrobe and slippers and heaved a small vessel of cracked corn over the corral for the cows. His pet cows, Rosey and Casimir the cow. Merle bent over the split rails and kissed their nose. The cows were exceedingly fond of showing their affection and took turns licking Merle across the face. The two cows liked anybody who gave them something to eat, and looking through the corner of their big eyes, were not bashful in sticking out their tongues all the way.

Merle went back inside. The screen door slammed on the worn hinges. Some of his stiff joints had loosened. He percolated the pot of coffee and gave two slices of white bread a ride inside the toaster, for some buttered toast with homemade strawberry jam. Then he proceeded to get dressed.

He pulled his navy-blue paving pants off the wooden peg. The leather belt with its patina brass buckle of the Barber Green 879, was served through the loops. But before he slipped on his britches, he lowered his white boxer underpants in the kitchen's arc light, and smeared tinea ointment all around his crotch and family jewels. The hot weather had spurred on a feisty case of jock itch; he'd fought the relapses over the last two summers.

Merle had noticed a tiny speck of blood, on the seat of his white boxers. Hemorrhoidal tissue had leaked in the night. He did not bother changing the white boxers. After bouncing around all day on the self- propelled paver box, there would be a lot more bleeding. He would soak in the bathtub that evening, the warm water sprinkled down with mineral salts, then pat himself down with a second tube of cream. But at least some of Merle's problems had waned away, because in the soppy jungles of Vietnam, he went through a full tube a week for jungle rot between his toes, executing bang-bang 11 Bravo tactics with his leathernecks in wet boots.

Sitting on the kitchen chair, Merle slipped on two pairs of fresh white socks. He always wore double cotton socks for paving, extra cushion inside his boots, just as he always wore long sleeves on the hottest days. The only place he'd ever rolled sleeves, was up in I Corps when he was hunting men, because of the oppressive humidity and the monsoons.

Down below along Route 100 on the paving job, the crew of Ranger Asphalt Company had a blazing fire going in the metal barrel. They were drinking coffee, eating cider doughnuts, and having small talk before the paving run began.

Merle took a good look at himself in the parlor mirror. Sure, he bore the long scar of war, was missing an eye, but still found himself handsome. Those plastic men sure did a great face lift, and all these years later, he still had some of the tightest apple cheeks in town.

Merle departed home. He toted the black lunch pail. Passing the corral, he rubbed Casimir's ear. "Moooo!" said Casimir the cow.

The blue Ford came to life. The black rubber wipers whisked away the dew. Merle slipped her into gear and motored toward the fire barrel. A blanket of stars was still casted above Smuggler's Notch. He putted through the village of Stowe and pressed toward the storytelling around the fire barrel. Johnny Terejko had been telling a story around the fire, and a stream of orange sparks soared towards the morning stars.

Merle Long was on top of his game. He drove with his arm out the window. Summer breeze fluttered his blue long sleeves. Perched high on the truck's seat, he considered himself the most fortunate man in the world. He would change nothing. The definition of his character had been forged through a Vermonter's poorness. He was tough as nails and could take the punishment. His rare cheerfulness was tempered around the small things of life.

There would always be the war stories only divulged to the night confessors. Things taken with him into the tomb. Tales which had died inside him around the fire barrel.

But he had his Dolly Dagger who stood by his jagged edge, certainly the love of his life. And he was still part of the paving crew, where big horsepower iron put down roadbed, and a man could smell the pungent aroma of melted tar.

He'd forgotten most of the bad times, after the RPG from the NVA soldier, caused the two circuits on the surgery table and all the suffering. And it was almost never, say, when he dwelled on the time he'd signed on the dotted line for the United States, and the hippie war protestor on a street in the Capital district, called him those names and spit in his face, after he got all banged up in a combat zone.

IF YOU ARE ABLE,
SAVE FOR THEM A PLACE
INSIDE OF YOU...
AND SAVE ONE BACKWARD GLANCE
WHEN YOU ARE LEAVING
FOR THE PLACES THEY CAN
NO LONGER GO ...
BE NOT ASHAMED TO SAY
YOU LOVED THEM,
THOUGH YOU MAY
OR MAY NOT HAVE ALWAYS...
TAKE WHAT THEY HAVE LEFT
AND WHAT THEY HAVE TAUGHT YOU
WITH THEIR DYING
AND KEEP IT WITH YOUR OWN ...
AND IN THAT TIME
WHEN MEN DECIDE AND FEEL SAFE
TO CALL THE WAR INSANE,
TAKE ONE MOMENT TO EMBRACE
THOSE GENTLE HEROES
YOU LEFT BEHIND...

WRITTEN BY MAJ. MICHAEL DAVIS O'DONNELL
FROM VIETNAM, ON JANUARY 1, 1970
HE WAS REPORTED MISSING IN ACTION
ON MARCH 24, 1970

Ace Machine Shop

"Go ahead," said the librarian, "take it."

"Are you sure?"

"It's not a big thing," she told me. "It's over three days old. Take it along."

"Alright then," I told her. I folded the Berlin Free Press in half, stuffed it under my arm, and went out of the library.

It was very hot. I pedaled two miles home. The newspaper, four ripe tomatoes, and a wedge of watermelon rode in the bicycle's basket.

A paddle fan in the kitchen was chopping air. A sea of cool breeze sailed from the blades. It was very satisfactory. I read the free news. The fan caressed the newspaper. I fanned the pages.

Many items filled the classified boxes. You could find a lot of good things in that part of Connecticut. There were a lot of bargains around. But because of all the Russians and Greeks in the area, you needed to move fast. The Greeks always responded right away on big-theme gold necklaces. They were fond of boats too. The Greeks were crazy for just about anything with a hull.

A black box caught my eye. Somebody had a Dell desktop computer for nice money. They were only asking $250, and that's before the asking price got worked over by hungry callers for a bargain.

I called the number. The phone rang a long time. The ringing in your ears, sounded like a phone ringing in an empty factory. Its bells carried on in the forenoon, and I was ready to abandon the receiver. But then machine picked up, and a man's voice was on tape: "This is Ace Machine Shop. We must be busy on the machines. Please leave your name and number, and I'll return the call. Fred."

Figuring I'd dialed in error, the receiver was clicked down. I said nothing. A buzzing filled the wire.

Checking the small print, this time under powerful reading glasses, it was discovered the sequence of numbers was correct. So, again I dialed the same number, and the same ringing in the vacant factory prevailed, and Fred's voice came back over the machine.

"Fredie," I said to the machine, "This is Paladin. I'm calling about the computer you had listed in the classified." I left my name and number and hung up the telephone.

The heat was really coming on. I sliced a tomato. A slice of white bread was procured from the bread box. I gave myself the luxury of a single slice of American cheese. For months I'd been of ill health — a tragic mistake on the ski slopes of waning winter, had broken many bones. It had arrested the task of physical labors, and the piggy bank was low. This was the precise reason for inquiring on a used computer.

I ate the sandwich under the spinning of fan blades. Then I retreated to the outdoor lounge and fell into deep sleep. The pockets of shade coming down through the grove of old rock maples, felt good on the bones of my leg. Convalescence was well seated, gaining strength by day, and riding the bicycle presented almost no pain. But I was low on money and eating like a bird, although I simmered home-made soup on a weekly basis, with a hardy stock derived from cattle bones.

I slept for many hours. The sun had shifted in gradual angles and was now leaning toward the West. I awoke from sound sleep. Insects were buzzing in the trees. They were working in the canopy of green leaves. I trudged from the sun splashed lawn, past the screen door. My joints were stiff from sleep. Jingling of bells began from my telephone.

"Hello," I said yawning.

"Hello Paladin! This is Fred. I see you called this afternoon. Sorry about that — I was in a meeting."

The wall clock in my kitchen read straight up at 8:00 PM. I was surprised Ace Machine Shop was still milling steel at this hour. It had been a chain of three sweltering days, so my conclusion was that they were in contract production, to be still burning candles in that kind of heat wave.

"Fredie, I see you have a computer for sale?"

"Oh yes, we have two for sale. Both are Dell Windows 10. Fine machines my friend, fine machines."

"Were those computers from your office?"

"No… not that. My brother-in-law and myself sell a few computers on the side. Roger is excellent at refurbishing computers. We make them new again."

"Yes, that's fine. I've been looking for a Dell desktop in Windows 10."

"That's what they are," informed Fred. "They are office models, well built, and all gone through. And let me tell you something — these computers are all factory Dell, not a monitor whacked off from there, or a salvaged keyboard from another junk."

"Are they fast enough?" I asked. "Nobody wants some old dinosaur that takes all day for a boot up."

"Fast? These babies got 2.6 Ghz of processor rams," bragged Fred.

"That's over my head," I confessed. "I'm just coming off typewriters."

"Ghz is short for gigahertz. That's one billion cycles per second," beamed Fred. He was tapping the telephone's receiver for effects. High in the rafters against the skylight, black flies were trapped below the glass, buzzing in the doldrums. Below on the chestnut floors were hundreds of dead flies that had succumbed from the heat wave inside dead air.

"Knowledge is paramount. I'm a writer, and I'll be looking for suture threads to sew up stories. Accuracy is more important than speed."

"These computers have the world covered."

"Maybe so Fred, but you can't see tears running off somebody's cheeks, or hear the quiver in their voice box on the computer."

"Amen," said Fred. "I know it's true."

"It's true." I told him. "Even back in the old days, writers rode for days on horseback, just to write a single sentence."

"Isn't that something."

"Isn't it though?"

"When can you come down?"

"How about the weekend. Heavy rains are predicted through Friday. Driving in downpours can be silly business."

"Quite understandable, my dear friend," said Fred. "Take no needless risks, and thou Lord will bless you."

In this late hour of a heat spell, a curious thing was revealed. Fred's drift over the wire, was suddenly stricken in religion. Certain rings punctuated in the phonics. You could feel his faith in the situation. There were deep currents of a man's measure of things in Fred's voice, a rhyme that had been around the printed black lines of a bible.

"I'll give you a heads-up when I'm hitting the highway," I promised Fred, "and so sorry about calling last time, and disturbing your meeting."

"Oh heavens," exclaimed Fred, "no problem — we close down the shop every Thursday afternoon and have a meeting right there inside with the Witnesses. We study the Bible."

"Hallelujah," I told him.

Save for the chop of white caps in the sound, the sea was flat and the heat waves still blanketed the town and the factory. Fred pushed a corn broom across the chestnut floors and swept up all the dead flies under the skylights. The smothering heat had crisped their bodies. Many of the black legs had broken free. The broom spruced up everything. Fred dumped the sweepings into the trash bin.

Then he worked the broom between the wood folding chairs of his improvised church. Fred folded a clean white bath towel over the bible. He lit a smoke. Dove grey wafts of smoke rose in the dead heat. Soft rays of evening light spilled down through the sky glass, and the three rows of empty chairs were soldier straight in the heat wave, for the next wave of practicing religion inside Ace Machine Shop.

The Last Straw

Joe laid on the beach. He was on his back and his arms were wide in the sun. The warm sands seeped up through the beach blanket and caressed his back. Joe reached off the blanket and scrunched some sand through his fingers, then wiggled his toes. It was very satisfactory therapy. He felt like a million bucks.

A sea of green breakers rolled across the Fort Lauderdale beach, and the combers tumbled into a white foam, a million bubbles breaking into thin air. The sounds produced by the lapping sea across the sandbar, produced a melody of relaxation to the people's ears, and the wayfarer of sun bathers on the blankets drifted into half-sleeps and went far away to dream worlds. Within the sea of people, sandpipers darted along the sheets of shoreline, pecking feverishly into the wet sands, and low overhead were seagulls soaring and riding the soft breeze. Some of them seemed frozen in time, motionless in the thermals of air draft.

Next to Joe on the blanket was Martha. Two years back in time she had been Joe's bimbo. That's because Joe was still married at the time, and they were committing adultery. But now that Peggy had filed on Joe, and everything went through with exactly half of Joe's pockets empty, Martha fit into a new category. She was his official girlfriend.

Joe liked Martha. He especially liked her full and wet lips. He'd never kissed lips that put out like that. The first time they embraced and felt her moist tongue, he almost passed out. Joe knew right then Martha was for him.

All of Joe's friends tried to warn him about Martha. They'd told him that she had too much baggage. They'd heard she chewed up three men and spit them out. That Martha had used the same divorce attorney out of Manhattan, to rake all those men over the coals. But Joe was too blind by love. He thought he might be in mad love with Martha. She had nice lips and wore fantastic per-fume and kissed nice, and she had the sweetest voice, and gave Joe long back rubs on the shag carpet. Joe figured he'd found true love after Peggy.

Joe and Martha had headed down to Fort Lauderdale for four weeks to become snowbirds. They stayed at Joe's place, a posh little condo pad over inside Golden Gates on the corner of NE 35th Street and Burning Tree Drive. From Joe's slider on the second-floor balcony, you could see the Coral Ridge Country Club wide and clear. Looking through the plate glass you could see the winding waters of the intracoastal with tiny islands dotted with palm trees, and far beyond miniature figures on the fairways of rolling green shanking white balls. It was truly a romantic view reminiscent of Golden Gates, and the first time Martha looked out through the slider she almost buckled at the knees.

At one time, Peggy's name had been on the deed. But after the divorce, she signed it over to Joe. Peggy kept the main resi-dence back north. She had her belly full of Fort Lauderdale, mostly because she never could seem to locate the right hairdresser, and it was not her kind of shopping. She liked pounding pavement in New York City with plastic, rummaging around the bins for high style cuts for a discounted buck; and her favorite shopping escapade was riding the wooden escalator inside the maiden Macy's near Time Square, and sailing up to the third floor where they had the most fantastic brassiere department in the whole world. Peggy could never picture going to Golden Gates on holiday all alone. After the separation, she relocated over with her daughter in Arizona.

Joe reached across the beach blanket, and clasped Martha's hand with his eyes closed. The sandpipers had moved closer to their blanket. The green sea was falling with the tides going out. It was the week after Christmas. They had been in Fort Lauderdale for two days now. In Joe's mind, they were just over one month late — he had planned for them to leave the day after Thanksgiving. He'd already bought the plane tickets on All Saint's Day, which falls every year on November 1st. But a few days before the Thanksgiving golden turkey and a day of watching the pig skin get thrown up and down the television set, Martha threw a kink into Joe's plans.

"Honey, I need to hit the brakes," said Martha hinting around.

"What?" said Joe. Everything was over his head.

"I can't leave next week for Florida." Her voice was stern and serious, and she dropped her chin and looked over her glasses at Joe.

"You've got to be kidding," exclaimed Joe. He pressed closer and waited for Peggy's answer.

"I'm sorry Honey. My daughters and I always start our Christmas shopping and wrapping the week after Thanksgiving. We've been doing it a long time, and it's in our blood. It's very special to me," said Peggy.

"How long will special take?" questioned Joe.

"About two weeks," said Martha. "But then Christmas is right around the corner." Martha told Joe how hard it would be not seeing little Ernie's face opening presents around the Christmas tree. Martha explained how fond she was of the aroma of needle bearing trees. She wanted to be around for stuffing red socks and being with her side of the family. She wanted Joe to hold off for a good month.

Martha would never know how much apprehension she injected into Joe's central nervous system. It threw everything into a tailspin. Joe needed to have their airplane tickets bumped up into Martha's time frame out of Logan Airport. The airlines clobbered Joe on price increase, and he took a beating on the tickets. He lost over two hundred dollars in real money, let alone that month in the sun and fun of Florida is just about priceless. Those were the first signs something might be funny. Joe had wondered if his friends might be right. He'd noticed a few small things that bothered him about Martha.

The worse trial on Joe's nerves, was Martha's insistence on the consuming of raw garlic cloves. She'd read in a health journal, that a regular intake of raw garlic can have a remarkable effect on the cleansing of toxins and promote good health. It was a sad affair Martha never took notes on the effects of bad breath.

But Joe had made counter moves and carried a war chest to ward away and mask some of Martha's garlic habit — he kept a clutch of Necco candy wafers, and mints, and chewing gum in his close whereabouts. There was no way Joe was going to let a runty white bulb that grows below the soil line, ruin the kissing of Martha's marvelous lips. Joe found out that Necco wafers worked best, and Martha never caught on he was offering the candy for other reasons. It seemed a few Neccos could subdue the effects of garlic on Joe, through kissing on the sofa into a few rounds in the feathers, and by that time both were sound asleep was when the fumes began seeping out of Martha's throat.

While counting off the days before Christmas, Joe's friends called with reports on the golf game. The weather at Coral Ridge Country Club had been spectacular. The greens were putting fast with a nice cushion, and the fairways were like green carpet. All the guys were all over their golf game. Melvin Botticelli made a hole in one when the fellas were locked in with wager, and he made a real nice chunk of money by the time they checked out on number eighteen. But because it was the golf pro's skin pot, and the tradition of the club dictated big winners of that kind of bread not only bought drinks for the foursome, but the tee-times just before and after your pack, and because a lot of names in that contingent were lushes, especially when they were sucking suds on somebody else's pockets, Melvin was lucky to break even. The guys had called from the country club too, and Joe could hear the laughter and merriment on the premises. All that was hard to take. He wondered out loud. Joe could almost taste their good times playing out without him.

But because their relation was still under one year, Joe still had plenty of patience, because his new-found love was more potent. They had discovered common ground. The couple had seated on lawn chairs on the clipped lawns of Tanglewood and taken in classical music as the musician's notes played into evening. He had all kinds of tender feelings in his heart, and Joe could feel Martha was a real keeper.

The sea gulls had pulled out. They were working a chum slick behind a party boat running beam-to with the chop. The tide was dropping, and the sandpipers had picked up the pace on the suddenly exposed sandflats; they pecked wild in the water riffle.

Joe and Martha packed it in for the day. They'd taken plenty of sun. They rolled the blanket and lugged the gear off in beach flops. Joe stuffed the gear into both bicycle's rear panniers. He cinched the folding umbrella to his rack. After they brushed the sand grains from between their toes, and slipped into tennis shoes, the lovers rode in echelon across North Ocean Boulevard. Their legs and ankles were sunburned like red lobster. It hurt them to pedal. They pedaled in short choppy strokes. They wheeled into Joe's condo pad and thrusted the front wheels into the sidewalk bicycle rack. It was a gated community, and all needs for worry and theft had been removed. Case-hardened locks were considered not necessary inside the compound of Golden Gates.

Joe poured twin glasses of white wine in Fontana Candida. It went down smooth against the sunburn. Joe looked out the picture window beyond the shade of his veranda, and there flying in open space off in the distance, was a pelican. The sky was a soft blue and the bold green fronds of the palms spread wide over the water feature, and many of the white golf carts were hugged around the clubhouse at Coral Ridge. Way across the lattice of palms and past the sixteenth green, Joe could see the classic outline of Melvin Botticelli's 1964 Chevy Impala SS parked next to the pro shop. It's pale Goldwood yellow popped against the lush green field of play. It was sure good to be back at his second home in Florida. He loved every second of the experience, and Joe truly felt blessed.

Joe had planned well ahead. That was like him. He'd bought a slab of wild red salmon from the market. Then he'd walked up the block to Sunshine Bakery and bought two Ciabatta rolls and two Brioche buns. When you had a bakery so close, there was no need to stack up and have your rolls go stale with blue streak.

Joe placed just about half of the salmon in the food processor.

It whirled a few seconds. The raw salmon had been converted to puree. Then Joe chopped up the rest of salmon slab on a maple cutting board with a kitchen cleaver. In a large bowl, in a far corner of the kitchen, Joe began making his secret recipe. With the salmon he sifted kosher salt, scallions, whole-wheat breadcrumbs, cilantro, a jigger of sesame oil, a dash of Adobo, shots of this and that, and two cloves of garlic minced for keeping Martha happy. With wet hands, he formed three husky patties.

Then he started in on the side dish. With a sharp knife with a strong back, he cut out long and stocky fries from a fat sweet potato. He refrained from skinning the peel. Joe rolled the fries in olive oil, patted them with salt, and carried the orange slices in a bowl out through the slider, under the veranda's shade, and flicked a spark into the gas grill. Joe had learned how to make knock-out fries after his divorce from Peggy. He'd quickly learned, Martha was not that good behind the range. Joe began flipping the orange segments with a spatula, turning them into golden fries.

The slider on the veranda next door slid open. Rudy Valentine walked out with a plate of red burger patties. Rudy was a nice guy, a short fellow with a wide smile who wintered over at Golden Gates out of Brooklyn. He was a native New Yorker, and when he talked everybody knew it too because his accent nailed him down to the borough. Acting on the advice of his tax advisor, Rudy always stayed just over six months to get resident status, so he dodged getting whacked with property tax. Rudy had pre-warmed the gas grill. He threw on a couple of burgers. After a while, the smoke from the burger's fat purled from the veranda's rafters and bellowed into space.

"Some weather, huh Rudy?" said Joe across the porches.

"You're not kidding," said Rudy. "We had the kids down for

Thanksgiving, and it's been just about perfect ever since. What a run, man."

Joe began filling the platter with fries. They were golden and done. Rudy flipped burgers on his side. He winced from the puffs of grey smoke; some of the plume had rolled into his eyes.

Down below, a tiny commotion broke. The screen door had slammed. Someone threw a rift of glass into the recycle tub. You could hear bottles bounce, but none broke and there was only a sudden mix of jangled sounds. The report of clicking heels was heard on the sidewalk below. Joe and Rudy clutched the railing and looked down off the balcony. Kelly Presley appeared below. She walked in a squirm and wiggle toward her white BMW.

"Holy Christ Almighty," said Rudy rubbing his high forehead, "what a package."

"You're not kidding," said Joe in disbelief.

Kelly sauntered towards the parking area. A bed of red bee balm hugged the sidewalk, their cherry petals riding high on four-foot stems. The red flowers complemented Kelly's peach toned summer skirt. It rode high and climbed as she walked.

Kelly slid into the sedan. The white door remained open with a wide view. Her skirt climbed and showed skin, and she swung her heels over the pedals. She averted to the balcony and gave the boys a wink.

"You see the way those mesh stockings hugged her thigh," said Rudy in pointed exclamation.

"I'm not blind," said Joe.

"I'm not kidding," said Rudy rubbing his ear. "I'd like to slip off her underpants and kiss her cheeks if she'd let me." Two horse flies buzzed around Rudy's head, and he swung blind at thin air.

A set of knuckles wrapped on Rudy's slider. It was Rhonda. She slid open the glass door a sliver, put her mouth next to the crack and jeered to Rudy, "I want cheese!"

"I'm making cheeseburgers," said Rudy throwing his hands up.

"Don't burn my cheese!" scolded Rhonda. "You burned my cheese last time. Make it nice!"

"You're letting in hot air," said Rudy in defense. The slider slammed shut, and Rhonda disappeared into her air-conditioned haven. The slider's green curtain swung and then arrested dead still.

"She's been on me all day," whispered Rudy across the deck space. "Maybe I should put fly paper on her burger — that'd keep her yapper shut for a while." Rudy crouched down behind the grill and chuckled to himself. "I'm not kidding man, she's been riding me harder than they rode Needles taking leather lash in his Kentucky Derby victory."

"I know that horse," said Joe.

"Listen," said Rudy, "my people have always been Florida people. My grandparents are Ocala stock, born and raised on the same grounds as Needles. That bay stallion is in my blood." Rudy pulled the cheeseburgers. They were cooked medium-well and melted to perfection.

"Sure, I moved to Brooklyn to chase the almighty buck. But there's only one Wall Street and picking winners in the stock market was my job. A man needs to support his family. But my heart's never left here in Florida, and I'll always love that horse. Needles was my dad's favorite, and that Hall of Famer will always be mine too."

"I've heard that poor skin was so banged up as a colt, busted ribs and bouts of pneumonia, the veterinarian worked his hide with so many jabs of the syringe, he was given the name Needles," explained Rudy.

"I never knew that," admitted Joe. "Very interesting."

"I'll bet you never knew Needles was running second to last in the Kentucky Derby, gobbled up the field of fifteen horses to make up those twenty-four lengths, and sealed victory going away," said Rudy with authority.

"Never had a clue."

"Well then you would never have known this — Needle's heart and hoofs are buried in the Garden of Champions, at the Ocala Breeder's Sales Company Pavilion. How's that grab ya?"

"Very sentimentally," said Joe. "I'm glad you told me."

Joe spun to go inside. "I'll see you in the clubhouse in the morning," offered Joe.

"Sounds terrific," said Rudy.

"Everything is terrific in Florida," said Joe. Looking across his shoulder, Joe could see Kelly Presley talking to a figure at the guard shack. Beauty in Florida was presented with many forms and amusements. Joe loved all of it across the board.

Joe quickly finished the salmon burgers on the inside range. They sizzled in canola oil. They finished quickly on the hot skillet. Joe sliced two Brioche rolls, slid on the fish cakes, sprinkled on some hoisin sauce and topped the load with spring greens.

Joe and Martha seated to dine. Joe topped off her wine. She was smitten in the flash of romance. A special light fell through the picture window. The condominium spread wide and spotless from the cleaning lady.

He toasted her with wine. Their glasses clinked. Joe wet his lips. It was a good vintage.

Joe kissed the inside of her wrist. He saw goose bumps run up her arm. Joe sunk his teeth into the salmon burger. It was out of this world, and Joe was finally back in his dream world.

Just then… the phone rang. The ringing startled and broke the moment. It was an ominous chiming of the bells, the sound carrying down the halls, and Joe was struck by premonition. You may call it foreboding. Martha took the call. Joe watched her face drop from across the table. It looked like she aged a million years in a flash. A voice on the wire, had arrested Martha into a countenance of gloom.

"You've got to be kidding," said Martha in seriousness. "When did everything start?"

There was a long pause. Martha slouched over the table, clutching the receiver. She pushed away the burger and fries. As if trying to squelch the tempo of misery, Martha slugged down her wine against wretchedness.

"Oh, the poor thing," said Martha in the shock of protest. "We'll be out on the next flight." Martha hung up the phone. She looked blank at Joe. Her fingers drummed a nervous tapping across the table's glass.

"What's going on?" asked Joe. He'd picked up on the next flight in their sentence block. Joe already felt painted into a vulnerable corner.

"Little Ernie's not well. He's been out two days from class. Veronica is taking him to the emergency room. I need to leave right now." Martha had already walked for the bedroom to begin packing.

"For heaven's sake Martha, let the doctors do their work. He's in good hands. Veronica will handle everything… let's wait until morning before —"

"We're leaving now. Veronica's husband got called out of town on storm duty in Maine."

Day bags were packed for the night flight. They got the 6:20 PM out of Fort Lauderdale. Good fortune had showered on them.

There had been exactly two seats open. Those two seats cost Joe a pretty penny on last notice. He threw his credit card down in repel. He felt like a man who'd just forked over big bucks for box seats at the ball game, thunder showers looming on the other end, and not sure what to expect or find on arrival.

The airplane sped into the night. Joe ate his salmon burger at altitude. He'd wrapped it in heavy white paper, as those procured in butcher shops for wrapping meat. Joe dutifully ate the salmon burger and looked out into the sable night; down below the spattering of lights marked civilization. Joe had muffled Martha's burger in his baggage. She had lost her stomach. That was too bad. The salvaged salmon burger would prove very satisfactory for Joe's breakfast the next morning, washed down with vendor's coffee.

The silver fuselage bore right up the seaboard. It was a non-stop flight; the pilots made fantastic time. They touched down at 9:32 PM on the runway of Bradley Airport.

A good hour before the hands struck midnight hour, the snow-birds pulled into Veronica's driveway. Several rooms were still enveloped in the casts of amber arc light. They saw two silhouettes peer from the den's window. The light post along the walk threw down a fan of spangled beam across the cobbles.

Martha pushed ahead; nervously advancing. A yule tide wreath hung on the lamp post, and the red ribbon rustled as the individuals making concern passed.

The wood door swung open before the report of a knock. Bobby appeared in the threshold. He was a man of brawn, with strapping shoulders. Veronica peered out from behind her man. She seemed to possess the nature of a sheep. Everybody seemed lost for words.

"Bobby?" said Martha in shock.

"The boss had a heart, Mom." Bobby always called her by that coined name. Nobody knew exactly why. It started off in the first dating. Veronica suspected it was about scoring points. "They cycled me out of storm duty to check on family. A guy from the southern sector filled my place." Bobby looked Martha in the eye as he made the revelation.

Veronica peaked out over Bobby's shoulder and said in a sheepish voice, "Thanks for coming… but I told you to wait on results." Joe was an expert on reading body language, and he didn't care too much for his tally. He smelled a coverup.

Bobby and Veronica had just returned from the Emergency Room. Wet tracks from Ernie's shoes were still on the tiles. The television set was casting blue luster in the parlor. Little Ernie sat on the sofa and stared into the screen. The lamp on the end table spilled over him fairy yellow, and a duffel bag of gear was beside him on the cushions.

"What's the prognosis?" asked Martha still in her coat and cable knit hat.

"It's not much, Mom," said Veronica blushing. "The doctor at the hospital gave us a set of instructions and released him."

Little Ernie had been home from school for two days with ailments. His nose was plugged. He'd been hacking away. Veronica tried cough syrup and chicken noodle soup for remedy. He was drinking plenty of liquids. Symptoms seemed in check. But then Ernie escalated. His temperature spiked. Veronica shook down the mercury. The glass read 100 deg. On the kisser between the lines. Ernie confessed he was inside the experience of hot flashes. The boy felt feverish to the touch. Veronica pushed the panic button — she raced Ernie to the Emergency Room in her automobile. The throng of rush hour pressed in the interstate, and the driver's advance was near mass exodus. Veronica escaped through side roads and cut-offs known only to locals, and she saved precious time in her mind.

There was no sugar coating inside the hospital. A registered nurse with bright red hair and thin as rails, plugged little Ernie into the vital signs tower. Brushed into the white curtains, Veronica could see the screen wide and clear.

"His temperature is right on the money," said the redhead.

Veronica moved down the white curtains; she felt it rubbing on her legs. She took a closer look into the vital signs monitor. The reading of 98.9 deg was posted in bright orange numerals. She was relieved of worry, but perplexity nagged her.

She removed the glass thermometer from her purse. She shook it wildly and slid it under her tongue. In attempts to solve mystery with detective work, she went through this repertoire three times over. And on every measure, Veronica got a wide reading of temperature. Her thermometer proved worthless. Hence, a failure contrary to previous indications. When nobody was looking, Veronica chucked the mercury unit in the grey can of trash. She heard it slide down the barrel.

Veronica explained all this to Martha and Joe. Joe was flabbergasted. He could see a map of the United States in his mind. There was a line and arrow to his destination. It had proven as a dead end.

"It's basically just a bad case of the sniffles," admitted Veronica. She had a hard time getting out the truth. Bobby threw his arm around Joe and patted his back.

Both couples retreated to the parlor. You should have seen the look on Martha's face at the sight of little Ernie — she just about melted in her tracks.

"Oh, my Ernie!" her voice cracking. Grandma Martha shuffled across the carpet in miniature steps, her black shoes shuffling a million miles an hour, her arms spread in glee to the heavens, producing a pantomime much like that of a love-sick penguin. She threw a world of affection around Ernie and planted a huge wet kiss on his forehead.

The boy pulled back. He tried to wear a smile, but everybody except Martha could see it was half-hearted at best. The last thing Ernie wanted at this hour, was wet kisses and baby talk from Grandma. He's been through a tough day. They'd seen enough of each other at Christmas. He'd picked up on some kind of onion smell too. Smelling bad breath and having blonde, over-dyed hair brushed on your face at this hour, was a tragic experience. The brush of Grandma's hair remined the boy of steel wool. He wanted no part of it. All that was too much like a bad dream in daylight. Ernie was tired and getting cross, and the little boy wanted to drift off in sleep.

Ernie was just over ten years old, which has always been the Age of Reason. Even at his tender age of youth, he could see through Martha's emotion. He felt sorry for Joe. There was no need for all this affection. He knew about all the beach fun getting ruined on account of him. Guilt tread on him. He was mad at Martha. The boy had his own parents and recited his prayers at bedtime. He had plenty of people to watch over him and had vast confidence in his guardian angel.

Ernie leaped off the sofa and began his departure. He grabbed his duffle bag and moved across the carpet on stocking feet. He feigned away a sea of hugs. Veronica brushed her son's scalp with a pass of her fingers. Little Ernie reached up and gave Joe some skin. The man's hand returned high five.

Ernie headed upstairs. He tried using his forehead against the duffle's strap as a thump line, but his strength was lacking. He shouldered the canvas sack and headed for his bedroom.

In the sleeping quarters, he emptied the duffle on the bed. A mound of riding gear spilled forth. Ernie pulled his snowboard from the heap. It was a green board with an orange dragon. He rubbed his hands across the surface. He folded his ride pants and put away the socks and mittens. The goggles remained enveloped in a silken sleeve. Now he was talking. His father would take him to the ski runs that weekend. The people down below could not give the boy what he needed. His grandmother could not make provision. None of them could. Only the mountain could give back the boy's desire. His lust was for adventure, and in the mountains of green firs and white snows of powder, he could find his quest. Him and his buddies would figure it out, when they could get it on with a little jibber in the theme park.

The boy killed the lights and threw his head back. The soft pillow cradled his thoughts. He drifted off away into a dream world. Pleasant sights came to mind. Barriers seemed to fall away, and the wild feats were all touchable. He touched all of them in his sleep. He saw himself in the half pipe. He could hear the snow creeping under his board. Speed built in the plunge. He caught some air on the cornice lips and reached down for a little grab.

Ernie rolled over in his sleep. He thought he heard Joe laughing down below. He tugged the blanket and drifted back into sleep. Ernie saw himself catching some jib on the hard cookie. In a few quick turns he rode a steel rail to catch air. He floated momentarily in space.

Ernie looked back over his shoulder in sleep, and saw Roger speeding down the slope, reach down with his front hand and touch the toe box, and plant a kid's version of Korean Air. Shreddin' in the cookie, he watched Everett make a lame stab at a Mute Stiffy, lurch and stumble, catch his balance, and reach back on the board's tail and push out some butter, his chest thrusted forward in proudness. The gang hooked together in posse through the theme park, and all of them busted out some Fakie Ollie. Excitement filled Ernie. He had come full circle in his dreams. He was finally back in his element. Everything would be better now.

Ernie had not been dreaming. He'd heard Joe laugh. Joe was happy. He'd broke out in laughter near the front bed of shrubs under Ernie's window.

While nobody was looking and engulfed in conversation, Joe had snuck out the front door. He'd pulled out his cellular telephone on the sidewalk. A zenith of star cluster twinkled in the night. Joe exhaled a cloud of steam into the frosty blackness. His fingers quickly stabbed and punched numbers in the keyboard. There was a long string of ring, and finally the airline booking agent picked up.

"May I be of your assistance," marked the phone booking agent.

"You sure can," exclaimed Joe in excitement. "I need two seats out in the morning for Fort Lauderdale."

"Certainly Sir… let me take a look." There was a long pause. Joe pulled out his tablet and ball pointed pen, in order to record departure and flight number.

"I'm sorry Sir — all the morning flights are booked solid for Fort Lauderdale. But I can get you on a direct into West Palm Beach, departing at 10:05 A M.

Joe blocked away the receiver with his palm, and said sarcastically to the black night, "Lady, I don't care if you get me two tickets for the moon! Just get me out of this joint and get me back to my condo pad pronto Baby!" Joe snickered to the night. It felt good to blow some steam. Joe opened the phone line and said with composure, "Lady, I'd love to take those tickets."

The lady clobbered him again with the price. Joe shrugged it off.

He finished business and signed out. There was a genuine crescent moon in the sky. Joe looked at the moon. Long wisps of charcoal cloud banks floated at the horizon. The moon made the clouds appear three dimensional in the pallid glows. Joe sucked in some crisp New England air and went back inside to Martha's world.

Back inside the house, good fortune spilled over him. Joe was a lucky man. Martha and Joe were assigned separate quarters. Joe would take the couch. That would save him shelling out Necco wafers. Joe shoved a few in his mouth. They hit the spot. Joe was happy. Ernie really in fact heard Joe laughing. It was good and quite a relief not to be dealing with garlic breath under the circumstances. Joe kicked off his shoes, stripped down in the moonlight, and slept the night away in the parlor. He slept sound as a baby.

At the airport, Joe could not get his credit card out quick enough. The ticket agent checked the booking and shelled out the boarding passes. Joe wanted to end his predicament and suffering. That's why Joe sprung for Golden Gates in the first place. But he never dreamed in his wildest escapades, that he'd get gouged three times over in such short order for plane rides.

In this early hour, the thong of suitcase people had momentarily increased, and two dense rows of travelers were rushing through the revolution of turnstile gangs. Martha and Joe produced picture identification, went through electronic surveillance, and got patted down.

Joe got a window seat by chance. His number was over the right wing. Martha sat next to him. She slid into the seat, as if inserted with a shoehorn. She just about squeezed in between the arm rests. Her saddlebags bulged into the seating arrangements. The curve of her chubby thigh, brushed on Joe's leg. Joe had noticed it on the beach in the swimsuit. Martha had put on considerable weight.

Martha prepared for flight. Three bags of candy were stuffed into the folding seat pouch. She opened the zipper of her travel bag and looked down at a huge roast beef grinder. She'd procured it from a take-out vendor along the concourse, and it was loaded with mayonnaise and provolone cheese. Martha could not wait until the red warning lights went away, and she could dive into her goodies.

The plane lifted. Joe watched the water droplets sheath back off the wing, and he could see the wing's tip was flexing in flight at great length. These flying machines had always been for Joe, a window of trust into mankind's ingenuity. Nevertheless, he kept an eye on the rivets.

The plane landed right on time in West Palm Beach. Martha was sleeping. The white paper wrapper from the grinder was crammed into the seat's pouch, with the nest of open candy bags. Joe could see many candy wrappers on the floor, and her dress was covered in tiny specks of breadcrumbs. Joe thought Martha said something about garlic cloves for health reasons. He now could see otherwise.

The couple needed to ride steel to get back home. Joe flagged a taxi. A Jamaican of extremely dark skin pulled in. He was nearly jet black. The taxicab was bright yellow and sat on full-size Chevrolet. The Jamaican hit the meter and said, "Where to Mon?"

"The train station," said Joe.

"No sweat Mon." said the Jamaican wheeling out. "Plenty hot," he added with beads of sweat running his brow.

"That's Florida Man," said Joe.

It was a short ride. All of it came to small money. Joe stuffed a wad of money in the cabbie's hand with a big tip.

"Thanks a lot, Mon," said the Jamaican counting the bills. "I really mean it Mon, thanks a million."

"No problem Buddy," said Joe.

That was the most Joe had spoken since Hartford. A wall of silence had grown between him and Martha. It was still very hard for Joe to fathom. He'd just wasted over two days on this foolish trip across the United States on account of sniffles, not to mention a pocket of greenbacks.

It was always nice riding trains after an escapade on airlines, because the seating on the railroad was spacious and wide berth with nice tables in certain compartments, and you felt it right away after being crammed into a fuselage at altitude.

The train crept forward, and in no time flat, the conductor was putting it to the iron, speeding the steel wheels down the track bed. Joe liked trains. It brought back pleasant memories. Joe and Peggy rode the train with their kids. They'd ridden the very section of track and train depots many times over, and these sweet memories pulled sentimentalism and hurt on Joe.

It brought him back to an existence of tangible oaths. Importance accentuated. Reminiscing pronged at his conscious. He was enlightened of pacts whispered in three-way conversation long ago, when he vowed to take a women's rib under an invisible contract with the Lord. What was real, what always had been, tugged on old strings. He saw many things in new lights, old things and parts of him, covered and varnished with time. But now in his new revelation, the train streaming forward and throwing down the chugging of locomotive, Joe could see a strange importance as if projected to life on a cinematograph film.

Joe blinked a few times on the train. He caught a glimpse of his old shadow. He was dressed in a blue jumper gown. Somebody was counting down contraction numbers. Joe had already completed antiseptic scrub down. His wife was drawn with emotion. The nurse and doctor had stone faces. A very bright beam of coned light shone forth. A scalpel, surgical tools and chrome forceps, glistened in the wash of electric beam. Peggy was having a baby.

Joe remembered the umbilical cord being cut. The doctor feverishly tying the knots to form an infant's belly button. After all these years, Rebecca's first cries filled his ear — the doctor had applied light love taps for an airway check. He remembered wiping the afterbirth from Peggy's inner thigh, with a warm and moist terry towel. Joe could feel the grip of his wife's hand, clasping his bundle of excitement with love. All the worry and sweating of bullets on the delivery table, seemed to have vanquished in baby's birth, and a glow of motherhood fell over Peggy. Joe beheld the wash of victory across her face, the pools of brown-black eyes, her jet hair seeped in sweat beads of her labors. A relevance to fatherhood was looming Joe.

Martha was eating candy. She ate several in succession. Silence prevailed. Vibrations of the train's metal came through the floorboards. Joe gazed out the window. He drifted a little farther down the line.

Joe and Peggy were Armenians. The real thing. Their people were Christians since A.D. 301, when St. Gregory the Illuminator converted the people form Zoroastrianism. Joe knew the history. The Turks always had been Armenia's worst enemy. He knew for a long time that its faction of Kurds slaughtered up to 50,000 of his people like ants.

Joe acknowledged after the slaughter by the Kurds, advance of intercession was thrown across the bargaining table by foreign governments: the Russians, French, and Great Britain, scorned the Armenian's blood bath, and crossed borders to buckle the Kurds' oppression. The Russians themselves, infiltrated the forms of propaganda into the aggressors, with the psychological goals to weaken the Turkish state. These efforts brought precious time for the Armenian culture and permitted their wants for keeping a separate identity.

But when discovered the Armenians were affording the Russian army with clandestine support, the Kurds dished out Holy Hell — they drove most of the Armenian people into waste lands of the Syrian Desert, driven like cattle with a one-way ticket to their very extermination. They died of starvation, wilted like dead flowers from the painful effects of sunstroke without water.

Joe knew his people had always stood fast as fierce individualists, bolstered by a strong national pride of language, customs, and the walls of their vast churches. In tongue alone, no other language in the world had close ties to the dialogue of Joe's people. In the prominence of all those traits was the church, where they could seek comfort and might from the Lord.

The Bible lore put Noah's ark moored in the mountains of Armenia after the great flood, and the Armenians knew the best place to seek refuge of those being hunted, was the Highest of places.

Joe entered the church. The avenue of travel was through a daydream. His church was the Armenian Church of Saint Gregory. He could hear the patter of leather soles on the altar's stone floor. The shoes sent echo in the mouse quiet of the chamber. The pews were empty. It was a private event for family. It was the sacrament of Rebecca's baptism. There was a sharp picture of Joe's imagination in train compartment, and he could smell church flowers.

Joe remembered the priest. He was very serious. The priest had baptized all five of Joe's children. But because this was their first child, Joe was full of extra excitement. The baptismal reservoir in Saint Gregory's Church, was carved directly into the stone altar. It was oblong in nature and looked like a stone sink. And as you might have imagined, there was no drain plug on the bottom. This effect casted historical lineage about the scene, and looking down into the holy waters, one got the feeling they were way back in time. There were chisel marks in the stone, and the stonecutter must have hammered around for quite some time.

They didn't fool around in the old world of Armenian church. They immersed you right to the hilt in holy water, making certain all the evil spirit was washed away.

Joe had braced Rebecca's calves, still plump with baby fat. While still singing chants and reciting of prayer, the priest cradled the baby and plunged her into holy water. Joe had felt his hand go with the baby into the waters. Rebecca had surfaced from the cistern, spitting of water thorough her tiny glistening lips. Then the little girl shouted in happiness. She slapped the water and kicked her feet. Rebecca exclaimed something to the priest in baby talk, as if hinting she'd love to go for another free ride down under on the house. The ceremony had done its work.

The train cut its momentum. The conductor was breaking her down. The giant iron wheels called and screamed a pitch of squeal on the tracks. They were pulling into Pompano Beach Station. Martha cupped her ears. She found the clamorous din was very unsatisfactory on her nerves.

Three colored fellows departed the train. When you saw guys like that around, they were usually fruit pickers. Their boot toes were sheened from cutting through the orchard's long grass all day. Small brown briers with tiny thorns, were clinging to their pant legs. One of the guys was lugging a plastic bag of oranges.

Joe said to them, "You guys pickers?"

And the last guy carrying the orchard drops said, "All day man. We pick every day when it's coming on and getting' ripe."

Joe knew Pompano Beach Station well. A memory shook him from the seat. He wiggled out around Martha, crossed the aisle and took a long, hard look past the row of far side windows, sweeping the horizon line. It sure was still there. He could see the semi-arched backbone of the Merry-Go-Round, still cutting the skyline. Seahorse Amusement Park was still in action.

The train pulled away. Joe looked back over his shoulder out his window. The giant steel wheel was framed against the sky of dove grey.

"What's there?" questioned Martha.

"Oh, nothing really," said Joe, "thought I saw something." He never made eye contact. Joe turned and went back out the window into his own world.

Seahorse Amusement Park had been their favorite place. That was long ago. The kids were small then, and they were a family.

Many visions returned. They came very quickly, much like a deck of cards being cut and fanned out on the table. Joe could not believe the condition of his mind. In just a mile of track, hundreds of visions could be painted in his head.

Joe saw the hand painted sign of Seahorse Amusement Park. It was a colorful sign, with navy blue capitals and burnt orange shading. The park's logogram was a seahorse. The sea creature was painted on the sign, perched on its curved tail, with a boxed snout and horse-like head. They sold T-shirts and sweatshirts of the same signage, and they flew off the vendor's shelves. You could see a Seahorse Amusement Park T-shirt just about any place in Florida, and Joe once saw one on a guy's back in Shea Stadium at a Met's game.

Joe saw his family walk under the sign. His corporal shadow pushed the baby stroller. The Seahorse sign was in vast proportions of the figures and miniaturized his family. They were swallowed and mingled with the crowd.

He could smell cotton candy. Its sweetness filled his senses. Joe watched the lady with a marcel of blonde, over-dyed hair, wind the pink fluff of cotton candy on white paper spears. She had been spinning this cotton in the metal tubbed machine for years, and she could produce a wonderful head. It was like a giant bee's nest when finished. The lady clutched a second paper spear in her free hand, and when one was spun, she began another twirl job. The cotton candy sat in soldiers' rows inside a pushcart with plexiglass walls, and a single light bulb shone down over the forest of pink cotton.

The kids hovered around the cart in wonderment. It was a special treat for them to behold spinning. They had never seen a lady with circus-like attributes.

The magic brought happiness to the brood, and this swelled Joe's pride in fatherhood. It was a significant banner of accomplishment caught in time. Joe was still amazed with what was still in his head.

Other snippets drifted about in daydreams. Joe remembered the purchase of seven red candy apples from a five spot that gave back change. His family was tucked into a park bench along the midway. They licked the scarlet sheathing of the apples, until the candy waned and permitted the sinking of teeth into the apple's flesh.

Joe closed his eyes. The train hustled south. He felt part of his stomach drop — the Ferris Wheel at Seahorse Amusement Park was climbing exceedingly fast. Joe's four kids were besides him on the wood slats. Joe looked through the safety bar. He could see Peggy clutching the baby stroller. He watched her get smaller and smaller, then go out of sight on the high crest; and when the wheel rolled over, Joe caught glimpses of his wife below on the midway, and she got bigger and larger than life on the wheel's revolution to full circle, and thus Joe could embrace the spark of life in her eyes.

You could see a long way from the Ferris Wheel, for it was a monstrous wheel of spoken iron speeding with all colors of electric light bulbs, and you could feel your gut lift when she went over top dead center. In the grips of this daydream, Joe's kids inched closer in the quest for security; they savored both of Dad's arms across their shoulder blades, squeezing them in the embrace of affection. Joe was their security blanket and felt they would always be safe when lurking dark valleys in his shadow.

Joe could never forget what the Ferris Wheel had dished out. It happened when the attendant sprung the safety bar, and his son Nick raced down the gangplank towards his mother's arms.

See Nick run. He ran to Mommy. Nick speeding down the ramp. But he never saw the spike's head sticking from the gangplank and took a real hammering on the lumber. The blow drove his teeth into Nick's tongue. He bled profusely through his mouth. He was screaming bloody murder. His bright red blood flowed over his lips and pooled on the weather planks. In a few hours, most of Nick's blood had wicked into the furrowed grain and showed a circuit of maroon staining in the hot Florida sun.

Those were the days before Golden Gates. Joe made small money then. They were blue collar people who rented a hotel flat for a week on the cheap side of Fort Lauderdale. Joe paid out of pocked for Nick's stitches. The doctor went easy on him. Small boys heal quick. The next day, Nick was body surfing in the breakers. The salt water did a stupendous job in healing the boy's mouth. He only spit blood in the first few runs of the surf, then a light pink welting of scar tissue had begun its formation.

Joe looked at Martha. She was sleeping. She was exhaling and inhaling through her nostrils. Huge amounts of rushing air could be heard. It was good she was out cold. It seemed the more Joe thought about it, he liked Martha better sleeping these days. There was a lot less trouble then, until she struck a new-fangled idea while in wakefulness.

Joe pulled his wallet. He brought it slowly to his lap. Another check was made of Martha. She was still out cold. Her head was slumped in slumber. Joe opened the wallet. He went over the photograph of his five kids. They were side by side in a beach setting. Sentiments arrested Joe. Vast importance was about the man. He kissed the photograph, shoved it back in the wallet, and went off to other avenues of contemplation. Some of it was tempered in forming a plot.

Many things were on Joe's mind. Some of them were small things. But the muster of all these incidents goaded Joe and brought forth a clear manifestation. Sheets of evidence compiled.

Some things had been on the table since the first spark flew. Joe's friends had put out the warning of too much baggage. But Joe was blinded by Cupid's arrow. The poor guy must have been suffering from love sickness. But now Joe could see Martha's big full lips had not been worth the spending of so much hard work. Trying to quench garlic with Necco wafers for a sultry make out is one thing. But now the maintenance of Martha had become extreme, and Joe was beginning to wonder.

Other problems surfaced. For instance, a few days before Martha pushed the panic button for a boo-boo ride to see little Ernie, she'd called out Joe on his haircut. She said it looked scalped and could see choppy cuts.

Everybody at Coral Ridge Country Club knew Marvin Botticelli had the eye. You saw the ball go in with the hole-in-one shot. He'd set up beautiful body line gaps while restoring his yellow Chevy Impala. He's given all the money from his skins game to his buddies, even though they took their cuts with pulls down the throat. Marvin was a straight shooter and told it how it was.

Joe pulled Marvin aside in the club house and asked, "Hey Marvin — does my haircut look skinned up?"

Marvin took a good hard look. He gave the Armenian's head of hair a real evil eye. Joe's dark hair was thick as prime fur and glistened in the sun.

"Your hair looks great," said Marvin in confidence. "It's got a wonderful tight taper around the ears, and the cut flows out beautifully. Your barber is right on the money."

"Martha said it was butcher work."

Marvin took another look. "That?" questioned Marvin. "That's just a tiny cowlick from pillow sleeping. Try a brisk brush out in the morning, with a little hair dope."

The train bustled over the trestlework. Water was on both sides. Joe saw a painted turtle on a log. The turtle was loafing in the hot sun. The train passed very quickly over the lagoon. The turtle closed its eyes. The bright yellow marking on its shell showed bold against the silver-grey log.

Joe briskly rubbed his head. He liked his hair. He went over his scalp many times with his fingers. His hair still had the vitality of a young man. His roots tingled from the rub down.

Joe spotted Martha's candy bag. It was lodged between the seats. He slipped his fingers down very slowly — slow and deliberate, as to not excite any detection of crinkling sounds from the wrapper. Martha was still drifted away. Free candy was always a nice thing. Joe put the Werther's candy in his mouth. The old-world zest of caramel began melting away in his mouth box. Joe wished everything tasted like candy.

Joe could feel something. Vengeance might be the wrong word. Hard feelings were a better word. Some of the problems Martha caused were giant stumbling stones. It put Joe on the dark side of family. Those effects alone, drafted the need for rebellion inside the man. Keeping Joe home back east in the weeks before Christmas, brought about serious problems.

All of Joe's five kids made winter vacation at Golden Gates. They stayed with dad at intervals over the winter. Leah and her husband Tommy always took the week off which culminates on Christmas morning. This holiday for Leah, was more than fun in the sun. It was an extension of faith.

Leah was very beautiful. She was Joe's second daughter, and the youngest child. She was twenty-eight years old. They were planning conception in the very near future.

After the gifts had been opened on Christmas morning, Leah's favorite tradition was attending Saint David's Armenian Church. It had been a family tradition now for many years. The church was in Boca Raton. Joe and Peggy had begun winter worship there when the founder of the church, Father Zaven, was still on the pulpit. Many years later, Bishop Nareg took over the church duty, and it was his voice that had bonded all of Joe's kids in scripture. But Bishop Nareg had taken other assignment in Brazil. In the last few years of winter religion, Joe's family had listened to the new voice of Father Paren, but in the few short visits, they could not fully read the priest, and it seemed he was still trying to fill some of Bishop Nareg's shoes.

Saint David's Armenian Church was plastered down with white stucco and had cupped tile roofing. A sea of tall palm trees grew along the church, and the green spray of foliage marked very sharp against the whiteness. For those trained and sharpened to those things, the grey husked bark of the palm trees, juxtaposed with near exactness to the grey cupped tiles which adorned the roof. But like I said, people with sharp eyes are trained to spot these connections. Many people walked through the church's front door for years, and never made the connection. Their minds were not wired to operate with that kind of scrutiny.

Joe could see Leah. The vision in his memory was clear. She was seated next to him on the wooden pew. The glass chandeliers of Saint David's Church casted a yellow warm light over the assembly. Leah's skin tones danced and illuminated in the light. She had very beautiful olive skin, and her black long eyebrows fanned a spray of wonder across her brow. Her beauty could stop men in their tracks.

Leah slid closer to Joe on the wooden pew. He could smell the spring like scents in his daughter's hair. They clasped hands. Joe swung his vacant hand over their clasp. Leah beamed. A marvel of love broke across her smile, and her eyes revealed her feelings. Father Paren recited the gospel in a steady voice. Joe held his daughter's hand through the sermon, and beads of sweat formed in their palms from the Florida heat spell.

Joe had his memories. But they could have been more recent, if Martha had not come into play. She had ruined Leah's Christmas. Martha's insistence on Joe spending Christmas dinner on her side spoiled everything. Joe was troubled with his choice. Their romance was in its first year, and he had gone along with the program. Joe thought he'd struck a wonderful kind of love. But now he discovered, bouncing around on the train tracks, it had been masked in a charade, and was nothing more than a shallow love. A series of guilt came over him with Leah's absence, and Joe's blindness had suddenly lifted. He vowed to play by new rules.

Cheerless gloom of grey mingled across the track bed. Fog blankets had creeped inland. A mist of grey engulfed the track. Joe looked out the window. Miniature beads of dew sailed across the glass. Warm trade winds out of the Bahamas were streaming over Florida's cold snap, and frontal fog bands were forming on the seaboard.

Beyond the soldier-still legions of sea grass, and in a far field speckled with rows of tress, were more fruit pickers. In the grey mist, the figures were vague and sketchy, and they drifted in and out of the picture. Silhouettes of humped baskets and brimmed hats moved in the gloom. Human waves of pickers, marched in bee-like fashion towards the farm wagon. The figures waxed and waned in the fog banks. In a thread of pale sunlight of the bluff, a heaped mound was the crowning feature on the wood wagon, a mountain of thick-skinned oranges.

Joe pulled a sweater from the travel bag. The chills were getting to him. The cable knit sweater was very satisfactory against the cold snap. But no amounts of bundling could seem to brush away the foreboding on Joe's mind.

Martha slept away. She'd covered with a red trade blanket. The blanket was adorned with three rows of black stripes. Martha was still making tiny puffs and snorts though her nose. Her big full lips, caught in the queer flat lights of the fog bank, seemed to have lost a lot of charm in Joe's heart.

"Cypress Creek Station," called the conductor's voice over the wire. Joe could see the rush of trees falling into focus, and up the tracks the locomotive halted. It was a short stop. Only three people departed. They would be home soon. Fort Lauderdale was the next stop.

Joe hoped Rudy Valentine had taken the liberty, for an apartment check on Joe's pad. He'd given Rudy a key. The last thing Joe needed was an air conditioner blasting, with this kind of cold wave. It would be a tragic experience. He wanted no part of that kind of welcome. Joe's plate was already full, without the addition of more problems.

The train was enveloped in fog. It built speed quickly. The narrow bands of fog hugged the shoreline from Hollywood and ran north to Magnolia Park; and from a bird's eye view, the silver flashing of the speeding train could be seen down through the breaks of grey gauze.

Just then, Joe was seized by a vision — deep into the banks of fog… he saw Needles. The dead horse. The apparition grabbed him by the seat of the pants, and Joe started into the theater of mirthless vapors.

Suddenly, Joe had a keen awareness of the horse being buried alone. Six feet under at the garden of champions. When you think that far back in time — for Needles was the hero of Rudy's dead dad — all kinds of visions come into play. Joe could see the skeleton, collapsed over all the years of time, for the connective tissue and disc spaces had long waned, and a snake-like path of vertebrate swept below the hot grains of sand. Joe could see the eye sockets hollowed out from night crawlers, and the heavy boned structure around the orbits. Down below in the tomb of melancholy, the horse's skull lay perfectly intact. The white skull swept back in the golden sands, and the teeth were in states of near perfection. Yellow stains traced the molar shanks, and all of Needle's teeth were fixed to the jawbone. But Needles had been buried in a lone grave. No bones of blood lines accompanied the tomb. One was the lonely number. These thoughts not only drove chills up Joe's spine, but also revealed a sudden urgency with strings attached.

Joe would need to speak with Peggy. They'd never completed any arrangements. It was one thing for Peggy to be living in Arizona. She could stay on that side of the United States. But they would need to talk. Joe wanted no part of being buried all alone. The black stallion with the bit still in his mouth, had enveloped Joe with premonition.

Top priority loomed. Joe wanted the family on a singular plot. It was time for a vote. This outcome would be mandatory. They would be buried together. All seven in a singular grave plot. They might all need to bend. Joe was willing to throw in some chips. He was hoping Peggy would not play stubborn. That she'd want everybody in her mother's plot down in Sierra Vista. Joe was hoping he'd never have to be buried with his mother-in-law. She'd started some of the problems. But it would be better than nothing.

Joe formed a plan. On the grounds of Golden Gates, were three tennis courts. They played on clay. The courts were shielded from Joe's apartment by a grove of magnolia trees that spilled forth white flowers in the springtime. Joe used the courts many times. Joe never served. He never owned a racket since high school. Joe used the tennis courts for dropping dimes. Joe liked making calls in privacy from the clay.

Sometime over the next few days, Joe would call Peggy. He'd send out Martha on a wine run to the package store. He would scheme out everything for mid-afternoon of Arizona time. That's when his mother-in-law took a nap. Joe and Peggy could speak in privacy on the span of this time.

Joe would not be making plea to have Peggy return for another chance. She was the one who filed. He was just hoping all of them would be back together after the last lap, so they were back at each other's side in the end, six feet under where the garden worms con-ducted the tracing of underground burrows.

The last month, sure had been trying on Joe's nerves. It had been one thing after another. That list of things Joe found trouble-some. The sensation was like being pelted by hail. It was a painful experience. He could sense scars building. Joe could feel some of his patience slipping away.

Martha woke from sleep. She rubbed her eye sockets and fore-head with a moist face cloth procured from her Guatemalan satchel. The towel took away her lipstick. She pulled a makeup mirror and re-glossed in #677 Siren red of the Revlon people.

Martha gave Joe a blank stare. She looked right through him. Joe turned quickly. He did not wish to telegraph anything away.

Joe saw Leah. She had returned in a vision beyond the window. They were motoring along the sea-drive in a convertible automo-bile. A rouge of beauty spilled from his daughter. She was caught in a nimbus of orange radiance from the sun, seated rigid in proud-ness against the seat, and her complexion was throwing off a halo of confidence. Joe could feel it across to his driving station. He reached up through the open button on his collar shirt, clutched the crucifix on the gold chain around his neck, and thanked the Maker for such a wonderful daughter.

Leah reached in her jean pocket. She pulled a harmonica in C scale and played a few soft chords. The music was quickly engulfed by the automobile's slip stream. Then Leah began to sing. It was not the song's first reciting. It had been sung by another woman a long time ago, across the ocean in the parish of Gweedore. Although they were complete strangers and never knew of the other's existence, both women felt the same tugging of heart strings when singing the tune. Leah sang with an angelic voice — *I remember all the best days… We're on our way home.* Her voice sliced the atmosphere, and she sang the requiem with the motive of salvation for their destiny. But at the time, if I'm not greatly mistaken, this revelation had not reached the ears of Enya. The face of Manderley Castle was too distant for sounds to travel.

Joe thought he must be in some kind of supernatural experience. A religious apparition. Leah pointed out the window; and out beyond was the wafer of orange sun on the horizon, and banking in an arc up toward the heavens, Joe thought he must have seen over a thousand white doves.

Joe had seen enough. He looked forward in the train's compartment. Everything was clear. His sights were now fixed and specific. He'd been painted far enough into the Pandora's box. The time had come. Joe took a deep breath and cleared his throat. Joe had been thinking for quite some time now it was perhaps a good time to call it a wash and break off everything.

First Steps

He sure was a little guy. Its miniature feet took tiny steps. He would never win any kind of race. There must have been a fresh hatch of eggs. A thread-like tail dragged behind. The baby snapping turtle moved up the trap rock lane, searching the gifts of life.

Nick came down the fire road through the forest, his eyes watering as he sped under the grove of husky pines, the tires of his bicycle spitting gravel through the bends. Nick had spotted him way below, a miniature little fellow caught in the yellow beam of sun. Nick spun the bicycle around and studied the critter. Nick mopped away the tears with his wrist and hunched over the western bars adorned with tassel streamers, measured the tiny fellow. It was a snapper alright. Its shell was no bigger than a quarter. Nick placed him in his hand and looked him over. He was not like an ordinary turtle, who sought refuge in a shell with legs retracted and peeking out. This little guy was full of life and wanted to see the whole wide world.

Nick was only ten years old. He felt exceedingly old next to the baby turtle. His shoulders were pulled back soldier-square, and he marveled at the mystical revelation of life.

Fear was not a word in Nick's word box. Daredevils had come to him through the night confessors; the little boy began to think he was invincible. Nick still had a lot to learn.

Nick was on the trap tock flats below the dam of the lake. This blue lough was the water supply for the town of Sentry. They patrolled the road with trucks. The last thing Nick wanted was for the baby turtles to get squished out and snuffed with rolling rubber, in their maiden voyage of life. Precautions were taken. The body of water was a good three hundred yards up the lane, past under the silver maples, up over the bluff and around the bend.

Nick cupped the baby turtle in his palm, fingers clasped tight. With the free hand, he pushed the bicycle by the handlebar's stem, walking along his much-loved Columbia in his blue and white Keds high tops. One of Nick's strides comprised perhaps a couple hundred of his new friend, and it really was no sweat to give the tiny shaver some slack with a free ride.

Nick caught something out of place up the lane —another baby turtle was pounding the trap rock dust. That shelled bantam marched north too. Nick plunked him into his palm and rolled the bicycle ahead.

Another form grew. It was a baby leatherback. Nick was getting an eye for them. It reminded him of looking for Indian arrow heads with his Uncle Stewie. Nick quickly closed the gap. The turtle's miniature legs were doing double-time up the dust bed, and his eyes the size of pinpoints, tried to measure his adventure.

On the slope where the roadbed rose on the bluff, another figure of the hatch was making tracks. This little guy was the leader of the pack. He had convictions. He was full of enthusiasm, his neck stretched forward, and in baby turtle speed this little rascal was making tracks. Nick scooped him up and plopped him into the pig pile. He fought Nick all the way. Nick tapped his snout. He blew big puffs of air in his face. But there was no holding him down. Nick could feel those tiny claws digging at his skin, tickling his palm, and the turtle climbed his fingertips with no signs of hitting the brakes. The third turtle inside the clutch, made a tinkle in his hand. He had felt something and peered deeply into his palm. A puddle no bigger than a bead of dew, glistened near his lines of fortune telling.

Nick marched with the rascals through the bluff meadow of golden rod, down the deer run through the shore brush, and reached the water. A good chop had formed; and at the present time just below the Tropic of Cancer, a class-4 hurricane was clobbering Puerto Rico. The chop had piled up a bed of lake weed on the shore. Nick kneeled in the green mass. It was a nice sensation to have that kind of cushion, on a shoreline plastered with plompster size stones. His kneecaps relished the experience.

Nick measured the brood. He concluded it was time for their first plunking. They would need to survive in water. They would all need to go under. Nick clenched the first tiny shell between his thumb and trigger finger and gave him baptism of the lake. His fingers brought him down and under. Tiny bubbles came from the turtle's mouth. The baby turtle threw out its legs, froze in place as if jolted by electricity, and craned his neck into the peacock blue. With all four legs spread, he looked like a parachutist sailing in space, motionless in his new world. His wee eyes bulged in wonder, and its baby feet raked the water.

Nick plunked them one behind the other into the lake. Their common denominator was apprehension — each baby's advance mirrored in the same mimic — they all froze with cold feet on the first dive. The leader of the pack showed no special knack of being superior. He got stage fright too. Nick was wondering if he'd pushed them too far on the first wet run.

Nick plopped them in a nest formation. He fashioned a fort around the green-grey shells with agate size rocks. The leader of the pack scaled the rocks and climbed quickly the hump of green lake weed. All others followed. It was Follow the Leader, and the three infants scurried to catch up.

From the crest of the humped weeds, the baby turtles could see a long way. The lake looked to them, like a million miles across. White caps were dancing and painted an ominous picture. The baby turtles had seen enough.

They retreated down the face of weeds. Their tails dragged behind. They kept a stiff upper lip and held their heads high. All the baby turtles sought refuge under a slanted flat stone, where under was a sand pocket and miniature pieces of grey sticks and driftwood. The pack took another long look across the lake. The speed of the blow coming across the lake, caressed the awareness of the baby turtles, and the chop was breaking on the shore stones in the sounds of lapping. The baby turtles turned their claws into the sand grains and peered out in amazement. The fears of competition had rolled through them as through a gate, and with nerves eaten and lost in the vices of cold feet, it was clear at the present time, those little shavers were not ready to relinquish their guard and begin training for Seal Team Six.

If it keeps on rainin'
levee's goin' to break
If it keeps on rainin'
levee's going to break
When the levee breaks
I'll have no place to stay.
Mean old levee taught me to
weep and moan
Mean old levee taught me to
weep and moan
It's got what it takes to make
a mountain man
leave his home
Oh, well, oh, well, oh, well
Cryin' won't help you, prayin'
won't do you no good
Now, cryin' won't help you,
prayin' won't do you no good
When the levee breaks,
mama, you got to move
All last night sat on the
levee and moaned
All last night sat on the
levee and moaned
Thinkin' about my baby
and my happy home

—When the Levee Breaks
by Led Zeppelin

—When The Levee Breaks was originally recorded by Kansas Joe McCoy and Memphis Minne. The setting was Columbia Records of New York City, cut into vinyl on June 18th of 1929. Minne is credited with the songwriting and played lead guitar when cut on open G tuning. As tribute and love for her hero, blues singer Bonnie Raitt paid for Minne's headstone.

CHAPTER 1

I'd been hunting Mexicans since early morning. My feed roll was packed with 15 shots. But taking portraits of Mexicans, can be like dealing with rattlesnakes. They are camera shy with fears of getting pinched in some kind of paperwork, and you need to build trust. And then there are privacy laws and trespassing and common courtesy. I've been a rolling fixture on those farm roads for a long time and have a green light on a lot of tillable. But still; it's a tough game with subject matter on payrolls moving crop harvest production. You need to strike like lightning.

On this very morning, sixteen Mexicans were picking strawberries on the Szymborski Farm, another seventy-five-plus on Kuchta Farm. Just up Golden Road was a colorful platoon of Mexicans picking summer squash for the Boston market, and on the Paderewski place, four more were wielding hoes in the furrows. Sentery River Valley farming would fall flat on its face without Mexicans.

I finally caught up with some Mexicans. I had them dead to rights. They were on a water break from cutting kale with head knives and were sitting and stooped against Stampora's barn. They had retreated into a tiny sliver of shade against the barn's wall, and their shirts were sopped with sweat. Out of dignity to their conditions, I cut them slack. Figured it best they catch a wind, because they'd be worked until the sun began its descent beyond the far groves of silver maples. The camera remained slung over my shoulder. The exposure was getting terrible too, sun beams beating the kale blankets. I averted up through the crop rows. Pulverized dust rose and dusted my boots. I fired the truck's engine and motored down to the Szymborski Farm.

I've known Zelda May Szymborski for a long time. She's an old lady now. She sells strawberries in the back barn. You can see her from the road, but she appears as a match-box figure, lost in the huge proportions of the open barn doors.

I pulled into the barnyard. Zelda was standing in the shadows behind the plank table, and rows of red strawberries were necked in arrangements on the stand. It was very hot. There had been drought for three weeks running. The hottest kind of July. Heavy blankets of sweltering humidity. All the white people in the valley had stripped down to scant habiliment. Zelda wore a white T-shirt cut as a tank top. You could see the border line of a farmer's tan around both arms. She was wearing sand coloured straight legs with frayed threads, and white tennis shoes with toe boxes scuffed from shuffling the fertile grounds. Most of the farm bosses I'd seen along River Road were wearing white T-shirts and ball caps. Two of them were swigging bottled water from their ice chest, sitting in the GMC pickup cab with the driver's door kicked wide open.

But the Mexicans never had those luxuries. Their destiny was labors of picking all day in the glistening sun. They knew well the beaming rays were their arch enemy. The summer's sun would zap their strength and burn their skin. They took it standing and enveloped in sun vestments. The Mexicans dressed in long sleeve shirts, cowboy style handkerchiefs around their necks, and wide brimmed hats. All the clothing of colors painted a quilt work of spectrum creeping and hunched across the green crop fields. The Mexicans had evolved as farm workers over long spans, had learned and found strange comforts being covered on the hottest numbers summer could dish out.

When the season of humped bushel baskets of table vegetables waned, and the digging of spuds began in Indian Summer, most of the Mexicans donned colorful feathers from songbirds quilled in their hats. They collected feathers from roost stations around the crop fields, and their hat brims were soaked in brines of sweat that stiffened the brims.

"Good morning, Zelda," I said. We measured each other at close quarters in the old barn, and baby beads of sweat had formed on her upper lip. The signature zest of life was in her eyes. Tiny slivers of light twinkled from inside her iris rings, and crow's feet ran from her sockets.

"Hello Travis," said Zelda, "it sure is some kind of hot." Tucked into the shadows, an industrial floor fan thumped its big blades across the cloaks of dead air. The fan was trained, so the tail effects of electric wind caressed her station.

Zelda was born in Sentery. Her maiden name was Zgrodnik. She's a rock pillar of the town's lore. She'd shot marbles with boys on the old school yard grounds. She never left town and put down roots. The farthest she ever wandered was for a three-day trip to the New York World's Fair of 1964. Her brother Teddy got killed in World War Two on the beachhead of Tarwa. His battalion of the 2nd Marine Division had drawn straws for the first wave on Red Beach 2. The landing crafts skipped across the sea, leathernecks peeking over the speeding bow with confidence in the metal boat, when their hulls got snagged at low tide on the reefs. When the grunts went over the gunwales in feverish pitch, they leaped into the razor-sharp coral below the combers. They began the wild slosh through the sea, Japanese machine gun nests sweeping the lurching brown clad figures. Almost all of Teddy's platoon on the left flank got wiped out. Their corpses bobbed and spilled blood into the blue tropical waters. Teddy was bleeding too — he gashed his calf on the knife-like coral and opened himself like a zipper.

The field medic lashed the leg with gauzing, then taped a double-cross butterfly over the wound. Teddy met his maker that night in the midnight hour. The zips had breached the perimeter under blackness, and hand-to-hand combat commenced. A rugged Polish prime of nineteen, brawn built on the farm, Teddy grabbed a Jap around the throat and smashed his skull into a palm tree. He heard something snap in the night. But another Jap was on him from the back, and the zip buried his dagger into Teddy's liver. He bled out and slipped away just after sunrise. There were no medivacs in island jungle warfare of the old school.

Teddy Zgrodnik is buried in Sentery. He's on the north side of town, buried in White Cross Cemetery. His sister Zelda brings flowers on Memorial Day and Christmas. Once she pushed a red rose into the blanket of snow over Teddy's grave. A tiny American flag flutters his tombstone. Rock maples surround the cemetery, very old trees with rippled bark. During the fall migration when the thousands of black starlings descend, feeding wild on corn shucks missed by combines, the flock of marauders perch in the naked limbs over the tombstones; crazy screaming.

Zelda married her grade school sweetheart, Johnny Szymborski. They were depression products. They could reach back and tell you about meeker times, firsthand witness to a stale bread line at Kutzeba's Bakery. The sweethearts raised five boys and three girls. The five boys became the suture and backbone of Szymborski Farm.

Zelda bought her first electric toaster with S&H green stamps. The toaster still rests on her kitchen counter, its stainless steel buffed to a high shimmer. She still makes borscht soup from scratch. Until a few years back, before the last of her relatives died off in Czestochowa, the mushrooms for the soup came directly from Poland.

They were dried mushrooms strung on brown string. The bloodlines of the old country picked the mushrooms in the forest. The best picking was always in the seam where the evergreens and hardwoods mingled. The old-world people strung them out with sail needles; dried the hanks on wooden pegs in the pantry. Zelda's children liked to marvel at the shriveled mushrooms, and the foreign postmarks of Poland on the shipping box. It was hard to believe dried mushrooms could produce those tastes. Polish folklore said the mushroom's savor came from minerals in the forest. They were a cherished item, especially since they came by steamship from the old country. Zelda had the old recipe from her bloodlines, and her soup was a special treat around the farm.

I looked down across the ribbing of Zelda's white T-shirt. She had weathered the storm well. For a woman who had given birth to eight children, her tummy was flat as a board. It had been 54 years since she delivered her last child, a daughter named Elleen. It appeared at 92 years old, Zelda might be able to touch her toes.

"What variety of strawberries are the Mexicans picking this week?" I wanted to know.

"We just finished on Honey Eye and switched to the Jewel field." Zelda waved her arm across the barn's chamber; stacked across the back wall were white and green striped cardboard flats for the wholesale vendors.

Inside a small push wagon near the barn door, empty wooden baskets were heaped mumbo jumbo, and I could see spatter of crimson stains on the wooden grains of baskets — they were used containers.

"What kind of people return the basket?" I asked.

"Nice ones," she told me with a wink and a grin. There's a depression survivor for you — they'll take their hard learned lessons of thriftiness to the grave. It's their badge of honor.

CHAPTER 2

Zelda is a card. She has a squeaky voice like Minnie Mouse. She never had a bad hair day. It's all silver grey now, an old fashion pixie. She works long hard during the strawberry season. It's her task to sell the ripe berries. Her face is weathered and furrowed like the sunbaked fields of parched grounds, but her spirit still sparks with enthusiasm. Electric alive with gusto.

She'll answer all your questions — but will ask you back a few in return. You can find her out in the barn bays from early morning to dusk during the June berry season. She can never get enough of action. She dreams of moving crop production.

That very morning, Zelda had been peeking out the farmhouse curtains. She was making certain the Mexicans were on the move for picking rows, so sales would boom later in the barn. She saw Miguel putting along on the old Ford 9N tractor, pulling the other fifteen Mexicans who sat with legs dangling off the produce wagon. Three of them were women in long cotton field dresses, and the men sat exceedingly close to the women, chatting away enormously at ease in the daybreak. One Mexican was passing his fingers through the hair of Carmen Benedicta Morales Exavier, and the other hand resting upon her thigh.

Zelda watched Miguel cross the forlorn band of pavement on Golden Road. The dust plumes headed toward the far river. The constant pounding of the cart road through the long drought, had turned the roadbed into heavy dust. It produced the effects of moving in seas of talcum powder, a brown flour-like dust of several inches thick. A wafer of tangerine sun rose in the horizon; below the sun, the white sand bars ran the banks of the drought-stricken river.

Across the molted green reflections on the river, spewing from the bed of white sands, a campfire waned from anglers who had bottom fished for catfish on forked sticks in the night. The forge grey smoke purled and spiraled against the ring of fruit colored sun.

The Mexicans disappeared. They had turned south and behind the hedgerow, and Zelda could only see the faint veils of dust rising. She knew they were headed into southern Block Number Six for picking. This was the essence of Zelda's world — she lived under a bubble of proven lessons handed down over generations of farming. Traditions that could be grasped as reality. The giant bubble engulfed all farms of Golden Road in its sphere. The quintessence zenith for all the inhabitants of this existence, revolved around the concept of Adam and Eve, man and woman, the blessing and love of family. And that above all, the Lord would provide destiny through their labors of the soils. This was their world.

The picture I've painted so far, is only minute in scope of what the soils produced. Strawberry beds were a seasonal crop for June. The Szymborski Farm, and most of the other farms of Golden Road, based the year's net on potato crops. It's not what you may think — most of the million and million pounds of potatoes, went into potato chips. Wonka Potato Chip Factory had cornered the market. Every holiday season, all the potato growers in the valley, received a huge cardboard box delivered from United Postal Service. Each box contained 50 bags of family-sized Wonka potato chips. Enough chips to last well into spring with judicious eating habits. This sparked storytelling and joke telling around town, for Wonka Potato Chip Factory made the best tasting chips across the lands, and every farmer would have loved to think every potato chip came off his farm.

Although this kind of thinking crossed minds and was a partial paradox, everybody knew it was a community thing. That's why a huge white sign with black letters, driven in on the town's line read:

SENTERY
"Home of the World's Best Potato Chips."

This kind of farming not only required big tillable acreage and fleets of expensive tractors and harvesters — it demanded sound business practice. The Board Room of the Szymborski Farm was the kitchen table with all oak leafs in place. A very long oak table, stained and nicked and bearing the scars of cigarette burns, where millions of conversations had been spilled over time. Its power was wielded by Zelda and her eight children. Zelda's husband Johnny had not been in attendance for some 28 years. He died back then from lingering stumbling blocks after coronary bypass surgery. Zelda still had plenty of power inside the farm meetings. She was not only the longest standing member of the family enterprise; she was the founder along with her husband Johnny who now slept in eternal peace. True — the farm deeds and bank accounts had long ago been handed over to the children, under the vice of a law firm's eyes. Everybody took their cuts from the profits. But Zelda still held over fifty percent on paper and was not bashful about cutting deals. She still pulled strings on the inside, and it was commonplace for her to ring up the president of Wonka Potato Chip Factory on her dial telephone. She could still put on a business game face at her age and loved making money deals. Zelda May Szymborski is like a female version of Donald J. Trump, except I doubt very seriously she's devouring Quarter Pounders with cheese in the midnight hour, and the last thing on her mind is taking crash lessons on how to Twitter. No amount of conversation would convince her to take a garden side suite on the Upper West Side, even if it afforded a grand view of Strawberry Fields, and butlers with blue uniforms adorned with gold piping. She already had what no money could buy.

It had been an election year. The general public had learned superficial knowledge through the media. Some people had experienced feeling a burn from a guy named Bernie. We learned about a fellow named Little Marco. Some people out of the main loop, spun tin globes for several revolutions, but never were able to discover anyplace in the Gulf of Mexico, a little sister isle for Marco Island. There was a story about a crazy woman by the name of Pocahontas running around in the woods of Massachusetts, but nobody had ever seen her in war paint. Drawing blood had shown no lines into the Indian Nation. All tests proved she was a quack. Then the people from around the world, discovered that billionaire Donald J. Trump had a fondness towards fast food. Donald reasoned that every burger of the chain — business thinking — must be perfect to capture the customer's trust. Some voters figured if they cast Trump a vote, the new president might put the soft touches on secret service for a bacon and cheeseburger in the middle of night. All this kind of thinking and street lore had been steeped into people's thought patterns from media exposure, mine included. But the last thing on my mind was a hot burger with wheels.

The crux of my adventure that summer morning, was to capture the old lady's most valuable resource — to serve as a living example for others to follow. A photograph on developed film, backed by an indelible negative kept behind the husky hinges of my tumbler combination safe.

"Can I take your picture?" I wanted to know.

"Sure," she said in her squeaky voice, "Why not?"

Plans had been laid in advance. I knew from experience that the barn door faced east. In the wash of sunrise, it would be too bright inside the barn. During the afternoon with the sun shifted, long shadows would falter my plans; now in the forenoon the lighting was near perfect. I knew too my Mamiya 645 Pro would never let me down, and always freeze up the detail with razor sharp clarity.

The feed roll was packed with those 15 shots of Portra 160 — the finest available for bringing out those realistic skin tones. That knowing my camera and all its stops would give me breathing room for what has always been paramount for all artists — design and composition, inner positive tension, harmony, light, and juxtaposed signals of visual communications.

I jerked my gear with excitement from the truck, my Mamiya camera already fixed on the Bogen tripod. Then I set shop. Hanging inside the barn on the north wall, was a white sign of black letters, and mocha shading on the main text. It was of respectable size, hand lettered on tin stock, and readable at automobile speeds. The sign writer had laid out Szymborski Farm in the old school of arched format, straight Sans-serif letters, and cut the sign's perimeter with cresting and under-belly scallops. The lower line read: Established in 1949.

Under normal conditions, both winter and summer, the sign dangled from rusted chains along Golden Road. But during the strawberry season, the sign was fixed inside the barn, moved in out of the weather for sakes of nostalgia. It was a weathered sign, beaten from the seasons of New England, and brought a timeless charm of history to the patrons.

Soft light was beaming through the barn. I framed Zelda against the sign, as the deep shadows cut her silhouette, and the grey locks made radiance against the bowery's cast of blackness. I could see very clear and knew by instincts, how the weathered sign would play its crucial role in composition. That human observation would find harmony between the time-honored skin tones and the gouging and flaking of bulletin enamels, and thus be driven and sparked with emotional rescue.

There was an aura of old-world luster around the scene. I could feel it inside my gut. It was as though part of Andrew Weyth had been reincarnated. Looking at Zelda's grey hairs against the black shadow, reminded me of Weyth's dry brush technique with egg tempera. Through the ages, all artists have survived by these tabulations — they have been trained to see the world in other lights.

Urgency filled the barn. The wave of customers had paused. Nobody around. There was only silence under the rafters. I knew it would be now or never.

"Hold it right there," I told the old lady. Then I rolled the focus and plastered her with five fast ones across the kisser.

We never spoke again till that December. Zelda and I were shooting the breeze in the farmhouse kitchen. The furnace was roaring in the basement. Cover crops of winter wheat were fastened across the frozen fields, and Christmas trees were for sale on the Kuchta Farm.

"How do you like our president-elect Trump?" I asked.

"I'm not sure about that guy," she said in her squeaky voice, "He seems to be always getting in some kind of trouble inside the press." She said it in motherly tones, without conviction, as if trying to protect the president.

"Better be careful," I warned, tapping my knuckles across the table.

"About what?" grinned Zelda.

"Reading slanted journalism," I suggested. I refrained from using the pointed grammar of filthy liars for the mainstream media.

"We never went through all of this with Eisenhower," informed Zelda. "It was a kinder world then, and the news people went to great lengths for protecting the lands and selling honest news items.

"What do you remember best about President Eisenhower?" I wanted the know.

"That he brought back egg rolling to the White House lawn." Zelda seemed to lose a few years off her face when she made the sentence.

"Was it about watching all those kids in their Sunday best, rolling colored eggs from the Easter bunny across the grass with forked sticks?"

"Not that," said Zelda. She had a distant look on her face, and we took a short break of our sentence blocks. Zelda took a slug from her hot chocolate, and I scooped away a spoon of whipped cream from the mug's head. Drinking hot chocolate in winter was very satisfactory.

"Truman had a post-war food ration in place after World War II," added Zelda, "and it was good to know there was enough of eggs to go around."

"Was there a shortage of eggs during the depression?" I asked.

"Not until we killed the chickens," frowned Zelda.

"How did they die?" I begged.

"They died over the chopping block under the hatchet's blow," said Zelda in a stoic pitch.

"Is it true many of them died on the dead run?"

"It's true," Zelda said, "the victims ran around the barnyard in circles, like chickens with their heads cut off."

"I guess that's where the analogy came into play, man acting like birds caught in the hot flashes of pandemonium," I said to the old lady. Then I got back on the trail of killing, "Did you ever kill a chicken?"

"Only in summer once," shrugged Zelda.

"Was it easier with sleeves rolled up for dirty work in the wash of heat waves?"

"Golly — not because of that," cracked Zelda's voice. "It was because of the white snows of winter. Severing heads on the chopping block, brought on the streams of gushing hot blood baths across the snow. The warm crimson sunk deep into the snowflakes. The red evidence lingered for a long time. You didn't have to be a homicide detective to see that slaughter was committed."

"It's too bad nobody ever thought of putting down blankets of sawdust around the execution block," I suggested. "It would have sopped up a lot of blood."

"We did. We thought of those things. Thornton's Sawmill gave us all the bedding of sawdust we ever needed on the house. We plastered the site with grain shovels," told Zelda with her hands clasped. "But many of the chickens in the ecstasy of their death, especially the roosters, went for dead runs on beelines past the brinks of the sawdust field."

"Were the flock's feathers of all colors?" I asked.

"New Hampshire's has a russet-brown plume," said Zelda. "It was a bit too intimate for me to watch their execution at close range. The hatchet came down with a muffled thump and bit into the block grains, and the head rolled off by your feet. The bright red comb and wattle showed bold on the frame of snow blanket, and the yellow rings of their eye stared off someplace into lifeless space."

"Did scavengers work the chopping block?"

"The black crows were frequent flyers. They descended on the flecks of red snow, and they consumed the guts. The chickens themselves were cannibals, and we needed to keep them locked in their cages during the rites of butchering," told Zelda.

"Travis, you've been a visitor on this farm for years," recalled Zelda. "Did any of the boys ever mention the mystery of skulls?"

"Mystery of skulls?" I jacked up straight in my chair, ears perked.

"We never policed the heads," explained Zelda. "We left all the heads where they fell. On special occasions, like in preparation for the farm's 4th of July picnic, we slaughtered over twenty chickens," filled in Zelda. But by the next day, all the heads would be missing."

"Must have been a weasel, or maybe a vixen fox on a hunting trip for her kits," I mentioned.

"That's what we thought," said Zelda, "until our detective work blew holes in that theory —we set a trap."

"Was it a Victor 1 ½ jump trap?" I wondered.

"Steel jaws were not in the picture." Then Zelda told her story. "It's not a very pleasant story," warned Zelda. "Are you sure it should be spoken?"

"Sure, why not?"

"You may get bad dreams and nightmares," she told me. "As well, it's Holy Week before Christmas. Perhaps we should wait until —"

"I must hear it," I intervened. "The wild dreams never bothered me." Then I reminded Zelda, "I doubt the Lord will ever hold anybody accountable for the bloodshed of animal husbandry."

"I do not want the responsibility for bad nightmare," Zelda chipped in.

"Tell it," I told her. "Hold nothing back... tell me the story straight up."

"Alright then," she countered. "But it's not a story for the squeamish."

"Never mind," I prodded her. "Reveal everything."

"Alright my friend, here's how everything went down," said Zelda with a straight face.

"We waited for a new snowfall in the dead of winter. Then we staked out our scheme. Seven chickens had given their lives that day. A light dusting had prevailed all afternoon. Snow covered the barnyard. We gathered the seven heads in a galvanized tin bowl, the same bowl used for feeding chickens with cracked corn. But now by irony of events, their severed heads rested in the metal vessel. My brother Jimmy and myself set the trap. Jimmy was my oldest brother, and he had cooked up the scheme for a long time."

"The snow scene around the chopping block was trodden with boot prints laid down during the slaughter, and the spattering of blood. A section around the chopping block was drenched in crimson. A lone set of tracks darted outside the ring of beaten snow — a headless chicken had gone on a valiant run across the white blanket, and you could see the bird's imprint where it had flopped over in the snow. My other brother Jack's track followed the trail, where he had retrieved the bird."

"It was my job to carry the metal bowl. The bottom of the tin was covered with a heavy coating of grain chaffs. The seven heads rested on the dust in the bowl. In the flat queer light of passing day, the chaffs threw off a golden luster, and it illuminated a strange presence of death around the red heads."

"Outside the beaten ring of footprints, past the ring of fresh sawdust, was virgin snow. A canvas of immaculate white crystals, free of any footprints. It was here we set our trap.

My brother Jimmy grabbed the collar of my checkered Mackinaw. Holding me tight, he reached down and grasped the cuffs of my trousers, lifting my figure in the horizontal position over the blanket of snow."

"Clutching the tin bowl in a singular hand, I reached inside and began placing the chopped heads into the virgin snow. I set them out in semi-circle, as seen on a clock's face between the hands striking of between numeral nine and three demarcation. For a little girl like me, who had been practicing baking cakes in a wood oven under her mother's watchful guidance, the placing of heads was reminiscent of pushing M&M's into white frosting on a chocolate cake. The russet color of the plumes, jumped out on the fresh snow."

Zelda dug deeper into the story. Her brother Jimmy was getting hot around the collar, and the veins on his forehead had risen. He was laboring with his calves buckled to hold her steady.

"Move faster," Jimmy had told her.

"I'm moving," Zelda had defended. "I want to make a nice arc of colors in the snow."

"Golly! This is not art school," Jimmy had exclaimed. "Get moving."

"The bowl was getting heavy. The chicken heads had a lot of give in the plumes and were still warm. Your fingers sunk in around the necks. I pushed the heads into the snow. Great care was taken to align the silhouettes in profile. The yellow rings of their eyes, cast a supernatural aura across the scene."

"My eyes were big. The sensation of being suspended in space, tugged on my pectoral muscles. The last of the seven heads was most vivid — the rooster's tongue stuck out between a tightened beak. Rigor mortis had set in. His red comb and wattle contrasted sharp and clear on the white flakes."

She was glad the bird's eye was closed. It showed as a slit, and the eyelid had turned into a rim of grey. It was creepy looking into the windpipe. She twisted the bird's head to view inside the air tube. Its rim was coagulated with dried blood. Zelda shoved in the last head, and yelled up to Jimmy, "Get me out of here!" Back on her feet, she washed the blood from her hands, rubbing them brisk in a snow bath of flakes.

"I've taken snow baths while camping in the mountains," I told Zelda. Rising from the table, I struck a wooden match on the gas range. Both of us had run dry on hot chocolate. The blue flame boiled water. Zelda kept up with her story. I listened with my back turned. Her squeaky voice carried across the farmhouse kitchen.

"That night it got to me bad. My sleeping was fighting with tugging suspense. I was too wound up for sleep. The heads were pressing on my mind. There was a crescent moon, and plenty cold outside, and cold but no wind and everything frozen rock hard. The nocturnal hunters were out making the rounds, and they could smell blood a long way off when the night combed," said Zelda. She tapped her finger twice on the oak table, and then spilled more of the storyline.

"I pulled back the covers and walked across my second-floor bedroom to the window. Keep in mind Travis, that the story I'm revealing took place inside this very farmhouse. The doctor delivered me in the back bedroom," and Zelda pointed down the hallway.

Her words through the squeaky voice, rolled back time. She was born and raised where my feet rested. A sense of antique history prevailed. Her words awakened sensual perception. I went over math in my head — the crux of her story had taken place nearly eighty years back in time. I stirred in heaping spoons of chocolate into the boiling water and became seated at the table. Rifts of steam rose from our mugs. Zelda revealed more —

"I pressed tight to the pane window. Patterns of hoarfrost

hugged the glass. A grey overcast sky had engulfed the night, and much of the moon's luster was diminished by the high gauze, as if trying to shine through wax paper. There were no shadows, only diffused light in the grey zenith, and the barn and trees appeared as darkened shapes. You could see the chopping block with the Hudson Bay axe dug into its face. The handle angled into night."

"But no matter how hard I tried to harness my night vision, the gloom was too dark and mysterious. So, I penned all my ambitions, crawled back under the snug covers, and slept sound until dawn for concluding evidence."

Jimmy had awoken his sister by knocking through our bedroom wall. She could hear him getting dressed, the creaking of boards, his boots clomping down the stairs. Sister followed suit.

"I'll never forget the look in Jimmy's face as we went out the door and down the porch stairs. A wide smile filled his face, and he gave me a big hug around my Mackinaw and said, "Let's see what we got in the trap Sis. He was so young and handsome, and it's a look I'll never forget about my big brother."

"We walked brisk across the barnyard. A set of fox tracks cut across the white snow, but they trotted between a gash in the barb-wire and struck out across the forlorn field of chopped corn stubble. The fox had proven himself innocent."

"We circled the chopping block, scouring the scene. We could hardly believe the evidence," revealed Zelda. She nursed a sip from her mug, and her eyes sparkled with excitement.

"We could not believe our eyes. All the heads were missing. Seven impressions in the snow marked the whereabouts. But no tracks were in the snow. Not a set. We walked in circles about the scene as to not disturb evidence."

Jimmy had stooped over in the crack of dawn. He'd gone down

on the knees of his brown canvas bibs. He looked very sharp and examined the scene. There were claw marks in the snow, the marking of sharp and deadly furrows. A bird of prey had descended in the night.

"Raptors with sharp claws must have swooped down in the night," said Zelda over her hot chocolate.

"I bent down and kneeled in the snow. Scouring the scene, claw marks had gouged the snow where the head was snatched. An image of the chicken's head was still sharp and clear in the casting of snow. The imprint of the curved beak was in heightened prominence."

"That solved everything with the mystery of skulls… or so we thought. Over the following summer and through the winter, heads would be missing. Not in the wake of all executions, but they were still being taken alright. When the bloody heads were not scavenged by the night stalkers, our chore was to rake up the remains. In summer we spaded the scraps into the till, and when the ground was locked up tight, the remnants were dumped into the below-grade garbage pail. You remember those — right? Those metal buckets with the funny-works foot pedal to open the trap lid," said Zelda.

The telephone began a long cry of rings. Somebody was trying to ring through. The bells sang in the old kitchen. Zelda never picked up. The telephone went dead, we looked each other the eye, and the storytelling carried across the kitchen table.

CHAPTER 3

"We thought the book was closed on the mystery, but two summers after our scheme in the snow, the final chapter played out in hard evidence. Mother Nature dealt the cards. It arrived in the form of a hurricane."

It was the biggest blow anybody had seen in a long time. She started out in the Caribbean when days of booming thunderstorms slowly dropped air pressure. A solid low formed over the blue swells, and the winds began the dance of swirling motion. A tropical cyclone had formed. While winds pushed the storm westward, an extended trough of low pressure formed, and hiding inside with its menace, was the birth of a hurricane the weather forecasters would handle Merle.

It was a fitting name for her, not only because in French she translated to black bird, but also too, because she ran up the coast with all the swerving moves of a black racer snake slithering over the forest floor. Merle started her boom-boom just off the Cayman Islands, always growing, twisting, always bearing up inside the Yucatan Channel. The vortex spattered driven rain across coastal Mexico and pummeled the board shacks of Espita. Her blow screamed across Havana, and shredded the flag flying on the common, the blue stripes and red canton and white star diminished to tattered threads. The cyclone was really spinning now inside her chamber, and miniature droplets of vapor rode thermals in the cloud banks. The blow ran on the south flank of Dry Tortugas, and it was sure a good thing the charter captains working a chum line for swordfish, had their sidebands turned and locked in Coast Guard frequency. The fleet, five boats operated by five owners with separate bank accounts, made it back inside in the nick of time — Merle was combing their wakes just off the horizon.

The fishing boats arrived at intervals. The first four inside Snipe Key got slips. The deck hands lashed them down and scurried up the gangplanks clutching the long strike rods and tackle. But the last boat inside was a 42' wide beamed plank job with perhaps the tallest flying bridge in the harbor, drew blank cards. In the pandemonium, every boat had taken anybody's slip in order to escape destruction. The crews along with other inhabitants, were already lying low where they figured they could ride her out best; they prayed and hovered over concrete floors in the basements, light bulbs glowing over their fear struck faces. But captain Moxie Mulligan was the last inside, and don't think in a million years he'd take a mooring. He was too seasoned for that kind of thinking.

Caught in the flashes of fatal danger, Captain Mulligan yelled to the crew, "Hold on!" The captain gunned the diesel Caterpillar and brought her to plane, his sinew laced forearm clutching the throttle lever, and rammed the *Siobhan Rose* up into a tidal slough. Her planked ribbed bottom, wide and squatted in the beam, was driven into the muck as if arrested by concrete, and she rested solid as ships on block cribbing when fixed for dry dock operations.

Merle skirted Key West, shot an azimuth around Miami, and screamed up the coast toward the Carolinas. But the backing winds tore up the Florida coast, and Snipe Keys was in the heart of this destruction. Moxie Mulligan's move of desperation, however, would grant *Siobhan Rose* a sweet salvation — she was the only boat to escape complete destruction. The others had been tossed like driftwood on white sands of the blown-out beachhead. And the next morning in the still calmness, an orange sun moored to the horizon, a lone pelican stood on the battered hull of the *Arrienne*.

"Don't forget," Zelda was saying, "those were the days before television, and our only communication was the radio set, and the police station. Our warning came at the last moment, and then she struck in the middle of the night, far into the hours of deep sleep. But nobody was sleeping, and the gusts had begun their work."

Merle ran the coast until Cape Cod, then beached with vengeance. She raked across the outer arm of Provincetown, the screaming winds putting a full-Nelson like hold on the whale watching fleet. Their black and white hulls bobbed like corks and chains tugged against town wharf, until they went beam-to in the howling blow and sunk into the mouth of frothing seas.

The eye of the hurricane looked over the roof of Neptune Bait and Tackle; she ripped it clean with the rafters, and it sailed into the sky as a discus soaring at track & field events. Cedar shingles trinkled into the sea. Then Merle exhumed the tackle shop's guts. A vacuum chamber lifted fishing tackle into thin air.

A few days later a couple of guys were carting storm damage from the Purgatory Saloon parking lot. They stood on the other side of town from the bait shop. Sprinkled across the lot, were casting plugs and Daredevil spoons, from the exhuming of the Neptune. The treble hooks of a red and white spoon had embedded into the high canopy of the town common's oak tree. It dangled in space. The chrome backing heliographed in the sun. Tourists concluded kids tossed the fishing tackle into the tree. But the height was far above the reach of adult arms, and the locals knew the real story. The horrible winds had tossed many plugs around, and the Daredevil was a testimony to the hell that swept through town.

Some of the plugs were still inside the plastic jacket boxes. Under normal circumstances, it would have been very satisfactory to find fishing gear. These implements were very useful. Just about everybody in a sea town went fishing. Even if you never wet a line, it would be impossible not to know somebody who was an aficionado of angling. But in the wake of destruction, busted windows and houses blown over, boats turned over with gashing holes poked in their ribs, and dock pilings torn from the sea bottom, there was no happiness in discovering somebody else's misery. The two guys boxed the fishing gear for the rightful owner.

Merle marched northward. She ran into a street fight. Another ridge of turbulence, high winds manufactured in the Maritime Provinces, swept high chop on the Bay of Fundy, and the blow ran across Aroostook County into New England.

"I'll never forget the sight of the police cruiser," said Zelda. "It was the calm before the storm. It pulled in at soft twilight, and the mellow glows brought out the righteousness in the officer's face. I was in my room and saw the black and white cruiser pull into the barnyard. I had a bird's eye view looking down on the bubble, and the police officer crawled in at a snail's pace. The sound of tires rolling over crushed trap rock came through the screen."

"My dad went out and down the porch stairs. We heard his boots clomp on the planks. He leaned into the open passenger window. We could see gesture and mouths moving, but too far for grasping any conversation. I had put things together from the seriousness of their faces, the moving of hands and body language. The police officer pointed on his watch. We knew it was coming then."

It was never a direct hit. The blow running out of the Bay of Fundy was not strong enough to shove Merle that far west. Nevertheless, high turbulence set up in the Connecticut River Valley, and hurricane force winds assaulted. There was no escape for Sentery. They were an overture for a good drubbing, screaming voices in the sea of grim clouds.

Zelda's father was under dilemma. Every man wishes to save his family. The test had arrived. Time was essence. No rehearsal was offered. His singular decision would deliver salvation or spell doom. The storm was marching.

Kasimierz Zgrodnik looked into his wife's fear-stricken face, and said, "Don't worry — everything is going to be alright. Grab some food and bottles of water. Find candles and matches and bring along the oil lamp. We're going to take it outside."

Then he put his arm around daughter Zelda, and said with a pinch of fear, "Tell the boys to get dressed in heavy sweatshirts. Wear something warm. We're going to take the blow in the root cellar."

Kasimierz led his family to their destiny. They changed position in the cloaks of darkness. They walked in a single file, out and away from the farmhouse. He thrust the flame of an oil lamp into the night, and its glowing ball of radiance waxed and waned in the breeze. Shapes grew bigger and larger, and shadows were casted and the lantern's beam through down a path for their destiny. Stars still twinkled in the night. But time was of central importance, for not far behind in the prelude of night, the hurricane was gobbling ground and spitting splintered wood, its winds howling with an appetite for destruction.

The root cellar was an earthen vault, under the stone silo's floor. Its purpose was to keep root vegetables in cold storage and bury blocks of river ice between thick layers of sawdust. You could extend the life of ice until May; but it was July now, and the ice had long melted, with sound beds of dry sawdust covering the chamber's floor.

The trapdoors of the root cellar were much like those found on ordinary farmhouses, as a shield over the stairs with descension into the basement. Twin wooden doors on stout hinges, where the lap-joints of one door closed on the other.

"You couldn't stand in the root cellar," said Zelda. "There was only room for sitting, and our heads poked just above the ground. It was like getting into a tomb. The root cellar was cribbed with planks. All of us were crammed like sardines, shoulder to shoulder. I was far right in the vault, reaching on feel and the senses in the raven night, and my shoulder was crushed against the planking."

"Then my father said, 'Light the candle,' to my mother, and she struck the match and caught fire to the candle. She'd taken a handful of Diamond matches, as we ran out of the kitchen. The candlelight flickered across our faces."

"Seven of us were in the catacomb vault, with my father dead center. Down the line, my sister Zuzanna was playing with her doll. Tosia was sucking her thumb. We were sitting on our haunches, and it was very satisfactory nested on the bed of sawdust, for it threw off a quality of warmth into your bones. It gave the sensation of sitting in a pillbox for shooting waterfowl."

Kasimierz spread his arms like wings procured from a guardian angel and embraced his family. He was continually casting sidelong glances, the letter of responsibility burned into his brow. He occasionally briskly rubbed his temples. Instincts forewarned of the marching plight. The shadows of his face were darkening, and his tight lips seemed to hold in check any doubts, even if swallowing some pride was involved. He knew some of the equation was out of his hands, where some may play out like the roulette wheel, spinning and clacking against the thong of leather, making odds against red and black squares inscribed with gambler's numbers. It seemed ominous foreboding was clashing with his fortitude. Kasimierz folded and pressed his weathered hands and began to pray. His voice was deep and marked with European block accent, and the meter of his words were slow and tempered with devotion — *Hail Mary, full of grace, the Lord is with thee. Blessed art thou among women and blessed is the fruit of thy womb Jesus. Holy Mary, Mother of God, pray for my family in these darkening hours, and may our Faith reign victory in your name. Amen.*

"My mother clutched the candle as seen in children making the procession of First Communion. The candlelight radiated a halo and caressed her countenance, and I can still see the red babushka over her head, the thick shock of bangs falling across her forehead and over the brow, the sparkle of light twinkling off her brown iris."

"Your story is painting vivid colors in my mind," I told Zelda. "It's very interesting. Was some of the candle burning in hopes of warding off flying insects?"

"Some of it was about bugs," added Zelda. "But most of the burning was for the fellowship of spirit. The atmosphere of flame seemed to vulcanize our will. At one point before calamity struck, four of us were burning candles in union. The effects of light danced high into the stone silo. The stone walls trapped light, much unlike the open night where light could run into eternal blackness, and the glow of flame cast a diffused amber into the vaulted ceiling."

There was very little warning. They became aware of the furnace roar of the storm. Great brown clouds swirled above the tilled land under the veil of night, and the curtain of woods filtered the blow. Strange music played in the forest, and the howling gusts rendered notes of Oriental wind-chimes through the limbs. Peering from the pillbox, the requiem summoned wonder into the inhabitants.

"'Close the hatchway!' said my father. Anxious hands carried out the task. We reached upward and sealed ourselves into the root cellar. A sensation of muffled air prevailed in the door's closing.

The shades of darkness deepened. It was jet black inside. All of us were squeezed in on our backs. The mingling of our clasped hands, echoed chants of nervous hope, my face buried into my mother's collarbone, girted the passions of love. We would take it as a family.

"The weathered doors were fabricated with inside cleats. They were screwed into spacer blocks and spanned the full length of both doors. During the loading of block ice, we roped back both doors from the cleat runners, as to protect workers from getting clobbered with a fallen door."

"But now inside with everything sealed tight, the cleats ran above our chests in the blackness. You could wrap your fingers around them, much like chin-up bars in a gymnasium. My father had lashed the doors with rope. He worked on his back in the darkness, serving the rope around by feel, and tying double-knots in excessive eagerness. We could hear him grunting in the night."

Annihilation had arrived. Mother Nature was in a giant dispute. The catalpa trees growing along the corn crib, could not take the blow; their wood was too soft and weak. Formidable winds sprayed a deluge of twigs across the barn roof, pattering the night shifts.

"Claustrophobia — there was none," said Zelda in tones of a steel voice. "Opposites prevailed. The casket of raven blackness, was our ride inside a time capsule towards salvation."

"We listened with perked ears. This part of the world was in a strange, off-world experience. Many things floated in space. We could hear them crashing, breaking into pieces, other things ricocheting in the theater of sable bedlam. We heard a giant tree crashing, the creaking as she went over, the rifle-shot of her limbs breaking, a muffled crump as heard while the ground buckles in the walking of light artillery."

Gusts of vixen winds began exhuming the silo; they screamed

wild. They swirled madly, and grains of sand blasted the sunken refuge. A ferocious blast drove into the kissed doors and began moves to disinter their very souls. The blow tested father's knot skill, and the doors chatted in clapping tempo — Whoom! Whoom! Whoom!

"'Grab the cleats,' yelled my father. We all reached up in harmony and fought the winds."

"My mother's elbow poked me. Fear had come knocking. We squirmed around for better hand holds. 'Don't pull the screws loose,' screamed my father, 'keep steady pressure… keep your head… hold it steady… hold it tight.' You could hear the terror in his voice."

"Some place off in the far tempest — was it the Kuchta Farm? — the report of glass shattered. Shards lanceted into the green rows of crop production. A chain of firecracker like pops sounded down Golden Road — the transformers on the power poles were exploding. Pop! — pop! — pop! The sounds walked down the road, and the last burst sent a shower of sparks into the sea of gloom."

"A weathered knot hole was directly over my head. Steams of fresh air seeped inside. Fresh air is a wonderful thing, in the face of pandemonium. I craned my neck and placed my eye as cupping a looking glass. You could see nothing, only the faint outline of the knot. Just then, gusts of winds combed the silo, and my eyeball was engulfed with corn chaff. I pulled back in reaction. I flooded my eye with a milk jar filled with water. Streams of water dripped off my chin. The blow rummaged the walls of stone, and I could feel pattering of more chaff on my chest."

"'Ugg! Ugg! —Ugg!' coughed my mother. She had grown feebleness of the windpipe from the wind-driven floor sweeps. I passed her the vessel of water. The sounds of her lips smacking, the gurgling down her throat, filled the sunken pillbox."

"In those days Travis, all the things for a woman's private needs were not on shelves. At lease for us country girls. Follow me?"

"I'm all over it," I told Zelda. I cupped my forehead and broke eye contact.

"Store bought S-napkins were scarce. Drug stores were miles. We had no automobiles. The red pickup's job was to tend the farm. We rode in once a month."

"Necessity is the mother of invention. We made our own. My mother procured rolls of batten cotton. I can still remember the soft light angling into the bedroom, sitting with Mum and aunt Maria on the white cotton bedspread of raised embroidery, and cutting batten strips. We cut cotton with big sewing scissors. My hands were not strong enough to operate scissors. We always had plenty of napkins to go around. It was my first year of puberty, and I'd use them. We stored them inside a tin box in the upper bathroom, and they were free for the taking in plain sight."

"I'd crammed a few in my pocket before we sought refuge in the root cellar. They would have other uses in emergency. The welted cotton could stop bleeding on superficial wounds. In my other pocket rested a bar of soap."

"A pinched breeze was still floating into the dungeon, and I snorted dust. So, I reached down in the blackness and tore away a good chunk of batten cotton; then I shoved it into the knot hole with my thumb. It thwarted the invasion dead cold."

But Zelda's efforts were childish notion, and short lived. Down in the blackness, her father had slackened the ropes, and slid his corncob pipe between the doors. Rushes of night shift caressed his stubble face. A siren wailed from the blackness.

Rain had been riding in the storm all evening. But now deluge fell. A metallic drumming played on the standing-seam tin roof on the silo. They listened to sheets of storm plunge across the crushed stone aprons. A distant rain spout pinged away. The family hunkered down under an olive wool blanket.

The storm slowly pulled away. A lull in the winds formed perception of security. Some of their guard had fallen. Sleep fell over them in the wake of Merle's siege.

But the storm was far from dealing out its punishment. Torrential rains lashed and clawed at ferocious pitch on the crop production. Crops were scoured to bare roots, miles of potato hills were exposed to elements, and in the days to follow, the sun would crack their skin and ruin their nourishments. They would rot from the inside out.

CHAPTER 4

All night it had blown out of the south, and the long lanky leaves of the corn had been parted away from the stalks. The winds worked the rows, and the dark green stems of the long leaves blew wildly as the winds killed them. All the tassels were shredded and lay to waste.

The winds blew both day and night for three days, and when it stopped half the corn cobs lay dead against the stalks. The tassels hung like burned brown strings that had been worked over with the sweeping of blow torches. Even the strawberry beds were pummeled to destruction, the weight of the plump berries sunk into the silted mud. The corn crop was gone that year along with most other colors of the harvest horn.

The only succulent leaves to survive the blow and seemed to flourish in the wake, were the lily pads growing in the pond near the village church.. They were big green saucers of life, and put out magnificent yellow flowers that summer, and the bullfrogs were extremely fond of croaking in their midst.

Skies opened in the wee hours. Platoons of ominous grey and charcoal clouds streamed at supernatural pace across the heavens, as if marching toward some other battlefield of distant lands.

A full moon sat in the night beyond the clouds. Its glow cast an eerie quiver down through the sea of grey drifters. It was hard to fathom the speed of which the platoons of clouds advanced. A man could hardly mark and behold the shapes, before other forms took their place.

The pallid moon spilled across the field crops of Paderewski Farm, and a world of destruction was revealed in its light. Mud glistened in the erosion troughs. Tiny brooklets of storm drain seeped toward the river. Huge channels were blown out through the riverbank, and it would be said many times over in the circles of Sentery, that over 100 years of soil building had slipped into the river. Brown currents swirled and ran the river, and all the farmer's labor sailed along toward the ocean. The hurricane's plundered booty would bear a heaviness across their hearts; but their emotional rescue would pan out with historical flaws, because it was never a white man who first broke ground. They were red.

The storm had done its work. A good three feet of loam along the river was at large. Vanished and gone. A massive ravine was blown out to the river, gouged down to bank run gravel. Moonlight fell on the field's hollow and played on three skulls and a basket of ribcage. An Indian burial site had been exposed. The dead hollow of eye sockets looked to the west, always facing promise of the next world through the setting sun. Trinket beads circled a victim, where flesh once housed a speaking voice box. A stone hatchet rested on the mud flats. Within the vicinity, hundreds of arrowheads were scattered about. The archaeological team from the university would have a field day. They would dig for weeks with hand shovels and trowels, barely containing their pent of hysteria.

A gentleman with khaki shorts and short sleeves, a felt crusher with a wide brim shading his eyes, got so caught up in the frenzy of unearthing works of primitive hands, ecstasy had driven him into pantomimes of melodrama. He was constantly pointing a finger toward the sky, reciting insightful hunches into thin air.

Word traveled quickly. The new find inspired a lust for treasure hunting across Sentery, and many figures were seen laying down zig-zagged paths over fields in hopes of stumbling on pay dirt. It took a special kind of eye to spot the chipped flints, and those with that possession, filled pockets with arrowheads.

A young boy with tousled golden locks and eyes of powder blue, found a spear point of purest white schist. He spotted the white stone sticking from the bank cut down to the river. It was at eye-level to the boy, and he marveled at the beautiful serving notch cut into the spear's head. He reached up and slipped it out of the bank with caress and holding his breath, and revealed it measured a length of eight inches.

Nobody in the circle of arrowhead hunters, had ever seen a white one, let alone hear of them. A man offered him a whole handful of arrowheads for the point — but the boy turned him down with cold shoulders. The man requisitioned the youth with another sentence block, pitched with exhortations of severe want. The boy never buckled. He simply walked away. His sneakers left a trail of footprints in the lands of sun caked muds. He kept the spear point in a safe box in his room, and often tumbled the prize in seclusion. His powder blue eyes got very big with Indian lore in the fondling of the white stone, and he often wondered if the red bloods it drew were from man or beast.

Kasimierz slept sound and snored. The other six were huddled and sleeping. The family had come to terms with the revelation, and they sensed the storm had waned. Hearing acute had formed this conception — the rain patter had ceased, and whistling winds were sailing about. They fought the temptation to seek refuge in the farmhouse. Lurking in the clutter of storm damage in the sable night, could be a tragic experience. They wanted no part of tragedy. Their body heat had multiplied many times over, and a wealth of security filled their retreat. It was a sensation that could not be bought. It needed to be earned with exposure to danger.

"We slept well into the breakfast hour. The crying of a siren had stirred us from sleep. I could see the daylight through the cracks.

My father opened the doors wide — they thudded with a loud report on the sleeper blocks, which rested them in anti-aircraft position. My father's figure was already walking through the stone silo's archway, when I reached back behind his avert, and pulled the plug of cotton batting from the knot hole," admitted Zelda.

The father passed a dead sparrow, as he pressed towards the farmhouse. The claws of the grey dead sparrow were clutching into thin air, and the bird was cuddled in a ball with his head tucked under. The other six closed on Kasimierz's heels, and they saw the dead bird. Zuzanna reached down and touched the sparrow. It was cold to the touch, and rigor mortis had set in. Her father saw her do that, and Kasimierz told her to stop messing around. The world before them had been swept and riddled with all the calibers of destruction. A marbled skyline of orange value hugged the horizon. Faint tracing of the moon still hung in the western zenith. A fireball of sun spilled rays of new hope across the land. All the worlds were in revolution, and a stiff wind rushed through the dawn.

Many birds were riding the high sky. They appeared as distant dots in the gale ceiling. It was impossible to distinguish any revelation of species. They were just birds, bands of daredevils riding the storm surge.

Not all birds survived. Nobody knows exactly what kind of shelter birds seek in that kind of storm. They could have never taken it in the treetops. They would have been blown from perches. Merle would have hurled them into the arch of heaven. Some took it under bridges, tucked into the iron webs of trestles. A few had scampered under the tin works of farm implements and slept impervious to the blow in the manifold chamber. Tiny songbirds huddled in dry brook beds, scooted up under the combs of undercut banks. All the nuisance pigeons had taken refuge in the barns, and nervously cooed the storm away.

A lone starling lay dead in the stubble. It did not appear as a bird under the effects of pesticide poisoning; it was not over on its back with claws clutched tight, and there was no wincing of pain around the beak. The black bird appeared to be resting in peaceful sleep, rolled over on its side and the purple hues of his plumes lustering in after-dawn. The top plates of his wing were disheveled, and black feathers were fluttering in the gusts.

"Many things laid destroyed. Broken parts and pieces were everyplace. Sculley Horton's windsock, which had served as a weather gauge for every blue overall farmer who motored Golden Road, had been goaded so severe by shafts of wind, that it dangled from the limb of a toad-squatted white oak some four miles distant of the confiscation zone," said Zelda. Her fingers were interlocked in prayer position, and she gazed through the pane window. Splendor fell across her face, and the silvers of her hair were bolstered in the radiance.

That very fall while partridge hunting, Rodney Breedlove spotted the red and white windsock in the tree. He immediately recognized the windsock as Scully Horton's.

He shouldered the 12 Ga. Double barrel and tried blasting the sock free. Twiglets exploded; the red and white fabric twitched. A trinkling of fall colors fluttered down. High brass shells were too expensive for blasting into thin air. Rodney felt sure if he were toting a .22 cal. Bolt action fixed with peep-sights, he could have nibbled twigs away and barked out the windsock.

Scully Horton had replaced the windsock. But it was a spanking new orange sock, and much emotion had been lost. The red and white sock had flown in homage to Poland's colors, and after that there was a lack of excitement in observing winds, because some of the sentiments had vanished in the blow.

Scully was an orphan; sure he was adopted, didn't you know that, of course he was. Wanda and Hughie Ogonozalek brought him home at age of five, but they never changed the name on the birth certificate. They just wanted an avenue for love and devotion, and Hughie found it foolish to cover up the little shaver was a love child from two sweethearts who began kissing at the County Fair, then got hot on each other on the green grass of a summer night.

"The Tomaszewski's barn took a beating," said Zelda. "But just the boards. The boys had the tobacco barn in open ventilation, and the side boards had been sucking wafts for the drying of shade grown. The howling winds fanned the barn's vents and popped nail sets like silly putty. Boards lay scattered like Merle was playing dominoes with giant toothpicks. When I walked through the silo's archway, the bright light hurt my eyes; and when I squinted a few times, the figure of Zbigniew Tomaszewski was across the road and looking thunderstruck at the barn's timber skeleton. He gazed upon the post and beams against a grey sky, and his body language was really bad."

"Later that week I overheard him tell my father at the barber shop, 'I'm so proud of the peg and joinery my forefathers cut into the barn's timbers — Merle could not budge their craftsmanship.' Zbigniew said it in the chimes of cheerfulness, and pride was washed all over his face."

"Everybody lost something. I can remember women crying for days in public without shame. But the most painful sight as we wandered in the hot flashes of bewilderment, was our fallen friend. She lay dead across the barnyard. She was over 100 years old. Her arm had been broken in the fall, and many joints splintered. The skirt of her root ball fanned in peacock fashion. A pungent smell of fresh earth enveloped the scene."

"The mighty chestnut tree had fallen. Its roots had hugged the barn, and casted a dapple of shade over the chopping block. We went through the motions of obsequies, our hands patting and caressing the furrowed bark, as if saying one-last vale to an old friend. It was a sad farewell. Everybody knew the giant was irreplaceable. Huge open space filled the blue sky, and the pangs of sorrow were hard to shake. The concussion had torn open the burly crotch of the chestnut's double leader and revealed hidden secrets. A catch of skulls had tumbled about. The tree had served as a nest chamber. My brother and I looked down in wonder. The mystery of skulls had been solved. Tufts of rabbit fur and mice bones were scattered. Feathers of many victims lined the nest. We gathered the skulls," said Zelda with a straight face.

"Chores pressed. Everybody toiled. Tasks loomed. Father's first mission was hearing farm machines run. The red and green iron spelled food and return of profit."

"But after we got combustion in the iron, our father cut us free, and we returned to the fallen giant. The leaves had flagged and wilted. Sets of tiny fruits that would have produced nuts, were still firm and the color of green apples. We counted the skulls. Fifty-seven pure white skulls, and you could look clear through the eye sockets. They had been picked clean. It was hard to find foil between thin air and the weight of skulls in your palm. They weighed almost nothing. Cranial stitching ran their heads, and the beaks had turned umber from the ages."

"Jimmy tumbled the skulls in a grain bowl. He was serving mechanic's wire through the eye sockets. His barbaric necklace took shape. The crude skulls formed a giant hank — it ran down to his belly button. My brother looked the part of nomadic Vikings while sporting the monstrous beads. Jimmy was twirling the white skulls draped across his copper-skinned chest, when I exclaimed in hushed tones, 'Look!' Perched on the beam header over the barn's door, was a pair of screech owls. Everything suddenly became crystal clear. We were rummaging the owl's quarters. The storm had destroyed their home," said Zelda in a strained voice.

Huge rings of yellow framed the owl's eyes. The bird's pupils looked upon the homespun candor of the farm moppets. The owls were in cryptic coloration of russet plume. They were very small birds and appeared almost tame. They could have been in states of shock. One of the feathered fellows was perched as quartered away, but its neck was twisted in circuit to measure their presence.

"Jimmy began speaking to them at close quarters. There was no reaction. Both owls remained riveted and silent creatures. They examined our countenance with the greatest of scrutiny."

The owl with its neck in mode of revolution, blinked its yellow eyes and perked his feathered capped ears. The mate gave a few putts and thrills, then sang a tremulous pitch of descending wail — the chords were reminiscent of a creature's rendition towards sorrow.

"The owls remained in sight for a few days. We saw them often sulking in the high rafters, perched and sleeping in the inky shadows. We left out table scraps for the outcasted owls, but they never touched a morsel. Hunting must have been good, their sharp claws sinking home. I guess our feathered friends found a new home, for they were never seen again," said Zelda with a dreamful look.

Then the dismemberment began. Zelda and her big brother Johnny worked the chestnut limbs, axe blows biting and spitting out chips. Tosia chipped in. She was still in diapers. Tosia dragged small branches. The workers had formed a burn pile in the barnyard. Her face was very serious, and she was all dirty from making patty cakes in the sandbox. She lugged a second load of tiny stick to the brush pile. Zuzanna was dragging brush too. But she made a game out of work, running around in circles with branches rising dust in her tracks. Kasimierz saw this from the kitchen window, and shouted out the screen door, "Przestań zachowywać się gtupio!" And he really meant the part about acting silly. The father yelled out the door again if she didn't get on the ball with work, Zuzanna would not get a homemade popsicle that evening. After that, Zuzanna started dragging brush double-time, and looked past the screen door for approval.

That night, the Zgrodnik family burned the brush pile under a spattered sky of silver stars. Kasimierz had fortified the ignition of fire, with a splash of diesel fuel from a tin cup. Red embers raced into the black night. The boys stoked the fire with dead snags. A crescent moon hung in the sky. The flames had combed the chestnut limbs, and a bed of cherry coals glowed a barbaric luster.

Zuzanna got caught throwing an old ear of corn on the fire. The tassels ignited in blue flames, and mischief was traced across her countenance. She grinned wildly across the bed of fire, and a rebellious spark shimmered in her eyes. Kasimierz had seen her throw the old corn in a wild streak, and exclaimed, "Zachowuj się Zuzanna ... albo idź wkrótce do tóżka!"

Zuzanna jumped back from the ring of fire. This behavior was nothing new. She pushed the envelope. Rules meant very little in her book. She had a lot to learn.

The week prior Zuzanna had wandered across the fragrant meadow, singing nursery rhymes to herself. Kasimierz had seen her blue dress against the orange faces of Indian paintbrushes, and while investigating saw Zuzanna pull on the donkey's tail. That stunt would cost her five days of popsicle treats.

Kasimierz had petitioned his family from the wreath of fire smoke and bade them for a soothing ride on the glider swing. Two bench seats faced each other, crafted of sound wood, painted white like they did in the old days, and the family of seven rocked the night away. It was a sound rocker with good ball bearings, and they glided over the grass under the old apple tree. Their efforts produced a soft breeze, and it was very satisfactory on the hot summer night. The gliding figures stole sideway glances at the ring of fire, which had settled into a deep, hot bed of scarlet coals. A halo of orange glow was cast about the iron implements, and the handle of the Hudson Bay axe bit into the chopping block, was well distinguished under the bed of silver stars. Beyond from the chicken coop, the chickens peered out through the mesh wire on the fire. They had no way of knowing, many of them would soon be under the axe head on the chopping block when the butchering commenced.

A sense of victory was enveloped over the glider swing. The Zgrodnik family had weathered the storm. They had beat the odds against Hurricane Merle. Pride was swollen over the seven survivors. Mommy draped her arms over Zelda and Johnny; the swing worked this was and that way in the night. A curtain of love had been accentuated in the root cellar, huddled tight against the blow.

Zuzanna was thinking about tossing an old soda crate on the fire. But she quickly recalled her father's warning in Polish about being sent to bed soon, and because she never wanted to miss a popsicle treat, Zuzanna kept her mouth shut and pulled back on her wild streak and kissed her doll under the crescent moon.

A few days later in the forenoon, a timber man showed for the chestnut logs. He was of huge proportions, big handed, and wore lumber-jack suspenders. He bucked logs with a six-foot crosscut saw. Its deep gullets cut with impressive speed. His big hands and square shoulders skidded the butt log up the ramp, reefing on the handle of a gear winch. He made three trips for five logs, because the overburden of pushing board feet, would have taxed the truck's suspension.

"The blown over tree left a huge hole behind… a crater as if walked by field artillery. We filled the hole and planted a tree. The chestnut blight was at large, so we planted a horse chestnut whip, which was resistant to the plague."

Zelda rose from the table. Stiffness had settled into her hips. She walked around and grabbed me by the high wrist, and said, "Follow me." She tugged me across the kitchen and threw back the curtain.

"A lot can happen in eighty years," said Zelda pointing across the homestead. A husky horse chestnut fanned across the barnyard. Its trunk was arrow straight with a solid root flare, and the canopy was well formed. Some of the branch tips caressed the barn's roof, and a wealth of shade fell across the stable. "Patience is a beautiful virtue," said the old lady, "and I'm glad I lived long enough to reap its harvest." We both walked to the tree and rubbed its bark.

CHAPTER 5

Tucked under the legs of my kitchen chair, was a white canvas satchel. I reached inside the flaps for Zelda's Christmas present. It was covered with glass and framed in white wood.

"Here's your portrait we took this summer," I said in the brush of preen. "Merry Christmas."

It's always fun to read recipient's faces when they look over forms of art. The artist's goal has always been to draw emotions. Zelda's face filled with cheerfulness, and she revealed, "I love it. It's a good picture of me."

Zelda's portrait moved well across Sentery. Many people wanted copies. I had 40 copies made, and they sold out for $20 apiece. I was sailing along pretty good, until the historical society put the soft touch on me. They decided they couldn't live without a full-frame portrait of Zelda Szymborski hanging in the library's carrel. They understood she was a living symbolism of a generation going extinct and wanted historical significance on the wall.

So, I made a special trip in person to Weizmann's in New York City. Maxie Weizmann asked about the setting, and we planned at length. We scrutinized Zelda's portrait. When a suitable luster and frame was chosen — I gave Maxie the green light.

Three weeks later the olive-green card arrived in the mailbox. It stated: Your order is ready. Please call the store at 212.786WEIZ. Because there's always adventure inside New York City, and there's never been anything like it for me to ride the Number 6 train in the sea of people, listening close and looking around and people watching, I went on the tracks into Penn Station.

Weizmann's nailed everything. Zelda's portrait was spectacular.

They set her up with a shell pink matting and white wooden frame set off with gold piping. It was out of this world.

But so was the price. I almost fell over backwards.

"That's steep money," I told Maxie.

"Listen my friend," said Maxie. "it's the finest work in the land."

"I agree," shrugging my shoulders.

"For Christ's sake," said Maxie, "we gave you hours of dodge and burn work on the house. Look how beautiful she looks."

"It's true," I admitted. "It's beyond my wildest hopes."

"Nobody can touch Weizmann's," said Maxie in sparks of glee.

"Listen Buddy," I told Maxie, "think we can go 10% on cash money?"

"Sure, my friend — why not? You've come a long way to conduct business. Let's ring you up with a fat discount."

The historical society was just about speechless. They cuddled around Zelda's portrait with rhapsodies of genuine admiration. The library's custodian fussed in great measure with steel tape and with the plumb of level, until Zelda's portrait hung in perfection. There was serene light of revelation in the room, and the combined effects of casting glances at Zelda's photograph, froze visitors in their tracks.

Because I donated the portrait, most of the profits went out the window. The bill at Weizmann's was $525 after the discount. So, with the printing charge of the 40 copies, and my train fare of a round-trip ticket through Penn Station, there was only enough left over in my pocket for a case of beer and three boxes of 120 film.

But my goal was never about green money. My quest with camera gear had been driven by pangs of passion. It was about being thankful for pulling into the barnyard for a shootout on that hot summer day. That I was fortunate enough to shove a huge ingot block into the gear train of Mother Time and arrest the scene dead still. That time was frozen for those crucial seconds, so the next generations could bear witness to when traditional values and principles were in check, framed against the strokes of 1-Shot enamel on a metal sign, laid down by hands driving a sable quill brush.

Mister, you could sure learn many things from the Old School. There's a certain authenticity in the lessons. It came about from pinching pennies through a depression. Even the wire people inside the news houses could have obtained vast knowledge. The messengers of media agencies would have found out Eisenhower brought back Easter egg rolling on the White House lawn. The news people would have heard through Zelda's voice how Dwight Eisenhower was the first president to have his hands tied with Amendment 22 of the Constitution, where time was limited to two full elected terms. Before that it was a reign of clear sailing for seats of longevity in the White House.

But the most important lessons the lacquer heads behind the news microphones would have picked up, was that in the winter of 1955, Dwight D. Eisenhower was the first president to conduct a news conference ever televised. That those predecessors of news agencies who once practiced genuine news coverage, cut their teeth on Ike.

It's important to remember too, that while Zelda and I were telling stories on the farm, the news hounds were all over Trump. They hounded him with all the angles. They pressed for numbers on tax returns. It was funny though, the general public never found out any more about the consumption of fast hamburgers and Kentucky Fried chicken, just what his cholesterol level was reading, and if President Trump was in any real trouble with the bad numbers.

Born May 15th, 1931 | Died February 19th, 2023

Eleanor Regina Smiarowski Co-founder of the farm "Old School" is a work of fiction. The town of Sentery never existed. The names of the Polish farmers are figures that never walked the earth. "Old School" is a tale of my imagination.

But there was a real hot summer day in the Connecticut River Valley, when I was hunting Mexicans who were wielding head knives, cutting kale for market. And I had them cornered, but gave them a pass from exposure on film, because they were crashed against the barn in the shade on break pouring sweat.

It's a real story too Pablo, that later that forenoon in the heat-wave I really did drive down the farm road and pasted the old lady in the kisser with five shots. She was a friend of mine. And that winter when the fields were all plowed and planted in winter wheat, I'd walked up the wood stairs of the farmhouse into the kitchen and gave the old lady her portrait for Christmas.

We sat there drinking hot chocolate and talking, and every so often we'd look out the farmhouse window, but we never did see Donald Trump pull in for a few squirts of ketchup on his Quarter Pounder, so we kept telling stories and throwing the baloney around under the winter sun of a Hatfield morning.

7 Poems for my Readers

Stephen Beck

High Noon Sweat

The sun was hot —
The air was dry —
The hay was now
Beckoning;
Long strands waived in
meadowland.

The sickle was sharp —
The farmer was ready —
There was work to be done:
The cow's life is precious thing,
'specially in the dead of winter.

Red Iron

Massey Furgerson shifting out gear,
September foretells winter times near.
Governor hunts the rhyme to master,
Motor mechanically thumping faster.
Reapers of amber shafts hay,
Farmer's work is through the day.

Tin knockers tapped a bullet-long hood,
Tractor working boarder of
viburnum wood.
Old metal filched the farmer's heart,
Grew in man from Red Iron's start.
Meadows flushed green in May,
Cashed in death to farm's cut pay.

Creaks and bleeds fluid the night away,
Red Iron sleeps in the old barn bay.
Farmhouse somnolents make
secret dream,
Terror creeps in the ghastly extreme.
Under gambrel of hewed chestnut beam,
The art of a solo executioner team.
Spider spins web on Iron's coat of
blood red,
Victims eaten alive in features of dread.

Sisters

Black on blades,
White on wheels.
Black leading out,
White riding shotgun —
Checkin' about.

Black Sister smiling wide,
Roller blades moving high.
White Pal rolling neat,
Rubber tires in the heat.
Sister switchin' times:

Black sweat socks,
Pulled from blades.
White tennis shoes,
Goes on blacks —
Done deals, for wheels.

Black's white teeth,
Beaming on bike seat.
White freckles sporting,
Seven silver hoops,
Bladin' blacks blades.

Black on bike,
White in blades.
Having funs,
And breakin' down,
Segregation.

—A POEM FOR THE SISTERS ON THE BIKE TRAIL.
WRITTEN ON SEPTEMBER 9TH OF 1999.

School's Out

Rickety rims,
Danced drunkenly;
Two lads,
Hand-me-down bicycles,
Zippered macadam's soft shoulder.

Fingers twisting,
Holding fast;
Fish poles,
Bridged between,
Handle bars.

Hard right,
Dirt path;
The dike resisted not.
Wheeled over top and out,
Of site.

Two boys,
In morning sun;
Taut lines,
With worms where,
Lunker catfish lurked.

—THIS POEM IS FOR ALL THE KIDS OF SUMMER.

Simple Math

Wednesday, 19 April 1995:

My craft is,
Poetry,
Is rendered useless today.

(A = f/m : The greater the force,
The greater the acceleration,
For the same mass.)

Words can not,
Heal,
Until the heart is open.

(A = f/m : Or is that aftermath,
Equals fortitude,
Over mourning.)

The wounds will,
Scar over time,
Knowing the revenge of justice is complete.

(A = f/m : No, it must be the answer,
Equals firing-squad,
For murder.)

For all who perished in the massacre … Baylee Almon and her tot classmates, who never even made the grade of Age of Reason … And in memory for those 62 Marine recruits, who at the instant of detonation were raising right hands to pledge allegiance for the United States, which is a strange macabre twist, is what took their very lives. (Equation: Allegiance = Federal/military.)

Swamp Serenade

Maestros begin!
A thousand notes of bird song,
Rose from the swamps desolation.
But marsh-land melody,
Came not from all beaks.
And the sentry birds only stared,
Riveted like mannequins in outpost of tree limb.

And there was this break … a long pause …
And silence was noted:
It came from back there,
In the tangled marshes backwaters,
Back where summer snakes sometimes slither,
Quite near that tufted stand of mush-
roomed hummock,
Where spiked-white flowers perched on stagnant,
Where two gazing orbs,
Peeped from under pads of water lily.

But still; there was more …
In thicket on swamp's shore,
There was that ambush site on the game trail,
Where those bound marks ended in failure,
Seeped in a pool of glistening blood.

— A POEM FOR E.A. POE

THE GOOSE BUMPS STILL RISE.

THE BLUETS

BY STEPHEN DECK.

LOOK! IT'S THE BLUETS!
THEY HAVE SPRUNG IN THE DUFF.
I DID NOT SEE THEM COME... DID YOU?
NOT I! NOT I!
THEY MUST HAVE SPRUNG IN THE FORENOON,
WHEN WE WERE OFF AND ABOUT.
ENJOY THE RAFTS OF BLUE-PLATOONS WHILE THEY DANCE,
THEY ARE SHY AND FAIR PETALS
SOON TO PASS.

LOOK! IT'S THE BLUETS!
COME QUICKLY TO SEE THEIR SHOW OF SPRAYS
THEY ARE WHAT YOUNG GIRLS DREAM OF IN SPRING,
TO SMELL, TO ADMIRE, TO WEAR IN THEIR HAIR.

A POEM IN MEMORY OF HOLLY PIIRAINEN,
WHO FORGED A NITCHE IN ALL OUR HEARTS...
WHO NOW LIVES WHERE ETERNAL FLOWERS BLOSSOM.

Ambush Love

ANNOTATIONS FOR THE DECEASED

The roses saw many things. They were at the murder scene. The wild roses saw everything.

It was very cold. The ground was frozen. It was winter, and it was my first day undercover, a detective working the murder of Holly Piirainen. The year was 1994. Many people were under Cupid's spell. Some were holding hands and others were kissing. It was February 14th, a day known affectionately as Valentine's Day. That's the day I went undercover and took up the cold murder trail, so the little girl knew we all loved her, and were not playing games.

A few days prior, I'd taken an oath of vengeance over Holly's grave. The rain fell as mist in the Fairview Cemetery, and kneeling on the blades of wet grass, we'd had our little talk. We'd be out for blood. Taking prisoners was not in the cards. Holly's dream had been to become a marine biologist, but the killer snuffed all that with his evil deeds, and he was going to pay dearly. Nasty medicine was in the cards.

The killer had abducted Holly, and drove to Five Bridge Road. He'd pulled off at the old railroad bed and slipped out of sight. He must have had a revolver on her, if I'm not greatly mistaken, and she was alive on the floor.

The railroad men had long removed the crossties and tracks. The abandoned train bed formed a causeway across the swamp, and at the far end grew a forest. The killer had driven down the gravel bed, killed the motor, and marched Holly to her murder in the forest.

Six months had passed since the murder. They'd found her bone pile at the end of October. It was now in the grips of dead winter. There was no snow cover. Dead leaves and brown grass. I walked down the track bed. I was on the cold murder trail. My instincts were drawn like wire. I was a professional woodsman and tracked many animals. My brain was hunting for evidence, and I was reading signs where melancholy had lurked.

The killer had been lucky. He'd dodged many bullets. The killer had brass balls — a nest of cottages was right there, and it was just past dead noon. One of the escape routes went straight up hill that would have zapped his speed; the other was wide open for some forty yards. Its mind-bending that he found the nerve, and that nobody ever saw anything.

The killer always thought he got away clean. But he made one big mistake. His escape was flawed, and somebody saw him. They actually reached out and touched him.

In those days, the path from the old railroad bed, was a thread-like trail along the swamp. It was hemmed on both sides by brush and presented only a thread wide enough for a singular figure. At night the trails were the circuit of racoons, and the beautiful mink with its silken fur.

The killer had killed the ignition on the old track bed. Both doors opened out of sequence.

The pair headed up the thread of trail. Holly was walking point. The killer perhaps, still had the revolver on her. Holly Piirainen was marching to her own death.

But there was a big surprise waiting for everybody. Holly was the first to pass through the trap. The thorns of the wild roses brushed her ankles. The same thorns used to weave a crown for Jesus. The most holy sign growing in this world.

The killer passed through next. The thorns reached out and brushed his trousers, and the needle points did their job. The killer from that point forward, was a dead man walking. The Holy Ghost had branded him with blood.

The murder played out. Holly's clothes were later found at the scene. The form of the shadow slipped here and there in the dappled shade. Holy Ghost can see through trees and stones. He knows all things before the hour is stricken. But making certain to miss nothing, the spirit shifted in the shadows and watched the hideous murder. He wanted to make certain all the evidence was stricken in the tablets, in order for the killer to have no angles of telling stories at the sentencing.

It was a very hot August day. Swamp beds are known to hold their heat. The killer lifted his trousers and fastened his belt buckle. He must have been nervous as an alley cat. Maybe he lit a smoke. Maybe he tucked the revolver behind his belt in the small of his back. He must have been moving double-time down the trail. The sweat must have been pouring off him and imagine how big his eyes were in the wake of crime.

But there was a big problem: he needed to pass through the Thorns of Christ, before his fingers touched the ignition key. The second time he passed through the bed of roses, the Holy Ghost reached out and tattooed him up with another lashing of thorns. His problems then grew a million times over, because his soul was now raven black and charcoal dead in his body.

The passing of the wild roses, had cut both ways in blood. For Holly Piirainen, it was her salvation. Long before the killer fixed his belt buckle and stuffed the revolver, Holly Piirainen's soul was in heaven. At ten years old, she had just brushed on the Age of Reason, and all children in that order get automatic Sanctifying Grace. From the Shadow in the forest, the blackbirds in the swamp now screaming wild, the Shadow snapped its fingers, for a squadron of Guardian Angles to escort Holly's soul into the Promised Land.

But for the killer, there would be no mercy. He got caught and all messed up in the rose bed by the Holy Ghost, and CPAC detectives were sniffing up his backtrail.

Perhaps in the wild intoxication of escaping the murder scene, he gave one backwards glance across the doom-soaked prose, before stabbing the gas pedal. Maybe his eyes stung by sweat, combed the dark penumbra of the murder scene … and thought he beheld the shadow. But the Shadow was like fog vapors, indefinite, vague and formless, and was the shadow of neither man or wild beast.

Perhaps the killer wiped his eyes of sweat beads and reeling in the hot flashes of panic again measured the forest. And there Shadow hovered behind the gloom shade of a noble white oak, and moved not, and remained silent in its presence.

Perhaps the killer in a brazen voice, nothing more than a mask over his bed of fear, waived the blued barrel of his heavy Smith & Wesson revolver across the forest, and demanded an inquiry, "Shadow — I am the Killer, and demand you confess your dwelling and appellation."

But there was only silence in the forest, and across the swamp it was very still. Even the blackbirds were all pulled back behind their breaks, their black eyes riveted against the blue sky, perched in fear on the dead snags of the swampland.

The Holy Ghost was too smart for that, and schooled in the vulpine charms. He offered no reveal for the killer's petition. The Shadow slipped up the margins of grey bark, and just like that in a flash, shot a silver streak through the cobalt blue zenith. It seemed too for those cunning in the stars, as if the orange ball of sun had pulled back, and thongs of a tangerine halo filled the sky.

The Holy Ghost had seen enough. The evidence and the verdict alike, were seated in a silken pouch of athanasia golden hems. Nothing was going nowhere. It was a done deal. The killer was sealed in murder.

Things looked very grave now. The killer himself had jumped back, when he noted the strange colours of orange sunbeam, and thought he saw a flash of a pink-silver star in the galaxies. Time, well, there was still some around, for the killer was still running on the fumes of free will. But his soul had already been stricken coal back in the needle-jabs of rose thorns, and no man is immortal. The Holy Ghost was holding a nice hand of cards now, because he knew it was only a matter of time before he could break out the nasty medicine and varnish the killer in ordeal for killing the little girl, all for the sake of twisted thrills on a hot summer day.

—Reader's note

The spray of thorns in the photograph, are the roses that brushed Holly Piirainen and the killer. It's been twenty-six years now since I went deep undercover down the trail. But the roses are still there.

It was a different place back then. Old washing machines were tossed on the side of Five Bridge Road, littered with dead beer cans, and the pinched trail hugged with wild roses. A hank of rosary beads hung from a tree limb, dangling over the place where the bone pile of Holly Piirainen was discovered. The rosary beads had an unbelievable emotional effect on me.

I miss the old look around the swamp. But that's just me. Detectives have their memories.

Afterword

Writing is hard work. There are no days off for the genuine writer. An allegiance to the alphabet hangs over them. Picture a salmon jumping up the falls of a river. Complex thoughts and ideas race in the writer's mind; and like the devoted fish, the writer who thinks with creative impulses, a lone figure who must distill those thoughts into a clear language for readers, and forever inhabited with characters and voices, must reveal their imagination in the spawning beds of books.

The four parts of every book are the breathing characters of the pages, the setting across our beautiful Mother Earth, plots that hook readers, and the impact of conflict. These are moving targets, and every writer paints their own canvas of this pictorial explosion in the reader's mind.

Every book is built from sentences. There are eight important parts to every well written sentence. It's like a combustion gasoline engine, which needs its pistons and guts to make horsepower. These parts are the nouns, verbs, adjectives, prepositions, pronouns, adverbs, conjunctions, and those interjections that can stand alone on the feet of their own letters.

Sometimes though, nevertheless, all the rules go out the window. I've got my own way of weaving stories. Something like Jimi Hendrix plucking strings on his Stratocaster, paying no heed at whatsoever to music sheets. Making his own rules.

My voice in writing, is like the language of Baltimore orioles. Specific meters of frequency response, where written speech patterns of linguistics, are prepared in very specific order, simultaneously elevating forms of artistic storytelling to the reader. A lyrical form of pictorial language, where the syllables of words move the tongue with a certain rhyme across the sentence. These silent voice patterns which strike the reader, are manufactured by deep thinking, and more precisely by crucial instincts, skills of a spiritual gift to know exactly what I'm looking for on paper. A way with words. After reading the twenty-three stories in this book, those story lines that captured a reader's imagination, now live and are invested in their vocabulary.

But there are primary building blocks in every story, that's not available in any rule books. It's called subject matter. Here, my friends, is where the real detective work and snooping around comes into play for the writer. It takes a sharp eye and keeping an ear into the wayfarers, and sometimes guts to lurk in dangerous places. Don't write down everything. Only write the things that grabbed you. What was really important in the storytelling.

It's hard to believe, that May Rain was inspired some 26 years back in time, when I trolled a Royal Coachman behind my aluminum Sea King, powered by an electric motor fitted with a hand-steering lever off the transom plate, streaming along in cheerful disposition on Ashfield Lake. I can still see the beautiful colors on the fat rainbows, and how they suddenly vanished in death of the fish. Little was it realized at the time, that subject matter lurked on the lake's bottom, and came back and surfaced in my after-dreams. This is how subject matter invites its own shadow into the manuscript.

That's why it's taken so long. All these stories when separated… are like a novella. Many are like baby books. They all tell their own story and are constructed from hands on subject matter. You need to visit these places and experience the adventure; then almost instantaneously for me, the percolation takes place. I can see the story in my brain. In almost every circumstance—the end of the story is laid out sharp and clear. A writer needs to spend a lifetime, to fills his baskets with classic subject matter. The things that rock the reader forward from the chair and move streams of emotion across the pages.

That's why my stories stand alone. They are premier stories. Nobody can touch them. And because I've worked the hardest and the longest with devotion and love, I'm the best writer standing. That's the way it is. I have no other way to put anything. And you need to think that way too, if you want to survive in a dog fight around the printing press.

The world of journalism has changed. There was a time, when the gates were open. Authentic mailboxes existed. Editors of the Big Five read your manuscripts. Stephen King could mail his manuscripts from Maine, directly into the hands of Bill Thompson, who worked for the Big Five and could personally coach his writers.

It was always my dream to cut my own book deal. Pull up a chair around a wood desk with Charles Scribner in New York City, fan out the manuscript and talk business. This I thought, and those dreams filled my head for a long time.

But then the Big Five pulled the plug. They made a universal decision in the book publishing industry, to seal the doors against writer's manuscripts. There was no direct avenue into a printing press.

Middlemen were invented. They were coined literary agents. This could have proven to be sound thinking. The editors of the Big Five were no longer swamped with manuscripts; literary agents were now the liaison between the writers and the Big Five, for a nice cut of the action.

But then the evil lightbulbs began flickering in their heads. It dawned on these literary agents, that they were now the gatekeepers into American literature. They could play favoritism and escort their owns kinds into publishing houses and leave other manuscripts untouched and lay dead for those they wanted blocked. The power they wielded went to their heads, and with a clear conscious jumped on imaginary thrones, and appointed themselves false gods. Progressive monopolistic literary agents with no checkmates to meddle in their cornered market.

Then the agents got more confused. They hoodwinked themselves into thinking they were the author. The literary agents became single minded and were only interested in publishing the books with topics and genre that had personal significance. With this absolute authority which was tethered into the Big Five — dictatorship — they made the final decision to what books hit the printing press. The rest would die with their discretion…no matter how the books were written.

Nevertheless, I moved forward with fortitude in my back pocket. The cross around my neck.

The Lord gave me the talents as a writer, and nobody was going to paint me into their corners of failure. *Land of the Story Tellers* was my life's devotion to writing. It takes a great deal of time and effort, to collect this wide gamut of subject matter. All the pen and ink drawings in this book, are the original artwork of author Stephen Deck. The image on the cover of this book is called *The Recluse* and was captured with a film camera in my big hands. The poems in this book span a long way back in time — I'd penned the poem of *The Bluets* in memory of Holly Piirainen, way back in May of 1994. Serious time invested. Important business. No agents from the publishing world, were going to block my path. Even if the consequences…were to pry it from their fingers.

So then, I rolled up my sleeves, and got down to work. I pulled down the executioner's veil and focused back on my dream. It was discovered there are many paths to publish a book. It was quickly realized, the literary agents have a huge reservoir of superstars and famous faces to publish, and us blue collar writers would need to seek out other paths to their readerships. Hope was never abandoned, however, and I kept my dreams of someday landing a literary agent and skating on the hallowed pond of The Big Five.

With no book contract as a safety net, I ventured through the Jungle of Alphabets, forged sentence blocks and invented places where verbs necked to nouns swam under the surface. I advanced with the Lord's gifts on my shoulders, never once thought about choking around the keyboard, and wrote this book all alone over many years. I've led my readers and fans through the dark forest of adventure, dead on the heels of protagonists who lived lives of courage and conviction and have reaped both seen and unseen scars to prove they were no story tellers.

This book was never about money. I'm a writer. My job is to write, and how I love my job. If there was no more writing, I wish to live no more. That's how things are in the nutshell. All this was stricken on the tablets long ago. God cut me out along those lines.

I'm a lucky guy. My English teacher in high school, Miss Kincaid, pulled me aside and prodded me as a freshman, "Stephen, you are a great writer. Keep up with your writing and stay with everything." I'll never forget those words. And that's the way I always thought too, right from square number one, nobody could touch me between the margins. My calling was to be writer. All the other agenda had little meaning and relevance.

I've got my own ideas how to tell stories, let alone how they are written. Every story or novel you ever read by this author, was first printed by hand in blue ink. Then it was printed two times over with the same blue ink, most times on junk paper. Then it was run through a typewriter for a clean pictorial language. I love that style of writing, and that's how I tell them. I've worn four brand new typewriters into the junk pile, and completely pummeled three editions of Websters American English Dictionary.

Over all those years, a small-framed guy who is mild mannered and known around the golf course as Jerry Hickle, was my typewriter repair man. He's been there in the thick and thin of things and was always there to drop hats for my repairs. Over all these years we've had a secret meeting place, where Jerry handed over a wad of Nakajima ribbons and correctable tapes, and I forked over some green backs in the parking lot.

Writing with antique machines is out of synchronicity in the modern world. Book printers want files. Many thanks to Mary Indomenico, who converted my typewriter manuscript into MS Word files. This was no small task, and she worked earnestly for 18 months on that conversion.

Special thanks to graphic designer Chrysti Orchulek for scanning the author's original pen and ink drawing into printable files, and converting my color art compositions into greyscale images for this second edition of *Land of The Story Tellers*.

Dear Readers, thank you for reading this book. I've pulled all the stops and done my very best to rise your emotions, and if I'm not greatly mistaken, have pulled back the curtains of adventure in *Land of The Story Tellers*.

Although I've had many great and much-loved writing instructors, the three writers that are responsible for grooming and accentuation of this writer are Edgar Allan Poe, Stephen Crane, and Ernest Hemingway.

As those three figures peer down through the fairy blue zenith, and behold their student in bodily form, faith prevails in the banner of credence…that I've passed all their tests and scored very deep and high on their measuring sticks, and they'll hold me down a seat around the Eternal Camp Fire, so the four of us can sit around the banks of cherry coals, poking the embers with green sticks where the beds glow across our countenance; and look each other dead in the face, changing tide and places to see who can spin the best yarn.

In going where you have to go, and doing what you have to do, and seeing what you have to see, you dull and blunt the instrument you write with. But I would rather have it bent and dull and know I had to put it on a grindstone again and hammer it into shape and put a whetstone to it, and know that I had something to write about, than to have It bright and shining and nothing to say, or smooth and well-oiled in the closet, but unused.

Now it is necessary to get to the grindstone again. I would like to live long enough to write three more novels and twenty-five more stories. I know some pretty good ones.

Ernest Hemingway
1938